HANGING FALLS

HANGING FALLS

A Timber Creek K-9 Mystery

Margaret Mizushima

**CROOKED
LANE**

NEW YORK

388 1044

Copyright © 2020 by Margaret Mizushima

All rights reserved.

Published in the United States by Crooked Lane Books, an imprint of The Quick Brown Fox & Company LLC.

Crooked Lane Books and its logo are trademarks of The Quick Brown Fox & Company LLC.

Library of Congress Catalog-in-Publication data available upon request.

ISBN (hardcover): 978-1-64385-445-8
ISBN (ebook): 978-1-64385-446-5

Cover design by Melanie Sun

Printed in the United States.

www.crookedlanebooks.com

Crooked Lane Books
34 West 27th St., 10th Floor
New York, NY 10001

First Edition: September 2020

10 9 8 7 6 5 4 3 2 1

For my siblings by birth and by marriage, with gratitude for your love and support

ONE

Friday morning, mid-July

A stitch in her side plagued Deputy Mattie Cobb as she jogged uphill, telling her that her level of anxiety and this form of exercise didn't mix. Running in the Colorado high country around Timber Creek had soothed her for years, but not today. Her mind kept jumping back to the one thing that made her so . . . well, she'd have to say frightened, excited, and nervous all at once.

Though Mattie rarely took vacations, starting tomorrow she'd scheduled a week off from her duties as K-9 officer in the county sheriff's department. It was unsettling enough to think about being away from work and outside her normal routine, but in addition to that, she and her patrol dog, a German shepherd named Robo, would leave early in the morning to drive to San Diego to meet her sister for the very first time.

Her *sister*! Just thinking about it took her breath away.

A few weeks ago, she'd learned through a DNA match on an ancestry database that an unknown family member was looking for her, and a flurry of emails had revealed that she had a sister and grandmother living in California.

It seemed impossible. Though she'd dreamed of finding family—or more specifically, her mother, since she'd been unaware the others existed—the thought of actually meeting this new sister and grandma scared her.

Mattie pushed herself up the steep path toward Hanging Falls, her feet crunching on stones as she took note of spots where washout had damaged the trail enough that it would need repair. She breathed in the moist air of the dampened forest. El Niño weather patterns had caused atypical levels of monsoon-like rainfall this summer in the Colorado mountains, resulting in floods throughout the high country. While at first everyone had welcomed the moisture—hoping the forests would recover from years of drought—now too much water had wreaked its own kind of havoc. In Timber Creek, when it came to rain and snow, it seemed like it was either feast or famine.

Mattie's K-9 partner, Robo, kept pace beside her. As they jogged, they alternated running on the easier footing in the middle of the trail with navigating the more challenging, uneven ground at the edge. Dealing with ankle-turning stones, clumps of foliage, and tree roots helped keep Mattie's focus sharp and her legs strong for the times when she needed to follow Robo off-trail during a wilderness search.

As she took in the scent that her brain classified as "wet forest," she wondered what the aroma smelled like to Robo. A dog would interpret scents in layers, dissecting each one and classifying it as it came to him: the crisp smell of fresh pine, the earthy scent of damp soil, the musky odor of decaying leaves and vegetation. And then there would be additional layers that Mattie couldn't detect with her inferior human nose—oh, a rabbit passed by here a few hours ago; there's a deer hidden in the forest over there; and hey now, Moose and Glenna are just up ahead.

The local district wildlife manager, Glenna Dalton, had invited Mattie and Robo to join up with her and her Rhodesian ridgeback, Moose, to scout out wildlife habitat and trail conditions prior to the start of hunting season. Mattie had been happy to go. She'd hoped the exercise would settle her nerves.

The pain in her side sharpened, and she knew she would need to stop soon to rest. She forced herself uphill, her goal the top of this last ridge where she could see what lay ahead. Surely the falls were around the next corner.

She pushed herself up the last fifty yards of steep slope, the pain turning into a blazing burn as she crested the ridge.

"Okay, Robo, let's stop here for a minute."

Robo threw her a confused glance before sitting at her left heel without needing to be told. He scanned the terrain while she smoothed the fur on his head, his nose bobbing as he sampled the air. Mattie wondered if he thought they were about to track a lost person or a fugitive as they often did.

Or maybe he was just searching for Glenna and Moose. She'd expected to see them when she came to this lookout and was surprised to find that she and Robo had fallen far enough behind that the pair had disappeared back into the forest.

Mattie puffed hard, taking in oxygen from the thin air. They'd reached a point in altitude right below tree line, and while the forest was still thick where she stood, the lip of the natural bowl that was their destination could now be seen about five hundred yards farther uphill, near enough to detect its stony rim, relatively treeless and littered with boulders and shale.

She'd been here countless times before, and she knew that the bowl at the end of the trail would be filled with a pristine, jewel-like lake fed by spring waters and snowmelt that spilled down a sheer thirty-foot drop, resulting in a spectacular cascade called Hanging Falls.

On her way up, the river below had been swollen and in many places even running outside its banks. Trails were washed out, and falls of all sizes crashed down rocky waterways as the abnormally high levels of snowpack continued to melt and rain continued to fall. Colorado Forest Service and Parks and Wildlife personnel would have to team up to make repairs as soon as the snowmelt diminished.

But right now, it was all she could do to battle the tightness in her chest and try to catch her breath. She clasped her painful side, going into a runner's lunge to stretch her psoas muscles and hamstrings.

"You should be able to do better than this," she chided herself. "Must be getting old and out of shape."

As Mattie stretched, her thoughts wandered back to her family. She knew precious little about them, but she felt like she'd discovered hidden treasure. Her sister, Julia Prescott, was thirty-five, four years older than Mattie. Julia lived in the southern part of San Diego with her husband, Jeff, and two sons, ages ten and eight. *Nephews!* And to top it off, their maternal grandmother, Yolanda Mendoza, lived with Julia. Her sister referred to their grandmother as Abuela, and that's how Mattie had begun to think of her.

It was almost more than she could take in and process.

She removed Julia's last email from her shirt pocket, one she'd printed and kept next to her heart. She unfolded the email carefully, thinking she'd read it so many times that she'd almost memorized it.

My dear little sister,

Even as I write this, I can't believe that we've found you. I've prayed for this for decades and still have trouble believing my prayers have been answered. I can't wait to see you next week and to hold you in my arms like I did when you were a baby. I have many old photos of our parents and us kids to show you, and I've made copies of all of them for you to take home when you have to leave.

Joey and Jason can't wait to meet their auntie. I cried all week after you told me that our brother Willie was dead and that you didn't know where our mother is. I guess it was too much to hope to be able to have all of you returned to me at once.

I understand when you say you don't want to share details about Willie's death until we're together. I feel the same about discussing our father's death. Some things are just too muddled to write down on a page in black and white. It makes it hard to see the gray that surrounds the circumstances. We'll have to talk about them when we see each other next week.

Abuela is beside herself with joy, though she has become very quiet the past few days. I think it's overwhelming for her to have found her cherished granddaughter only to discover that it's too late to ever see her grandson again. She's getting older, but she has never given up hope that she will still see our beloved mother again before her life ends. And now I have renewed hope that we can pool our resources and make that wish come true.

I'll text you directions to my house, and like I told you when we talked, both you and your dog Robo are welcome to stay with us. (I still have trouble imagining my baby sister as a K9 cop!) I know you mentioned finding a pet-friendly motel nearby, but we would love to have you as our guest. Please consider staying here with us, your family.

We love you and can't wait to see you.

Hugs and kisses,
Your sister, Julia

It broke Mattie's heart to think about Willie's death. Although she, her mother, and her brother had been kidnapped when Mattie was only two years old, Willie had been killed by one of their abductors only a few months ago. Her pain from that was still raw, and tears welled in her eyes.

It was nice of her sister to open her home to both her and Robo. Though Mattie didn't doubt the sincerity of Julia's invitation, a wave of anxiety engulfed her each time she thought about spending twenty-four hours per day with these dear people who were family—but still strangers.

She'd already made a reservation at a motel near Julia's house, where she and Robo could seek respite at the end of the day or whenever the circle of this new family began to close in on her. Although finding family was what she wanted more than anything in the world, she knew herself well enough to expect that it would not necessarily be all joy and comfort. She would need to take breaks to do her yoga and practice her breathing exercises to stay centered.

And if how she'd been coping lately was any indication, she was in danger of becoming a complete mess.

She folded the email and returned it to her pocket while she spoke quietly to her dog. "Okay, that's enough lagging behind. Let's go find Moose and Glenna."

Even though she felt like taking a much slower pace, she told him to heel and struck out at a jog to tackle the last five hundred yards. Once a high school cross-country track champion, she didn't like to come in last.

Boulders on the trail made a rough staircase to the top. Mattie and Robo left the thick stand of pine and hopped from one rocky surface to another as they breached the rim where the trail flattened out onto a slab of stone. On the other side of the rise, Glenna sat on a boulder waiting, apparently enjoying the view.

A dazzling lake filled with water the color of deep sapphire nestled in a depression surrounded by granite peaks under partly cloudy skies. The sun broke through the cloud cover in patches, sending shafts of light down in intervals, as if spotlighting some of the boulders while most of them remained in shadow.

On the far side of the bowl, Hanging Falls tumbled down a rocky chute and spilled into the lake, churning up the water beneath it. The falls were more violent than Mattie had ever seen them, fueled by the last deluge. Stark white snowfields cloaked the rugged peaks above the falls, ice melt adding to the runoff that fed the rolling water.

"Hey, Glenna," Mattie panted, trying to catch her breath without showing how winded she'd become. "You kicked my butt coming up here."

The unusual humidity in the typically dry Colorado altitude made Glenna's curly black hair frizz, allowing it to escape the ponytail she'd drawn together earlier at her nape beneath her floppy, wide-brimmed hat. "I haven't been here long. Only a few minutes."

Mattie suspected it had been longer, since she and Robo had spent upwards of ten minutes resting before their final ascent. Glenna was at least six inches taller than Mattie's five foot four, with a much longer stride, but still—that was no excuse for falling so far behind.

Mattie stretched against a boulder beside Glenna while Robo scouted the immediate area, sniffing grassy tufts and brilliant-purple wildflowers. "Where's Moose?"

Glenna gave Mattie a quick assessment with large hazel eyes framed by black lashes. "Are you okay?"

Mattie's shortness of breath embarrassed her. "Sure. I have a stitch in my side that got to me. I'll be ready to move on in a few minutes."

Glenna rose from the boulder where she'd been sitting and began to stretch her hamstrings. On duty, she was dressed in the khaki shirt-and-shorts uniform of the Colorado Parks and Wildlife Department, her long legs tanned from being outside during the summer. "Moose ran on ahead."

Even as Glenna spoke, Mattie saw the big red dog break out of the pine down below and gallop along the edge of the lake, leaping over stones. The strip of hair that grew in the opposite direction along the Rhodesian ridgeback's spine was a shade darker than the rest of his burnished coat. His black muzzle stood out and his ears flopped as he ran.

"There he is," Mattie said, pointing him out for Glenna and wishing she could allow Robo the freedom to take off and run to his heart's content. But her dog had cost thousands of dollars, purchased by the citizens of Timber Creek and donated to the sheriff's department to combat drug traffic in their community, and the responsibility of keeping him safe weighed constantly on her shoulders.

Mattie scanned the bowl in front of her, taking in the meadow surrounding the lake, its grasses lush and green from the plentiful rain and sprinkled with wildflowers of all colors. White water spilled out of the lake and coursed through a riverbed filled with wild rapids that would only gain momentum as it flowed downhill from here.

Glenna rose from her lunge. "Ready to go on down?" she asked. "We can walk."

"Sure." Mattie decided to let Robo run ahead. The grassy meadow looked safe enough to let him roam. "Go ahead, Robo. You're free."

That was all it took for him to break away at a lope, heading down the trail toward Moose. Glenna took the lead at a walk and Mattie followed on the narrow trail, avoiding muddy spots and puddles where rainfall had pooled in stony depressions. The gradual descent toward the lake afforded more time to recover.

"So . . . word around town is that you and Cole Walker are a couple," Glenna said. "Is that true?"

Mattie didn't like sharing personal information with just anyone, but she'd been working on being more open with others instead of closing them off. Her relationship with Cole still felt brand-new and maybe even a little shaky at times, but she could discuss it with Glenna. Mattie enjoyed spending time with the wildlife manager, someone who might eventually become a friend. "I guess we are a couple . . . yeah . . . we are."

Glenna threw Mattie a smile over her shoulder. "You don't sound too sure of that."

"Oh, I am," she fibbed, because she didn't want to get into details. "It's just that I'm not comfortable talking about it yet. We've only recently made it public."

The hazel eyes Glenna turned on her held a twinkle. "You don't have to talk about it if you don't want to. I just wanted to confirm that Cole was off the market."

Mattie smiled, thinking of the way Cole focused on her instead of the obstacles his family life had thrown up in front of them. "Oh, he is. Or as far as I'm concerned, he is."

"So my next question is . . . does he have a brother?"

Mattie chuckled. "Sorry, but no. Just a sister."

"Well, darn. Then let me know if you get tired of him."

The unmistakable deep-pitched bay that could come only from Moose resounded over the lake and echoed off the granite wall on the other side.

"Oh no," Glenna said. "What has he found?"

"Not a cougar, I hope." Concern for Robo pushed Mattie forward. Stepping off-trail to dash past Glenna, she sprinted toward the lake, shouting at the top of her lungs for Robo to come.

Glenna ran close behind, but downhill had been Mattie's specialty in high school. Her shorter legs and lower center of gravity allowed her to travel faster than taller runners whose stride outmatched her when going uphill. She pulled ahead on the smooth pathway, continuing to shout for her dog.

But Robo's familiar bark had joined the echo. Mattie reached the lake and took the trail along its edge where she'd last seen the dogs. The footing was rockier and uneven here, and she watched the path, shouting to Robo while she ran. She entered a band of pine that wrapped like a finger around the pool at the base of the falls.

Darn it! She hoped the two of them hadn't cornered a dangerous animal and gotten themselves into trouble. She imagined the worst, her heart in her throat, as she pounded along the path. The noise of the tumbling cascade filtered through the evergreens, growing in volume as she approached.

When Mattie broke through the trees, she spotted Moose and Robo crouched and barking near the base of the falls. White water spilled off a cliff, crashing over boulders, filling the air with a fine mist. Robo's bark sounded ferocious as he jumped at the water's edge, landing elbows-deep in the pool and then backing out to trade places with Moose.

Both dogs raced back and forth in a fury, their eyes pinned on a felled pine that lay partially underwater, its trunk upended but still anchored to shore by a root system that rose into the air. Mattie called Robo as she ran, but his attention was fixed on something within the submerged part of the tree and he wasn't listening.

Mattie raced the last hundred yards and came up to the dogs only a few paces ahead of Glenna. As she rounded the felled tree, Robo spotted her and came at once, his eyes bright and snapping with excitement. Mattie's first glance didn't reveal anything, and she allowed herself to relax, thinking it must be a squirrel or chipmunk that had taunted the dogs.

But Robo whirled to go back to Moose, obviously still drawn to whatever the ridgeback was barking at. In a stern voice, Mattie told Robo to "leave it" and made him come to her. Moose was so fixated on the tree boughs that he wouldn't break away when Glenna called him. She charged down to the water's edge to grab his collar.

Glenna captured Moose and had started to drag him away when surprise crossed her face, followed by a look of horror. She straightened, one hand on Moose's collar while the other went to her chest. "Oh no!" she said, loud enough for Mattie to hear over the roar of the falls.

"What is it?" Mattie shouted, reaching for the pistol she'd strapped into a shoulder holster under her loose shirt.

Glenna's eyes were still fixed on whatever she'd seen as she dragged Moose up the bank. "It's a body, Mattie. Snagged in the tree. Or at least I think it is."

Surely not a body. Mattie returned the pistol to its holster. She needed to subdue Robo and get him back under control. She feared he would leap into the water, which swept past the tree and into the torrent. "Robo, down. Stay."

He obeyed, panting, his eyes now pinned on her as he watched her every move. Glenna struggled to get control of Moose as he continued to bark and pull against her. With a feeling of dread, Mattie inched her way down the tree trunk, searching the water within the submerged branches.

Then she spotted it. White and bloated, facedown, bobbing about six inches below the water. One arm floated upward, its hand swollen like a puffer fish with sausage-like digits. A body, hung up in the snag of branches and debris from the felled pine. The current rushed against it, threatening to loosen the tree's hold and wash it away at any minute.

Below this point the river ran in rapids and white water until it spilled out of the bowl and rushed downhill, where it joined with other streams and runoff. If this body slipped from its mooring, it would be damaged as it bounced over the boulders in the riverbed. And if it floated past the rim to the next falls, it might be lost forever. Mattie couldn't let that happen.

She raised her eyes from the grisly sight and looked at Glenna. "We need to get it out."

TWO

For the past few weeks, it had been tough sledding for Cole in his vet clinic, and he'd grown tired of it. With the exception of his office manager, Tess, who was always cheerful, everyone he employed had been giving him the cold shoulder. Of course, his other two employees happened to be teenagers—one his very own daughter, for Pete's sake—and the two happened to be friends, so that didn't help any.

The girls weren't exactly being disrespectful. Cole could've managed open hostility better than this stony-faced silence. He enjoyed his work and he liked to joke around under the right circumstances, like when he and the kids were mucking out stalls, cleaning cages, or just hanging out between client visits. Their sudden distance had lasted longer than he'd thought it would, and it chafed him like an ill-fitting harness on a workhorse.

Preparing for his next client, Cole assembled his mobile X-ray system in the back room. He'd yet to meet this woman who'd recently moved to Timber Creek. Her female German shepherd was scheduled for hip films that would be sent to the Orthopedic Foundation for Animals for soundness rating. When he'd commented to his older daughter, Angela, that he was excited to meet another German shepherd like Robo, she'd responded with a withering look before turning away to update his last client's records on the computer.

He'd thought he'd built a solid relationship with his sixteen-year-old, but during the past few weeks she'd turned into someone unfamiliar. Or maybe her behavior held hints of familiarity that concerned him. If he was being honest, she might be treating him with the same touch of disdain he'd received in the past from her mother, his ex.

The older Angie got, the more she looked like her mom, too. Tall and thin with white-blond hair and blue eyes, Angie seemed to resent her own appearance, because her anger toward her mom was something else the kid happened to be dealing with this summer. And one thing he knew for certain was that mentioning the mother-daughter similarity to Angela was the wrong tack to take.

His other teen employee, Riley Flynn, whose freckle-faced countenance often wore a broad grin, came through the door from the equine treatment area and startled as if she hadn't expected to see him. Though she'd worn a pleasant expression and had almost smiled when their eyes met, she quickly rearranged her features into a flat mask that looked nothing like her typically animated appearance.

"Hey, Riley. Are you done with sweeping the cement pad?"

"Yes, sir," she said, staying the course she'd set toward the inner office. "I'll ask Tess what to do next."

"I could use some help here."

Riley paused her march through the room and placed her hand on the side braid that she wore her unruly brunet hair in for work. "Okay," she said, sounding unsure of herself as she glanced toward the door that led to the reception area, where Angie was working on the computer.

Cole had decided that Angie was the leader in this disagreeable situation, and Riley's response only added confirmation. "I've got a new client coming in named Mrs. Vaughn. She's bringing a female German shepherd that needs hip X-rays. I could use some help with that."

A twinkle of excitement sparked in the girl's eye before she extinguished it. "Okay."

Tess usually assisted Cole with procedures, and he hoped that inviting Riley to help would extend an olive branch. He knew why the two girls were mad at him, but he didn't plan to do anything about it.

Angie resented that he'd fallen in love with Mattie; she'd made that point very clear when they'd talked about his new relationship a few weeks ago. Angie had evidently enlisted Riley to join her side—easy to do, since Riley's widowed father had also begun to date, a situation that didn't please her either. Cole realized these were tough issues the teenagers had to deal with, and he hoped to wear them out by showing them he was still there for them, no matter what.

Cole gave Riley one of his most charming smiles. "Go get the lead aprons and gloves. There are three sets, and we keep them in the utility room. I'll get the X-ray plates."

The girl headed for the door to the utility as Tess entered the room from the small-animal treatment area. Tess wore her hair short, spiky, and colored an unnatural shade of red, sometimes with blue tips on the end. Today was one of those times—red and blue. "Ruth Vaughn is here," she said.

"Great. I'm just about ready. Riley's going to help. Could you get a radiation monitor for her to wear? She's getting the aprons and gloves."

"Sounds good. She can learn to help hold."

Cole had been lucky to hire Tess ten years earlier, and she'd been a godsend when his ex-wife, Olivia, left him and his daughters in the lurch. His family had faced some tough adjustments, but Tess had been there to teach both Angie and his nine-year-old, Sophie, various jobs at the clinic to keep them busy after school before he found his live-in housekeeper, Mrs. Gibbs.

Life had been rocky back then. He hoped things would smooth out again soon, because it wore him out when his loved ones were unhappy.

Cole placed a set of X-ray plates beside the machine and followed Tess through the small-animal treatment room and into the main office. A tall woman who wore her dark-blond hair in a large bun at her nape below a small cap of white fabric waited in the lobby. Several towheaded kids peeked out from behind her calf-length blue skirt and white apron, while a young girl about Angie's age, dressed in garb like her mother's, stood holding the leash of a gorgeous German shepherd.

After Cole extended his hand and introduced himself, the woman raised her gaze to his briefly before diverting her eyes.

She returned his handshake with the tips of her fingers and responded in a demure voice, "And this is my daughter, Hannah."

Cole received another tentative fingertip handshake from Hannah, who was the image of her mother from head to toe. Both wore white anklets and black lace-up shoes that reminded him of those worn by his grandmother in her later years.

And then his eyes were drawn to the shepherd. Obviously female, with a graceful head and smaller boned than Robo, she sat beside Hannah's left heel, her sharp gaze watching his every movement. When he looked at her, she opened her mouth slightly in a pant as if overcome by a sudden case of nerves, though she remained quite still otherwise. Like Robo, she was predominantly black with mahogany markings.

"Wow," Cole said, with a smile for Hannah. "Your dog's a beauty."

Hannah returned his smile with a slight upward tilt of her lips, then lowered her face in the same demure manner as her mother.

"Her name is Sassy," Ruth said, her voice a quiet contralto that made Cole strain to hear. "I have her records here."

She reached inside a denim bag she wore slung from one shoulder and brought out a booklet that she offered to Cole. He took it, flipping it open to see a birth date and completed-vaccination list. Everything looked up-to-date.

He handed the booklet to Angie, who remained seated at her reception desk. "Could you set up a record for Sassy while I get started?"

While she took the booklet from his fingers, Angie looked beyond him toward Hannah and gave her a welcoming smile. Cole had to hand it to his kid: at least she could maintain a warm attitude toward his customers while still freezing out her dear old dad. Hannah responded differently to Angie than she had to him, meeting Angie's gaze directly, her face now lit with a friendly smile.

Cole turned toward his treatment room, holding the door open for the family to enter. "Let's take Sassy here to the table where I can take a look at her," he said to Hannah as she passed through the door.

Now that Ruth and her children were mobilized, he could count three of the small ones, each of a different size but all with light hair—two girls in pigtails wearing pint-sized versions of their mother's dress, and a boy with a bowl-shaped haircut dressed in a blue chambray shirt and denim pants with an elastic waist instead of a zipper. He resisted the urge to tousle the boy's hair as he passed by, sensing that the child's shyness might make any kind of boisterous gesture unwelcome.

He watched Sassy walk to the exam table, her gait steady and even. While she possessed the sloping hip that matched the breed standard for a German shepherd, her legs moved well at the joints, and there was no apparent limitation when she walked.

Movement on the other side of the room caught Cole's eye. Riley slipped through the door and tried to melt into the wall, looking toward Cole as if seeking permission. He gave her a nod before speaking to his clients. "This is Riley. She helps out here at the clinic."

Hannah and Ruth both said hello and then turned back to Cole, Hannah's gaze lingering for a bit on Riley.

"I see that Sassy just turned two," Cole said to Ruth, referring to the birth date he'd seen on the shepherd's vaccination record. "You're thinking of having some puppies?"

Now Ruth raised her face to meet his gaze. "That's why we need the OFA test."

It sounded like this woman had some experience with breeding shepherds. "Did you purchase her, or did she come from one of your own litters?"

"The breeder I bought her from said he would guarantee she passed this hip test and he'd replace her if she didn't." Ruth smiled slightly, and the bit of animation transformed her bland face. "But I don't know how we'd ever do that. The children and I couldn't give her up."

"Do you know the OFA ratings on Sassy's parents?"

"The father was rated excellent and the mother good. The breeder had pups from a female that also had an excellent rating, but I couldn't afford one from that litter."

"I know what you mean." Cole had been watching Sassy while they talked, and the dog had settled back down to sit at

Hannah's heel without being told. She scanned the room, taking in everything, but she seemed unusually calm compared to most dogs that came to the clinic for the first time. "She has a pretty laid-back personality?"

"She's been great. She adjusted well to the kids, and Hannah works with her constantly. Sassy's made a good pet for our family."

"Is it okay if I give her a treat to make friends?"

"Certainly."

Cole went to the counter where he kept his dog treats, picked one from the jar, and walked over to Sassy, keeping his voice low and his words slow to limit agitation. He offered his hand, palm down, the treat tucked inside his fist. Sassy sniffed his fingers daintily and touched his hand with her tongue, as soft as a butterfly kiss.

He opened his hand so she could take the treat, then followed up with firm strokes to her neck and back. She didn't offer any sign of fear or resistance—well socialized, even temperament. Cole looked at Hannah. "Can you help me lift her onto the table? She'll be happier if you do."

Hannah nodded, bent, and grasped Sassy around her chest, lifting the front end of the seventy-pound dog while Cole reached to lift the shepherd's hips and place her on the table. Sassy's toenails clicked against the stainless-steel surface, and she broke into a light pant.

Cole stroked the dog with one hand while he removed his stethoscope from his lab coat pocket with the other. "If you'll hold her there, Hannah, I can take a listen."

The *ker-thump* of Sassy's heart was steady and regular, and her lungs sounded clear. He examined her eyes and found them to be healthy looking and responsive. He turned to Ruth. "She looks like she's calm enough for me to try to do the X-ray without sedation. And her heart and lungs sound good, so if I have to slip her a light sedative, she should do fine. I need you to sign a release form just in case."

"All right."

Before Cole could go to the pass-through to ask, Tess entered the room with the paperwork.

"Thanks, Tess." Cole picked up a muzzle made from red nylon straps. "I'm going to slip this on her so that no one gets bit when we position her for the X-ray. It won't hurt her, and it'll ensure that we don't get hurt either."

Hannah frowned as she nodded. Cole went ahead and positioned the muzzle on Sassy, adjusting the straps so that they were comfortable. The dog appeared willing to cooperate, making him even more impressed with her temperament. He could hardly wait to tell Mattie about her.

Tess got the necessary signature, laid the form on the counter, and turned to Hannah. "I can take Sassy's leash now. She's going to the back room for her photo, and we'll take good care of her."

As Hannah relinquished the leash, Ruth spoke up. "If Hannah goes with Sassy, I'm sure she can get her to cooperate."

Although the procedure involved holding a dog on its back, Cole typically didn't have a problem getting a calm dog like this to lie still. A little belly scratching often did the trick. "I think Sassy will do fine. The exposure to radiation for an X-ray is low, but let's have Hannah stay in the lobby with the rest of you."

Cole followed Tess and Riley into the back room, where they already had Sassy sitting on the thick pad below the X-ray machine. Riley was petting the dog while Tess coached her. "Low and slow, Riley. That's what Dr. Walker says will keep a dog calm."

Ah, Tess. Thank goodness someone enjoyed employee training, a task that made Cole cringe. "Sassy looks comfortable," he said. "Let's get her to lie down."

Sassy's obedience training became obvious when she responded to Cole's first command. He let Tess show Riley how to gently press Sassy onto her side, and they took turns, one petting her while the other donned a lead apron. Tess laid the gloves within reach. Cole positioned the generator over Sassy's body and then put on his own protective apron.

Though Sassy was well-groomed, she began to shed hair that floated from her body and clung to the spongy pad. Cole could tell she was nervous but still consolable.

Tess told Riley to put on her gloves and kneel beside Sassy, far enough back to stay out from under the generator. "Rub her chest right here to keep her calm."

A quick glance told him that Tess was ready, and without needing to say a word, they worked in unison to position the plates beneath Sassy's hips while swiftly turning her onto her back. Tess soothed the shepherd with her voice and scratched her belly with one hand while capturing her front legs with the other. For a split second, Sassy resisted, but her heart didn't seem set on it and she stopped struggling almost at once.

Positioned at Sassy's hips, Cole reached forward to take hold of the dog's forelegs, using his arms to stabilize her body while Tess slipped on her leaden gloves. Then Tess took over while he slid on his own protective mitts, quickly adjusted the generator over Sassy's hips into the perfect position for the X-ray, and made sure the remote switch was near his foot. In one swift motion, he grasped Sassy's hind legs, stretched her into place, and stepped on the button to capture the shot.

They released Sassy and she rolled to her side, panting but not even shaken enough to try to get away. She lay still while Tess and Riley petted her and told her what a good girl she was. Cole felt certain the films would be fine and they wouldn't need to redo them, but he told Tess to wait while he checked.

Cole's X-ray machine had been more affordable than the newer digital models, so he took the plates into his darkroom to develop. Placing the films into the tank full of fluid, he set the timer and went back to where Tess and Riley waited with Sassy.

"What did you think of that?" he asked Riley.

Riley's eyes were bright with excitement. "That was cool. You guys did that really fast."

Cole exchanged a smile with Tess. "We've had a little bit of practice, and Sassy is a model patient. You did a good job too, keeping her quiet."

Petting Sassy, they chatted for a few minutes, and Cole was happy to see that Riley had adjusted her attitude toward him. Now he needed to work on Angie, a tougher nut to crack.

The timer bell dinged. Cole went back into the darkroom to remove the film from the tank and held it up to the light to study. It looked good. Deciding that the Vaughn kids might want to see the result, he carried the X-ray with him, signaled that all was well to Tess, and reentered the exam room, where he clipped the film onto the light box.

While Tess and Riley brought Sassy, he opened the door into the reception area and invited the family to return to the exam room. "Angie, if you want to see the X-ray, come join us."

Angie hesitated, and Cole tried a disarming smile as he held the door open for her. Evidently unable to resist seeing the X-ray, she moved through into the exam room without making eye contact. Sassy was back in Hannah's care, and the girl had hunkered down beside the dog with her arms around her. Tess had removed the muzzle, and Sassy wore a smile on her face that matched Hannah's.

Cole enjoyed showing the kids the landmarks on the film: the white strips of dense bone and the darker images of soft tissue. He asked Ruth if the children could have suckers, and she allowed it. Even the shy boy murmured thank-you when he selected his treat.

"I'll contact you with the results when I get them," Cole told Ruth as he ushered them back into the lobby to say good-bye. Then he marked the bill so that Angie could handle taking payment and went back to help Tess and Riley with cleanup.

"That went well," he said as he disassembled the X-ray system. "Thanks for helping, Riley."

"Gosh, thanks for letting me. Sassy is so sweet."

"She's a beauty, isn't she? If all goes according to plan, maybe we'll get to see her puppies in a few months."

Riley's freckled cheeks bunched as she grinned. "Sounds awesome. Who's the dad going to be?"

"Well . . . I didn't ask." Cole had thought of Robo, but he belonged to the Timber Creek County Sheriff's Department. He supposed that any future breeding arrangements would be an executive decision and not just up to Mattie.

"Maybe Hannah would let Angie and me come out to her house to see them when they're born."

"Maybe." Cole pictured the subdued girl in the old-fashioned dress and worried about how she might be received at Timber Creek High. He had an idea of something that might help but knew it wouldn't fly if he suggested it to Angie right now. "Hannah and her family are new in town. She could probably use a friend or two before school starts. Maybe you and Angie could call her and invite her over to the house some afternoon."

Riley nodded, a faraway look on her face as she considered it. "Why do they dress like that?"

Cole kept his reply neutral, hoping his kids, including Riley, would be willing to see the people beyond the clothing. "I don't know, but I bet it's a religious choice. You can probably talk to Hannah about that after you get to know her. She's probably just an ordinary girl like you."

The muffled slam of the clinic's front door carried through to the back room, followed by a booming male voice. It was almost noon, and Cole had thought they were done for the morning. He looked at Tess. "Were we expecting someone else?"

"No one else on the schedule until one thirty." Tess started for the exam room to check things out just as Angie met her at the door.

Distaste pinched Angie's face. "Dad, Parker Tate is here to talk to you. He doesn't have an appointment."

"Thanks, Angie." Parker was a pharmaceutical rep, new to the company that had hired him, and this was only his second visit to the clinic. "Send him into the exam room, and I'll talk to him."

Angie disappeared, and Cole hurried to place the last piece of his X-ray system into its case and close the lid. He went into the exam room as Parker was entering through the other door, holding it open and speaking to Angie over his shoulder. "Okay, darlin'. I find it hard to believe you don't have a boyfriend, a pretty girl like you. But it gives a poor old boy like me lots of hope."

Cole's hackles rose, and he studied the man with a sharp eye. Teasing teenage girls was harmless in most cases, and he was used to hearing it from the older men who were dads themselves. But Parker looked like he was in his early twenties, probably only six or seven years older than Angie, and he had the edgy features of a fox on the prowl.

Call it father's intuition or purely gut instinct, but whatever it was, Cole's previous tolerance of the sales rep soured to instant dislike. "What brings you here today, Parker?"

Parker turned his cobalt-blue eyes toward Cole, shifting his expression from a leer to a smile, though not fast enough for Cole to miss it. He must have read Cole's disapproval, because he instantly sobered and adopted a deferential attitude just shy of genuine. "Thanks for seeing me, Doc. I was driving through town and thought I'd stop by. I've got some samples to give you, and I thought I'd see if you need to order anything."

Cole crossed his arms over his chest. "All right, we have about five minutes."

Parker displayed evenly spaced white teeth in what looked like a practiced grin, placed his briefcase on the exam table, unsnapped the latches, and opened the lid. The kid wore his hair styled and gelled into a sweep on top that Cole guessed had him standing at the mirror often to make sure it stayed in place. Some might think him handsome, but Cole thought he looked like trouble.

Parker took several boxes from his case and lined them up on the table. "I brought you some new heartworm pills you might want to try and a chewable vitamin that smells like dog candy."

Cole scanned the labels on the boxes, deciding that both products looked like something he could dispense, but he didn't feel like placing an order today. "These are the samples?"

"Sure are. I can give you a discount on an order of twenty boxes or more."

"Thanks for these. I'll take a look at my inventory and get back to you if I need anything more."

"Hey, that's fine, but I can get you discounts if you order directly from me," Parker said, removing a business card from inside his case and offering it.

Cole took the card, going toward the door as a sign that the meeting was over. Parker caught his drift and snapped up the case to follow, which might have put him back in Cole's good graces if he'd walked through the lobby and exited like a good lad. Instead, he paused to take one last shot at Angie.

Parker flashed his phony grin. "Hey, gorgeous, remind the doc here to call me when he needs to order supplies, and I'll bring you something nice the next time I come to visit."

Seated at her desk, Angie straightened and stared at her computer screen, her cheeks flushed. One look at his daughter's body language told Cole she wasn't having it, but she seemed embarrassed by the attention and unable to come up with a reply.

"Make sure you call first for an appointment, Parker," Cole said, wanting to prevent him from showing up at a time when Angie and Tess were at the clinic alone. "I'm not always here, and it'll save you a wasted trip."

Parker gave him a salute. "Will do, Doc. I hear you've been keeping pretty busy these days."

Puzzled by what he meant, Cole raised a brow.

"I heard you've got a new girlfriend you've been running around with." Parker smirked as if sharing a joke, one that Cole didn't think funny.

The grapevine in Timber Creek is going to be the death of me yet, Cole thought, as Angie's scowl told him she didn't consider the joke funny either. He glared at Parker and opened the outside door to show him out. "Don't always believe what you hear when you gossip."

But Parker wouldn't leave it alone, and evidently thought they could bond if he exercised his sense of humor. "Now, nobody's blaming you, Doc. Fall is just around the corner, and you're gonna need someone to warm your bed when the snow starts to fly."

These were not the type of comments his daughter needed to hear, especially now, and Cole's irritation toward the guy spilled over to the boiling point. He grasped Parker by the arm and marched him through the door, closing it firmly behind them. "Listen, bud. That's my daughter in there, and I want to make it clear that I don't like you insinuating things in front of her or toward her."

Parker pulled his arm free, and the way he flexed it told Cole he might have squeezed a little harder than he'd meant to. "Hey, man. You don't have to go ballistic. I was just fooling around."

Cole backed off, trying to cool down. "Maybe so, but your way of kidding is inappropriate, especially when you should be paying attention to business. Take some words of advice, or you'll lose this job before you even get started."

That must have struck a nerve. The kid tried to look chastened. "Sorry about that, sir. Would you like for me to apologize to your daughter?"

Parker seemed smart enough to realize that customer complaints could put a fork in his career path, but Cole wasn't impressed by his remorse. "Just go. And it's best if we do business by phone in the future."

As he watched the guy drive away, Cole drew a breath and wondered if he'd overreacted. This cold war with Angie had him on edge, and he guessed he needed to meet the problem head on. No more waiting.

But first, he'd better go back inside and see what kind of damage control he needed to do now, or if it could wait until he found the right time to sit down and work things out with his daughter.

THREE

Mattie squatted beside the lake, using her cell phone to snap photos of the body snagged within the pine boughs. Robo huddled near. He was less agitated now that Glenna had tied Moose to a tree and made him stop his baying.

Glenna came up behind her and spoke loudly enough to be heard over the roar of Hanging Falls. "How do you propose we do this?"

"Do you have any rope in your pack?"

"Nope. No straps, no nothing."

Mattie thought of the dogs' leashes when she heard the word *straps*. "Can you swim?"

"Not well."

Mattie wasn't exactly a strong swimmer either, and the thought of entering the swift current just yards away from the crashing falls scared her.

"That water comes off the snowfield, and it's barely above freezing," Glenna said. "It'll take your breath away. We need water rescue personnel in wet suits."

Mattie took her last photo and stood. "That we do. But it'll take hours before they can get here, and if the body breaks loose from this tree, no telling where it will end up."

Glenna nodded agreement as she stared at the corpse. Mattie studied it too, but since only the upper back could be seen from her vantage point, she couldn't determine its gender. Pink slashes marred its white skin, blurry under the water. Pine boughs shielded its lower half.

"Cold water preserves a body," Glenna mused. "As long as the water level stays the same, this pine tree isn't going anywhere."

At least five feet of trunk and a bit of root system anchored the fallen pine to the bank, even though its narrowing top stretched about twenty feet into the water. Clouds hung heavy and gray, threatening rain.

"I don't think we can count on the water not rising," Mattie said. "There's another storm brewing."

A loud crack came from the falls. A dead tree bobbed up at the base and spun so that its heavy end swung their way, and the strong current pushed it like a battering ram toward the pine that held the body. It smashed into it, making it shudder. Robo leapt to his feet, barking and dancing nervously at the edge of the water.

Mattie sucked in a breath as she watched the body disappear out of sight beneath the pine, and only when it bobbed back up again did she exhale. "Okay, that does it. We have to get this body onto the bank."

She scanned the area, searching for deadfall beneath the grove of lodgepole pine. "What if we make a pole that we can lay beside the pine tree?"

Glenna nodded as Mattie shared the rest of her plan. "I think we can make it work."

Mattie hurried to her pack and grabbed the Leatherman tool that Cole had given her. She rarely went into the high country without it, and when she was on duty she carried it in her utility belt. Together they hurried into the trees beside Moose, who barked when they passed.

With Robo running out in front, they found a dead pine with a narrow trunk and dragged it down to the lake. Most of the limbs had been stripped already, and Mattie set to work whacking off those that were left. Soon she made a pole that was light enough for Glenna to handle by herself.

In the meantime, Glenna had calmed Moose enough for him to be taken off leash. He obeyed her command to lie down and stay while she tied his leash to Robo's to make a long strap.

After Mattie carried the pole to the lake's edge, she sat and stripped off her shoulder holster, hiking boots, and socks. She'd worn lightweight hiking pants and a short-sleeved khaki work shirt, and she decided to leave her clothing on to protect her from the pine's bark and branches. A cool breeze wafted downhill from the snowfields and made her shiver. She could only imagine how cold the lake water was, and she planned to stay out of it for the most part.

"Ready?" she asked Glenna.

The game warden frowned. "I'm ready when you are."

Mattie picked up one end of the pole. "Let's see if we can position this at the edge of the pine without disturbing anything."

Mattie slid the tip of the pole into the lake, upstream near the edge of the fallen pine. She kept an eye on the body and the bobbing tree trunk as she and Glenna guided the pole into place. It felt more stable than she'd even hoped for.

Taking up the newly created strap, Mattie moved to the broad trunk of the pine. "I'll see how this works," she said, placing one bare foot on it. "Hold steady."

Rough bark and brittle twigs poked her bare feet as she climbed onto the tree trunk and crouched. She rose slowly, finding her balance before edging down toward the water. Heel to toe, as if she were taking a sobriety test, she stepped onto the floating pine. The icy surge lapped at her feet, numbing them in an instant. A wave of dizziness rocked her as the swirling flow caught her eyes. She refocused on the trunk, gripping it with toes she could no longer feel.

The pine bucked and swayed but held her weight with a minimum of sagging. Inch by inch, she crept until she could sense the white body beside her. Like a gymnast on a balance beam, she bent her knees and knelt.

The body bobbed two feet from her, but her perch was too precarious for her to lean far enough forward to accomplish what she wanted.

Careful to avoid the jagged broken ends of branches, Mattie placed her palms on the rough bark and lowered her legs into the rushing water, gasping as the icy liquid swept up to her waist. She couldn't bear this frigid temperature for long.

The swell rocked the body outward and then sucked it back toward her so that it bumped her thigh, making her shudder. With a buckle of the two-leash strap in one hand and a handle in the other, she leaned over the sickly white torso, straining to keep her head above water while she reached downward to embrace the corpse.

They dipped and swayed in a macabre dance. Her fingers numb, Mattie felt a dull sensation of slick rigid flesh, like a frozen wet fish. At least the cold water had preserved the body enough that she was spared the odor of decomp. She turned her head, her cheek kissing the water as she closed her eyes and clamped shut her chattering teeth. Her chest now beneath the surface, it was all she could do to breathe. She focused on taking short breaths, panting through her nose while keeping her lips tightly closed.

Her arms encircled the torso, and she fumbled to put the buckle of the strap through the handle at the other end, her hands so numb she had to feel her way by pressure cues alone. She didn't dare rise out of the water without securing the strap, because she'd never be able to force herself to hug this corpse again.

After a few seconds of blind groping, she sensed that she'd threaded what felt like an eye of a needle and tugged gently on the strap to test her assumption. She was rewarded with resistance that told her she'd succeeded. Forcing her frozen fingers to hang on, she rose to sit, clumsy as she reeled in the strap to draw the circle tightly around the body's torso.

Now, the pole. Leaning forward, she did her best to wrap the strap several times around the pole that lay along the other side of the body. The pole's narrow diameter allowed her to accomplish it without having to dunk herself in the icy water. Mattie focused on the task doggedly until she'd tied a square knot. Then she struggled to make her frigid fingers clip the buckle onto the second leash handle to reinforce the security of the knot.

By this time, Mattie was shivering hard and having trouble keeping her balance on the tree trunk. A glance told her that Glenna stood by holding her end of the pole. "Okay," Mattie shouted above the noise of the falls. "See if you can pull him in."

Glenna took a few slow steps backward, and the strap tightened between pole and corpse. For a moment, it looked like the corpse would break free of the pine boughs and follow, but then it hung up and wouldn't budge.

"Just a minute," Mattie shouted. She raised her foot, placed it against the body's shoulder, and gently pushed it out and away.

Glenna pulled, and the body went with the pole. Mattie focused entirely on the process, but she looked up when something crashed at the base of the falls. A huge log the size of half a tree bobbed up from the churning water and, like a missile, headed her way.

"Pull!" Mattie shouted to Glenna, her first thought being to get that body out of harm's way. Mattie tried to raise her legs out of the water so she could scramble back down the tree trunk to land, but it was as if they'd turned to lead.

Another glance told her the log would strike the pine trunk about five feet from her position. She didn't have time to reach shore. Grabbing on to any branches she could reach, she drew a deep breath and hunkered down on the trunk as it swayed in the current.

Boom! The log rammed the pine, making it buck and then dip below the water. Mattie tumbled into the lake, its icy flow reaching for her, breaking her clumsy grasp on the pine's boughs. The crashing water bombarded her ears. A glacial fist closed around her chest, forcing her to release her breath. She fought the reflex to gasp for air.

She flailed and kicked as the rapid flow sucked her beneath the pine. Unable to think, she rolled into the tree. Broken branches jabbed her face. Boughs entangled her arms.

Disoriented, she lashed out against the current, not knowing which direction would take her to the surface. She thought her lungs would burst.

She sensed a splash beside her, and a surge of displaced water rocked her into the trunk of the pine, banging her head. Sparks flared at the backs of her eyes, which she dared not open. Pine needles pricked her face.

She felt the furious churning of water beside her . . . the bump of a warm sensation against her arm. She reached out blindly, clutching with stiff fingers. Her dull sense of touch told her she'd grabbed a handful of fur. Robo? She willed her unco-ordinated fingers to hold on and started kicking her feet with all her might.

At the moment when she couldn't resist gasping for air any longer, her head breached the water's surface. She sputtered and coughed, still holding on to Robo while he paddled furiously to stay above the water. Her weight pushed him below the surface. She panicked but immediately regained the presence of mind to release him. He rose up beside her, his head bobbing on the surface.

She tuned in to Glenna screaming behind her and realized she was in the space between the felled tree and the corpse, which remained lashed to the pole. She grabbed the end of the pole and kicked hard as Glenna started reeling it in to shore. Robo swam alongside, making her giddy when she knew he could make it on his own.

Mattie clung to the pole while Glenna hauled it to land. Still gasping air in great, lifesaving gulps, Mattie cleared her vision. Soon she could sense the shallow water a few feet from the lake's edge. She touched down a split second before Robo, and she hugged him with one arm as she dragged herself out of the water.

Robo gave a mighty shake, scattering droplets of the frigid water, while Mattie crawled a few feet up onto the rocky shore before she collapsed. Robo was on her in a second, licking her frozen face with his soft warm tongue and wagging his furry body as he nuzzled her arms and hands.

Her energy and strength had been drained, but she gathered him into a hug. Her teeth chattered and her body shivered hard against him. Even though his fur was soaked, he felt warm beneath the wetness. Convinced he'd saved her life, she kissed his muzzle while he licked her cheek.

Still clutching the pole and struggling to pull the heavy corpse from the lake, Glenna was shouting at her. "Mattie! Are you okay? Talk to me."

Mattie drew a shuddering breath and tried to speak through her chattering teeth. "I'm okay. Just a second."

She leaned against Robo and used him to push herself up to stand. She stumbled toward Glenna as she briskly rubbed her forearms. Though not up to par, she lent enough strength to help tug the corpse to land. Denim pants dragged from where they were caught on heavy work boots. Otherwise the corpse had been stripped bare.

"Thank God you made it out of there," Glenna murmured, as she dropped the pole and helped Mattie scoot the body, face-down, away from the water. "I'll make a fire here in a minute."

Though they were surrounded by wood, the forest was damp and soggy, so Mattie didn't hold much hope for a blazing fire. As she shivered, she studied the back of the corpse, noting that the pink marks on its back appeared to be welts and slashes. Whip marks?

"Let's turn him," Mattie muttered, clenching her quivering jaw.

When they rolled the bloated corpse, she confirmed that it was indeed male. Slash marks crisscrossed the dead man's chest.

She forced herself to examine his face. She couldn't tell how old he was, but he had a close-cropped dark beard along his jawline and dark hair. He stared at the sky with round opaque eyeballs, the lids nibbled away by water life. His nostrils had suffered the same fate, revealing the creamy gleam of cartilage beneath what was left of his nose.

"I think he's been dead a while, but I can't tell," she said, talking to herself as much as to Glenna.

"Good grief, Mattie. Look at the marks on his chest."

Her vision still blurred, Mattie swiped moisture from her eyelids to focus. Pink cuts stood out against his white, bloated flesh. Any residual blood had been washed away, but the letters looked as if they'd been carved with a knife: *PAY.*

"What do you think it means?" Glenna asked.

"Your guess is as good as mine."

FOUR

Mattie huddled by the fire that Glenna had started by using a ferrocerium rod tool to throw a shower of hefty sparks onto a packet of compressed, dried tumbleweed, which she'd brought with her in her backpack. Mattie had to hand it to her—the game warden was better prepared for a backcountry emergency than she. Glenna had used plenty of pinesap-soaked bark and twigs from a pile of deadfall to feed the fire until it was large enough to add branches and logs.

After making sure the fire was banked and that Mattie was warming beside it, Glenna had left to go downhill to radio for help. She'd been gone an hour. Though the heavy clouds looked low enough to touch, they'd still shed no rain. Mattie leaned in close to the fire, toasting her clothing front and back, making it steam as it dried.

She removed her sister's soggy note from her pocket. The paper appeared too fragile to open, so she tucked it inside a small zippered pocket on the outside of her backpack. No matter. She could print another copy when she got back to the office.

Her teeth had stopped chattering, and she decided to walk down to the water and further examine the corpse.

With Robo staying close by her side, she dug out some latex gloves from the bottom of her backpack, slipping her hands into them as she walked toward the body. She wanted a closer look at the pants gathered at the man's feet. Maybe there would be a wallet or some source of identification in one of the pockets.

She stared at the word *PAY* on his chest, wondering what it meant. She thought of the obvious: the man could have been tortured and then killed in order to pay for some transgression—or some perceived transgression. With murder involved, you couldn't make assumptions about the victim's guilt.

She knelt at his feet and started sorting out the pants, which were turned inside out and gathered at his ankles above heavy leather boots. As she worked the denim pants up on the swollen legs, she was able to reveal the waistband and placket. *This is odd. No zipper.* The placket was still closed, held together with five medium-sized navy-blue buttons.

She slipped her hand inside one pocket and then the other, finding nothing, but she noticed that the pants seemed to be hand sewn. They had the wide seams that reminded her of the clothing her foster mother used to make. She checked down by the boots and confirmed that the hems of the pants had been hand stitched.

His boots looked store-bought. They were made with plain leather and had no fancy tooling. Smooth, rounded toes. The boots had been saturated while in the water, and there was no way to tell how old they were. Perhaps when they were removed, there would be a brand name or something useful to try to follow up on.

A crash at the waterfall signaled another huge log coming. Mattie rocked back on her heels to watch it circle and roll at the base of the falls until it righted itself and blasted into the current headed toward the pine. It smashed into the trunk where Mattie had removed the body, moving the tree sideways and ripping up the rest of its root system. The felled pine teetered, tearing away from the edge of the lake foot by foot until at last the forceful current snatched it and pushed it toward the stream.

Thank goodness we moved the corpse out before that happened. Mattie walked back to the fire, picked up her rain poncho, and carried it back to the dead man. She couldn't stand letting him lie there exposed any longer. As she spread the poncho over his torso, she squatted near his shoulders to arrange it over his face and noticed a purple birthmark on his neck. It covered the left side, roughly the shape of a kidney. *Should help identify him,* she thought as she tucked the waterproof fabric under his sides to anchor it.

She went back to the fire, stripped off her clammy gloves, and placed them in a waxy evidence bag that she removed from her backpack. Robo had stayed with her, going back and forth but keeping his distance from the dead man. Now she patted her leg and squatted, folding the dog into her arms and hugging him against her chest. She buried her face in the fur at his neck, dry now but smelling funky with a mixture of lake water and smoke.

"You're the best, you know that," she murmured, kissing him on the silky fur between his ears. His was the bravest soul, and she counted herself among the most fortunate of law enforcement officers to have him as a partner. He'd saved her life more than once.

After finding a treat for him, she spent some time throwing his tennis ball—his favorite reward—even though carrying out this ritual felt bizarre in the presence of a corpse. Afterward, they sat side by side in front of the fire, Mattie feeding it with sodden sticks that sizzled and popped as they dried in the flames. Every few minutes, another log or clump of deadfall came down the falls, and she wondered what the terrain was like up above. Obviously flooded and letting go of dead stuff—nature's way of cleaning house.

She glanced at the corpse. Had this poor man been carried down through the falls before lodging in the pine tree? Had someone buried him up above, thinking he would never be found, only to have Mother Nature intervene?

Mattie scanned the ledge at the top of Hanging Falls, and a flash of movement caught her eye. *What was that?* She searched the ledge but couldn't detect anything out of the ordinary. A single pine jutted out of a rock formation, pointing upward at a wheeling hawk. A mountain jay flickered from one of the pine's limbs and left the bough waving.

Maybe that's all she'd seen—just the normal motion of the forest. She continued to pet Robo as an eerie sensation stole over her. Standing guard over a dead body was unnerving, but surely she wouldn't let her imagination get the best of her. Still, she felt like she was being watched. And if that was the case, she and Robo would be clear targets sitting here in the open by the fire.

After picking up her backpack, she rose to her feet and strode off toward the trees. "Robo, come."

Once they were within the shelter of the trees, Mattie drew a steadying breath and scanned her surroundings. On the other side of the lake, sheer granite walls rose above a boulder field that would challenge even the most skilled rock climber. No place to hide there.

Her eyes were drawn again to the terrain near the falls. She'd climbed to the top of that ledge before, and she knew the path to be steep and rocky. There was a faint trail made by people who had blazed their way up, but not one that the Forest Service maintained.

She itched to take Robo up to explore. If someone was watching, it would be from the ledge. That, coupled with the movement she'd sensed earlier, led her to believe that her suspicion might be right.

Is this man's killer still in the forest?

If she could leave the body and explore the ledge, she was certain Robo would pick up a scent trail and track the observer. But she couldn't leave the body, especially not on a hunch.

She brushed her fingers along the handle of her Glock and hunkered down beside Robo. Her dog didn't seem to be alarmed— no raised hackles, no alerting to the forest. She sighed as she settled in beside him. Maybe this hinky feeling was all in her head. For now, there was nothing she could do except watch and wait.

★   ★   ★

An hour later, she felt relieved to see Glenna and Moose crest the top of the rise and jog down the trail that led to the lake. While Mattie waited, she had built a fire pit and lined its perimeter with a circle of stones before laying some twigs and kindling inside. She'd placed a log halfway into the fire down below until it dried and its end blazed; then she'd carried it like a torch up to her new fire pit beneath the shelter of the trees. She made certain her fire blazed cheerfully before letting the one down below go out.

Her clothing had dried for the most part, so she'd donned a light jacket retrieved from her pack. Off and on, a smattering of raindrops had fallen, keeping the forest wet enough to make tending the fire a challenge.

She'd lost the eerie feeling of being watched, making her wonder if that's all it had been—a feeling. She walked down to meet Glenna, raising a hand in greeting as she approached.

Glenna gave her a once-over with a concerned gaze. "The fire's out. You all right?"

"Sure. I moved it up into the shelter of the trees. I felt exposed down here."

Moose and Robo greeted each other with sniffs and a tussle while Glenna told Mattie the plan. "Sheriff McCoy will organize a posse to bring Detective LoSasso up. They should arrive within a couple hours. I see you covered the body."

"Yeah." Mattie led the way up into the trees toward her fire. "I don't know if it was real or imagined, but I had a feeling I was being watched. So I moved up here."

Glenna frowned as she held her hands out above the flames. "Did you see anything?"

"Maybe some movement. I'd like to climb up there and check it out."

"When the others get here?"

Mattie didn't know when they would arrive. "I'd like to go now. This damp forest is ripe for holding scent. If anyone's up there, Robo will find the track. Would you guard the remains?"

"All right. If you think you should go."

She needed to be on the move again; she'd had enough waiting. "It shouldn't take long."

She slipped on her backpack and headed for the falls. Robo gamboled alongside, eager to run, while Glenna called Moose to stay with her. Mattie had already mapped her course. She found the sloping channel she'd planned to use and started to climb. Robo swept around her to lead the way, and she followed, using boulders, tufts of grass, and bushes as handholds.

When the terrain evened out on top, she could look down on the lake and easily spot the body covered with her yellow rain poncho, but Glenna and Moose remained hidden in the trees. Robo was sniffing everything, burying his nose in rocky cracks and plants. He lifted his head to sneeze but shook it off and went back to the business he was born to do.

"What do you smell, Robo? Can you find a bad guy? Let's go find a bad guy!" Mattie continued the chatter that raised Robo's prey drive. If there had been a human up here, it wouldn't take him long to pick up a scent and then follow it.

Robo moved his head side to side as he quartered the area, moving around the tree that had caught Mattie's eye earlier. He sniffed his way closer to the falls. Tons of water rushed over the edge, and the sound of it crashing down to the rocks below filled her ears. A wave of dizziness struck her as she watched the water pour over the cliff.

She tore her eyes away from it to study Robo. His movements short and choppy, he sniffed, his head wagging back and forth as he homed in on a scent. His excitement transferred to her when she realized he'd found the track of a human. She'd been right. Someone had been in this area and had probably watched her from behind that very tree on the ledge.

Robo struck off from the ledge into the terrain beyond. Summer rainfall had turned this area into an alpine swamp. Trees had tumbled, their tangled roots snaking out in all directions. A temporary lake filled this basin, created from snowmelt and rainfall that had drained down the granite peaks from above. Water rushed through the swampland to the lake, and a torrent flowed from there to spill off the cliff, clearing out some of the deadfall as it went.

Mattie hurried to follow her dog, stepping on tussocks of green grass to avoid falling into the muddy glop. Robo quickly led her onto higher and rockier terrain. Nose to the ground, he zeroed in on the track with no hesitation. She struggled to keep up, not wanting him to get too far from her protection.

Without a leash, she jogged behind Robo, staying as close as possible, her eyes flicking between her dog—so that she could monitor his body language—and the treacherous ground beneath her feet. As far as she knew, there was no way out of this basin except the way she'd come, and there appeared to be few places to hide up here except among the sparse trees.

Hackles rose on Robo's back, making the hair prickle at the nape of her neck. This was her dog's signal that he'd closed in on his prey. She hated to interrupt his search, but she couldn't let him rush into an ambush. "Robo, wait," she said softly.

When he paused, she caught up and took hold of his collar. In a near whisper, she encouraged him to move forward. "Okay, find the bad guy."

They'd done this before, this teamwork between handler and dog, edging through the forest, facing danger together. Time stood still as once again Mattie touched her service weapon. The trees grew thin here against the side of the basin, and she felt exposed.

"Hey!" The male voice came from up ahead. Near. "Hey! Call off the dog. I surrender." His words were drawn with a southern accent, making his *I* sound like *ah*.

What the heck? Surprised, Mattie ducked behind a tree, pulling Robo in behind her. With a burst of adrenaline ratcheting up her heart rate, she searched the forest, but she couldn't spot the guy. "Timber Creek Sheriff's Department," she shouted. "Do you have a weapon?"

Metal clanged against rock, the sound echoing off the granite wall.

"I threw it down. I'm unarmed."

Threw it down? Mattie looked upslope, scanning the boulders and rocks above her.

"Here," he called. "Here in the tree."

And then she spotted him—at the base of the wall, halfway up a pine with spindly branches that didn't offer much cover. She couldn't believe it. She had no doubt that Robo would've led her right to the base of the tree, but the guy was surrendering just at the sight of her dog.

She didn't trust the situation. Was the guy trying to draw her in to shoot her? But as quickly as the question surfaced, she decided the answer was no. Why would he do that when he could've drawn a bead on her as she approached? "Is that your only weapon?"

"Nothing else on me. And that knife I threw down isn't mine anyway," he called back to her.

"Show me your hands," she shouted.

He adjusted his seat on the tree limb and raised his hands, palms out.

"Keep your hands where I can see them." Mattie told Robo to stay and crept forward, moving from tree to tree for cover. She glanced behind to check on her dog and found him peeking out from behind the pine, watching her from where she'd left him. At least he was staying put.

Satisfied that Robo would obey her verbal commands, she drew her service weapon. She didn't know if it would be necessary, but until she could get this man on the ground and determine that he was unarmed, she didn't want to take any chances. He'd watched her earlier and he'd fled when she and Robo climbed up here, not to mention that he'd been carrying a knife, the type of weapon that had been used to carve letters onto their victim.

She crouched and moved to a point where she could see the guy more clearly. He looked to be in his twenties, with shaggy brown hair reaching almost to his shoulders. He wore a ragged denim jacket and jeans. Dirt smudged his thin cheeks below deep-set dark eyes that looked like burning holes.

After covering the last few yards to the base of the tree, she kicked the knife away so that it would be behind her. She didn't take the time to examine it, but on first glance it looked like a large buck knife with a fixed blade. "Come down from the tree slowly, and keep your hands where I can see them."

"Did you tie that dog up?"

He must be really afraid of dogs to react this way. "You don't need to worry about him as long as you do what I tell you."

Keeping his hands raised to grasp the branches above, the guy inched his way down the tree. He wore a pair of high-top tennis shoes that were muddy and worn and looked like they'd seen better days. Once he reached the ground, he raised his hands above his head and turned to face Mattie, his eyes shifting between her and Robo.

Mattie wanted Robo beside her, because she needed to holster her gun to pat this guy down. Even though she believed he was too afraid to try anything stupid, she was still alone in the forest and didn't want to take any chances. "I'm going to call my dog. Keep your hands in the air and don't make any sudden movements."

The guy blanched under the dirt on his face. "Don't let him bite me."

"Stay still, just as you are." Without glancing away, Mattie called Robo to come to heel. Within a split second, she felt Robo brush against her left leg. "Stay," she told him.

"I am!" the guy yelped, evidently thinking she was talking to him. He kept his hands held high.

Even though apprehending a fugitive like this was one of the most dangerous duties a cop had to perform, Mattie had to suppress the urge to laugh. "Good," she replied. "Now keep your hands up and spread your legs. Do you have any weapons or needles on you?"

"I don't use needles. I don't carry a gun or anything. I found that knife in the forest . . . seriously. It's not mine."

Mattie locked his hands in hers at the top of his head and began to pat him down, starting at his armpits. She noted how skinny he was around his rib cage. When she reached his waist, she encountered a bulky object hidden by his shirt and jacket. "What's this?"

"My pack."

"What's in it?"

He hung his head. "Just some food. Some personal stuff."

She thought his posture meant there was something in there that he didn't want her to find. "I'm going to lift your shirt and remove this pack."

As she grasped the hem of his shirt, her fingers brushed a strap. She tugged on it to move the pack around toward his back and found the buckle. The fanny pack felt like it definitely contained something. Holding on to the strap, she let it dangle toward the ground until she could set it down gently. She finished frisking the guy and backed off, stooping to pick up the pack.

The entire time, Robo had stayed where she'd left him. A quick glance told her that he stood with his head up, ears pricked, alert and on guard. Robo weighed in at about one hundred pounds. Big and dark, he often frightened a perpetrator, but he looked beautiful to Mattie. She backed up until she was beside him again.

When Robo tracked a bad guy during training, he always got to take a bite at the end of the exercise, something he loved. Of course, the officer assigned to lay down the track during a training session wore a protective bite suit, which this guy didn't, and Mattie was pretty certain that Robo was smart enough to know the difference. Her dog was being remarkably patient under the circumstances. She murmured, "That's right," to reinforce his good behavior, and then "Watch" to let him know his work wasn't done yet.

"Okay," she said to the guy in her gruff cop's voice. "Who are you, and what are you doing up here?"

FIVE

After lunch, Cole and Angie dropped Riley off at her house before heading out to his next appointment. Angie scooted over from the middle to sit by the window when Riley stepped out of the truck.

"I'll call you later," Riley called to her as Angie pulled the passenger's side door shut and waved.

Cole leaned forward so that Riley could see him and waved too. He waited a few seconds while Angie strapped on her seat belt.

"Thanks for coming to help," he said, as he headed for the highway.

"You didn't give me a choice." Angie stared out the window.

Angie wasn't normally mean-spirited, and Cole had to believe that she wanted to repair their relationship. This girl had been through a lot in the past year: her parents had divorced, her best friend had been murdered, her little sister kidnapped, and now her dad had fallen in love with a new woman. Angie loved Mattie too, Cole had no doubt about it, and he hoped that affection would help win her over in the end.

Cole turned onto the highway to head north out of town. He drove past his own place and set a course for the ranch owned by two brothers who raised cattle and horses. It was about five miles away, which gave him time to start a conversation with his daughter.

"I'm sorry that Parker was rude to you," Cole said, glancing at Angie sideways. "I told him not to come by again. Let me know if he does."

Angie was still gazing out her window. "What did you do, take him outside and punch him in the face?"

Cole huffed a short laugh. "No, but I wanted to. Luckily, I controlled myself."

Angie granted him a thin smile, the first she'd given him in weeks, and it encouraged him more than it probably should have.

"We can't control what people in this town gossip about, Angie. All we can do is try to control our reaction to it."

"You told me that before." Angie turned away from him again.

"Sorry for kicking a dead horse, but it seems like good advice."

Angie sniffed—whether in disdain or in agreement, he couldn't tell. He preferred to believe the latter, although he realized he might be delusional.

Unsure how to initiate the discussion they needed to have, he decided to test the waters. "Angie, I know you're upset, but I hope you're ready to talk about it again. What are you thinking these days?"

She shrugged, not giving him eye contact. "I'm thinking that men are all alike."

Ouch! He hoped she wasn't putting him in the same category as Parker Tate, but it sounded like she just had. "We might have our subtle differences."

"Sure you do."

Angie could dole out her share of sarcasm. "Let's talk about me specifically," he said.

She gazed out the window. "Okay, Dad. Let's talk about you."

"If there's one thing in the world you and Sophie can count on, it's that I love my kids. You guys are number one in my life, and you always will be."

Angie looked at him, her face stony and her jaw clenched. She looked like she had something to say but couldn't bring herself to do it.

"Say what you're thinking, Angie. I want to know."

"You can say that, Dad."

He waited for her to go on, but she didn't. "What? You don't believe it?"

She shook her head and looked away. "I do believe you love us, and you say you put us first. But . . ."

"But what?"

"You've always got things going on in your life."

It stung to hear the same old story, first told by his ex-wife, coming now from his daughter's lips. Cole took a moment to think about it instead of allowing himself the knee-jerk reaction of getting defensive. True, he stayed busy with his work and volunteering as part of the county sheriff's posse. But Angie was busy with school and extracurricular activities and friends—he could go on and on. Things that enriched her life, things he wanted her to participate in.

"I think we all keep busy, Angel, but that doesn't mean we don't love each other. And if I'm not mistaken, we make sure we have meals together as often as we can, and we work together at the clinic. That's why I asked you to ride along with me this afternoon." Cole paused, thinking life wasn't always work alone. "Maybe we need to make more time to play together—I don't know. But spending time with each other will always be important, no matter who else comes into our lives."

"But Dad, why do you have to complicate things by falling in love with Mattie? We can't handle adding someone else to our family. Why can't you just stay friends and keep things the way they are?"

She sounded close to tears, and Cole felt grateful she'd articulated what really mattered to her. He tried to listen to the fears that lay beneath the words. "I wish I could explain the ways of love. I really do. But sometimes I think I don't understand it any better than I did when I was your age."

He paused for a moment to examine her. He still thought of her as his daughter, his little girl, but she was sixteen now and had grown into a lovely young lady. As far as he knew, she had yet to find her first boyfriend. Had her parents' divorce stunted her interest in developing a relationship with the opposite sex? Was that something else he should add to his guilt list?

"I'm not sure yet if the feelings I have for Mattie will lead to adding her to our family." He hoped lightning didn't strike him right here in the truck, because truthfully, asking Mattie to marry him occupied his mind a lot these days. "If Mattie and I do decide to marry, you and Sophie will be an important part of that decision. I can promise you that neither of us would take it lightly."

"It's hard enough to deal with having one mom. I don't want to have to deal with two."

"We're repairing the relationship with your mom, Angie. I have faith that we can work things out with Mattie too."

Angie shrugged, and as she stared out the window, Cole sensed that while she wasn't ready to agree, he'd at least opened the door to them talking about it. That was a big step, and maybe he should back off and talk about the work thing.

"When I was your age, life was simpler. You know your grandparents . . . Grandma nagged your granddad, and he teased her back. I used to wonder if they even liked each other, but they always stuck together during the hard times. We didn't have much family playtime. We worked together on the ranch, Granddad yelled at us if we did something wrong, and he didn't waste time telling us if we did things right. With him, no news was good news." Cole glanced at Angie and smiled, hoping she was at least observing him from the corner of her eye. "And he certainly didn't waste time telling us he loved us."

Angie glanced at him, some of the edges on her face softened.

"So when I had kids, both of you girls, I don't think I really knew how to interact with you. Your mom is a good mom." When she made a noise as if to disagree, he hurried on, wanting to stay on track and finish what he had to say. "Now, I know you've had your differences, but she was good with you when you girls were little. And it was easy for me to just do what I knew how to do: work. I let your mom handle the child-rearing. But you know what? I didn't know what I was missing. I loved you girls, I loved my family, but I didn't know how important it was for us all to spend time together. And I didn't know how much I lost out on during those early years."

"I'm afraid you'll slip into your old habits," Angie said in a hushed voice.

Cole paid attention and received the message loud and clear. He knew it was important not to jump in with reassurances that to her were empty promises. "I can see how you'd think that. I probably look like a lost cause to you."

Angie glanced at him. "You're okay."

"I'm trying, but sometimes I do better than others. I know you have friends you like to be with too, and I appreciate that you come home to dinner in the evening as often as you do."

"Are you saying I shouldn't go over to dinner with my friends?"

"Absolutely not! You're welcome to spend time with your friends, because you don't overdo it. You know what I mean? We all have our own interests, our own commitments, and our own friends. You have more going on in your life than I did when I was a teenager. I'm happy that you're committed to family and to your little sis. I'm thankful that Mrs. Gibbs makes a nice home for us all to live in together. But I also know that each of us has to venture out into the world too. That's just the way of life."

Angie looked down at the floorboard. "I know you want to go out with Mattie more than you do."

"Hey, Mattie and I are both homebodies. She's the one that suggests we get together at our house instead of going out. She wants to be with you kids as much as I do." Balancing a new relationship while making sure he didn't neglect the kids had become a challenge, and Cole was grateful that Mattie seemed to love being with his kids—though lately Angie had spent more time in her room than before, and her absence hadn't gone unnoticed.

They reached the entryway to the ranch, where his next appointment awaited. Cole slowed, turned, and bumped over the cattle guard beside the sign that bore the name *Double K*. The place was owned by brothers Keith and Kevin Perry, two rough-around-the-edges men whom Cole had worked for off and on for several years. Both were in their sixties, and rumor had it that their wives had left them years before they moved here to start ranching. Evidently neither had found someone else to spend his life with, so the two of them lived in a single clapboard ranch house that had grown more and more run-down over the years.

Angie changed the subject to the business at hand. "What are we going to do here?"

"Float a stallion's teeth."

Angie remained silent at first while they bumped along the washed-out lane, filled with potholes, that led to the house, barn, and corrals. "What does floating teeth mean?"

Cole thanked his lucky stars for teenage curiosity. "A horse's upper jaw is wider than its lower, and they chew with sort of a circular motion. Kind of like grinding their food between two flat stones. But as they age, they develop sharp edges on the outside of their upper teeth and the inside of their lower ones that have to be knocked off so they don't bite the inside of their mouths and can still chew their food. We use a tool called floats that grind off the sharp edges."

Cole had been at this business long enough to manage on his own, but he'd wanted this time alone with Angie, and he hoped he'd made a little progress. He suppressed a sigh as he parked outside a barn made from rough-cut lumber that sat beside an arrangement of steel-pole corrals.

The older brother, Keith, came from the barn, his lips pinched around the wad of snuff he always kept tucked inside his lower lip. Cole had never seen him without it. Keith wore denims, a plaid shirt that might not have seen a washing machine in weeks, and low-heeled cowboy boots slouched over at the sides to compensate for his bowed legs. His dark hair was streaked with gray, his moustache and beard even more so.

Cole exited the truck and headed toward the back to round up his supplies.

Keith spit a stream of tobacco juice off to the side before speaking. "Hey, Doc. How ya doin' this summer?"

"Doing well, Keith. Have you met my daughter Angie?" Cole completed the introductions while Angie stayed on the far side of the truck and said hello.

Cole kept up with Keith's running conversation about the rainy weather while he gathered power floats, a tray full of sedation drugs and syringes, and all the paraphernalia he would need. He handed the tray of drugs to Angie, picked up the rest, and followed Keith inside the barn. Since the day was cloudy, the inside of the barn was dimmer than usual. He scanned the ceiling and spotted a light. "Okay if we turn the light on in here, Keith?"

"Sorry, Doc. That light burned out—oh, let me think . . . I'd say about a year ago."

The stocks, a metal stanchion designed to hold horses still so they could be worked on, were set close to the doorway, so Cole thought he could make do. There was a shelf cluttered with cans of all types of balms, ointments, and pastes that ran along the wall, covered with dirt and oily grime. A black live-stock whip hung from a nail, beside which he spotted an electrical outlet on the wall. "All right. Angie, I'll plug in here, and maybe you could just hang on to the tray until I need it."

She nodded, looking around with a frown at the mess of hoses, boxes, old tires, and lord-knows-what piled against the walls. Then she rearranged her features into the neutral mask of a pro, giving Cole a sense of pride. She was turning into a great assistant, and he was glad he'd brought her along.

Until he heard the trumpeting neigh resounding from the back of the barn, followed by hoof strikes against a box stall.

Keith chuckled. "That'll be *Rojo Caliente* tellin' us what he thinks. Kevin's trying to get a halter on him. He's a handful. Just as red-hot as his name."

Cole felt a sense of alarm. "Is this a new stud horse you've got, Keith?"

"Sure is. Bought him down in New Mexico. Got a big, stout hip on him and a heavy-muscled chest. Threw some of the prettiest foals you've ever seen last year."

"Quarter horse?"

"Yeah. Red sorrel, stands a little over fifteen hands, and pure muscle. Quick as a cat on his feet, but his personality is another thing. Watch out when you're working on him, Doc. He likes to bite."

His alarm escalated to full alert, and Cole looked at Angie. "I want you to stand outside the barn until we have Rojo inside the stocks. And then stay beside the doorway until I get him sedated."

Angie nodded and headed out the barn door, reassuring him that she'd do as he said. He wished he had a nickel for every time he'd discussed safety while working around animals with his kids.

Another pickup pulled up outside, and with a quick glance, Cole read the sign on the truck: *Randolph Farrier Services*. This was something he'd not expected. "You got plans to shoe some horses when we're done here?" he asked Keith.

Meanwhile, the aforementioned Rojo Caliente continued to kick up a fuss at the back of the barn, followed by cursing and shouts that Cole assumed were coming from Keith's younger brother, Kevin.

"Thought we'd have Rojo's hooves trimmed while you had him sedated."

"I didn't schedule time for that."

"That's okay. If you can just leave me a little of that sleepy paste, we can manage." Keith turned away before Cole could respond and headed down the alleyway toward the back of the barn. "I'll go see if I can help Kev."

Cole thought Keith meant a mild sedative he dispensed in paste form to his horse clients. He heard Angie exchange greetings with the newcomer before the man entered, lugging a case full of tools, which would include various sizes of nippers, rasps, and right- and left-handed hoof knives.

The farrier gave Cole the once-over with narrow-set gray eyes separated by a nose bridge so pinched it reminded Cole of an Afghan hound. After he set the heavy case down on the ground with a thud, Cole introduced himself, extending a handshake.

"Pleased to meet you, Doc." The man wiped his palms on his jeans and returned Cole's grip with a callused, work-hardened hand. "Quinn Randolph."

Cole began to feel uncomfortable as Quinn continued to study him with an unblinking gaze. "Are you new to town, Quinn?"

"I'm from Hightower. Starting to come over to Timber Creek quite a bit."

Cole had several horse clients around Hightower. Odd that their paths hadn't crossed before today. "You been in the business long?"

"Just started up on my own a few months ago." Quinn withdrew a wallet from his hip pocket and riffled through cards inside it until he found what he was looking for. "Here's my card. I'd appreciate it if you could mention my name to some of your clients."

Cole read the card before placing it in his pocket. It included a list of services: hoof trimming, shoeing, and hoof shaping and balancing.

A stall door at the end of the alleyway banged open and a large red stallion rushed out, for the most part dragging his handlers rather than being led. He reared, pawing the air until Kevin snapped the chain on his halter and brought him down. Kevin was smaller than his older brother but built like a professional wrestler with wide shoulders, stocky and strong. The two were compatible in that Keith tended to make the decisions while Kevin seemed most comfortable working with the animals.

The men had hooked two different lead ropes onto the stallion's halter and managed to guide him, snorting and stamping, down the alleyway toward the stocks. Cole noticed Angie peeking around the doorway, her eyes widening as she took in the fractious animal. She pulled back to disappear again behind the wall, staying well out of the way.

"We've got our hands full with this one," Cole murmured to Quinn.

The farrier gave Cole one of his hard stares as he muttered, "Not a horse born that I can't handle."

Cole had to wonder what methods the man used that made him so sure of himself. He himself planned to use sedation, because this stud horse would never tolerate the dental procedure without it. "Have you had this horse inside the stocks before?" Cole asked as the men approached with the animal.

"Nah," Keith said, his eyes on Rojo. "When we bought him, they said we'd have to sedate him to do any vet work on him or mess with his feet. But Kevin plans to work through that with him. We just haven't had him long enough yet."

Cole wished Kevin a whole lot of luck and hoped he could make progress with the stallion in time. But for today, he'd stick to his original plan. He removed three bottles of sedating drugs from his smock pocket and drew up a combination of xylazine, medetomidine, and butorphanol into a cocktail that would sedate Rojo while allowing him to stay on his feet.

He approached the horse on the younger brother's side, holding the syringe ready. "Kevin, let's have you hold the lead strap and let him circle while I step in beside you and give him the shot."

Rojo bared his teeth and snaked his head toward Cole, but Kevin yanked the lead chain to arrest the movement before the horse could bite. Cole stepped in quickly beside Rojo's neck, close enough that he couldn't strike with those heavy front hooves. He used his free hand to stroke the horse's neck and find the vein, which he occluded with pressure so that he could inject the sedative intravenously. Within seconds, the drugs started to work.

Cole moved back out of the way. "Get him into the stocks."

Rojo followed with sluggish steps, stumbling on the last few as Kevin positioned him inside the rectangular stanchion. He swung the heavy side bar closed, securing the latch at the back.

"This horse needs a few come-to-Jesus sessions," Quinn said as he leaned against the wall.

The words were said in an ominous tone that Cole didn't like, but he chose to ignore them. Just then his phone rang inside his pocket. He ignored it as well and hurried to position the stallion's head high enough at the front of the stocks so that he could insert a dental block that would hold his jaw open.

A quick exam revealed the sharp spines on the edges of the stallion's teeth. Cole grasped the handle of his dental instrument and removed it from the bucket of disinfectant that he was soaking the business end of the floats in, positioned it in Rojo's mouth, and turned on the power. The floats whirred as the tungsten carbide bits ground and smoothed the teeth into a flatter surface.

Quinn was talking to Keith. "You met your new neighbors yet?"

"Afraid so," Keith said. "We don't neighbor much. What a bunch of weirdos."

"That's for sure. Women and girls dress in garb that makes them look like a bunch of nuns."

Cole figured Quinn was talking about the Vaughn family, the ones he'd met in his clinic this morning. The family had impressed him as being cordial and nice. He turned off the floats to feel the teeth on the lower arch, which still needed a little more grinding. He'd probably be better off if he stayed out of the conversation, but he couldn't allow himself to do it. "I suppose they have the right to dress the way they want. Met Mrs. Vaughn and her kids at the clinic this morning, and they seem like real nice people."

Quinn stared at him while Cole turned the floats back on, filling the silence with noise from the instrument.

Quinn raised his voice, directing his comments to Keith. "There's more than just that one family living there. They've got at least five trailer houses lined up and a passel of kids running around. Did some shoeing for a fellow named King who says he's a horse trainer."

"Horse trainer." Keith spat tobacco juice in a way that showed his disgust. "That's a bunch of nonsense. Doubt if they know what they're doing."

"The men dress funny too. Pants that button, suspenders, blue shirts, like it's their uniform. They wear funny-shaped beards along their jaw like those Mennonites you hear about."

Cole stayed out of the rest of the conversation while he tackled grinding Rojo's upper dental arch. As soon as he was done, he turned to Quinn, saying, "He's all yours," before gathering his equipment to pack up. Angie helped him carry his things out to the truck and climbed into the front while he finished up with Keith, providing the medetomidine paste he'd requested earlier. The Perry brothers were going to need it with that horse.

Through the doorway, Cole could hear Quinn lecturing Kevin about how to tie a horse, throw him down, and show him who was boss.

Cole waved a hand toward the open door. "Just so you know, I'm not a fan of treating a horse that way. It's one thing to tie up a leg to work on him, but it's another to try to throw him and roll him. It would most likely result in an injury, either to the horse or to yourself."

Keith rolled his eyes. "Kevin won't stand for that anyway. He's just letting the guy flap his mouth."

Cole nodded, said good-bye, and stepped up into the driver's seat. He pulled his phone from his pocket, saw that the call he'd ignored earlier had come from Sheriff McCoy's cell phone, and dialed him without checking the voice mail.

Sheriff McCoy's deep baritone answered. "Cole, did you get my message?"

"I called you back without listening to it."

"We've got a situation that I need some help with from the posse."

Oh no. He didn't have time for this today. "What's going on, Sheriff?"

"Deputy Cobb and Glenna Dalton are up at Hanging Falls. They've found a body, Cole."

His heart dropped. He hated the thought of Mattie up in the wilderness with a body and felt pressed to go help her. "What do you need from the posse?"

"I need to get Deputy Brody and Detective LoSasso up to the falls and maybe one man to ride along with them."

"I'm away from the clinic now, but I'll call Dad and see if he can get some horses and gear ready for you. We'll need a horse to pack out the body too, won't we?"

Angie turned and stared at him, her face filled with surprise, obviously listening to his side of the conversation. He kicked himself for not keeping a closer watch on his words.

"Yes, we'll need a packhorse, but I don't have all the details yet."

"I'll call you back as soon as I know what our schedule is," Cole said, before ending the call.

"What's that about?" Angie asked, her face set in a concerned frown.

Cole felt like he should tell his daughter what was going on and see if he could enlist her cooperation. "That was Sheriff

McCoy. Mattie told me last night that she and the game warden were going up to Hanging Falls today. Apparently they've
found a body."

"Oh my gosh, Dad! Whose?"

"Don't know, sweetheart. But I've got to call Grandpa to
get things set up for taking people up there."

"Do you need some help?"

He would never allow Angie to ride up to a crime scene
like this, but it pleased him that she'd offered to help. "Thanks,
but I think Grandpa can take care of the horses. I'll have to see
who's available to ride up with the team."

Angie slipped him a sideways glance and settled back in her
seat while Cole pulled away from the ranch and set a course
back to Timber Creek. She probably knew he was the one most
likely to volunteer, because after all, this was Mattie who
needed help. "You were planning to go over to Riley's house
later this afternoon, right?"

"I guess."

As Cole brought his truck up to speed and dialed his dad,
he knew Angie wasn't a bit happy about the situation. He was
sorry, but right now he had his hands full, and there was nothing more he could do about it.

SIX

"You won't let that dog bite me, will you?" the guy said, his eyes fixed on Robo.

Robo opened his mouth in a slight pant, revealing his sharp teeth.

Mattie wondered if the man had had a previous run-in with a K-9. "If you don't make any sudden moves or try to touch me, you have nothing to worry about. Now what's your name?"

"Name's Brown. Tracy Lee Brown."

"Okay, Mr. Brown. Tell me what you're doing up here."

"Campin'." His southern drawl was evident, even on the single word.

Mattie found that hard to believe. She waved a hand in the general vicinity of the basin above the falls. "Up here?"

"Nah, not up here. Down below the falls."

That sounded more believable. "So what are you doing up here today?"

"Just takin' a look around."

The way Tracy Lee's eyes kept shifting from Robo to her and back colored her opinion of him. He certainly looked and acted suspicious, and she had to remind herself not to jump to any conclusions. His fear of dogs could be the sole reason for the shifty eyes.

"Why were you on the ledge watching me earlier?"

He wagged his head. "I wasn't."

"I know you were. I spotted you there, and that's where my dog picked up your scent."

"I wasn't really watchin' you on purpose. I started to come down and saw you there, so I decided to stay where I was."

"Why not come on down?"

He cleared his throat. "Didn't want to run into anybody today. I . . . I just went for a hike. All I want to do is get back to my campsite."

Robo might be making the guy nervous, but he wasn't solely responsible. Mattie decided that Tracy Lee was clearly hiding something. "Where do you live when you're not camping, Mr. Brown?"

"Don't have a permanent home this summer."

"Where was your last place of residence?"

"Down near San Angelo." He paused, flicking the fingers of his right hand as if they were a release valve for some of his nervousness. "Texas."

"When did you arrive here near Timber Creek?"

"Maybe the first of June. I've been here most of the summer."

"Camping?"

"Yeah. Pretty much campin' most of the summer." The fingers of his right hand continued to twitch.

"Do you have a camping permit?"

He looked startled. "Do I need one?"

Mattie was fairly sure he didn't need a permit in this part of the national forest, although living on government land was illegal. No permanent address, camping, and his unkempt condition added up to squatting in her book. This was something the Forest Service needed to look into. "Depends on where you camp. You'll have to take me there."

He flicked his fingers again as he stared at Robo.

This guy knew more than he was saying, and she wasn't ready to believe that he'd found the knife he'd been carrying. She had a right to take him to the station for questioning, and she could probably justify looking into his pack without permission, but it was always good protocol to ask first. "You say there aren't any weapons in your pack here, right?"

He nodded, but he looked even more worried.

"Mind if I take a look inside?"

He puffed out a breath. "I guess you can. Nothing illegal in there."

Mattie picked up the fanny pack and opened the zipper. First thing she spotted—a bag of marijuana and a pipe. She sorted through the rest of the stuff: beef jerky, granola bars, candy, and bags of trail mix. All a person needed to satisfy the munchies. There was also a roll of cash in an outer pocket, which Mattie left untouched and zipped securely in place. "You do know it's illegal to possess weed on federal land, don't you?"

His mouth fell open. "What?"

"In Colorado you can possess a small amount of marijuana for use in your own home, but it's against the law to smoke it in a national forest." Mattie recited the code, watching his face fall. "Is anyone else up here camping with you?"

He shook his head. "I'm alone."

"Did you see anyone come up here during the past week?"

His gaze didn't quite make eye contact. "Nah, I haven't been at the falls for a couple weeks. My camp's over a mile away."

Mattie decided to be done with the polite approach. "I'm having trouble believing you, Tracy Lee. You see, I think you were watching me earlier, and I think you know we fished a body out of the lake by the falls."

His eyes widened, and he clamped his lips shut.

"What do you know about that body?"

He was shaking his head even before she finished the question. "Don't know nothin' about a dead man."

And yet he knew the corpse was a man. "I think you do, Tracy Lee. I think you know plenty."

"No, ma'am."

It was time to end the questioning. Detective Stella LoSasso would pick it back up later at the station. "Clasp your hands on the back of your head, Tracy Lee."

"Oh, shit." Though he complied, his comment told Mattie he'd been this route before. She'd bet money this man had a record. Time would tell what all was on it.

"Robo, guard." Robo shifted, lowering into a fierce crouch that would scare anyone, digging his toenails into the ground as if to launch, while Mattie moved behind Tracy Lee to stay away from his reach. She figured he was too frightened of Robo to try anything, but it never hurt to play it safe. She snapped a cuff on one of his wrists and then the other before letting her captive lower his arms in front. They had some rough terrain to journey through on their way back to Hanging Falls, and with her partner at her side, there was no reason to force the man to walk with his hands cuffed behind his back.

"Robo, out," she said, releasing him from his stance.

Robo looked disappointed, as he released his bunched muscles only slightly, still keeping his gaze fixed on Tracy Lee. She'd used up her supply of gloves and didn't have an evidence bag with her, so she picked up the knife with two fingertips by the very end of the blade and placed it lengthwise on top of the snacks inside Tracy's fanny pack. She would have to carry it that way until they reached the others down at the falls.

"Let's go," she said as she pointed the way.

He headed out tentatively, evidently not wanting to turn his back on Robo. "Don't let that dog bite me."

"He's a professional, Mr. Brown. Haven't you figured that out yet?" As Tracy Lee began to walk away, Robo gave her a glance that she interpreted as asking permission for one of his favorite parts of the job. "Go ahead. Book him, Robo."

Robo trotted forward, his head high and his tail waving, eager to escort their prisoner by walking near the man's left heel. Tracy Lee let out a squeak that sounded like a mouse and drifted to the right while he tried to walk and keep his eyes on Robo at the same time.

Since Mattie followed behind, she allowed herself the pleasure of a smile. Sometimes her dog cracked her up. And she loved him more than words could express.

As they broke out of the timber and approached the swampy drainage basin, a flash of lightning followed instantly by a roll of thunder shattered the air. Rain spattered and turned rapidly into a downpour, the frigid drops soaking Mattie's jacket at once. The dark sky had finally broken open, and this elevation—near tree line—was a most dangerous place to be.

She scanned the area for a boulder under which they could seek shelter. It was best to just hunker down and wait for the storm to pass, but from the looks of the sky, that might be a long time.

★ ★ ★

Cole and his party crested the last ridge on the Hanging Falls trail. Lightning cracked nearby on the peaks, injecting the smell of ozone into the air. Cole's mount, a bay gelding called Duke, tucked his tail and spooked, hopping to the side and making Cole pull the reins tight so he wouldn't set off the other horses in the string. Mountaineer, the packhorse Cole was leading, plodded along behind, his placid nature providing a steady example for the other horses.

As the dark clouds dumped a torrent of rain, he could hear both Brody and Stella muttering curses behind him. Keeping a tight rein on Duke, he turned to check on them. Stella LoSasso, unused to riding horseback but gaining experience during her tenure as Timber Creek County's only detective, wore a green slicker several sizes too large for her that almost swallowed both her and her mount. The slight woman sat hunched in the saddle on the back of a gentle palomino mare named Honey.

"How are you doing, Stella?" he called over the rush of the pouring rain.

"I've been better, that's for damn sure," she replied, looking at him from under a droopy hood that covered her long auburn hair.

Brody, more comfortable around horses, rode behind her on a black-and-white paint mare named Fancy. Ken Brody was a tall man with broad shoulders and a gruff exterior, but over the past few months of working with him, Cole had learned that his tough outer layer and machismo attitude covered a softer heart that cared a lot about justice and his fellow members of the human race. He also wore a sheriff's department slicker, although his fit his large stature better than Stella's fit her.

"Ken, is everything okay?" Cole called.

"Yup, but we better get the hell off this ridge."

"Heading downhill now."

Having grown up on a ranch near Timber Creek, Cole had been to Hanging Falls countless times. It was an easy hike or ride on a well-groomed trail with a beautiful, pristine spot to enjoy at the end. Hard to believe someone would sully it by killing a person up here.

He leaned back slightly as Duke picked his way down the rocky trail. Cole was anxious to see Mattie, and he searched the stand of trees down by the lake, hoping to spot her. Two forms materialized from the trees—a person and a dog—and they moved down toward the lake before stopping. The dog ran around with excitement when he spotted their party and began to bark.

Cole could recognize that bay anywhere—Moose. *The person is too tall for Mattie. Must be Glenna.*

As they approached, a yellow spot near the lake assumed the shape of a covered body. Cole reined Duke through the downpour toward Glenna and dismounted when he drew near.

Glenna's drenched, floppy hat did very little to protect her from the deluge, and the curly dark hair that typically frizzed around her face lay plastered against her cheeks. At least she did receive some benefit from the lightweight rain jacket she wore, though she looked chilled standing there in her shorts and hugging herself with her tightly wrapped arms.

A bolt of lightning struck a lone pine on the far side of the lake, followed by thunder that echoed off the rim. "Is there someplace we can take shelter?" he asked Glenna.

"Follow me." She turned and headed back into the grove of pine she'd come from. Apparently loving the rain, her big Rhodesian ridgeback gamboled in front of her.

Cole glanced behind to make sure Stella was still upright and forward in the saddle, but Brody had evidently helped her dismount. She was following Cole, her slicker a few inches from the ground, while Brody led both horses.

Leading Duke and Mountaineer, Cole spoke up so that Glenna could hear. "Where's Mattie?"

Glenna glanced back over her shoulder. "She climbed up to the ledge above the falls about an hour ago. She thought someone was watching from up there earlier while I was gone, and she wanted to take Robo to check it out."

Alarm shot through him. This was what scared him most about loving Mattie—when it came to doing her job, she never hesitated to put herself in danger. She'd thought someone was watching . . . and so she'd gone up to investigate. Alone and no doubt hoping to catch the guy before he got away. And now she'd be at the upper elevation, exposed to lightning.

Glenna reached a huge boulder and turned. "There's not enough room for the horses, but I think we can shelter here until the storm passes."

"So where exactly did Cobb go?" Brody asked as they squatted around the base of the monolith, making themselves as low to the ground as possible.

"There's a steep trail that leads to the ledge where the waterfall spills over," Glenna said. "She went up there."

A frown of concern etched itself into the hard planes of Brody's face. Rain dripped from his hood. "This ground is saturated. And this amount of rainfall will probably cause the lake to rise. Once the lightning stops, we're going to need to process this scene and pack that body out before the trail becomes impassable."

"Mattie and I took photos before she covered it," Glenna said.

Not knowing where Mattie was and if she was okay, Cole couldn't stand to wait. "I'll climb up and find Mattie."

"Going up there now would be foolhardy," Brody said, his voice a deep-pitched growl. "Cobb's smart. She'll find a place to take shelter and come down when she can."

As if to punctuate Brody's words, a simultaneous clap of thunder and crack of lightning struck nearby. Cole could feel the hairs on his forearms rise in the electrified air.

"Don't take an unnecessary risk, Cole," Stella said.

Times like these made him think of his kids. They needed him. Though his ex-wife had tried to recover from her depression, her mental health was still a work in progress. If something should happen to him, he couldn't count on her to raise the girls alone. Clenching his jaw, he decided to wait ten minutes to see if the lightning would let up, and he leaned back against the boulder, the cold chill of the stone immediately seeping through his slicker and into his back.

While they waited, Glenna filled them in on Mattie's daring retrieval of the corpse, a tale that made Cole's skin crawl. He imagined what it would be like to plunge into that icy water beside a dead man.

The thunder and lightning gradually rolled away toward a neighboring set of peaks. Although rain still fell from the darkened sky, they determined it safe to venture away from the boulder. Cole led the horses toward the lake, tied them to a lodgepole pine near the grove's edge, and joined the others beside the corpse.

He glanced at his watch. It was after six, and they were losing light fast. The noise of the falls pounding the rocks drowned out all other sound. He scanned the area next to the cascade and thought he could spot the faint trail Mattie had used.

"I'm going up to find Mattie while you process the scene," he told Brody, and turned to leave before anyone could protest.

Rain continued to beat on the hood of his slicker and drip from the foliage beside the trail. Cole started to climb, discovering immediately that his slick-soled riding boots provided little traction on the slippery path. Grabbing on to bushes where he could to help keep his balance, he edged upward.

At the top, he found a whole different world than the last time he'd been up here. The entire drainage basin was on the move, water streaming down to pool at the bottom in a lake the size of the one below the falls. It had devoured trees as it spread, some of them still standing, others leaning at crazy tilted angles.

Floodwaters dragged some of the felled trees downward in a relentless liquid march. Even as he stood on the ledge beside the falls, a pine slipped over the spillway about ten feet away and crashed against the rocks as it rode the watery chute into the pool below.

"Good grief," he muttered under his breath. He headed toward the narrow stand of evergreens near the basin wall.

He'd not gone more than twenty feet when he spotted two people emerge from the trees and head his way. A dog that could only be Robo trotted jauntily beside the lead person, someone too tall to be Mattie.

As they drew near, he could see Mattie in back, and a weight fell from his shoulders. He raised his hand in a wave, which she returned, telling him she'd spotted him too. Neither Mattie nor the guy in the lead wore a raincoat, and they both looked soaked. He could tell that the guy wore cuffs by the way he walked with his hands close together in front.

So Mattie found her peeping tom. With a huge sense of relief, Cole waited at the top of Hanging Falls for the woman he loved and her prisoner.

SEVEN

The rain slackened to a chilling drizzle, but the damage had already been done. Mattie kept one eye on the edge of the lake as it inched up closer to the corpse. In the past half hour, the width of the waterfall had tripled, closing off the trail beside it. Tons of water poured over the ledge.

The recovery team had finished scouting out the lay of the land and taking the photographs they would need. They'd also enclosed the remains in a body bag, getting it ready to strap onto Mountaineer's packsaddle.

Though it was midsummer, the heavy cloud ceiling obscured any sunlight that might still be available, making Mattie shiver. Nightfall would come early. She kept one eye on Tracy Lee Brown, who sat cuffed under Robo's watch a short distance away while she huddled with the others to make plans.

Brody eyed the lowering clouds. "This sky isn't going to clear anytime soon. We won't have time to get down before it's too dark to see."

"We'll just have to use flashlights, because we can't stay here," Stella said.

"That trail was rough before," Glenna said. "With this much rainfall, no telling how much more of it has been washed out."

"I think we can make it," Cole said. "I'll lead the way."

Mattie felt torn. She was wet, she was cold, and a large part of her wanted to return home. Ever since they'd found the body, her mind had been focused on her duty as a law enforcement officer. But since she'd returned to this spot by the lake, she'd been thinking of her sister and grandmother. She was scheduled to leave town in the morning to go to California, and yet . . . there were so many things she and Robo should do to assist the investigation. Perhaps she should delay her departure for a day or two.

"This guy," she said, tipping her head in Tracy Lee's direction, "says he's got a campsite near here, and I think we should search it. He's the closest thing we have to a suspect, and I think we need to go to his camp sooner rather than later. Maybe we could shelter there overnight."

"There are six of us," Stella said. "What kind of tent does he have? I doubt if it could provide shelter for all of us."

Mattie conceded that this would be true. She started to speak, but Brody cut her off.

"Don't even think about splitting up, Cobb. We stick together. If this guy isn't our killer, then there's someone on the loose who could still be up here."

"I believe that body was buried up above and came down the falls," Mattie said, thinking out loud. "But it was too flooded for me to go in there to search. Robo and I still need to do that."

"Tomorrow's another day," Brody said.

"But you leave on vacation tomorrow," Stella said to Mattie.

Brody raised a brow as if the thought hadn't occurred to him. "Well . . . we'll have to make do. But right now, time's a-wasting." He looked at Cole. "Let's get the remains strapped to that packhorse and get off this mountain."

Mattie thought Cole looked relieved as he turned away to help.

★   ★   ★

The trip down to the trailhead was grueling, and by the end, Mattie's legs were trembling, from both cold and fatigue. She and Robo had led the way, lighting the hazardous trail with a flashlight. Cole had followed her, leading Mountaineer with his grisly burden. Brody had insisted that Glenna use his mount, and he'd hiked at the end of the line behind Tracy Lee Brown, who'd remained sullen and silent.

By midnight they'd slipped down the last hundred yards of the muddy trail into the parking lot at the base. Mattie had never been so relieved to reach level ground.

Brody had used the satellite phone to stay in contact with Sheriff McCoy. The sheriff's Jeep, Deputy Garcia's cruiser, and the coroner's van were waiting at the parking lot when they arrived, their headlights creating a dazzling sparkle in the mist. McCoy stepped out of his vehicle and came forward to greet them.

Deputy Garcia exited his cruiser to join the sheriff, moving forward to take custody of Tracy Lee. McCoy had decided to keep him on a forty-eight-hour hold at the jail for questioning. During that time, the head ranger with the Forest Service could determine what charges would be brought against him for the possession of an illegal substance on federal land. Garcia left, taking the bedraggled Tracy Lee Brown with him.

Cole dismounted and led Mountaineer behind the van, where a grim-faced Dr. McGinnis opened the doors. As coroner of Timber Creek County, the local family physician would take charge of the body and have it transported to the medical examiner in the neighboring county, since Timber Creek was too small to retain those services.

Brody and Cole worked together to move the body bag from the packsaddle onto a stretcher and then up into the van, while Mattie, with Robo at her side, stood back with Stella and the sheriff. She huddled beneath the slicker Cole had given her and struggled to keep her teeth from chattering.

"Deputy Brody has kept me apprised of the situation, so we don't need to meet at the station tonight. You two are free to go home," McCoy said to Stella and Mattie. "Detective, let's meet at seven o'clock sharp in the morning."

Mattie unclenched her jaw, which resulted in a quiver as she spoke. "I'll be there too. I plan to delay my trip for a couple days. Or as long as it takes for Robo and me to do what we need to."

McCoy studied her with an unwavering gaze. "I won't pretend we don't need you. But I won't ask you to postpone your vacation."

"Y-you don't have to." Mattie tried to control her shivers.

McCoy shrugged off his jacket and draped it over her shoulders. "Then go home now and get warmed up."

Before she could say anything, he turned away to go talk to Dr. McGinnis.

"Are you sure you want to play it this way, Mattie?" Stella asked as she moved closer. "I know how much this trip means to you."

"I'll still go. But the first forty-eight hours are the most important to the case, so I'll stay and do what I can. Keep your fingers crossed that the rain stops so Robo and I can get back up to the falls."

"Do you have some whiskey at home?"

"No." The only alcohol Mattie kept at her house was the rubbing kind, aside from a stash of beer she kept handy for Stella. Having been raised by an alcoholic and knowing that liquor and she didn't mix, Mattie never kept the hard stuff around.

"Do you want me to bring some over? I think a hot toddy before bed would do you some good."

"I'll stick to hot chocolate, but thanks anyway."

Glenna called to her from across the parking lot, where she stood beside her pickup. "Do you want a ride home, Mattie?"

She and Robo had caught a ride with Glenna and Moose that morning, so her own unit was still parked in front of her house. Before she could answer, Cole called back to Glenna, "I'll take Mattie home."

"Hmm . . . looks like there'll be no need for that hot toddy after all," Stella said, her grin apparent in the glow of the surrounding headlights. "See you in the morning, Mattie."

Stella chuckled as she walked away to join the sheriff. The detective often teased Mattie about her growing relationship with Cole, and by now Mattie had grown used to it.

Cole came up, leading Duke and Mountaineer. "I'll load the horses, and then we can go. Here are the keys to the truck. Go ahead and get it started so it'll warm up."

Leading the other two horses, Brody joined Cole at the back of the horse trailer while Mattie unlocked the truck, loaded Robo into the back of the cab, and climbed into the driver's side. She perched on the edge of the seat while she fired up the engine, then ran around the front to the passenger's side.

She pulled the sheriff's coat tightly around her and sat shivering, hugging herself while she waited for the engine to run long enough to warm the heater's outflow. A musty odor tainted with firewood smoke from her damp clothing filled the truck's cab. Trying to watch Cole from the back window, Robo darted back and forth behind the console, still energetic despite his trek in the mountains.

She could hear Cole decline Brody's offer to help unsaddle the horses before they said good-bye, and then Cole opened the driver's side door and stepped up into the truck to take his seat.

He looked at her with concern and reached out his hand. "How ya doin'?"

She slipped her cold fingers into his warm grasp and spoke between chattering teeth that she'd given up trying to control. "I got chilled this morning and haven't been able to warm up. Even the hike down the mountain didn't do it."

He flipped on the seat warmers, turned up the heater, and began to rub her hand. "You need to get out of those wet clothes. I think I have a clean coverall in the back. I'll get it for you."

Cole leaned between the bucket seats, nudged Robo out of the way, and began rummaging around. "Here," he said, laying the coverall on the console. "Let me help you get your boots off."

He exited his side of the truck and dashed around the front to hers. Mattie had shrugged off the sheriff's coat and set it aside and was now wrestling around to pull off her slicker, twisted and pinned beneath her. By now, the heater's warm output had combined with the humidity to fog up the windows. All of the others had pulled away from the parking lot, leaving them alone in the dark.

Cole opened her door and reached for her boots, untying the laces and pulling them off her cold feet. He stripped off her wet socks while she succeeded in shedding the slicker. "Unzip your pants," he said.

This was no time for modesty, and besides, Cole had seen her without clothing several times before. But still, this level of intimacy was unfamiliar, and a warm flush rose on her cheeks, the first warmth she'd felt since she'd hovered over Glenna's fire this morning.

She unzipped and bridged off the seat enough to wriggle her wet pants down to her thighs. From there Cole grasped the waistband, his warm fingers creating a frisson of pleasure and a cascade of memories. He tugged her pants off.

"Under different circumstances, darlin', this could be a lot more fun," he murmured, giving her legs and feet a brisk rub-down as their eyes met. "Here, hand me that coverall before I get too distracted."

Torn between welcoming the distraction and the shivers, Mattie grabbed the coverall and with Cole's help quickly pulled the dry garment up to cover her legs. She slipped her shirt over her head, and in response to his muttered "Lord, have mercy!" she snorted with laughter. She held his gaze, flirting with him as she shrugged into the upper part of the coverall and slowly zipped it closed. It amazed her how fast she could switch from embarrassed to flirtatious when she was with this man.

He was tucking the extra pants length over her cold feet and placing them against the heat vent. "I don't have any spare socks, so keep these cold puppies right there. Is that coat dry enough to cover you?"

"It'll work." Actually, the few minutes it had taken to change into dry clothes and the touch of his hands had definitely helped warm her blood. Her teeth were no longer chattering.

He placed his hand at the back of her head and drew her close for a kiss that warmed her a considerable amount more. "Is that better?" he murmured against her lips.

"Much," she replied, kissing him again.

He smiled as Robo barked, ending the kiss. "I've been needing that all day."

She touched his cheek. "Evidently I have too."

He closed her door gently, trotted around to his side, and climbed in. He diverted some of the heat to the defroster and began wiping the inside of the windshield. "I'll get that heat back on your feet full force as soon as I can."

"It's all right," she said, loving this man for always thinking of her well-being, something she'd experienced only from Mama T, her foster mother, before meeting Cole. She shifted to sit cross-legged, tucking her feet under her before settling into the warmth of the bucket seat. "This seat warmer is already doing the trick. This is heaven."

"It certainly is," he said, putting the truck in gear before reaching for her hand. "We have ten miles to go, and I have you all to myself."

Robo settled down in the back and went to sleep while they rode in silence, Mattie savoring the cocoon of warmth and love that Cole had spun. But then her mind went back to the dead man she'd fished out of the lake. She wouldn't be able to push aside the memory of his cold flesh and the terrible marks on his body anytime soon. What significance did the word *PAY* carved on his chest have? Would it eventually give them a lead?

How were they going to identify him and notify his family? Family notification had gained much more significance during the last few weeks since she'd found hers.

"I'm going to have to call Julia and tell her I can't leave for a couple of days," she said, worried about disappointing her sister.

"I heard you tell the sheriff." Cole gave her a sympathetic glance. "Sorry this has come up at the last minute. But good grief, Mattie, a body in the lake? So you're sure it wasn't an accidental drowning?"

Cole must not have seen the condition of the corpse before coming up the trail to find her. He'd helped the department time and again with their investigations, and at this point she felt no hesitation whatsoever in discussing the case with him. "We're sure. He has marks on his torso that might have been made by a whip of some kind. And someone carved the word *pay* on his chest."

"*Pay*?" Cole frowned as he considered it. "As in payback for something?"

"Who knows, but I think that's probably it. For what, I have no idea."

Mattie thought it over for a few minutes before breaking the silence. "That guy Robo tracked down could be the man who killed him, but I don't want to jump to any conclusions. We can't even be certain the knife he was carrying was involved."

He frowned at her. She knew he worried about her more than he should, because they'd been down this road before, but at least he was holding his tongue tonight. To put his mind at ease, she told him how the guy had surrendered as soon as he spotted Robo. The tale seemed to restore some humor to his expression.

Cole tossed her an amused smile. "It's a little hard to believe the guy's a vicious killer when he caved at the sight of a dog. Although I have to give Robo his due—he can look pretty scary when he wants to."

Mattie agreed and returned the smile, enjoying their companionship. "There's one thing about the victim that was unusual—besides the marks, of course. His pants were denim, but they looked homemade."

Cole got a funny look on his face, and he shifted his attention between her and the road as he spoke. "I met a new client this morning, a woman who came in with a German shepherd." He went on to tell Mattie about Ruth Vaughn and her children and their manner of dress. "I doubt if their clothing was store-bought. And at a farm call I made, a farrier showed up and talked about my clients' neighbors. Said the men wore pants that looked homemade. No zippers, only buttons."

Mattie remembered the placket in their victim's pants and the five navy-blue buttons sewn there, an image that gave her a much-needed spurt of adrenaline. "I think you've just given us a lead, Cole. The sooner we can identify this man, the faster we can gather information about him."

She reached for her backpack to get her phone. "I'll text Stella tonight about it, and we can get on this early tomorrow morning. Where does this family live?"

"I don't have their address off the top of my head, but I can get it for you at the clinic."

"I'll let her know. We've got to check missing person reports and do some research before we go out there to talk to them," Mattie said, while she texted Stella.

The streetlights of Timber Creek cast a warm glow on the horizon as they approached the town. Mattie hated for her time alone with Cole to come to an end. Cole evidently did too, because he slowed more than necessary when they reached the last curve into town.

As they passed the lane that led to his house, Mattie thought of his kids. "How are the girls?"

"They're fine."

This time Cole didn't look at her, which seemed unusual, since the road was straight and free of traffic. "What did they do today while you were gone?"

"Angie spent some time with Riley, and Sophie was at home with Mrs. Gibbs."

Yep, he was definitely avoiding her gaze. "And how was Angie today? Is she any friendlier?"

"We had a talk. She's starting to come around."

"Did she tell you exactly what's been bothering her?" Mattie had her suspicions that Angie was upset about Cole developing a relationship with her, and his behavior seemed to confirm that.

"She's having trouble with all the changes in her life. You know, the trip we took to Denver a couple weeks ago for the kids to see their mom was against her wishes, although I was proud of the way she conducted herself. Sophie is happy with the way things are going, and Angie will come around."

Again, no eye contact as they drove into the town limits. "She's upset about you and me, right?"

This time he looked at her before moving his gaze back to the road. "I think what upsets her most is change. It has nothing to do with you. She loves you."

Mattie knew Angie and Sophie were fond of her, but the thought of causing them discomfort made her heart ache. "Would it help for me to talk to her?"

Cole shook his head. "Not right away. Let me see what I can do over the next few days. Maybe after your trip, we could all sit down together. We'll see what feels right then."

She gazed out the window, the mellow feeling from being with Cole melting away. Falling in love with this man had been the absolute best thing that had ever happened, but she didn't want to reach out for that blessing at the expense of his children.

Cole extended his hand, palm up. "Don't worry, Mattie. This will all work out. Angie cares too much about you to take a hard stand. She's just struggling with a lot of stuff right now. We'll be okay."

"Her happiness means a lot to me."

"I know. Me too. But you and I have a right to happiness too, and we can work this out for the best for all of us."

Mattie turned to him, and their gaze met for as long as it could before he focused back on his driving. He turned onto the street where she lived and pulled up to her small home, a snug one-bedroom made of adobe bricks covered with tan stucco. After turning off the engine, he drew her as close as the console between them allowed.

His kiss was meant to reassure her, but instead it created a mixture of sadness and foreboding. Would the joy she found with this man last? Or would it be as fleeting as the other moments of happiness in her life?

Robo awakened and popped up in back, pressing his nose between them. Cole ruffled Robo's ears and gave Mattie one more quick kiss before opening his door to get out. "Let me help you inside."

Only time would give her the answers to her questions, because for now, the only thing she could imagine was to stay the course. It would take more gumption than she had in her to push this man and his kids out of her life.

EIGHT

Saturday Morning

Mattie awakened to the warm, orangy glow of sunrise in her room, an infrequent phenomenon this summer. She'd worn her winter sweats to bed and cuddled under the quilt Mama T had made for her as a high school graduation gift, warming up enough to fall into a deep sleep. Though the night had been short, she'd slept without nightmares, which had dwindled during the past month.

But as she stretched under the covers, the horrible image of the dead man filled her mind. She shook it off, threw back the covers, and reached for Robo, who'd arisen from his cushion to greet her. He placed his chin on her knee, allowing her to pet his fine head and kiss him between the ears before he whirled to run into the hallway, obviously anxious to go outside.

She'd slept with woolen hiking socks on her feet, and she padded after him to open the door to the backyard. Though this side of her house had a western exposure, she could tell that the entire sky was awash with shades of rose and pink reflecting off the storm clouds that hung over the mountains.

Robo ranged around the yard, which was enclosed by a seven-foot chain-link fence topped with razor wire that the county had installed to protect him. Mattie went around to the side gate to make sure the heavy-duty lock on it was secure and undamaged, and while she was there, she admired the streaks of color throughout the sky.

The red sky might be beautiful now and the gentle sunshine welcome, but it didn't necessarily bode well for the rest of the day.

After letting Robo back into the kitchen, she fed him his kibble and then made herself a peanut butter and jelly sandwich for breakfast. She never invested in a lot of food, relying on energy bars, peanut butter, and bread as her staples.

Her cell phone jingled on the counter top where she'd left it. She glanced at the clock—quarter to six. Unfortunately, in her line of business, early-morning calls often brought bad news and a flurry to get to work. But not always. One person in her life called frequently this time of day. Mama T. And caller ID said her foster mom waited on the other end of the connection.

"Good morning, Mama."

"Good morning, *mijita*."

Mattie never tired of the endearment. Being called *my little daughter* by her Mama T was one of the small pleasures in her life. "I see you're up with the sunshine this morning."

Mama chuckled. "Always. Are you packed and ready to go?"

The words reminded her of a different phone call she needed to make before going to work, the one to her sister, one that wouldn't give her much pleasure. "I have to put my trip off for a day or two, Mama."

"Oh no! Why is that?" Her disappointment was palpable; Mama T had been almost as excited as Mattie for her to meet her sister and grandmother.

"I have work that I need to do."

Mama scoffed. "*Mijita*, no work is that important. You must go today."

Although she didn't want to tell Mama T the details, she shared that they had found a body in the wilderness. "Robo and I need to search for evidence, and there was too much flooding up there for us to do it yesterday. Maybe with this break in the rain, we can get it done today."

"I don't like the sound of that." And indeed, her foster mother sounded worried. "You must be careful. Don't take any chances."

"I won't, Mama. That's why we came home last night." Mattie didn't add that she'd come down from the high country against her wishes. "I need to call Julia and tell her I'll be a couple days late."

"Your poor abuela. She'll be so disappointed."

Mattie didn't want to make the situation into something worse than it was. "Not as long as she knows I'm still coming. I'll be able to leave soon, Mama."

After talking for a few more minutes, Mattie wrapped up the conversation, ending it with a promise that she would come by before she left for California to pick up some tamales that Mama T had made for her to take with her, a gift for her new relatives. She glanced at the time, which was now six—five o'clock in California. Maybe too early, but she needed to make the call before going to work.

She swiped to her contacts and tapped the entry for Julia. She listened to the phone ring several times and was mentally constructing a message when her sister suddenly connected the call.

"Mattie, good morning! Are you already on the road, *mi hermana*?" Julia's voice was low-pitched and rich, and like Mattie, she had no Spanish accent unless she was speaking that language. She sounded sleepy and spoke in a hushed voice.

"I'm sorry I woke you."

"I was only dozing. I woke up about a half hour ago, so excited that this day was finally here. Just a minute." Mattie heard Julia speak quietly to her husband and then in a normal tone when she came back on the line. "There, I moved into the living room so we can talk. Jeff is going back to sleep."

Mattie wasn't sure how to begin, so she decided to just say it. "Julia, I need to stay here another day or two. I'm sorry to have to wake you up with this news, but I wanted to tell you before I have to go in to work this morning."

"Go to work? But you have today off . . . your vacation starts today."

Mattie hated that her sister sounded upset. "I know, but we have some urgent business I have to take care of before I go."

"What do you mean, urgent business? What could be so urgent?"

"We've had a homicide in our county, and I need to do my part of the investigation before I leave."

"Can't someone else do it, Mattie? This is your vacation."

"Timber Creek is a very small town. Robo and I are the only ones who can do this type of work." Mattie tried to reassure her. "I'm still going to come."

There was a long pause before Julia spoke. "Abuela and I were just talking last night, saying we want to come see where you live and meet your people someday soon. Maybe that time is now."

That took Mattie by surprise. "You're always welcome, but that's not necessary. At the latest, I can leave in a few days."

"No, we can't take the chance. What if you still can't leave by then?" Julia sounded adamant. "If we leave this morning, we'll be able to see you by midday tomorrow. By the time we get there, maybe your work will be done."

Mattie wasn't certain she could finish by then, and much as she wanted to see her family, she didn't know if this was a good idea. The case would probably consume the entire weekend. She explained as much to her sister.

"Well, we'll be able to have Monday together then," Julia said. "And if you can only spend part of the time with us, that will have to do. We have so much to tell you, so much to share. We can't wait indefinitely, Mattie. Abuela never sleeps late. I'll start packing now, and we'll be on the road within a few hours."

Mattie still didn't know for certain if she could delay her vacation time to next week. Maybe under the circumstances, her sister was right. If Julia and her grandmother were willing to make the drive, so be it. If she had to work, at least she would still have her mornings and evenings with her family. "My house is small, and I don't have beds for you. I'll make a reservation for tomorrow night at the local motel. You'll be comfortable there."

"What's the name of it?"

"The Big Sky."

"I'll make the reservation, *mi hermana*. You take care of your business today, and we'll see you soon."

"Text me when you stop for the night so I know where you are," Mattie said. "And Julia, thanks. I can't wait to see you."

"I love you, *mi hermana pequeña*. Is your work dangerous?"

"Not really." The thought of the rushing water, the fallen timber, and the many unknowns associated with investigating this crime scene gave her a twinge of anxiety. "I love you too. Be safe as you travel."

As they said their good-byes, tears stung Mattie's eyes. It was hard to take in, having family who would drive across the country to be with her. She planned to go up to Hanging Falls and finish her work today, no matter what the conditions. She needed to be able to spend time with Julia and Abuela when they arrived.

Mattie hurried to dress for work while Robo watched her, his eyes eager. She would skip their usual morning run, since she knew he would get plenty of exercise when they headed into the high country.

"Are you ready to go to work?" she asked, as she removed her service weapon from its safe in her closet.

Robo pivoted, his toenails skittering across the hardwood floor as he scurried through the living room to the front door, where a clean leash hung doubled on the knob. She'd sent the contaminated one to the station along with other pieces of evidence.

Robo snatched his leash and came trotting back to her, the blue nylon strap dangling from his mouth, while she went into the kitchen to get the gallon jug of fresh water she'd prepared before dressing.

"All right," she said, taking his leash from him. "Let's go load up."

She carried the leash to her unit while Robo rushed ahead. She opened the rear compartment of the Ford Explorer that had been converted to meet her dog's needs. He hopped in and circled so that he could watch her secure the jug that contained his water supply, check her other supplies, and close the hatch. By the time she climbed into the driver's seat, he was standing at the front of his cage, ready to navigate. She smiled at him, her spirits rising.

Her phone signaled the arrival of a text. She checked it while she turned on the engine. It was from Cole, and it included the address of the woman he'd mentioned the night before. The rest of the message told her he loved her and he would see her later. She wondered when that would be, knowing she had a full day's work ahead of her.

It took only a few minutes to drive to the station. Although it was a quarter to seven, Brody's cruiser and Stella's silver Honda were lined up beside the sheriff's Jeep. She hurried to unload Robo and followed him to the door, where she made him wait to allow her to enter first, her way of reminding him that she was alpha in their small pack. As a high-drive male shepherd, Robo needed frequent reminders that she was boss or he would try to take over, a problem that could be hard to reverse with these high-energy patrol dogs. It was best to stay on top of his training at all times so that she didn't have to worry about it.

Rainbow, the daughter of two hippies who'd settled in Timber Creek and the department's unlikely dispatcher, sat at her desk on the other side of the lobby. She favored colorful, flowing, tie-dyed tunics over leggings, and today was no exception. She wore her headset atop her long, blond hair, which was tied back with a purple chiffon scarf. Mattie gave Robo permission to greet her while she went to clock in.

Rainbow leaned over the dog as she fondled his ears and cooed, making him grin. "Hey, Mattie," her friend greeted her as she approached the desk. "What are you doing here?"

Even though she'd arrived early, Mattie felt pressed to meet with the investigative team, but she still needed to touch base with Rainbow, who'd helped her out many times when she truly needed someone. "I'm not going today after all. My sister and grandmother are coming here so I can get some work done on this investigation."

Rainbow's eyes widened with surprise. "Oh my gosh. We always need you and your boy, but I don't know. There's something wrong about you losing part of your vacation."

"I'll get the days back another time."

"You're more driven than I am. Maybe I can meet your family while they're here." Rainbow raised a finger as she listened to her headset.

She didn't have time to wait, so Mattie signaled Robo to follow and went back to the staff office to get a cup of coffee. "Let's go to the briefing room," she said, and he took off in that direction. When they entered, she found the others had already gathered.

"Good morning, Deputy," McCoy greeted her. "Thank you for being here."

Brody raised a brow and gave Mattie a nod as she took her place at the table while Robo settled in beside her.

The briefing room was serviceable, sparsely furnished with several rectangular tables, plastic molded chairs on aluminum frames, and a rolling whiteboard upon which Stella had already begun laying out the case.

She'd written *John Doe* at the top of the board, and she'd deviated from her typical procedure of posting a photograph of the victim. Mattie remembered the man's missing eyelids and nostrils, which had been nibbled away by aquatic life.

"We have very little to go over this morning, so we'll share what we know and establish our plan for the day," Stella said. "I received some positive news from CBI lab this morning. Our victim's hands were starting to deglove in the water, but they were able to salvage the skin on the fingers and get prints."

Mattie knew the process. The term *deglove* referred to when the skin on the hands became so waterlogged that it peeled away like a glove. Sometimes the victim's prints could be captured by slipping the skin from a finger onto a technician's finger and then taking a print from the tissue by rolling it as they would that of a live person. "How long do they estimate the body was in the water?"

"Probably two to three days in very cold water," Stella said. "The skin sloughs much faster in warm water."

"We're lucky for that, then," Mattie said, thinking she could vouch for how cold the water was. "I take it they're running the print."

"It'll take several hours to run through the database, but we hope to have an identity by noon," Stella said. "Unless we get it sooner than that by following Cole's lead."

"I have his client's address now." Mattie took out her cell phone and read it aloud for the others.

"Out east of town," McCoy said. "If this man has been dead for two days and if he resided near here with his family, why haven't they reported him missing?"

"Good question," Stella said. "I guess it's possible they don't know he's missing yet. Which means we'll have to break the news that we believe their loved one is deceased—subject to verification, of course. We'll also have to interview them to get all the information we can."

"And to see if we can rule them out as suspects," Brody muttered.

Family always needed to be looked at in a homicide investigation, which Mattie felt was a shame, but the fact remained that victims of murder often knew their killers.

"Mattie and I can team up to do it," Stella said, sending her a look. "And maybe we can poke around a little while we're at it."

"We can if we go first thing," Mattie said, feeling the pressure of all she needed to get done that day. "I also need to get back up to the falls to search for evidence."

"I should be a part of that," Brody said.

Mattie nodded at him. "With this break in the rain, the runoff might have subsided enough to get in there."

"Anything else, Detective?" McCoy asked.

"Not at this time. We'll have more from the lab later today."

McCoy nodded. "Then let's get to work. We have a lot to get done during the next twelve hours."

NINE

Mattie turned off the highway onto a crude and narrow private road, barely more than a dirt track, through short and stubby pastureland. The grass was green from the rain but lacked the lush density and length of an irrigated meadow. A cluster of buildings about a half mile away marked their destination.

As they drew near, Stella verbalized what they could both see. "Looks like five trailer houses and a barn with some corrals."

The homes were all single-wides and lined up next to each other. The barn was a modular affair made from pine board-and-batten siding with an A-frame metal roof. Horse runs surrounded it, and although Mattie wasn't sure how many there were, it looked like the runs were attached to indoor box stalls, several of them filled with horses. Corrals made of panels made the place look thrown together or at least temporary, because as she and Stella drew near, she could tell that someone was building more permanent corrals beyond the paneled ones.

A tall man came out of the barn as Mattie pulled up and parked. "We might as well start here," she murmured, dreading the interview. Giving a family notification of death was never easy, and this time it was made even more difficult by their not knowing the identity of the deceased.

The man was dressed in blue denim pants held up with suspenders and a light-blue chambray shirt with white buttons. He wore his dark beard cropped to about an inch in length, covering only his jawline. A hat with a broad, circular brim sat on his head, and a black patch covered his right eye. He watched them park, and as they exited her unit, he lifted one hand in greeting, his facial expression pleasant.

"Hello," Stella said, rounding the front of the SUV. "Are you Mr. Solomon Vaughn?"

This was the name Cole had given them for his clients: Ruth and Solomon Vaughn.

"No, I'm not," the man said, walking forward and extending a handshake. "I'm Isaac King, but Solomon lives here too. Can I help you?"

Another man came to the doorway of the barn, carrying a push broom. He was also tall, thin, and, save for the eye patch, dressed and groomed as a carbon copy of Isaac. Mattie had the immediate impression that these folks must practice the same religion, although she was unsure at the moment exactly what that would be. The second man set his broom aside and came out to join them.

Isaac turned and lifted his palm in a gesture toward the new man. "This is Solomon."

Solomon's dark eyes searched Mattie's as he extended a firm handshake first to her and then, when Mattie introduced her, to Stella. Mattie could tell he wondered why the police had come to his property, but he didn't ask.

Stella edged her way into the interview. "It's nice to meet you both. You're fairly new to Timber Creek."

"Yes," Isaac said. "We've been here about two months now, just getting started building our place. We hope to call this home for many years to come."

"It's a beautiful site to build on," Stella said, indicating the mountain range to the east.

"Yes, I'll enjoy God's masterpiece every day during morning and evening prayers," Isaac said, his smile crinkling the corner of his uncovered eye, giving him a warm and friendly appearance despite the pirate's patch that he wore.

A woman rounded the corner of the first trailer, followed by a girl and a dog. Even though they were dressed in unusual calf-length blue dresses with white pinafores and caps, it was the dog that caught Mattie's eye—a gorgeous German shepherd with the sculpted head and fine bone structure of a female.

Solomon glanced at the two and introduced them as his wife and daughter, Ruth and Hannah. Both women offered handshakes, although Hannah dropped her eyes as if bashful when she stepped up to shake Mattie's hand. The dog seemed attached to the girl more than the woman, so Mattie murmured a compliment about the dog, and Hannah gave her a shy smile in return.

"This is Sassy," Hannah said, glancing up to meet Mattie's gaze before leaning over to pet her dog. At that moment, Robo barked from inside the unit, making Sassy's head go up in alarm. She growled and barked a warning, leaving Hannah's side to head toward the SUV, where Robo continued to sound off. Hannah hurried after her dog, calling her back and making her obey, while Mattie went to her car and told Robo to stop.

Both dogs settled after their brief outburst, but evidently Solomon had already had enough. "Hannah, take Sassy back to the house, please."

The girl did as she was told without protest, perhaps more readily than most teens, but under the circumstances, that might be too quick a judgment. Perhaps the girl didn't want to aggravate Robo either. Ruth had stayed, and Mattie rejoined the group.

"Are there others living here besides you?" Stella asked, sweeping the threesome with her gaze before settling on Isaac.

"Yes," Isaac said, his voice deep and solemn. "We have five families living here, all sisters and brothers sharing in our new lives in this new land."

His grand manner of speech made Mattie wonder if he was a preacher. At the same time, movement at the barn door caught her eye and two other men appeared, one older, with pepper-and-salt hair and the same coloring in his beard, and the other quite young, maybe in his late teens or early twenties, his hair and beard sand colored. Both men hung back by the barn.

"Is anyone in your group missing, a man who might be in his twenties?" Stella asked.

"No one is missing," Isaac said. "All were present and accounted for at morning prayer."

"All right," Stella said. "So everyone who moved here two months ago is still here?"

Ruth smoothed the side of her skirt with her palm. "One young man left recently, but he's not exactly missing. He left to return home to his parents. He decided this wasn't where he wanted to live after all."

"His name?" Stella asked.

"Luke," Ruth said. "Luke Ferguson."

"Does he still have extended family living here?"

"Not any relatives by blood," Isaac said. "But we're all family here."

Mattie thought these people might be able to identify their victim, since the men's manner of dress, hairstyles, and beards seemed to match.

"Did Luke have any identifying marks such as tattoos or birthmarks?" Stella asked.

"He had a purple birthmark on his neck," Ruth said, placing her palm on the left side of her own, in exactly the same spot as their victim's birthmark. "Why do you ask?"

Mattie observed all of them closely while Stella continued— not just the three in front of her but also the men who stood outside the barn listening. This would be the most important time to detect responses that might indicate guilt.

"We found a young man who's deceased, and it's possible it might be Luke," Stella said.

"Deceased?" Ruth echoed, looking stunned.

"Where?" Isaac asked, his face registering surprise. "When?"

Solomon's brow knit with concern, and the two men at the barn walked out to join them. The younger man looked especially worried, and he took off his hat and held it by the brim at his side. Everyone seemed genuinely alarmed.

"This young man we're trying to identify was found in the mountains up by Hanging Falls," Stella said. "Do you know the place?"

"Why yes," Isaac said. "Several of us rode up there a couple weeks ago to give the horses we're training some trail experience."

"Was Luke with you then?" Mattie asked, wondering if the young man had been familiar with the spot where he'd been buried.

The older man who hadn't yet been introduced was nodding as Isaac answered. "He was with us. It was shortly afterward that he decided to go back home."

"Did he say why he wanted to leave?" Mattie asked.

"He said he missed his old way of life," Isaac said, his appearance saddened. "I counseled with him extensively, but he was adamant. You see, he'd only joined us when we moved here."

Mattie wondered about transportation. "How did he leave? Was he driving his own car?"

"No," Solomon said, frowning. "I dropped him off at the bus stop in Hightower last Wednesday. Are you certain this person you found is Luke?"

"No, we're not certain," Stella said, her face sympathetic. "We're still trying to identify this young man. We came here because of a suggestion that his clothing and style of beard might be similar to yours. And in fact, that appears to be the case."

It seemed like an awkward thing to bring up, and Mattie felt uncomfortable with it, but profiling of one kind or another often led to more information as long as one kept an open mind. And none of these folks seemed to take offense.

"How can we help you?" Isaac said.

"Do you have any items of Luke's? Toothbrush, hairbrush, comb? Even any items of clothing might help," Stella said.

Isaac turned to the older man. "This is Ephraim Grayson. Luke stayed at his house. Ephraim, do you know if Luke left anything?"

"No, ma'am," Ephraim replied, looking at Stella with dark and serious eyes. "He shared a room with my son here. Abel, did he leave anything in your room?"

"No, sir." Abel shook his head, looking at his father. "He didn't have much, but he took everything with him."

"Do you have a photograph of the man you found?" Isaac asked. "Perhaps we could help you that way."

Stella hesitated, and Mattie could understand why. They each had photos on their cell phones, but those were hard to look at. Stella glanced her way as she removed her cell phone from her pocket and started swiping the screen. "We think this young man had been in the water for a while, so this photo-graph is going to be hard to see, but I have a close-up of the birthmark on his neck."

Isaac squared his shoulders. "Let me look at it first, then. Perhaps the others won't need to."

When Stella moved forward to show Isaac the picture, his face became grim. He drew a deep breath and stepped back, as if to put distance between himself and the image. "I'm afraid that looks like the mark on Luke's neck. It might very well be him. God rest his soul."

Each of the others murmured the same words. Mattie could see various amounts of shock on their faces, Ruth's holding the greatest. "Oh dear," she said, looking at Isaac. "What should we do? Should we contact his parents?"

"I can certainly do that," Isaac responded, looking at Stella. "What do you think I should tell them?"

"I prefer talking to them myself," Stella said. "If you'll give me their contact information, I'll make the call."

"I'll get it." Ruth turned and hurried back toward the trailers.

Mattie had an idea. "Could I see where Luke slept?"

Ephraim looked at Isaac and, after receiving a slight nod, turned to his son. "Abel, take the lady to show her your room. Tell your mother I said it was okay."

"Just one moment, Abel." Mattie went to the back of her unit while Robo pinned her with his eyes and danced in place. She felt bad telling him to stay, but after opening the hatch, that's what she had to do. His look of disappointment made her feel even worse. She knew he wanted to work; it's what he lived for. "Later," she told him. "You'll get a turn later today."

She grabbed her fingerprint kit and followed Abel down the row of trailers. As they passed the second one, Ruth stepped outside onto the wooden deck that had been built in front of the door. Another blond woman dressed like her stood at the doorway, a worried look on her face.

Ruth came down the steps when she spotted Mattie. "Would you like this number?" she said, holding out a slip of paper.

"If you'll take that to Detective LoSasso, I'd appreciate it," Mattie replied, eyeing the other woman and hoping for an introduction. She took a few steps closer, giving Ruth incentive to make it.

"This is my sister, Mary," Ruth said.

Mary nodded and said hello while Mattie exchanged greetings and decided that she could see a family resemblance between the two sisters. Several young boys and girls, some blond and some brunet, stood clustered behind Mary, who obviously seemed set on blocking their way and keeping them inside the house. Mattie couldn't get a head count, since some of the kids were peeking out from behind Mary's skirts, but she thought there were six or seven. The kids appeared curious, and they looked clean and well dressed in their matching blue-and-white outfits.

Mattie turned back to Abel, who'd waited politely, and followed him to the third trailer, where he mounted the steps of a wooden deck similar to the one at Ruth's house.

He opened the door and spoke to someone inside. "Mother? I've brought a guest."

Abel stood aside, holding the door for Mattie to enter. A short woman, her sandy hair wound in a bun at her nape underneath a white cap, turned from the sink, grabbed a dish towel, and dried her hands. Her eyes widened as she took in Mattie's uniform, but she extended her hand, saying, "I'm Rachel."

Mattie introduced herself and shook Rachel's still-damp fingers. "I'm sorry to show up unannounced like this, ma'am, but I need to see the bedroom where Luke Ferguson slept. I won't take but a few minutes of your time."

Rachel looked at Abel, a question in her eyes, to which he responded, "Father said to allow it. The police think that Luke might be dead."

Her hand flew to her mouth as her eyes widened. "Oh my dear heaven. How could that be?"

"We're in the process of trying to identify the person we found to confirm whether it's Luke or not," Mattie said. "If I could just see the bedroom, I won't be long."

"Of course," Rachel said. "Abel, show the officer your room."

As Mattie followed Abel through the kitchen and into the living room, she found it awash with children of all ages, all dressed alike and occupied with various activities. A towheaded teenage girl in a chair read aloud quietly to a dark-haired boy, two other dark-haired youngsters worked on activity books, and a bright-eyed and smiling toddler with sandy hair fiddled with building blocks inside a playpen. All eyes turned Mattie's way as she entered the room.

A woman with brunet hair streaked with gray beneath her white cap looked up from her sewing machine, where she appeared to be working on pants made of blue denim. "Oh," she said, as if startled. "Hello."

From behind Mattie, Rachel made the introduction. "Deputy, this is Naomi, my sister."

Naomi raised her eyebrows, sending a questioning look Rachel's way, but she murmured a polite greeting.

"Go ahead and take the deputy on through to your room, Abel," Rachel prompted, before giving a quiet explanation to Naomi.

Naomi gasped as Mattie followed Abel's stalwart form down a narrow hallway and into a tiny bedroom. The curtains were drawn and the light dim, so she touched the overhead light switch with the tip of one finger. A quick glance told her she was in luck. Twin beds with polished wooden headboards had been placed against opposing walls, with small bedside dressers in between. And on each dresser stood a table lamp.

"Which bed was Luke's?" she asked.

Abel pointed to the one on the far wall, and Mattie crossed the room to inspect the lamp's switch, growing more excited as she peered under the lampshade. She'd found what she'd hoped for: a toggle switch that needed to be pressed back and forth to operate. The perfect spot to dust for prints. And in addition to that, the slick surfaces of the dresser and headboard offered a secondary source.

"Has anyone else moved into this bedroom since Luke left?"

"Not yet. I've had it to myself."

Rachel appeared in the doorway, and Mattie addressed her directly. "I want to look for prints on the lamp, the dresser, the headboard, and on the wall beside the light switch, if I could. If I can get a clear print from here, we could see if they match the person we found. Is it all right if I do that?"

Rachel's face showed concern, but she said, "If it will help you, go right ahead."

Mattie looked at Abel. "I need to take your prints too, so that we can eliminate you from the ones I recover. Is that all right?"

Abel nodded his agreement. "Sure."

"I appreciate your cooperation. I'll need for you both to sign release forms."

Since neither of the two indicated that this was a problem, Mattie opened her kit, gave them the forms to sign, and then set to work.

★ ★ ★

After leaving the property, Mattie turned onto the highway and headed back to the station, eager to drop Stella off so she and Brody could head up to Hanging Falls.

"Good job finding a source for prints," Stella said. "We'll get them to the lab as soon as possible and see if we have a match."

"Most of them were partials or smudged, but there was one good one on the back side of the lamp and a few on the back side of the headboard that look complete." Mattie hoped they would soon have a definitive ID on their victim.

"What was your overall impression of the people we met?" Stella asked.

Stella was a great one for lecturing about not jumping to conclusions, so Mattie proceeded with caution. "I thought their reactions were genuine when we broke the news, and I didn't see any obvious signs of deception that rang any alarm bells."

Stella was nodding, which Mattie took as agreement.

She continued. "The style of dress, hair, and beards along with Isaac's comments about prayers led me to believe they're a group that practices the same religion, and Isaac King appears to be their leader."

Stella gazed out the windshield, her eyes narrowed and lips pursed, the posture Mattie recognized as the detective's thinking mode. "I had the same impression."

"When I went into their homes, I met three other women—Ruth's sister, Ephraim Grayson's wife, and her sister. There had to be at least ten or twelve children inside the two homes, all dressed alike. From what I could tell, things within the Grayson home were clean and tidy, and Rachel's sister was sewing a pair of denim trousers."

"What did you make of all that?"

"The pants were similar to those worn by the men and our victim." Mattie looked at Stella and gave her a thin smile. "There are lots of children living there, and I don't think we've even met all the adults yet. But I can't help but compare what I observed here today with photos and videos I've seen of different polygamist groups from Colorado City and other places across the nation. They look similar."

"Fair enough," Stella said. "Matches my opinion. Did you have any impressions that would make you concerned about the welfare of the children?"

Mattie remembered the children's curiosity, and though many of them appeared shy, she hadn't observed anything outside the norm. "Not at first glance. They were clean, looked healthy and engaged, seemed happy enough, but that's a hard judgment to make, since I haven't had a chance to talk to any of them."

"I have a feeling we'll be visiting these folks again with more bad news very soon," Stella said with a grimace. "And if so, we'll need to set up interviews with all of the adults and older children. We can assess their welfare during that process."

It all sounded to Mattie like a monumental task, and one that might not be completed by tomorrow afternoon. Wrapping up this investigation before her family arrived didn't seem possible at the moment. "So . . . polygamy is illegal in the state of Colorado," she said, thinking aloud. "How do these groups get away with it?"

Stella raised a brow. "By not using legal means for marriage. The men might have a marriage license and legal ceremony with one wife, typically the first, and then they form spiritual unions with the others. Unless there's proof of someone breaking the law, we pretty much have to leave them alone. At least, that's how it works here in Colorado."

"Key words: unless someone breaks the law. Murder factors strongly into that guideline." Mattie held Stella's gaze for a few beats before looking back to the road.

"Yes," Stella said, settling back into her seat and looking out the window to brood, something Mattie expected from the detective at this stage in the case. "Yes, it certainly does."

TEN

Cole received a call on his cell phone that had been forwarded from his clinic line, and he answered with his official greeting. "Timber Creek Veterinary Clinic."

"Is this Dr. Walker?"

The voice sounded familiar, but he couldn't place it. "Speaking."

"Oh, hello. This is Ruth Vaughn."

"Hello, Ruth. I won't have Sassy's results until at least midweek."

"Oh, yes . . . you told me that. But that's not why I'm calling. I wondered if you were working today."

"I am, but I'm not at the clinic." Cole didn't typically keep his clinic open on Saturdays but reserved the morning for catch-up from the week. He'd just driven up the lane from his clinic to his house and hoped to visit with his daughters before leaving on a farm call. They'd been asleep when he left early this morning, and he wanted to see them before the morning got away from him. "I had to reschedule some folks yesterday afternoon, so I'm running ambulatory."

"Oh . . ." Ruth sounded disappointed.

In a hurry, Cole parked in the driveway, hit the button to open his garage door and exited the truck, heading for the inside door to the kitchen. "How can I help, Ruth?"

"We have a gelding with a split hoof, and this morning he's turned up lame. Our farrier is coming to work on him, but we hoped you could take a look to see what you'd recommend."

"I can work you in right after my next appointment. Say, in about an hour; would that be okay?"

"Oh yes," Ruth said, sounding relieved. "And thank you so much. Do you need directions?"

"No, I drove past your place yesterday. I know where you are." Cole entered the kitchen, found it empty, and walked on, seeking his kids. He said good-bye and disconnected the call as he made it to the den, where he found Sophie watching television, snuggled up against Belle on the Bernese mountain dog's cushion.

"Hey, Sophie-bug." Cole perched on the edge of a chair near her. "What ya watching?"

"My show." His nine-year-old didn't even look at him but stroked Belle's head absently, her eyes glued to the TV. While her older sister resembled their mother, Sophie took more after him with her brunet curls, brown eyes, and a sprinkling of freckles across her cheeks. Her once-stocky child's body had lengthened and thinned this summer, as she'd been growing like a four-week-old puppy.

"What's your show?" Cole asked, looking at the screen filled with a bunch of cartoon dog characters.

"*PAW Patrol.*"

"Do you want to record it and come ride with me?"

"No thanks, Dad."

He could tell he was up against a better opponent and had no hope of gaining her attention. "Where's your sister?"

"In her room."

"Mrs. Gibbs?"

"Don't know."

This conversation was going nowhere, and Cole felt pressed to move on. "Okay, little bit. I'm going to see if Angie wants to go with me. If you change your mind, I'll be leaving in about three minutes."

"Okay. I'll stay here."

All this without her looking at him even once. Usually she was more engaged than that, but Cole took consolation in the fact that you couldn't fight *PAW Patrol.* He headed for the stairway and met Mrs. Gibbs coming down.

His resident housekeeper had been a lifesaver ever since his sister Jessie found her. Cole had been at his wits' end, trying to run his practice and take care of the kids right after Olivia left. But the kind lady, a transplant from Dublin, had moved from her daughter's home in Denver and taken them all under her wing, Cole included. She governed them with a great deal of wisdom and humor, having had years of experience raising her own daughters.

"Hello, Dr. Walker," she said, her Irish brogue always a pleasure to his ear. "I was tidying me room and didn't hear you come in. Do you need something to eat?"

"No, I'm fine until lunch. Just looking for Angie."

"Young Miss Angela has been in her room most of the morning. I think you'll find her there," she said, one eyebrow raised as she moved past him and headed for the kitchen.

Cole knew she was privy to the problems he was having with Angie, and he also knew that the lady was one of Mattie's biggest fans. But he doubted if she would get into the middle of things unless he asked her to, and he hoped he could manage this on his own without calling in the second-string quarterback.

He knocked on Angie's door. When there was no answer, he knocked louder. "Yeah?" he heard her say, so he opened the door and peeked inside. She was lying on her bed with a book, plugged into her iPod with earbuds, one of which she'd removed and was holding between her fingers.

"Hi, Angel. I'm looking for company while I make my calls. Want to go with me?"

She eyed him. "Do you need my help?"

"Nope. Just want your companionship."

"How long will this take?"

Surprised that she actually seemed interested, Cole dared to hope. "Only a couple hours. We'll be back in time for lunch."

"Is Sophie going?"

"She says not. Does that matter?"

"Just wondered." Angie turned off her music and removed the other earbud. "I guess I'll go. Let me change." She was still wearing the tank top and boxers she used for pajamas.

Cole grinned, letting his pleasure show. "Can you be ready in a few?"

"Sure."

Cole closed the door, hurried down the steps, and joined his housekeeper in the kitchen.

Mrs. Gibbs was zipping the lid on a soft-sided cooler. "I packed you a snack."

"You're the best." He checked the cooler's contents while giving Mrs. Gibbs a quick one-armed squeeze. Bottles of juice, a baggie full of grapes, a small sack of pretzels, and individually wrapped cheese sticks. Very healthy—Angie would like it.

Angie came downstairs carrying a backpack and wearing jeans and a pink tee. She had pulled her blond hair into a pony-tail. "Ready to go," she said.

"Excellent." Cole picked up the cooler. "Thank you, Mrs. Gibbs. We should be home about noon."

Once they were situated inside his truck, Cole drove down the lane toward the highway. He didn't want Angie to think this was another of his attempts to hold her hostage while he talked to her about Mattie. He'd been honest about his agenda and truly did want to spend time with her on a busy day. "Music or no music?" he asked, his finger hovering over the button for the sound system.

"My music," she replied, unzipping her backpack and tak-ing out her iPod.

"Go for it," he said, thinking, *Geez, I hope I can handle this.*

After she hooked it up, the jolting rhythm of some type of rap or hip-hop or whatever that Cole could barely stomach filled the truck's cab. He gave Angie a tight smile as he turned onto the road and headed for his first appointment.

★ ★ ★

An hour later, they turned onto the dirt track that led to the cluster of buildings that made up the Vaughn place. "This is where Hannah lives," Cole said to Angie as he turned down her music, which she'd started again when they left the last place.

"Looks like a bunch of trailer homes." Angie switched off the music. "I wonder who else lives out here."

The sudden quiet inside the truck came as a big relief. Sometimes spending quality time with a teenager could be a tough job. "Maybe we'll find out."

"What do you have to do here?"

"Look at a cracked hoof on a horse." As Cole pulled into the area in front of the barn, he spotted the rig that belonged to the farrier Quinn Randolph.

"Oh no, it's that Quinn guy," Angie said. "After he was making fun of these people, they've got him out here working for them? Don't they know?"

Cole liked that his daughter had grown indignant about the situation. "I doubt if they do. But maybe this is the best way to change his attitude. You know, once he gets to know the Vaughns are nice people, he'll stop poking fun at them."

Angie sent him doubtful look. "Maybe . . ."

Ruth Vaughn and a tall man with an eye patch came from the barn, and Cole stepped out of the truck to greet them. After saying hello to Ruth, he extended his hand toward the man. "And you must be Solomon?"

"No," Ruth hurried to interject. "This is Isaac King. He's in charge of the horse training."

"Glad to meet you, Isaac." Cole shook hands with the man, who responded by voicing his gratitude to Cole for making the trip out to help on a Saturday.

Angie rounded the truck from the passenger's side, and as Cole introduced her, he noticed a faint look of disapproval cross Isaac's face. The man greeted her politely, though, before turning his attention back to Cole. He decided Isaac's disapproval might be because Angie was wearing jeans and a T-shirt, so different from the dresses that Ruth and Hannah wore.

Cole thought Angie's choice of clothing very appropriate, considering the more revealing tank tops and shorts he knew she and her friends favored during the summer. Isaac didn't know about the many times Cole had gone round and round with his daughter to get her to dress *this* way when she worked with him.

Different strokes for different folks, Cole thought as he shifted his attention back to the job at hand. "Ruth said you have a horse with a cracked hoof," he said to Isaac as he walked to the back of his truck to gather supplies.

"That's right," Isaac said, following Cole. "This gelding's hooves were in need of a trim, and we had the farrier scheduled to come out today anyway. But this morning the horse came up three-legged lame, and I appreciate you taking a look to see if we should do anything special to reinforce the hoof. I had Quinn start on one of the other horses."

Cole heard Angie say hi and turned to see Hannah approaching from the row of trailers, her eyes on Angie and a big smile on her face. The dog, Sassy, left Hannah's side to deliver a tail-wagging greeting to his daughter. Cole waved to the girl before gathering hoof testers and a hoof pick and then turned to follow Isaac to the barn, leaving Angie as she walked over to join Hannah.

The barn was a well-constructed prefab with rows of box stalls on each side of a concrete alleyway. Down at the far end, it looked like Quinn Randolph had set up shop and was holding the raised front hoof of a brown mare between his knees while he trimmed curved clippings from the hoof with a pair of nippers.

"The gelding we need you to look at is in here," Isaac said, leading the way to a box stall where another tall man with a dark beard and round-brimmed hat was cleaning out the bedding around a sorrel gelding, who stood supporting most of his weight on three legs. The horse held his right hind leg cocked, guarding the hoof. The way he stood with his gaze turned inward told Cole all he needed to know about the pain the poor guy suffered.

Isaac introduced the man inside the box stall as Solomon Vaughn. Cole paused a moment to exchange a handshake, while Isaac stepped up and clipped a lead rope onto the gelding's halter.

"I'll take a look here in the stall," Cole said, knowing he didn't need to watch the horse's gait. "You don't need to lead him outside."

Cole trailed his hand along the gelding's back and bent to examine the crack. It ran a couple of inches along the coronary band at the top of the hoof and looked long and deep enough to be painful. Cole slid his hand to the hock, hoping the gelding had been trained to let someone work on his feet, and was rewarded when the big horse complied by lifting his sore foot and allowing Cole to hold it over his thigh.

The sole of the hoof was already cleaned, so Cole clamped his hoof tester down on various spots to see how the gelding would react. No flinching or withdrawal, which told him the bottom of the hoof was sound and an abscess unlikely. The pain was coming from the crack in the coronary band and would probably respond well to treatment. He released the hoof and let the gelding touch it down gently on the ground.

He was explaining his opinion to Solomon and Isaac when Quinn and another man came to the stall door. Cole went on to describe his recommended treatment. "I'll clean out the crack, cover it with some antibiotic cream, and wrap it in a sweat. We'll give him some oral antibiotics and some phenylbutazone paste to help him feel better, and I think this will heal up in a few weeks. He shouldn't have any problems."

"I have an Easyboot in the truck," Quinn interjected, looking at Isaac.

"An Easyboot won't do him any good," Cole said. "The sole of the hoof is sound. It's the crack that hurts, and an Easyboot won't make any difference for that."

Quinn clenched his jaw and gave Cole a look but didn't argue. Cole figured he'd just interfered with a sale, but the farrier would lick his wounds in private.

"I'll need a bucket of warm water and some meds and vet wrap from the truck." Cole left the box stall with Isaac trailing behind.

"Should I hold off on having his hooves trimmed today?" he asked Cole.

Quinn evidently thought he'd been asked the question, because he was the one who answered. "He'll do fine if we do it today. I can give him something so he won't feel a thing."

Cole paused and turned back. "What would that be?"

Quinn's eyes shifted away as he answered. "I have some tranquilizers I keep on hand when I need them."

"Who dispenses them to you?" Cole asked, curious as to which vet distributed the drugs.

"I have a friend that prescribes it," Quinn said, before turning away and speaking to the man who'd been helping him. "Do you have another horse for me to do while the doc works on this one?"

Cole interrupted before the man could reply. "I'll paint some lidocaine into the crack, and that should take care of the pain well enough for you to trim his hooves. You don't need to dose him with a sedative."

"All right." Quinn squinted a look at him before following the older man down the alleyway, making Cole believe the farrier would do whatever he wanted to. After observing Quinn here and at the Perrys' place, he was certain he wouldn't be recommending this guy's farrier service to any of his other clients.

Out at the truck, Cole noticed that Angie and Hannah were nowhere in sight, but a whole bunch of younger children and about six women had materialized from somewhere and were playing a game of Wiffle ball out beyond the trailer homes. A few of the women had tied up their skirts to knee height and were playing with the children.

Ruth joined him from a clothesline where she'd been hanging clothing to dry, identical blue-and-white garments in a row. "Hannah took Angela inside our home to show her the kittens."

"Oh no," Cole said, smiling at her as they walked back to the barn together. "You've got a litter?"

"Siamese kittens. Eight weeks old."

"Uh-oh, I know what Angie's going to be talking about on our way home."

Ruth gave him a soft smile. "Don't worry, I've got this litter sold. But I have another cat that's due anytime now, if you're interested."

"So you're not only going to be in the puppy business, but you're also raising Siamese cats?"

"That's right. I try to help out with our income where I can."

They'd reentered the barn and ended their conversation, but Cole found it interesting that Ruth had found a cottage industry to help with expenses. During his years of experience, those of his clients who were backyard breeders took special care with their animals and raised well-socialized pets for others, although he was well aware that wasn't always the case. He didn't know Ruth well yet, but her treatment of Sassy placed her in the responsible-breeder category.

"Do you mind telling Angie that we'll be leaving in about ten minutes?" he asked Ruth, before turning to the task at hand.

★ ★ ★

When they got back in the truck and were headed home, Angie was all smiles. "There were seven, four boys and three girls. And they were all so sweet. One of them fell asleep in my lap."

Cole's heart lifted, glad that Angie had had such a good time. "Nothing cozier than a sleeping kitten. But when they play, those little claws are like needles."

"That's for sure." Angie raised her hand and showed him the tiny red scratches on the back of it. "They've got the bluest eyes."

Cole smiled, thinking the cat's eyes were probably about the same shade as Angie's.

"Hannah showed me the different color patterns. The mother cat is a seal point. Do you know what that means?"

Cole nodded. "Dark-brown face and ears, cream-colored body."

"Do they teach you that stuff in vet school?"

"I must have picked it up somewhere. Ruth said they have another female that's pregnant."

"Lily. She's a chocolate point."

"Milk-chocolate color, which is a dilute of the seal point," Cole interjected.

"If you say so." Angie grinned. "You're right about the milk-chocolate color. And the father is a blue point. Do you know that one?"

Cole did but decided to let Angie describe it. "What does that one look like?"

"It's a real pretty color. Hannah calls it slate gray. His name is Smokey, and I think I like his color the best." Angie gazed out the window for a minute before turning back to look at him. "When Lily has her kittens, do you think we could get one, Dad?"

He'd known that was coming. "They're selling the kittens, you know. It wouldn't be free. And there's plenty of free kittens that need homes that we could adopt."

Angie nodded, her face falling into a look of disappointment that made Cole wish he'd given her a different answer.

"Why don't we think about it?" he said. "We also need to talk it over with Mrs. Gibbs. Adding another pet inside the house affects her too."

"And Sophie, but she would say yes."

Cole grinned. "That's a sure bet."

Angie was silent for a moment before changing the subject. "Hannah has seven brothers and sisters, four boys and three girls, just like the kittens."

"That's a big family."

Angie nodded. "She shares her bedroom with the girls, and the boys sleep out in the living room."

Cole was surprised. "Don't they have another bedroom for the boys?"

"Her mom's sisters have the other bedroom, and then her parents have their own room, of course. That's three—all the bedrooms the trailer has."

"I see."

"They're going to build a house as soon as they can."

"That'll give them more room."

Silence again, and Cole was happy that Angie didn't want to fill it with music.

"Dad, can I take Riley out to see the kittens before they go to their new homes?"

Cole had bought Angie a used Toyota Corolla after she obtained her driver's license, and she was enjoying the freedom that her own wheels had given her this summer. "Sure, but make sure Hannah clears it with her mom first. Did you get her phone number?" And then he felt silly for asking, because of course she would.

"She doesn't have her own cell phone. Her parents won't allow it. But she gave me the number for her house phone." A quick glance told him that a concerned expression had taken over Angie's face. "I gave her my phone number, but she said she's not allowed to make calls. If I call her, though, her mom would probably let her talk to me." After another short pause, during which Angie seemed to be thinking, she continued. "They don't have a television or a computer. And Dad, she won't be going to high school. One of the other moms home-schools all the kids."

That didn't surprise him much after observing what he had so far. "Well . . ."

"Yeah, I know." It seemed as if his daughter had read his mind. "Thanks, Dad, for giving us the life we have. I know you work hard to provide things for us, and some of the time it must seem like we don't appreciate it. But just to let you know . . . I do."

Cole was touched, and he reached out to give her hand a quick squeeze. "Thanks for saying that, Angel. It means a lot."

They rode together in companionable silence the rest of the way home, during which he decided that it was a good thing to let kids see alternative ways of living in the world. Only with a variety of experiences could they make their own choices about what they did and didn't want in their lives. What a fine line parents walked when trying to protect their children while at the same time trying to offer them choices. No wonder the job grew exhausting at times.

ELEVEN

The investigative team met in the briefing room to discuss Tracy Lee Brown and decide what they were going to do with him. Impatient to go search the area above Hanging Falls, Mattie stood near the table where the others had gathered, Robo sitting at her left heel. He raised his eyes to check her face, evidently catching her mood and expecting her to leave the room at any moment. When she did, she knew, he would be right beside her.

"No warrants out for his arrest," Brody muttered, as if disappointed. "He's got a record, but only misdemeanors—vagrancy, loitering, trespassing, petty theft—homeless type of stuff. Apparently he receives disability income from the government and withdraws it from an ATM when he can—thus the three hundred and twenty-five dollars he had in his fanny pack."

"Why the disability checks?" Mattie asked.

"He says it's from a back injury he received on a construction job over two years ago," Stella said, shaking her head slightly. "I wasn't able to get any more out of him than you did, Mattie. He says he had a falling-out with his family and doesn't stay in touch with them. I called the number he gave me for his parents' home, but it's been disconnected. Says they probably use cell phones now but he doesn't have their numbers."

"The knife he carried is old and rusted around the handle," McCoy said. "The lab found no sign of human blood on it. He swears he found the knife in the forest near the creek a couple months ago and he uses it to gut fish."

"So what's his status? What do we do with him now?" Mattie asked, knowing full well what the answer would be.

"We have to let him go," McCoy said, meeting her gaze. "I know he's the closest thing we have to a suspect, but we have absolutely no reason to hold him. He even had enough cash to pay his fine for marijuana possession."

Mattie nodded to let him know she understood, even though the situation frustrated her.

"Cobb and I can take him up to his campsite and see if there's anything there that warrants an arrest." Brody's chair screeched against the beige linoleum floor as he stood. "If there is, we'll bring him back down with us."

"All right," McCoy said. "Check in after you've searched his campsite."

Eager to leave so that she and Robo could do their work, Mattie turned, murmuring, "Robo, heel." He moved with her as she strode from the room.

★　★　★

Mattie, Robo, and Brody followed Tracy Lee Brown through the forest. Although clouds were starting to build above the western mountains, clear weather had held all morning and the trail had been passable. The swollen river rolled downhill, crashing over boulders in the riverbed and spraying whitecaps into the air, and though it surged at its banks, it spilled over and flooded in only a few spots. They'd left it behind to follow Tracy Lee across country for what Mattie estimated was about a half mile.

"Here we are," Tracy Lee said as they dropped into a small clearing with a stream running through it.

She scanned the area and finally spotted an olive-green tent, like the kind found at an Army surplus store, sitting about fifty yards away, partly hidden by pine at the edge of the clearing. "No one else here?" she asked.

"Nope. Just me." He'd been uncommunicative throughout their hike, responding minimally when spoken to.

Robo lifted his nose to the air and sniffed, but Mattie didn't observe any changes in his attitude that would cause alarm. She went ahead and followed Tracy Lee into the campsite, which was set up around a fire ring filled with dead coals and ashes. A blackened grate, skillet, and coffeepot sat askew beside the rocks that encircled the fire pit. A fishing pole leaned against a nearby spruce.

It took only a few minutes for Mattie and Robo to sweep the site, including inside the tent. Disappointed that this outing had led to a dead end, she went back to talk to Tracy Lee. "We're going to ask you to stay put here for the next few weeks."

His deep-set eyes shifted away from her. "I move my camp-site around every week or two."

"We just want to be able to reach you if we need to, Tracy Lee. You know, make sure you're okay."

"I can stay as long as the fishing holds up. If I run out of food, I'll have to move."

Brody spoke up. "Someone will be up to check on you within the next day or two. Be here then."

Tracy Lee toed the ground, his eyes downcast. "Okay."

Mattie hated to walk away, thinking the man would disap-pear as soon as their backs were turned, but she had hours of work to do.

She and Brody struck a course across country that soon intersected the trail to Hanging Falls. Once on the trail they kept a fast pace and arrived at the lake within a half hour. Mat-tie was relieved to see that the falls had narrowed again and that the trail to the upper basin looked passable, though changed by the flowing water. Bushes had been washed out, more rocks exposed, and the footing looked muddy and slippery.

"Let's go, Robo," she said, letting him lead the way. He hopped from rock to rock while she and Brody struggled up the cliff beside the waterfall. The cascade sprayed them with cold droplets, saturating her clothes by the time she made it to the top. The black hair on Robo's back glistened with moisture.

Runoff from yesterday's rain had subsided, and tufts of grass now peeked through puddles. Mattie stepped carefully as she made her way down toward the lake's edge, winding through fallen timber and deadfall. Robo trotted ahead, leading the way until she called him back. She huddled with her dog and Brody beside a pine that still looked healthy—its trunk thick and strong and its needles green—on a patch of relatively dry ground.

"We might as well start here." She shrugged off her backpack and hung it from a tree branch. As she scanned the terrain, she pointed to the swollen stream of water that rushed from the lake to plunge downward in the falls. "This is where I thought a body might wash out. I want to do a grid search in this area."

Brody grunted his agreement.

Taking Robo's blue nylon collar from her utility belt, she bent and unbuckled his everyday collar that he'd worn to travel up the mountain. This alone told him he was going to work, and he trotted around in excitement until she fastened the collar at his neck. Then he stood at her feet, looking up at her face, awaiting a command.

She removed Robo's collapsible bowl and filled it with water from her supply. It seemed strange to provide him with water when they were surrounded by it, but moistening her dog's mucous membranes to enhance his scenting ability before an evidence search was a valuable part of their routine. Once he'd taken a few laps, she began to pat him and chatter in a high-pitched voice that revved up his prey drive.

Bending to pat Robo's side while he danced on his front paws in excitement, Mattie scoped out the terrain. She decided to put Robo on a long leash and run a grid that encompassed ten-foot sweeps near the edge of the rushing stream. Once they reached the end, she would turn her dog around and he would sweep another ten-foot-wide section, sniffing and looking for evidence as he went. Brody would follow doing a visual sweep.

After receiving a nod from Brody indicating that he was ready, she led Robo downhill to the edge of the water and gave him the command she used for evidence detection. "Okay, Robo. Seek!"

Robo put his nose to the ground and started quartering the area, his head moving back and forth. Mattie guided him gently, covering the strip of ground along the edge of her imaginary grid. She tried to stay on the grassy tufts but ended up slipping off into the muck more often than not. Soon her boots were caked with mud.

They worked their way down sixty yards and then turned to head back, ten feet higher and moving into the trees. Brody turned and moved along with them, scanning the ground as they worked their way back.

On the third pass, which ran deeper into the timber, Robo paused about halfway down, stuck his nose into a hole in the ground, and sat. Mattie's pulse quickened as she bent to pet him. "What did you find?"

A stunted spruce had toppled and now lay perpendicular to the water, its roots exposed. The entire area contained pits and depressions from uprooted trees, but this one looked slightly different, and Mattie wondered if it could have been their victim's shallow grave. The hole that Robo indicated was small, about the size of a gopher hole, and something that would never have caught the human eye.

Mattie knelt beside Robo, hugging him close and murmuring endearments near his ear while she scanned the sky, considering whether they should call in a forensic unit but deciding they didn't have time. "It's going to rain again soon, Brody. Don't you think we should process this by ourselves?"

Brody glanced at the heavy clouds. "Let's do it."

They both took cell phones from their pockets and snapped photographs of the hole and the surrounding area while Robo sat and watched.

"When this spruce went down, it could've exposed enough of the grave that the body could wash out." Mattie lined up a shot that showed the proximity of the tree to the depression. "This might just be an air hole. We've either got another body or something that was buried with our victim."

Brody pulled a pair of latex gloves from his utility belt. "We'll see."

The muddy ground made for easy digging, and a shovel wasn't necessary. Brody removed the soil handful by handful, working to enlarge the hole as he dug deeper. Soon after he started, he rocked back on his heels. "I've hit something. Take a picture before I dig it out."

With Mattie snapping photos, he carefully excavated what looked like a piece of fabric, the color of which had been obliterated by mud. As he uncovered a wadded-up ball of the stuff, Mattie could see shades of blue peeking through the brown.

"Is it a shirt?" she asked, thinking of the shirts worn by the men she'd met this morning. Blue chambray, white buttons.

"I think so." Brody leaned back. "One more shot of it, and I'm going to take it out."

After Mattie took the picture, Brody lifted the fabric free from the mud and slowly straightened it, laying it carefully on the muddy ground. When it took shape, they could see that it was indeed a shirt, and through the mud, some of the buttons glinted white.

"This is the type of shirt the men wear at the place where Luke Ferguson was living," Mattie said. "I'd bet money this came off our victim."

"I won't bet against it, but we'd have a hard time proving that."

Mattie snapped a photo, and then Brody reached for one of the pockets. "I'm going to see if there's anything in here that could be useful."

As he probed the pockets with gloved fingers, a look of satisfaction consumed his face. He pulled something out, letting what looked like a muddy chain lengthen and dangle from his fingers. There was some type of pendant on it.

Mattie snapped a photo and leaned forward to examine it closely. It was one of those necklaces that teenage girls favored, a heart broken in half with a jagged edge down the middle. She felt a burst of adrenaline as she realized what it was. "I don't want to wipe it off in case there are prints, but I think beneath the dirt it says *BFF*," she said. "Best friends forever. It's something girls wear at school. Someone else, a best friend, has the other half of the heart. This could lead to something, Brody."

Their eyes met while they shared a moment of silent celebration.

A smile quirked one corner of Brody's mouth. "Now all we gotta do is find the person with the other half."

TWELVE

Mattie spent another hour searching the rest of the pine grove that lined the upper lake. As she and Robo moved higher up the drainage basin, the trees became thicker and the footing dryer, but her dog didn't hit on anything else.

She stopped to rest at the edge of the grove, her legs tired from scrambling over the rugged terrain and fallen timber. A rumble of distant thunder made her look up at the lowering clouds. "The storm's moving in, Brody, and we're done here. We'd better get to safer ground before the lightning sets in."

"Are you satisfied we've found everything we're going to up here?"

"I think so. I'll let Robo travel off leash on the way down to the falls, and we'll see if he hits on anything new."

Mattie unclipped Robo's leash and told him to seek, flinging out her arm to encompass the area, and he took off. She and Brody followed, taking the middle ground while Robo hunted with his nose, working back and forth.

Once they reached the trail beside the falls, Mattie officially signaled an end to the hunt, telling Robo what a good boy he was and taking off his evidence detection collar. After snapping on his everyday collar, she let him go out in front while they slid their way down the path. She was wet, cold, and muddy.

Lightning began to crack up on the peaks they'd just left, and it began to sprinkle. Mattie led the way over to the pines before shrugging off her backpack and opening it to retrieve her raincoat while Brody followed suit.

She'd been thinking of Tracy Lee Brown. Had he packed up and moved his tent already? Or was he staying put like he'd been told?

"Brody, what do you say we hike over to Tracy Lee's camp and see if he's still there. It'll only take an extra twenty minutes, and we can stay off the open parts of the trail where we might attract a lightning strike."

"All right. Won't hurt to see if he plans to stick around."

As the sky opened up and poured on them, Mattie and Robo led the way down the trail until they reached the spot where they needed to cut across country. Despite the rainfall, they made fast progress going downhill.

The campsite looked drab, wet, and deserted. Tracy Lee was nowhere to be seen. The tent had been taken down, and all his belongings were packed inside or lashed onto the outside of a backpack that rested against a tree trunk beside his fishing pole.

As they made their way into the campsite, Mattie called out. "Hello! Tracy Lee, are you here?"

No answer. She raised her brow at Brody. "I guess this answers the question about whether he plans to stick around or not."

A hinky feeling consumed her as she scanned the area for any sign of the man. He'd had no weapons at the time they'd left him, but he could have hidden a handgun out here somewhere. Brody placed his hand on the Glock he wore on his utility belt.

Robo darted around the campsite, sniffing, which gave Mattie an idea. "Where's Tracy Lee, Robo? Let's find the bad guy."

Robo had tracked this man before, but he seemed to sort through various scents before he chose one to follow. With his nose to the ground, he trotted through the dripping forest, heading downhill. Mattie hurried after him, and Brody fell in behind.

They'd traveled only about fifty yards when the hackles on Robo's back rose, making Mattie's neck prickle. This wasn't exactly what she'd expected, since Robo knew Tracy Lee by this time, and his reaction set off her alarm system. "Tracy must be close," she murmured to Brody. "Or someone else."

Brody drew his handgun and Mattie grabbed Robo's collar, making him slow down. She walked beside him as he sniffed his way along the scent track, nose to the ground. Although she kept her eyes peeled, they came upon the horrible sight all at once. When Robo led her around a dense spruce tree, there it was, right in front of her.

His boots inches off the ground, Tracy Lee Brown swung from a rope slung over a lower branch of a tall pine and tied to the trunk. Though it looked grisly, Mattie couldn't take her eyes off his face. Above the knotted rope at his neck, his tongue protruded from his mouth and his eyes bulged, his skin purple and bloated.

"Damn it to hell," Brody muttered. "I didn't see that coming."

Mattie hadn't either, and a tremendous swell of anger and guilt washed through her. Tracy Lee's hands were tied behind his back. There was no doubt this was a homicide. And she and Brody had left him out here to face a killer alone. "I had no idea his life was in danger."

"Shit, Cobb. He was packed up and ready to get the hell out of Dodge. He never said anything, but he must have been afraid. Why didn't he ask for help?"

"Maybe he was a part of Luke's murder and his partner turned on him." Mattie felt responsible for the man's death, no matter what the circumstances. Rain dripped from the trees onto her hood. "It's wet, but Robo can still track scent. We need to follow the person that left here and catch this guy."

"Wait a minute. You can't take off half-cocked, Cobb." Brody threw her a look that challenged argument as he shrugged off his backpack, unzipping it to access the satellite phone. "I'll call this in and tell them to check the trailhead for vehicles. Then we need to process the scene as best we can while we wait for a recovery party."

Torn between her duties to this dead man—preserving his crime scene or tracking his killer—Mattie tried to think of a compromise. "Let's photograph the scene and get him down from that tree. Then Robo and I should try to find a track and follow it as far as we can. With this amount of rain, the track could get washed out."

"You shouldn't go without backup." Brody narrowed his eyes at her, ending the discussion while he made the call.

Mattie took out her cell phone to start taking pictures of the scene, conscious of the pressure from both the passing time and the falling rain. She felt she owed it to Tracy Lee to track down his killer. When Brody disconnected with the sheriff, she stated her case. "Robo and I are a team, Brody. We can handle tracking on our own. And we left this man alone and exposed. He deserves justice."

"Damn it, Cobb. Someone has to stay here." Brody began to search the ground, which was covered with pine needles, cones, twigs, and branches, apparently looking for prints that would be hard to find here. "And there could've been more than one guy. In fact, there probably was."

She knew that having to wait while she and Robo tracked the killer was what bothered Brody most. He was a man of action and didn't like to be the one left behind.

Mattie hardened herself to the images while she framed shots of Tracy Lee's body. "You'll have to search for prints and work the scene before the rain washes everything away."

"Go ahead," Brody said, sounding both disgusted and resigned. "I can handle this. Go see what you and Robo can find."

She nodded, pocketing her cell phone and reaching into her utility belt for Robo's tracking harness. After rapidly changing out his equipment, she gave him a drink from his water bowl. She wanted to hurry and get away before Brody changed his mind.

"Once I get a radio signal, I'll check in at the station," she said.

"Maybe you should take the sat phone."

She thought about it for a brief moment. "No, you'll need it to guide the others. I'll be okay without it."

The chatter Mattie used to excite Robo worked its typical charm, making him dance and circle her legs. The soggy ground was perfect for trapping skin cells that a fugitive would slough off as he fled, and she thought the track would be fairly straightforward. "Robo, search! Let's find a bad guy."

With his nose to the forest floor, Robo began to circle the crime scene, sorting through scents and then apparently rejecting them. She had begun to wonder whether she was wrong about the rain not having washed away the track yet when he pricked his ears and took a few steps forward, sniffing furiously. Within a few more steps, he seemed to vacuum up scent that led somewhere and began to follow it, an invisible track with an occasional footprint in the rocky soil.

"There are some prints over here," she called to Brody as she trailed her dog.

"I'll get them," he called out to her. "Watch your back."

Mattie raised her free hand in farewell and then concentrated on Robo as he led her downhill and away from the tree. Hanging Falls would never be the same to her again.

It was like trading a little slice of heaven for a big chunk of hell.

★ ★ ★

Robo led Mattie downhill for about a mile. Sometimes when the trail was especially rocky, he scrambled around, sniffing the soil and foliage as if he'd lost the track. But he always picked it up again, and Mattie knew that he was battling the elements as much as she was.

The scent track led diagonally back to the main trail beside the river. When she left the shelter of the pines, rainfall pelted her shoulders and head. Her cold feet squished inside her saturated boots. Robo seemed less and less sure of himself, and she feared the rainfall had dispersed the scent, making it harder for him to detect.

When they crested a rise that afforded a view of the downhill terrain, Mattie told him to wait. In this spot, the trail dropped off steeply and then traveled beside the river for a span, but the scene below had changed drastically since they'd hiked up earlier this morning.

The river boiled and frothed over boulders as it tumbled to the curve where it typically flattened out and ran more sedately downhill. But not now. It had swelled beyond its banks and flooded the trail, pooling in an area at least one hundred yards across. Her heart sank as she realized the recovery party would now be cut off from the upper part of the trail, unless they could find a way around it.

Even though she could guess the outcome, Mattie asked Robo to continue the search. He led her the fifty yards it took to reach the edge of the flood and then paused to sniff back and forth. Eventually he sat and looked up at her.

She knelt beside him, hugging him close, as she praised him for the job he'd done and contemplated what he was telling her. The trail ended here. The fugitive or fugitives had passed this way before the river flooded the area.

Mattie asked Robo to come with her as she went back uphill to a thick pine where they could shelter while she reconnoitered their position. Robo nudged her thigh, his signal that he wanted to play with his tennis ball, his reward at the end of a mission.

She ruffled the hair at his neck while she knelt beside him. "Sorry, buddy. It's too dangerous to play here. A treat will have to do."

While she retrieved several baked-liver treats from a pocket on her utility belt and fed them to him one by one, she watched the floodwaters surge and swell. She pulled her radio from her pocket and pressed the button to open a channel.

To her relief, the sheriff responded.

"Deputy Cobb," he said. "What's your status?"

"I'm about halfway down from Hanging Falls. We've lost the scent in some floodwaters that have blocked the main trail. I estimate our fugitive passed here two to three hours ahead of us. Are you at the trailhead yet?"

"We're beyond there and on our way up." Their connection had started to break up, and the sheriff's voice faded in and out. Mattie strained to make out his words as the rain pelted the ground, raising a loud clatter. "I sent a cruiser here as soon as Deputy Brody called in, but there were no vehicles in the lot and there've been none since."

"There's a flooded area here about the size of a football field that's going to cut you off."

"Repeat that. What did you say?"

Mattie shouted above the noise. "The trail is flooded here. See if you can circle around!"

"Copy that." Static and a trail of broken words that Mattie couldn't understand followed. Then, "Cole might know an alternate route."

She assumed Cole was with the sheriff on his way up the hazardous trail, and she tamped down the fright that bit of information gave her. "Watch out for flash floods." She spoke slowly, articulating each word carefully. "The river is out of its banks."

The connection went dead, and she could only hope the sheriff had heard her warning. After scanning the torrent below, she asked Robo to come with her and set off into the forest, heading away from the river. She needed to find a way to reach Cole and the others so she could guide them safely uphill away from the flood.

THIRTEEN

The wet and bedraggled recovery party of four clustered in a small knot at a spot on the trail above the river, which ripped down the canyon, carrying whole trees along with it. Cole watched the sheriff try to communicate with Mattie and then put his radio back inside his pocket under his slicker, his frustration evident.

McCoy looked at him. "Mattie says the trail is flooded above and we can't get through. Do you know an alternate trail?"

Cole wished he did. "There isn't one that I know of. But we need to get out of this canyon, that's for darn sure."

Glenna spoke up. "I think I can get us around this. There's a game trail off to the east, not too far from here."

Cole was glad the game warden had been able to come with them. She was relatively new in town, but she'd spent a lot of time out in the field, and for a newcomer, she knew her way around the nearby forests well, maybe better than he did.

"Shall we wait and see if the waters recede?" McCoy looked at Stella, who sat slumped on her mount, her face pinched with apprehension. "It's important to get up to the site as soon as we can, but I'm not willing to risk your lives while we do it."

"If we can get farther away from this river and find a way up, that would make me happy," Stella replied.

Wherever Mattie was, that's where Cole wanted to be. "If we backtrack out of this canyon, do you think you can find the game trail from there?" he asked Glenna.

"I think we can head across country from there. It depends on how bad the flooding is."

McCoy nodded at her. "Go ahead and take the lead."

Cole reined Duke downhill behind Glenna, and the gelding stepped out at a smart pace, evidently happy to be homeward bound. Mountaineer trailed behind on a lead, carrying a packsaddle that contained an empty body bag and tarps.

The trail had turned into a muddy sluice, dangerous underfoot, and the horses' shod hooves slid off slippery stones with a clang as they picked their way downhill. The downpour beat against Cole's Stetson, rolling off the brim in an annoying trickle, even though it protected his face. The turgid river roared off to one side, and he hated having it flow downhill at his back, knowing full well that a wall of water could come down the canyon at any moment, sweeping them off the trail into its maelstrom.

He kept an eye on the rock walls, looking for a path the horses could traverse, but every crack and crevice had turned into a stream that flowed over the rocky terrain down toward the river. He began to feel desperate as he searched for a way to climb away from the flood.

Farther down the canyon the rock wall widened out, creating a flatter grassy space near the river. It was already filling with water, but Cole thought they could still cross if they hurried. On the other side, he could see where the forest sloped gradually uphill toward higher ground.

"There," Glenna shouted to Cole, pointing out the terrain in front. "Do you think we could get through there with the horses?"

"I'm certain we could."

McCoy reined up beside him and shouted above the noise from the river. "It's flooded, Cole!"

A flash flood could take out this route at any minute. "We can make it. But if we don't move now, we'll lose our chance."

"Go ahead." McCoy turned to Stella. "Stay close to the packhorse and hold on tight."

Cole saw her grip the saddle horn as he turned away and nudged Duke downhill and off the trail toward the standing water. Duke balked at the edge, refusing to enter the flooded glen. Cole wished he were riding Mountaineer instead—that mountain pony would go anywhere and do anything asked of him.

As he continued to tap Duke's sides with his heels, he pulled Mountaineer up close, hoping the steady gelding's proximity would give Duke enough heart to take a step. It worked. Duke gathered himself, tucked his haunches under him, did a few little dancing steps on his front feet, and then leaped into the water, fanning up a huge splash, evidently thinking he could jump the fifty feet ahead of him in one fell swoop.

Sheesh! Cole made a mental note to give this guy more experience crossing waterways before counting on him in this kind of weather again.

Mountaineer plodded into the flooded area behind Duke, and together the two horses led the way across, the water rising up to their knees in one place but no higher. The other horses followed without protest, apparently deeming the way safe when their cronies led the way.

Once they reached dry land, Cole turned to check on Stella. "You okay?"

Still clinging to her saddle horn, she nodded. "I'm making it. Just lead on, Macduff."

Glenna struck out into the forest and Cole followed, scanning in all directions, wanting to keep his bearings. The last thing he needed was for them to get lost or stranded.

He missed his friend Garrett Hartman more than ever. Garrett knew the woods around Timber Creek better than anyone, and he usually accompanied the sheriff's posse on this type of mission. But he was recovering from a head injury he'd sustained last month, and though the doctors believed he could make a full recovery in time, he'd been sidelined for now.

Taking note of the landmarks along the way—a crooked pine struck by lightning here, a huge boulder with a straggly tree growing from the top of it there—Cole followed Glenna through the rugged country, angling away from the river as they went. They left the canyon behind and climbed a ridge, seeking Glenna's game trail that would lead to higher ground.

When Cole crested the ridge, he stopped behind Glenna to study the view. Farther downhill away from the river, a flash of movement caught his eye. Riders? Before he could be sure, they disappeared into the trees.

Cole pointed to the spot. "Glenna, did you see movement down there?"

"I didn't. Was it a deer?"

"I think it was someone on horseback."

The sheriff rode up beside Cole and reined to a stop.

"Abraham," Cole said to the sheriff, pointing toward the site. "I think I just saw riders headed downhill, but then they disappeared."

"How many?"

"I couldn't tell, maybe two." Cole turned to dig his binoculars out of his saddlebag and trained them on the evergreens before sweeping the terrain beyond. "I can't see them anymore. Here, take a look."

McCoy raised the field glasses to his eyes. "This is not the kind of day for a pleasure ride. Mattie said she followed a scent track on the main trail beside the river until it ended in a flooded area. This could be our killers. How far away is that? A mile, a mile and a half?"

"I think so, and some rough country between here and there." Cole wished he could've glassed the riders before they disappeared. "I only caught a glimpse of them. Let me look again."

After taking the binoculars, he focused doggedly, trying to determine what kind of trail existed over the rise. There appeared to be a faint cut through the trees. "I think there's a game trail through there."

"Are you sure you saw riders and not elk?" McCoy asked.

Cole remembered the image well enough to be sure. "Yeah, they were riders."

McCoy looked at Stella before dismounting. "I'm going to peel off and head down that way. See what I can find. The rest of you go on up to the crime scene." He retrieved the satellite phone from his saddlebag. "Here, take this so you can contact Deputy Brody. You can also check in at the station if you need to."

"All right," Stella said, her brow furrowed with concern. "Be careful."

"I'll go with the sheriff," Glenna said, looking at Cole. "That game trail is just a little farther east. You can't miss it."

Cole used the binoculars to scan back uphill where he thought the game trail might run. "I think it runs up inside that draw. We can find it."

McCoy finished transferring the phone into Stella's saddle-bag before stepping back up into his saddle. "We'll stay in touch by cell phone if we can."

Cole hated for the two of them to strike off on their own, but he knew it was important that they do so. He echoed Stella's advice. "Be careful."

"You too." McCoy reined his mount downhill, and Glenna followed. Cole watched them ride away for a moment before turning Duke toward the draw, which he hoped harbored a passable trail.

★　★　★

Mattie jogged downhill on a faint game trail, following Robo through the forest where the footing was actually better than it was on the main trail. Needles from pine and spruce provided absorption into the rich soil rather than the relentless runoff that led to the river. And the timber around her provided shelter from the pelting rain.

Reaching inside her slicker, she pulled her radio from her shirt pocket. The farther she traveled downhill, the better her connection would be. She whistled for Robo and told him to wait while she checked in with the sheriff.

"Where are you now, Mattie?" Apparently he'd dropped his usual formal way of addressing his deputies in favor of speedy communication.

"I'm on a game trail east of the river. It's free and passable. Looks like a good way to get above the flood."

"Glenna and I have split off from the others and headed downhill, trying to catch up with some riders that Cole spotted. We're east of the river too."

As soon as he said he'd split from the others, concern washed through her. "Are you closing in on them?"

"We started off at least a mile behind them, and the going is rough. I doubt if we can catch up. I hope we can find out where they leave the forest and see if we can at least get some prints or something." McCoy paused. "Try to call Cole and see if you two can connect. Then take them up to the site."

"Will do." Mattie ended the transmission and took out her cell phone. Relieved to see she was low enough in altitude to have service, she dialed Cole, who answered right away. "Where are you?" she asked.

"Stella and I are following a draw uphill on a game trail about a half mile east of the river. With any kind of luck, we can follow this for a while and end up above the flooding. Where are you?"

"Somewhere uphill from you. When I get to a vantage point, I'll see if I can spot you."

"Sounds good. Stay in touch."

Mattie hated to end the call and lose contact, but there was no good reason to keep the line open. She returned her phone to the pocket inside her slicker. "Let's go," she told Robo, and he trotted out in front as they continued downhill.

After about five hundred yards of relatively clear footing, the trail entered a boggy area where Robo suddenly showed an interest in the ground, putting his nose down to sniff. When Mattie caught up, she could see the horseshoe prints that had caught his attention. She took out her cell phone and took a few photos. Looked like more than one horse.

"Good boy, Robo." She ruffled the fur at his neck. "Let's go. Let's find a bad guy."

The scent track continued on down the game trail, and Mattie was certain these were the same people the sheriff now followed. It was impossible to tell whether or not they had murdered Tracy Lee Brown, but the lone fact that they were in this part of the forest was enough to raise suspicion.

Robo had definitely tracked the killer or killers from Tracy Lee to the spot on the flooded hiking trail where he'd lost the scent in the water. Perhaps the fugitives had made it down that part of the trail but had been forced to head east lower down, where the flooding most likely began.

Mattie followed the game trail into heavy timber, and pine boughs brushed her arms on both sides. Robo was bobbing along at a trot when he stopped suddenly, one front paw lifted, poised in midstride. He sniffed the foliage to his right, poked his nose into some brush that grew at the edge of the path, and then turned to look at Mattie while he sat.

She took hold of his collar and knelt. "What did you find?"

She parted the grass carefully to avoid touching whatever her dog had smelled. A brown pharmaceutical bottle lay at the base of the stems.

"Good boy, Robo," she murmured as she reached for a pair of latex gloves inside her slicker pocket. She shrugged off her pack and dug out an evidence bag from inside. She hoped there would be fingerprints. The glass surface would be perfect for them.

As she picked up the bottle by its narrow stopper, she read the label: *Rompun (xylazine) 100 mg/mL Injectable. A sedative, analgesic, and muscle relaxant for horses.*

Cole can tell me more about it, she thought as she dropped the bottle inside the bag and sealed it.

After securing the evidence inside her pack, she gave Robo another treat and then moved on downhill, knowing that he was on track and would tell her if he found any other items inconsistent with the environmental norm.

As always, she counted herself lucky to have such a remarkable partner. Not everyone could count on their partner to sniff out evidence. She smiled as she remembered the many times she'd struggled to connect with human law enforcement officers. Only after she'd been assigned Robo had she grown to fully trust someone else.

After they broke free from the thick grove of pine, they came to a point where Mattie could overlook the draw. About a half mile below and coming out of a grove of aspen were two riders and a packhorse, and she recognized the familiar color patterns of Duke, Honey, and Mountaineer.

She waved, but evidently Cole's attention was focused on the trail, and he didn't see her at first. But as she continued, he glanced up and waved back. It was strange that in this huge forest, Cole and she would find each other on the same game trail. Then she decided that maybe what was even stranger was that after all these years with both of them living in Timber Creek, they would finally meet and fall in love.

Perhaps they were destined to be together from now on, throughout the rest of their lives. At any rate, that's what she would choose to believe. She hoped Angie would come around to the idea of her dad developing a new relationship soon.

"Let's go meet Cole and Stella," she told Robo, and started off down the trail. "We'll have to leave this track for the sheriff and Glenna to follow."

FOURTEEN

They reached Tracy Lee Brown's crime scene by late afternoon. The rain had slowed to a drizzle, but the lowering sun didn't have enough power to punch through the cloud cover. Mattie's breath hung in the air as they placed Tracy Lee's corpse into the body bag.

Brody had found and photographed prints that looked like they came from the same boot. Flat sole with no tread, round toe, square heel—could be made by a riding boot. Cole had determined that there were two sets of horseshoe prints down at the bog on the game trail, but it looked like only one person had been at this crime scene.

Before loading the corpse onto Mountaineer, the team huddled around the fire, warming fingers and toes to prepare for the long ride down the mountain. Brody threw another damp log into the flames, and it snapped and sizzled.

Stella held her hands out to warm them above the fire. "CBI lab notified me that our first victim's fingerprints match those you took at the Grayson home, Mattie. We've tentatively identified him as Luke Ferguson, awaiting DNA confirmation. I reached his parents, and here's a surprise—his mother said they weren't even expecting him to come home last week."

That didn't make sense. "Solomon Vaughn said Luke planned to take the bus home, but his parents weren't expecting him?" Mattie asked.

"That's right. She said they hadn't heard from Luke for weeks. And the last time he called, he sounded happy and content. She was surprised to learn that he planned to return home."

"But his mother has an item with his DNA?"

"A hairbrush he'd left and a toothbrush, so once our lab gets that processed, the ID will be definite. But the print match lets us work under the assumption that our first victim is Luke Ferguson."

Guilt over Tracy Lee Brown's death washed through Mattie again. "We'll need to see if there's a link between Luke and Tracy Lee. Why were they both killed here in the same area?"

"Two different MOs." Frowning, Brody nudged the partially lit log with the toe of his boot so that it settled deeper into the flames. "We can't be certain these two homicides are linked."

"I guess you're right," Mattie said. "So far they're linked only by proximity."

"Tracy Lee swore he had no idea who Luke was at the time I interviewed him," Stella said. "But I'm afraid he probably knew more about his homicide than he would admit."

"Tracy Lee hid and spied on us yesterday afternoon," Mattie said. "Do you think he could have observed Luke's murder?"

"I suppose that's possible." Stella fell silent, as if thinking before she spoke. "But how would Luke's killer know that? Tracy Lee was with us the entire time we had him in custody."

Mattie wished she'd never left the man alone at his campsite. "Cole, when we were on the game trail before we met you, Robo found a bottle of Rompun in some brush at the edge of the path."

Surprise lifted Cole's brow. "Rompun's a brand name for xylazine. It's a powerful sedative and analgesic for horses. I'd say up here beside a game trail would be the last place you'd find a bottle of it."

"Robo found it soon after we started following the horseshoe prints."

Stella spoke up. "Why would someone use Rompun on their horses or carry it with them up here?"

Cole frowned. "Good question. I use it for surgeries or to immobilize a horse for a procedure. I don't dispense it to my clients. It's nonnarcotic but dangerous to humans." His gaze met Mattie's. "It suppresses respiratory function and can result in death to humans."

Mattie nodded, recalling what it had been like when she and Robo were dosed with a large-animal tranquilizer in her backyard a few months ago. They'd barely made it through the experience alive.

"So it would be hard for someone to get ahold of this stuff," Stella said.

"Right." Cole's eyes narrowed as if he had remembered something.

"What are you thinking?" Mattie asked.

"I met a farrier yesterday who said he had access to horse tranquilizers through a friend, although he avoided telling me who."

Stella jumped on the words. "What's his name?"

"Quinn Randolph. He's from Hightower and he's building a clientele here." Cole's frown deepened. "He was out at the Vaughn place when I went there this morning, and I know he'd been there before."

"Meaning he might have known Luke," Stella said, her brow knotted as she gazed into the fire. "That's useful information, Cole. Any other customers of yours who might have the drug?"

"Like I said, I don't dispense it to my customers, but I suppose someone could get it through another vet."

"How about the Vaughns or the others that live out there?" Stella asked.

"I've only been out there once, but I don't think they have tranquilizers available, or at least no one said so when Randolph brought it up."

"I need to make some phone calls to veterinarians in Willow Springs." Stella gazed into the fire for a moment before addressing Cole. "Any other way a layperson could get it?"

Mattie watched Cole's expression change as he thought about it. She could tell he'd thought of someone else.

"Rompun requires a prescription from a vet for a layperson to get it. But there was a drug rep in my office this morning that would have access to it and might even carry it with him. He's new to the area, and he's about the same age as Randolph. It's a long shot, and the guy probably has nothing to do with this, but you might see if the two happen to know each other."

"What's the name of the drug rep?"

"Parker Tate. He works for a company out of Willow Springs, and I'm one of the vets in his territory." Cole looked at Mattie, his expression sheepish. "He made some off-color comments around Angie and I got a little hot under the collar, so I'm not the one to ask for a character recommendation. Told him not to come back to the clinic again unless he had an appointment with me."

Mattie approved of his way of handling the situation and gave Cole a nod.

"How old is this guy?" Brody asked, his eyebrows pinched in disapproval.

"I would say early twenties."

"We made another find up above Hanging Falls this morning, or I should say Robo did," Brody said. He went on to describe the shirt and best-friend necklace. "Made us wonder if there's a girl involved."

"A teenage girl," Mattie said, further refining the thought. "It's the kind kids share in junior high around here. Luke seems too old to be interested in that sort of thing. Quinn Randolph or Parker Tate too, for that matter."

"We know there's at least one teenage girl that knew Luke," Stella said. "The Vaughn girl, the one with the dog."

Mattie and Cole chimed in together as their eyes met. "Hannah."

We would remember the name of the girl with the dog, Mattie thought. "There was also another teenage girl inside the Grayson house, reading a story to one of the younger kids."

"We'll need to go out there first thing in the morning and interview them," Stella said to Mattie. And then to Brody, "When we get back tonight, let's search for the farrier and the drug rep online."

Brody nodded.

Stella thought for moment. "I'll ask our lab to test both of our victims for xylazine, just on the off chance that it was used on either of them."

"If it's present in both, it would give us a link between the two cases," Mattie said.

"And give us a lead on two persons of interest," Stella said.

Brody sloshed water on the fire, making it smoke. "Let's douse this fire and head home. We've got a lot more work ahead of us."

And a long way to go to get home, Mattie thought, hating the idea of leaving the warmth of the fire. *And only a half day to work tomorrow before my family arrives.*

Her family! Her stomach fluttered.

She and Robo might be finished with the work they needed to do in the high country, but she wanted to help Stella with interviews tomorrow morning. Luke Ferguson was someone's son and family member, well liked by the people he lived with. She wanted to do her best by him and bring his killer to justice.

And in the case of Tracy Lee? Well, a part of her felt responsible for his death. He might have been sneaky and a bit of a voyeur, but now she realized he'd been vulnerable, maybe even afraid. Had she called attention to him by bringing him in for interrogation? Were she and her colleagues somehow part of the reason he'd been killed?

She wouldn't be able to rest easy until she had some answers.

★ ★ ★

Halfway down the mountain, Stella connected a call to the sheriff and learned that he and Glenna had followed the trail of two riders until it led back to a wide spot off a dirt road farther east from the main parking lot. There they'd found tire prints in the mud worthy of casting. From the depth and shape of the prints, it looked like a truck and trailer had parked and then turned around to go on down to the highway. Boot prints—flat sole, rounded toe, square heel—and horseshoe impressions had also been taken.

One valuable piece of evidence became apparent at the truck: both riders wore the same size and shape of boot. That cleared up why the prints at the crime scene had looked like they'd come from only one set of boots. Apparently, if a shoe fit two suspects, they might have their pair of killers.

Mattie was surprised by how relieved she felt when she learned that the sheriff had arrived safely at the end of the trail. Why had she been so worried about him? After all, the sheriff was an experienced and competent lawman, so there shouldn't have been any need for concern. And Glenna had been there as backup.

But the man had been her mentor, someone she could count on, and her world wouldn't be the same if something removed him from it. Law enforcement was a dangerous profession, and you could never count on a fellow officer's safety during an investigation.

Besides, Sheriff McCoy represented the closest thing to a father figure that Mattie had ever known.

Cole trailered the horses to his home while she took Robo directly to the station. Before they parted, he made her promise that she would call him when she finished work.

Brody and Stella took their laptops into the briefing room to dig for information on Quinn Randolph and Parker Tate while Mattie fed Robo in the staff office and wrote her reports. When he finished eating, he curled up on his red cushion beside her desk and fell asleep within seconds. After she printed her reports and left them in the outgoing tray, she considered waking him but decided to leave him in the office to sleep.

She found the others still in the briefing room, comparing notes on what they'd found online. Sheriff McCoy glanced at her when she entered and gave her a smile that made her feel warm and welcome. "Where's your partner?"

"Asleep," she told him as she closed the door behind her. "He'll track me down if he wakes up and I'm not there."

Before she could make it to the table where they all sat, the harsh sound of Robo's toenails scraping the door echoed through the room.

"Ha!" Stella said, her eyes on her computer screen. "He has his Spidey sense on even when it looks like he's asleep. He's one tricky character to leave behind."

Mattie turned to let Robo into the room, using the moment to hide her flushed cheeks. Stella knew only the half of it. Her dog had become increasingly difficult to work around whenever she and Cole wanted to be alone in her bedroom. Even though she considered Robo the most obedient dog she'd ever seen, her bedroom door had gained many new scratches on the outside veneer in the past weeks. Apparently his down-stay wasn't good enough to go the distance.

While Cole had been dealing with Angie learning how to share her father, she'd been dealing with Robo. Kids!

After she opened the door, Robo trotted into the room like a king, giving her a glance as he passed. He went directly to the chair that Mattie usually sat in and waited for her to settle. Then he circled a couple times, lay down to put his head on his paws, and sighed. She figured he would be asleep again soon.

"Look at this," Stella said, turning her laptop so they could see the screen. "Check out the boot."

The screen showed a website for Randolph Farrier Services, upon which a rather narrow-faced guy was pictured wearing leather farrier's chaps, posed with one boot propped up on a blacksmith's anvil. There it was in plain sight: a leather boot with a rounded toe, which probably also had a square heel and flat sole, although she couldn't tell for certain from the angle of the camera.

"It would be hard for him to deny he has this style of boot." Mattie clicked on the other website pages but couldn't find any other shots of the farrier's footwear.

"There's only a head shot of Parker Tate on the pharmaceutical company's website, so no shot of his boots," Stella said. "Let me show you."

The screen filled with the photos of several company employees, and Stella pointed out the one captioned *Parker Tate*. He looked to be in his early twenties, his hair gelled into an upsweep in front, his eyes flirting with the camera. Mattie withheld her opinion that the guy looked like he thought a lot of himself.

"Hmmm . . ." McCoy mused.

"Real ladies' man," Brody muttered, turning his computer screen toward Mattie and Stella. "Here's his Facebook page."

Party shots filled the photo section. Parker's involvement with many different female friends was readily apparent, as was his penchant for drinking and bars.

"The farrier doesn't do social media," Brody said, pulling his computer back in front of him. "I'll see if I can find anything else about him."

McCoy excused himself to take care of some business in his office while Brody and Stella focused on their laptop screens, so Mattie decided to update the whiteboard on the Luke Ferguson case. They'd picked up a lot of valuable information during this long day.

When she mentioned it to Stella, the detective gestured toward the printer. "I'll print a photo of Tracy Lee too. We need to set up his case."

The photo of Luke Ferguson that showed his damaged face had been printed and pinned to the top of the whiteboard. Mattie added the evidence that Robo had uncovered and then began a list of persons of interest, beginning with Quinn Randolph and Parker Tate. As she added the names of the folks at the compound—the term she'd been using in her own mind for the place—and the list grew longer and longer, her heart began to sink. They still had a lot of work to do before her family arrived.

After she retrieved the printout of the mug shot they'd taken of Tracy Lee when they booked him last night, she pinned it to the second whiteboard. Thankful that they didn't need to use one of the ghastly, distorted images that his face had morphed into above the noose, she stood back and studied the photo for a minute.

Thin cheeks, unkempt straggly hair, deep-set dark eyes that looked like burned-out holes—this photo finalized the shift her brain had made to classify Tracy Lee as victim rather than perpetrator. Why hadn't she seen it before? The eyes she'd seen as furtive had become sunken holes of misery.

The man had been living a life of bare existence out there in the forest, smoking weed and eating whatever fish he could catch. That and the small stash of junk food he carried with him in his fanny pack. Where was his family? Would anyone care if he was alive or dead?

"We have to find Tracy Lee's family," she murmured.

"Sheriff McCoy's working on that now," Stella said, looking up from her screen. "He'll take care of notification."

Brody sat back in his chair and rolled his neck on his shoulders, making the bones pop. "Let's wrap it up for the night. My eyes are so blurry I can hardly see the screen. I'll come in early and pick it up again."

His eyes *were* bloodshot and strained, and Mattie remembered they'd been at this now for two days and two very late nights. She stifled a yawn as she agreed to come in early too.

"Come in when you want, but we'll plan on meeting together by seven," Stella said. "We'll get out to the place where Luke lived by eight. Maybe we can finish up out there within a couple hours before we move on to Randolph and Tate."

"All right." Mattie bent to rest her hand on Robo's side, and he awakened slowly as if from deep sleep. His eyes opened and focused gradually before he raised his head to stare into hers. "You want to go, buddy?"

As if someone had pressed an on switch, he scrambled to his feet and headed for the door. Mattie said good-night and followed, removing her cell phone from her pocket as she went. In the staff office, she sent Cole a text saying she was about to leave. Before she could put her phone back into her pocket, it rang in her hand. Cole.

"You're still up?" she greeted him.

"Yeah. Got my chores done with the horses, and everyone else here went to bed. Mrs. Gibbs saved some dinner for us. You want to come eat it with me?"

She smiled, the phone next to her lips. Since he'd seen the bare expanse of her refrigerator, Cole often lured her to his house with the promise of food. Dinner at home would have been a peanut butter and jelly sandwich. "I'd like that. We'll be there soon."

FIFTEEN

As she loaded Robo into her SUV, flashes of lightning chased across the sky and thunder rolled in an uninterrupted chain like distant artillery fire. A chill breeze carried the scent of rain. She was grateful they'd finished their work in the high country, because another night of rainfall appeared to be in store.

After driving the mile out of town to the Walkers' lane, Mattie turned in and followed it to the log house, a two-story with a covered front porch. She parked under the cottonwood tree outside the yard.

As was customary, Cole had been waiting for her outside with Bruno, his Doberman pinscher. Robo had begun his happy dance in the back compartment as soon as she'd turned down the lane, and now he acted like he was beside himself, jumping back and forth in his compartment, pressing his nose to each window. After ratcheting on the hand brake, she popped open the front door to his cage and let him bail out behind her.

Robo and Bruno wrestled each other around the yard while she and Cole met halfway on the sidewalk.

Cole took her in his arms. "Mmm," he murmured against her hair as he hugged her close. "So happy to see you when there isn't a dead body involved."

She groaned. "I'll say. It's been wild, hasn't it? I can't believe it sometimes."

A breeze had sprung up, causing a chill that made her shiver. Well, that along with the memory of Tracy Lee Brown's distorted face.

"Let's forget about death for a while," Cole said, tucking her under his arm and guiding her up the sidewalk to the porch steps. "Your family arrives tomorrow. Have you heard from them yet?"

Mattie took out her cell phone to check her text messages. "Here's a text from Julia. Oh my gosh, they're in Green River, Utah, tonight! About five hours away. She says they'll try to get on the road by nine in the morning. They'll be here around two."

Cole tightened his arm to draw her closer. "Are you excited?"

Mattie couldn't define her exact feelings. "Excited, nervous, scared, you name it."

"They're going to love you."

She felt her lips quiver slightly as she smiled. "Julia already says they do."

A huge gust of wind hit the side of the house, followed by the splatter of raindrops on the sidewalk. Robo and Bruno came running to the shelter of the porch.

Cole chuckled as the dogs bounded up the steps. "You'd better get up here, you two. At least they have enough sense to come in out of the rain. Did Robo eat?"

"I fed him at the station."

"Let's go inside and have our dinner, then. I'm starving. You hungry?"

She acknowledged that she was, told Robo to heel, and made him settle at her side. Cole grabbed Bruno's collar, and they led the two straight through the den and into the kitchen, a routine familiar to both dogs and a signal that it was time to abandon their roughhousing.

Though they tried to be as quiet as they could, Mattie heard a door open and close upstairs as she crossed the threshold into the kitchen. She released Robo from heel position so that he could go drink from Bruno and Belle's water bowl, as he was wont to do each time he visited, and looked back to the doorway just as Sophie came around the corner.

The child's brown curls were tousled, and she was wearing a turquoise set of shorty pajamas that had a tiny rose print on the fabric. She carried a bedraggled toy rabbit that she still cuddled with at night but typically left it in the bedroom during the day.

Although Mattie had never had a favorite toy—in fact, she'd had very few toys of any kind during her childhood—she figured nine was not too old to use a stuffed rabbit for comfort when needed.

With Belle trailing behind her, Sophie peered up at Mattie. "The storm woke me up."

"It's a noisy one, isn't it?" Mattie said, reaching out to place her palm on the child's curls. She couldn't resist touching Sophie, because she couldn't have loved this little girl more if she'd given birth to her herself. "Why don't you come in and sit with your dad and me while we eat our dinner?"

A glance at Cole told her he was giving her his perplexed look, one eyebrow quirked. Maybe he'd planned for the two of them to have dinner alone, but she couldn't send Sophie back upstairs. She led the child over to the table while Belle raised her chin and allowed Robo to greet her with a lick. Rarely did the older dog join in on the two boys' shenanigans, as she preferred to carry herself much more sedately through life, queen of the pack.

"I'm hungry too," Sophie said, taking her usual seat. Belle plopped down next to her in her spot on the floor, apparently not at all disturbed by the booming thunder that accompanied the storm.

"I'll get you a plate," Mattie said. "You can share some of mine."

"There's plenty of food for everyone," Cole said as he closed the door to the microwave on a plateful of food, pressed the button to reheat, and headed back to the refrigerator. "You want a little spaghetti left over from dinner tonight, Sophie-bug?"

"Yeah."

"Say *yes, please*," Cole said, as if by rote, while he retrieved food from the fridge.

"Yes, please," Sophie echoed, with a grin for Mattie.

Mattie smiled and tucked an errant strand of the child's hair behind her ear. "Do you want a glass of milk or water?"

"How about Pepsi?" Sophie asked with a twinkle in her eye.

"That would be a no," Cole said.

"Then water, please," Sophie replied, grinning at Mattie. "Just testing."

"It might be late, but your old dad is still awake and alert," Cole said, placing a spoonful of spaghetti on a small plate.

Mattie was filling water glasses when movement at the kitchen door caught her eye, and she looked to find Angie poised at the threshold. The girl wore a long, oversized tee over boxers and a tentative expression on her face, evidently trying to decide if she would enter or not. Mattie felt certain that Angie had spotted *her* and was now hesitant to come in and join her family.

Their eyes met. Normally, Mattie would go to Angie to give her a hug, but she felt reluctant to press herself on the girl, who lately had been sending out powerful vibes demanding that she be given some space.

"Hi," Mattie said softly. "Did we wake you up, or did the storm?"

"I was awake when I heard Sophie leave her room."

"Come on in, Angel," Cole said, beckoning with his hand and a smile. "We're having a midnight snack. You hungry?"

While Angie paused, apparently torn, Mrs. Gibbs—pin curls framing her face—suddenly materialized behind her. She placed an arm around Angie's waist and nudged her into the room. "Well now, this is a fine thing. There's no sleep to be found during this storm, I tell you. I said to meself, sounds like everyone's down there in the kitchen, and I'm about to miss out on a slice of that cake I made today. I got meself out of bed and came down here right smart, lickety-split."

"Lickety-split," Sophie echoed, evidently liking the sound of it. "Can we all have cake?"

"Well, of course, my fine friend," Mrs. Gibbs said. "That's why I made it. Angela, dear, would you be so kind as to get us some forks and small plates?"

Grateful that Mrs. Gibbs had arrived to force Angie into the group, Mattie turned away to fill more glasses with water. She tried to keep a low profile as she carried drinks to the table and spread them around for everyone. By this time, Cole had heated dinner plates for the two of them and a small one for Sophie. "Angie, Mrs. Gibbs, do either of you want a plate of spaghetti?"

"No thanks," Angie murmured.

"I don't want to spoil me appetite for cake, so no thank you, kind sir." Mrs. Gibbs carried a domed cake plate over to the table, making a dramatic display of setting it down and sweeping off the cover. "Voilà!"

Two-thirds of a gorgeous double-layer chocolate cake slathered with rich fudge frosting sat in the middle of the table, looking good enough to inhale. Smiling, Mattie placed a knife and spatula on the table beside Mrs. Gibbs before slipping into her chair.

"Hooray!" Sophie cheered, opening her mouth wide enough to expose half-chewed spaghetti.

"No shouting with your mouth full, little bit," Cole murmured. "And no talking either."

Cole exchanged an amused look with Mattie before tucking into his dinner, while Mrs. Gibbs served large slabs of cake and started passing them around the table.

"Your sister and grandmum arrive tomorrow, right, Mattie?" Mrs. Gibbs said as she handed her a serving.

Mattie's stomach danced uneasily as she set her cake down beside her dinner plate and glanced at the clock. It was well after midnight. "That's right, Mrs. Gibbs, although to be exact, it's officially today already."

"Ach! It is indeed. Are you excited?"

Mattie took a breath, thinking she could be honest about her feelings with this lady—and with this family too, for that matter. "Excited. And nervous."

Mrs. Gibbs stopped midreach as she was handing Cole a piece of cake and studied Mattie for a brief moment before sending her a look of encouragement. "I can see how that would make someone a bit nervy. You don't remember either of them from your childhood, right?"

"That's right." Mattie looked into Mrs. Gibbs's eyes and saw sympathy there. "I've tried to remember them, but I must have been too young before we were separated."

"Did you separate like Mom and Dad?" Sophie asked, her face alight with curiosity.

"No, not like that." Mattie had never shared details of her childhood abduction with the kids, although they knew a bit of her history. She glanced at Cole before expanding on her answer. Concern creased his face, and he lifted one shoulder in a quick shrug. "My mother and my brother and I got separated from my sister when I was about two years old. Even I don't know everything about how that happened."

"Will your grandma tell you when you see her?" Sophie asked, putting her fork down and giving her complete attention to Mattie.

"I think she'll tell me what she knows. I hope so." Mattie's breath caught, and she felt suffocated by the ache in her chest. Sometimes it surprised and overwhelmed her how much it still hurt to think about how the Cobb brothers had destroyed her family.

Sophie must have sensed her distress, because she reached out and touched Mattie's hand gently. "I hope so too."

Cole cleared his throat and placed his warm hand on Mattie's shoulder. "Everything's going to be all right. It'll be good for you to get more information, because you're the type who wants the whole story, not just part of it."

Mrs. Gibbs spoke up. "You just wait. All will be well, and you shall have a lovely time together."

Mattie showed her gratitude with a thin smile. "I hope so," she said, looking down at her plate, but not before noticing that Angie gazed at her with concern.

"When will they get here?" Sophie asked.

"Early afternoon," Mattie said.

"I have an idea," Mrs. Gibbs said, as she picked up her fork and filled it with a generous bite of cake. "Why don't you bring your family over for dinner tonight?"

That came as a surprise, and Mattie shook her head. "Oh, I couldn't impose."

"It's not an imposition, dear." Mrs. Gibbs looked thoughtful as she chewed her cake and swallowed. "It's important that we get a chance to meet your family while they're here, and what better time than during dinner? Besides, maybe we can relieve some of the pressure on you. You know, divert the conversation for a few hours."

Mattie wasn't sure about that. How could she explain the relationship she had with this family to the family she was meeting for the first time? Could she tell her sister that this was the family she hoped would become hers someday? Probably not.

"Please, Mattie." Sophie looked eager, her freckled cheeks bunched above her smile. "We want to meet your sister and grandma too."

"That's a great idea, Mrs. Gibbs," Cole said. "Unless you'd like to cook dinner for all of us at your house, Mattie?"

The sparkle in his brown eyes told her he was teasing her.

"Oh, pshaw," Mrs. Gibbs said. "Now that's what I call an imposition. Of course you don't have the time to shop and cook, Miss Mattie, although I'm certain you would be entirely capable if you were taken with the idea. You'll all come here for dinner, and I won't take no for an answer."

Mattie scanned the faces of those around the table, lighting on Angela's last. There was no animosity in her expression whatsoever, simply a reserved mixture of curiosity and concern.

"You should come," Angie murmured, "or Mrs. Gibbs is going to pitch a fit."

Mrs. Gibbs snorted. "Aye, that I will."

With a warm feeling of acceptance, Mattie agreed. The alternative would be for her to take her family to Clucken House or the Main Street Diner, which she would save for the next night. "Thank you, Mrs. Gibbs. What time should we be here?"

Mrs. Gibbs put on a victorious smile while she made plans and they all ate their food. Mattie regained her appetite as she let Mrs. Gibbs take over. When Cole pressed his hand just above her knee, giving it a squeeze beneath the cover of the table, her heart filled with gratitude for this new chapter in her life.

Cole and Mrs. Gibbs had a brief scrap over who would fill the dishwasher, but Cole insisted that he would do it, and the lady backed down. "Come on, Sophie dear," she said. "Take your dishes to the sink, and then let me tuck you back into bed."

"Will you read me a story?" Sophie asked, as she put her dishes on the counter. "I'm not at all tired."

"Sure." Mrs. Gibbs led the way toward the stairs, encircling Sophie with her arm. "Chocolate cake in the middle of the night was probably a bad idea for both of us. I'm not tired either, but maybe we'll get that way if we lie down together and read. Say good-night to everyone."

Good-nights were exchanged as the two left, but Mattie was surprised that Angie held back and didn't take advantage of the opportunity to slip away. Mattie gave the girl a tentative smile, hoping she was starting to warm back up to her. Angie had acted like they were friends until the past few weeks.

In response to Mattie's smile, Angie's lips tweaked upward in a short, quick response, as if they did so automatically, before she turned away to carry dishes to the sink. Mattie helped her clear the table.

Cole was busy rinsing and stacking dishes inside the washer. "Are you tired, Angie?"

"Not really." Angie leaned against the counter and, head tilted down toward the floor, ran her bare toe along the grout between two of the slate tiles. She looked up at Mattie and caught her watching her. "I was wondering something, Mattie."

With some trepidation, Mattie tried to assume an open posture. She didn't know what Angie wanted to talk about, but if the girl was willing to open the door to communication again, she wanted to meet her at least halfway. "What's that, Angie?"

"What happened when you got separated from your family? I mean, I know your mom left you and your brother when you were kids. You said you thought she did that to protect you. But what happened before that?"

Cole closed the dishwasher. "Maybe Mattie doesn't want to talk about it, Angel."

"Oh." Angela gave Mattie a stricken look. "I'm sorry."

"No, it's okay. You have the right to ask, and you're old enough to know." Mattie hated to share her past with anyone, but Angela had been through some tough times this past year, and she was mature enough to treat the information with respect. Mattie couldn't tell her everything, but if she wanted to strengthen her relationship with this girl, sharing some of her secrets might bring them closer. "The problem is, I don't remember much about the years before I was six. But I don't mind talking to you about it."

Gathering her thoughts, Mattie cast her gaze around the room. "Let's sit back down at the table."

"I was just wondering about how you and your mom got separated from your sister is all. I didn't mean to stick my nose in your business."

Mattie sat back down in her chair while Angie took her seat. Cole drifted over to join them, drying his hands on a towel that he carried with him. He knew all her secrets, and Mattie felt his sympathy.

"I don't remember much about the night that John and Harold Cobb abducted me, my mom, and my brother, but I do know that Mom had left my sister Julia with my grandmother that night. That's why she wasn't taken along with us." Mattie crossed her arms at her solar plexus to control the flutter. "Eventually, Harold Cobb brought all of us here to Timber Creek to live. For most of my life, I thought he was my father."

"Was he good to you?"

"No, Angie, he wasn't." Mattie felt shored up when Cole placed his hand on her shoulder. "He abused all of us. When I was six, I called the police the night that he tried to kill my mother. Sheriff McCoy was one of the deputies that responded."

Mattie hugged herself as she felt her inner tension build, making her feel taut as a spring. Cole squeezed her shoulder.

Her eyes huge, Angie leaned forward, hugging her own belly. "You don't have to talk about it if you don't want to, Mattie."

Mattie shook her head. "I'm okay, Angie. Really I am. It just shakes me up when I think of it, even now after all these years. The police came and arrested Harold Cobb, and my mom had to go to the hospital. My brother, Willie, and I ended up in a foster home, together at first, but when Mom was released from the hospital, she didn't come back to get us. Eventually Willie and I got split up and sent to different homes."

Angie's brow knotted, her sympathy evident.

"I felt abandoned by my mother then, but now I think she was afraid. Like I told you before, I think she thought her leaving would protect us. And it did, at first. But then Harold Cobb's brother got released from prison after he served time on a different charge, and he found Willie and killed him."

"And he's in prison now." Angie already knew that part of the story and looked relieved to be able to say it.

"That's right. He was looking for my mother."

Angie frowned. "But you don't know where your mother is, right?"

"Right. And my sister doesn't know where she is either."

Angie leaned back, her face filled with sorrow. "Oh man, I'm so sorry all that happened to you when you were a kid, Mattie. No one should have to go through something like that."

"Isn't that the truth?" Mattie reached her hand across the table, and Angela clung to it with hers. "I guess that's why I chose to go into law enforcement. I don't think anyone has the right to do bad things to people against their will. And all children should be protected."

Cole removed his hand from Mattie's shoulder and, placing it over both hers and Angie's, gripped theirs tightly. "I admire you for overcoming the hardship of your past, Mattie, and for choosing to do right by people."

She shrugged as she gently pulled her hand loose to break up the pile. "It doesn't take much to try to do the right thing. Anyway . . . my sister says that our father is dead, and she's going to tell me how he died when we're together."

"Do you ever think about changing your name?" Angie leaned forward again, putting her elbows on the table.

"All the time lately. This is still pretty new to me, but I don't think I'll keep the name Cobb much longer."

"What's your real name?"

"Our last name was Wray."

"R-A-Y?" Angie asked, spelling it out.

"No, W-R-A-Y." Mattie traced the letters on the tabletop, thinking what it would be like to be called Mattie Wray. She liked the sound of it, and the name Cobb had brought her nothing but pain, even though that was the only name she'd ever known.

"You'd have the same last initial as us," Angie said with a slight smile.

"Sure 'nuff," Cole murmured.

"I hadn't thought about that." Mattie's shivers had quieted, and she was able to lean back in her chair. "I hope to learn a lot more about myself over the next few days. Julia's bringing pictures, and maybe that will spark some memories. And no telling what my grandmother can tell me about our parents."

"I hope you learn lots of good things," Angie said, her eyes filled with the old friendship Mattie was used to.

"I'm sure I will." But she had a suspicion that the circumstances surrounding her father's death were not all good, or at least that's what Julia's email had led her to believe. She scooted her chair back a little, and it scraped against the tile. "Unless you want to talk more, Angie, I guess I'd better be going home. I need to get up early in the morning."

"No, that's okay. I'm sorry if I made you stay too late."

Angie seemed to be more apologetic than usual, making Mattie wonder if she might feel bad for turning a cold shoulder the past few weeks. But whatever the reason, Mattie was glad they'd shared these few moments together; it gave her hope that it would be a new beginning.

"No worries, Angie. I'm glad we had a chance to talk. And we can visit more after I meet with my family, if you want. Maybe things will become clearer for me then."

★ ★ ★

Wanting to make sure Mattie was okay after that intense conversation, Cole walked her to her car. "I hope that wasn't too hard on you," he said, putting his arm around her waist.

"She needs to know some of what happened, enough for it to make sense for her. Not everything."

He knew she was referring to the type of abuse she'd suffered from Harold Cobb, different from the kind he'd dealt her brother and much more personal. Mattie liked to keep that part of her life private, and as far as he was concerned, it would always be her story to tell. "It's up to you to decide when and how much of your past you want to share."

Mattie went around back and loaded Robo into his compartment while Bruno watched dolefully from the ground. Cole opened the door of the Explorer and handed her up into the driver's seat. "I hope it goes well for you tomorrow when your family arrives. I'll be thinking about you."

Mattie reached to place her hand on his cheek, a gesture that always made his heart expand with love. He covered her hand with his and leaned forward to give her a good-night kiss.

They ended the kiss, and she turned the key to start her car's engine. "See you for dinner about six," she murmured.

He watched her drive away, wishing she could stay the night. He worried about her when she had this much going on in her life. Would she be able to sleep, or would her insomnia kick in? Would she withdraw from him like she had in the past?

As he walked up the sidewalk to his house, his mind filled with the ghastly images of the two most recent homicides. He wondered again if it was wise to fall in love with a cop—but then, it was too late to worry about that now. There seemed to be little he could do to control his heart's willful choices.

SIXTEEN

Sunday morning

Mattie was driving to the station when her cell phone rang. It was Mama T, and she connected the call.

"Good morning, Mama."

"Will you leave for California today?"

Mattie realized she'd neglected to tell her foster mom about her change in plans. "Oh gosh, I got busy at work and forgot to call you. I'm not going to California after all. Julia and Abuela are coming here."

"Oh, *mi cielo*! When will they get here? Where will they stay? Will I get to meet them?" Mama's excitement escalated with each question. "You must bring them for dinner."

Mattie explained the details and assured her foster mother that she would indeed bring her guests by for her to meet. "You're number one on my list for them to get to know, but it's too much trouble for you to fix dinner for us, Mama. You have a houseful of kids to cook for."

"Mattie, for you, it's no trouble. How about tomorrow for lunch? The kids are going to summer day camp this week, and they will be gone all day."

"Will you let me help you cook?"

"No, no. You have enough to do. You can help me serve when you get here. And I'll use the tamales I made for you to take to them."

After they discussed the menu, which included a taco bar complete with homemade tortillas and a variety of Mama T's homemade salsas, Mattie ended the call, her mouth watering. So now she had two meals planned for her new family. She could prepare a simple lunch at her home one day, then rely on local restaurants for the rest.

And in a pinch, there was always takeout pizza at the Pizza Palace.

She arrived at the station, and after a team meeting to get organized for the day, Mattie and Stella drove out to the compound. They turned onto the rough lane that led to the trailer homes, and as they approached, figures outside in the yard began to take shape. People, both adults and children, were sitting in chairs lined up row upon row. There were at least forty people present, perhaps more, the large majority of them kids. Isaac King stood before the gathering, speaking from behind a podium.

"Good Lord," Stella muttered. "I think they're having a church service."

Mattie cringed as she pulled into a spot outside the barn, parking away from the group. She hated interrupting their religious service and felt she should have anticipated this possibility. After all, it was Sunday morning.

"Let's sit here until they're done," Mattie said, as she set the parking brake and turned off the engine.

Stella glanced at her watch. "We can sit for a while, but we don't have all day. We need to free you up by two. And maybe we should go listen anyway."

A tall man Mattie recognized arose from the front row and headed their way. "That's Solomon Vaughn."

She and Stella exited the vehicle to greet him. Dark circles under his eyes made him look tired.

"We're sorry to interrupt your worship service," Stella said as she shook hands. "But we have news about Luke and need to speak with you and some of the others."

"Let's go into the barn," Solomon said, lifting a palm to usher them toward the doorway. "We'll talk inside, where we'll be less distracting to the children."

Once inside the barn, Mattie scanned her surroundings, noticing a black buggy whip with a long handle leaning up against one of the stalls, not too unusual in a livestock barn but still noteworthy. There were also some medications lined up on a shelf near the horse stocks. Trying not to call attention to herself, she edged over to scan the labels, but none of the containers were marked as xylazine, and they all held tablets or paste.

Solomon watched her, but he didn't comment. Instead, he seemed intent on hearing their news. "You have information about Luke?"

"Yes, our victim's fingerprints match Luke Ferguson's," Stella said. "I'm sorry for your loss."

Solomon looked down at the concrete floor. "I feared that would be the case. Poor Luke."

Stella made a sound of agreement. "We need your help with our investigation. What can you tell us about Luke?"

Solomon raised his gaze, his tired eyes widening. "There isn't much I can tell you. I met him for the first time about four months ago at a congregational meeting in his hometown. At that time, we were planning our move to Timber Creek, and he expressed interest in joining us. We took him in as one of our own."

While he spoke, Mattie looked down at his footwear, but today he was dressed in a black suit and wore plain brown dress shoes, not at all like the boots that would have left the prints at Tracy Lee's crime scene. She wished she could recall what kind of footwear the men had worn yesterday when dressed in their work clothes.

"How did he fit in here?" Stella asked.

"Just fine. We train horses, both for saddle and for pulling carriages, and Luke had a great deal of experience he brought with him. He lent a good, solid hand to the job."

"Did he develop any ill feelings toward any of your group members? Or vice versa?"

Solomon shook his head. "Nothing like that. He had a good head on his shoulders and got along well with people. We all enjoyed having him with us and thought he would stay."

"What changed? Why did he decide to leave?"

When Solomon shifted from one foot to the other, Mattie thought it was his first sign of being uneasy. "That's something I don't know. He counseled with Isaac about his feelings, and those discussions are kept confidential."

"Did Luke make friends with anyone outside the group? Someone from town?" Mattie asked, needing to know who else they should be looking at.

"Why yes, he did," Solomon said, frowning. "He seemed friendly with the farrier that comes to our place and asked to drive the truck into Timber Creek to meet him for dinner a few times. I'm not certain it was dinner, but maybe drinks at the bar. I have sometimes wondered if that became a temptation to leave our way of living."

Mattie was shocked to hear that Luke and Quinn Randolph might have had a friendship. "So he was allowed to go into town on his own?"

The lines deepened between Solomon's brows. "Of course. We do not keep our young people prisoner in any way. They're free to learn about the ways of the world and make informed choices about the path they want to take in life."

Stella cleared her throat lightly. "Mr. Vaughn, what is this religion that Luke was practicing with you?"

Solomon's dark eyes connected with Stella. "We are a fundamentalist group and call ourselves the Brothers of Salvation."

"And was Luke raised in your fundamentalist beliefs, or had he joined your group to learn more about them?"

Mattie thought Stella had asked sensitive questions in a nonthreatening way. It would be good to be able to glean as much information as possible from Solomon in case Isaac King was unwilling to share the reasons why Luke had decided to leave.

"Luke had not been raised in our ways, but our path interested him, and he believed he wanted to join us."

"Are there any others from town that Luke befriended?" Stella asked.

"None that I know of. He would have been free to make friendships with anyone, though."

Mattie was thinking of the BFF necklace. "Do you know if he had any close friendships with girls or young women?"

Solomon straightened as if in affront. "We're all family here. Luke was befriended by all of us."

"He was a young man who might have been thinking of having a girlfriend or even a wife," Mattie said, pressing for a more specific answer. "Do you know if there was someone he considered special?"

"No." The word was clipped, and his eyes shifted away from hers.

"I know of two teenage girls who live here," Mattie said, gazing toward the congregation still seated in front of Isaac King. "Hannah and a girl who was at Ephraim Grayson's house. Are there others?"

Solomon shrugged. "Several others."

"We'd like to speak with Hannah before we leave, if that's all right with you," Mattie said, watching for his reaction. It might tell her something about the relationship his daughter had had with Luke. "You or your wife should be present when we do."

Solomon raised a hand as if to stop her. "There is no reason for you to upset Hannah. She doesn't know yet that Luke is dead."

"You haven't told her?" Mattie asked, surprised.

"There was no reason to tell her, since we were not certain ourselves."

"Are you afraid she'll take it hard?" She began to think that Hannah might be the girl they were looking for. She was fifteen, perhaps a bit old for that type of jewelry, but not if she'd led a sheltered life.

"We decided not to tell any of the children yet. Several of them might take it hard, since Luke was very well liked by all." Solomon shifted his gaze and stared out the door, his lips pressed together in a downward turn. "Ruth and I will have to tell Hannah now."

Mattie wanted to interview the teen before her parents had time to coach her. If Hannah had shared the BFF necklace with Luke, she might be able to provide more information about him than anyone. And if she wasn't Luke's girlfriend, she would probably be able to point out the girl who was.

"It's important that we speak to Hannah this morning before we leave." Mattie glanced at Stella. "Perhaps you and your wife can break the news to her while we speak with Mr. King. Then we could talk to her afterward."

Solomon rubbed the back of his neck. "I don't want you to involve Hannah in this. She's an innocent, and she doesn't know anything that I can't tell you myself."

Mattie thought his concern wasn't too unusual for a protective parent. But his belief that his daughter didn't know more than he did? Well, it didn't hold water. Hannah was closer to Luke in age, and teenagers often knew more about each other than their parents. "We still need to talk to her," she said, adding firmness to her voice. "This is a homicide investigation, Mr. Vaughn. It's important."

Solomon seemed to back down, though his face still showed his disapproval. "Of course. Ruth and I will speak to her as soon as the service is over."

Stella glanced at her watch. "And when might that be?"

"Very soon now." Solomon pressed his lips together in a thin line as singing wafted through the open doors into the barn. "This is the closing song."

"One more thing, Mr. Vaughn," Stella said. "Does the word *pay* mean anything to you in relationship to Luke?"

Solomon's brow shot up. "Pay? As in pay a debt or pay back money owed?"

"Yes, P-A-Y."

"Pay," Solomon uttered, as he appeared to think. "I don't have any idea. I doubt if Luke owed anyone money, but that might be it. He was a young man who came to us with very little. He earned a small wage here in addition to room and board, but he might have borrowed money from someone he met in town."

"One more thing, Mr. Vaughn," Stella said. "Do you know a man named Tracy Lee Brown?"

Solomon paused as if thinking. "No. I've not heard that name before. Should I recognize it?"

"Not necessarily. Mr. Brown was killed up near Hanging Falls yesterday."

Solomon's eyes widened. "Could it have been by the same person?"

"That's a possibility. Where were you yesterday afternoon?"

"I was right here, working with the horses." His eyes jumped from Stella to Mattie and back. "Everyone can attest to that. Ask anyone."

Stella nodded. "Just needing to ask the question, Mr. Vaughn. Did anyone from your group leave for a long period of time yesterday afternoon?"

He shook his head adamantly. "No. No one went into town for anything. We were all here."

Mattie watched the Brothers of Salvation through the doorway, noticing members rise from the chairs, some of them moving toward the trailer homes. She wanted to interview Quinn Randolph before Julia and Abuela hit town, and she felt pressed to move on.

"It looks like Sunday service is over," Mattie said, "and here comes Mr. King. After we talk to him, we'll speak with Hannah, and then there will be others we'll want to talk to. Should I go ask people to stay on the property?"

"People will stay here today. We share a noonday meal together, so no one is planning to go anywhere."

Isaac came through the doorway, his face etched with concern and his hand outstretched toward Stella. "Good day, Detective." After shaking hands with Stella, he offered a handshake to Mattie. "Deputy Cobb. I assume you have news about Luke."

"Yes, sir," Stella said with a somber expression. "We've identified the person we found as Luke Ferguson. I'm sorry I don't have better news."

Isaac's expression turned grave. "I was afraid of that."

Solomon stretched his hand toward Isaac as if in appeal. "They want to speak with members of our flock, including some of the children. The older girls and Hannah specifically."

Isaac's gaze sharpened as he looked at Stella. "And why is that?"

Stella met his gaze with a sharp one of her own. "Our investigation has led us to believe that Luke could possibly have formed a friendship with a teenage girl. Nothing more. We need to follow up on that possibility."

They were banking on a young girl having shared that necklace with Luke, but in reality it could have been given to him by anyone. The lead might pan out and it might not, but they had to ask the questions, and this type of group living situation seemed to be the place to start. At least until they gained further information that would send them elsewhere.

"And what if that goes against her parents' wishes?" Isaac asked, evidently wanting to press the same issue Solomon had.

Stella gave him the same answer. "This is a homicide investigation, Mr. King. We need to follow every lead we come to if we're going to find Luke's killer."

Isaac appeared to be mulling it over. Even though Mattie wanted to tell him they could get a warrant if necessary, she stayed silent. She and Stella typically avoided confrontation on that issue if at all possible, and she didn't want to appear threatening . . . yet.

"All right," Isaac said. "If Solomon approves, you may go ahead."

His statement made Mattie wonder just how much control this leader had over the Brothers of Salvation. That, coupled with other, more subtle signs she'd observed.

"I don't think we have much choice," Solomon said. "I'll go discuss this with Ruth."

Isaac watched Solomon walk away until he left the barn and turned out of sight. "Luke's death will hit our people very hard," he murmured. "Although we're not unused to persecution."

His words struck Mattie as significant. "Do you think Luke's death could have anything to do with persecution, Mr. King?" she asked, thinking the words *hate crime* but not wanting to say them aloud before Isaac did.

"It's quite possible," Isaac said, looking at Mattie. "Luke had been spending more and more time with folks from town. We've faced persecution before in other places when people who don't understand our ways became aware of us. It's quite likely he mingled with the wrong sort of person."

"Do you know of anyone specifically who could have meant Luke harm?" Stella asked.

"Not anyone I can name," Isaac said, "although he came home one night pretty shaken up. Evidently someone waited for him outside the bar and got in a few punches before they left him in the alley."

This was the first Mattie had heard of this. If it was true, she would've thought the night deputy, Cyrus Garcia, would have mentioned it in morning report. "When did this happen?" she asked.

"A couple weeks before Luke decided to go back home."

"Were the police notified?"

"Luke didn't want to file a report. He picked himself up, brushed himself off, and came home. He said he would quit going out at night."

"Did he say who did this to him?"

"No, he wouldn't name names, although I had the feeling he knew the men who did it."

"Men? How many?"

"He said two. He said one held him while the other delivered the blows."

Mattie grew irritated that this hadn't been mentioned before. "Why are you just telling us this now? Why not yesterday when we first spoke to you?"

Isaac raised his brows and spread his hands in front of him. "Yesterday, we weren't positive Luke was dead. I consider everything Luke said to me confidential, and I saw no reason to tell you this before. You know it now. That should suffice."

Mattie wondered what else Isaac knew. "We need to know anything else that happened to Luke while he was here. What else can you tell us?"

Isaac rubbed one side of his beard along his jaw, his face creased with sadness. "I can tell you that Luke became unhappy staying with us shortly after we moved here. He wanted to experience the world, and I think that's why he decided to come with us in the first place. His parents are good people and had instilled strong values in the young man, but once I got to know him, I could tell he wanted something different than a religious life. I counseled with him and tried to show him the right path, but he seemed determined to stray. I wish I could have done better at showing him the way."

That was all well and good, but Mattie wanted names. "Can you think of anyone specifically who befriended Luke?"

He took a breath and straightened as if shoring himself up. "I don't want to point a finger at anyone, but I do think you should talk to Quinn Randolph, our farrier. He befriended Luke, and quite possibly . . . Well, I'll just say he's the one you should talk to."

Stella leaned forward. "What were you going to say, Mr. King? And quite possibly . . ."

"Well, I try not to judge others, but it's a weakness of mine. I started to say that he quite possibly played a role in leading Luke astray, but it isn't my place to judge. Only God can pass judgment."

If he's guilty of murder, the court system can too. Mattie kept her thought to herself, since it might be too cheeky to say aloud. Stella might appreciate the statement, but not Isaac. "Was there anyone from Luke's past that he might have been afraid of? Someone who could have followed him here from his hometown?"

Isaac shook his head. "Not that I know of. If there was, he never mentioned it to me."

"Does the name Tracy Lee Brown mean anything to you?" Mattie studied Isaac as he thought it over.

"That's a name I would remember . . . sounds southern," Isaac said, stroking the beard on his chin. "But I've not heard it before. I know of no one by that name."

"Did Luke ever mention the name to you?"

"I can tell you that he definitely did not. Like I said, I would remember it if he did."

"Do you have any idea as to what the word *pay* would mean in relationship to Luke's death? P-A-Y?" Stella asked.

"Why do you ask that?" A puzzled frown creased Isaac's brow. "Was there a note found or something?"

"I can't say," Stella said, her eyes pinned on his face. "Does it mean anything to you?"

"Maybe he owed someone money? Perhaps another question for Mr. Randolph."

"All right, Mr. King." Stella turned toward the door. "I appreciate the information you've given us, and that's all I have for you now. But if you think of anything else that might help with our investigation, please call me."

Isaac extended a handshake to Stella. "I will. This is a terrible thing. Our people will be crushed."

Mattie thought Isaac looked sincere as he spoke.

He started to leave but turned back to ask, "Who else will you want to speak with?"

"We'll speak with Hannah now and decide who we want to talk to next after her," Stella told him.

Isaac nodded, and Stella watched him stride through the doorway and out of the barn before turning to Mattie and speaking in a low voice. "No reason we should tell him our lineup."

They'd decided on the way out that they should speak with Abel, Ephraim, and possibly the teenage girl Mattie had seen at the Grayson house. Rachel and her sister Naomi were also on the list. "Do you have reason to suspect Isaac or Solomon?" Mattie asked.

"Not yet, but both of them pointing a finger at the farrier makes me question if they might have discussed this prior to our arrival. But let's see what the others say." Stella started walking to the doorway.

Mattie took her cell phone from her pocket. "Wait a second. Let me get a picture of this whip and those medications on the shelf. I want to see if Cole sees anything there that's similar to xylazine."

Stella waited for Mattie to finish. "C'mon, let's go around by the side of the barn and get some photos of the truck and trailer tires. Then we'll head over to the Vaughn house."

"Can you remember what kind of boots the men had on yesterday?" Mattie asked. "They have on dress shoes today."

"They were wearing a leather-topped work boot, with leather lace ties and a shallow waffle tread. Not the slick sole we're looking for."

Mattie gave her a thin smile. "Good job, Detective."

Stella shrugged, an uneasy look on her face. "And now I'm certain we've got a group of polygamists that have settled out here. How's that for detecting?"

"Yeah . . . it's pretty clear, isn't it?"

"I know polygamy doesn't necessarily mean the presence of more violent crimes, but keep an eye open for signs of abuse, child brides, that sort of thing. Otherwise, let's stay in our lane and focus on the investigation."

Mattie had already thought of all this and had planned to keep an eye out. "Got it."

They left the barn to go take their pictures.

SEVENTEEN

As Mattie led Stella toward the Vaughns' home, she checked in on Robo. The sun had climbed higher in the cloudless, brilliant-blue sky. She'd left the air conditioner in his compartment turned on, but she wanted to make certain he was comfortable. When their feet scraped the gravel next to her unit, his face popped up in the window, ears pricked, blinking sleep from his eyes.

No panting; he's fine. "Good boy," she told him through the glass. "You wait here."

He plopped his rear end down and watched them pass by. Mattie figured he would be asleep again soon.

"You've got a good partner there," Stella said with a half smile. "I wish I'd had even one partner who was that obedient. I might still be working patrol."

"You like being in charge."

In acknowledgment, Stella turned the full wattage of her smile on Mattie briefly before settling into professional mode as they approached the Vaughn home. "Why don't you take the lead on this one? You can read kids this age better than I can."

"You do all right," Mattie conceded, thinking Stella had gained more experience with interviewing kids since joining the Timber Creek team. "But okay, I'll start."

As they reached the wooden platform that served as a porch, the door opened. Solomon stepped out and spoke quietly. "Hannah is very upset. I'm not sure it's a good idea for you to talk to her just now."

Mattie didn't want to pressure the girl, but she didn't want to miss this opportunity to interview Hannah before she talked about Luke's death with the others. And Mattie felt certain that Isaac was already breaking the news to the other children.

"I think Hannah's comfortable with me, Mr. Vaughn," Mattie said. "It's important that I speak with her now. We won't take long."

"Let me see," he said, looking doubtful. "Perhaps if you wait here, she'll be able to come out for a few minutes."

"Could we come inside?" Mattie asked, not letting him close the door on them. "It would be much better for Hannah if we talked to her in her own home. In her bedroom or perhaps at your kitchen table. And of course, with you and your wife present."

Solomon hesitated before giving a reluctant nod and holding open the door for them to enter. "Hannah's in her room with Ruth. Please wait here in the kitchen."

A pot of something that smelled delicious simmered on the stove. After Solomon left, the woman Ruth had introduced as her sister Mary bustled through the living room beyond the half wall that divided the two spaces. She was wringing her hands as Mattie introduced her to Stella but pulled them apart long enough to offer a handshake as she murmured, "How do you do?"

"We're distressed over this news about Luke," Mary went on. "But please, please take a seat at the table. May I offer you something to drink? Water? Lemonade?"

Both Stella and Mattie declined.

Beyond the half wall, Mattie could see another woman sitting in a rocking chair knitting, a small square of work hanging from her needles and brushing against her pregnant belly. Her blue eyes met Mattie's briefly before her gaze dropped back to her work. Like the others, she was dressed in blue with a white pinafore, a white cap covering the crown of her blond hair. She looked like a younger image of Mary, perhaps in her twenties.

Mary evidently noticed Mattie looking. "This is my sister Elizabeth," Mary said. "Perhaps you should go to the other room, please, Bess. The officers are going to talk to Hannah here in our kitchen."

Setting her knitting aside, Elizabeth scooted to the edge of the chair and braced herself against both arms of the rocker, pushing herself up to stand. She looked to be at least eight months pregnant, her enlarged midsection pushing against the fabric of her pinafore. She turned to disappear down a narrow hallway, and Mattie noticed three Siamese cats of various shades lounging on the sofa and blinking their blue eyes at her. One of them lay draped along the back cushion and presented a bulging belly that promised a large litter of kittens.

Mary scurried around the kitchen like a nervous little hen, stirring the simmering pot on the stove, washing a few dishes, and wiping counters while they waited. At her insistence, Mattie and Stella took seats at a long, narrow table with a great many chairs around it that sat next to the wall.

Stella tried to gain information from her. "We're asking everyone if they know anything that might be useful in our investigation of Luke Ferguson's death. Do you have any information that might help us, Mary?"

Mary darted a glance toward the hallway before shaking her head. She opened the lid on the pot and stirred its contents again as she answered. "I saw Luke only at Sunday luncheon, so I know very little about him. He liked to play ball with the kids, and Solomon said he knew a lot about the horses. There's nothing more that I know."

"Do you know anyone who might have wanted to do him harm?"

Mary still faced the stove, but her shoulder muscles stiffened beneath her blue dress. "Absolutely not. He was a good boy."

"Only twenty-one years old," Stella said. "Had his whole life ahead of him."

Mary tapped the wooden spoon she was using against the rim of the pot, replaced the lid, and turned to face them. The rims of her eyes were red and brimmed with unshed tears. "I can't imagine anyone wanting to hurt him in any way. The world can be a wicked place sometimes."

In the back of her mind, Mattie had been pondering the fact that Ruth had introduced Mary as her sister and now Mary had introduced Elizabeth the same way. She wanted to ask whether they were actually sisters by blood or simply sister wives, but the question wasn't relevant to their investigation, so she held her tongue. But she couldn't help but wonder if polygamy had somehow been a motive for Luke's death. How did jealousy play out in these intermingled relationships?

Mary darted a glance toward the hallway. "Let me go check on Hannah and see if she'll be joining us."

She scurried away as if being chased, while Stella and Mattie traded glances with each other. Mattie had noticed a framed picture on the far living room wall, and she rose from her chair to get a closer look.

It was an eleven-by-fourteen photograph of Solomon, Ruth, Mary, and Elizabeth standing left to right with a group of eight children clustered at their feet, Hannah included. Solomon and the boys were all dressed in their Sunday best, black suits and white shirts with black buttons fastened up to their stiff white collars. The women and girls were attired in white shirtwaist dresses that came to midcalf and had high-collared necklines and long sleeves.

Had she seen this picture under other circumstances, Mattie would have interpreted it as a wedding photo, but in her gut she knew this was a family picture taken prior to Elizabeth's pregnancy. She was turning away to go back to her seat in the kitchen when Solomon led the way through the doorway with Hannah and then Ruth behind him.

Solomon narrowed his eyes slightly at her when he spotted her in front of the photo, but Mattie stood her ground. "I was admiring your family picture, Mr. Vaughn."

"Thank you." Solomon gestured toward his daughter, who was trailed by Sassy. "Hannah wants to talk with you now. Shall we go sit in the kitchen?"

Stella had stood when the Vaughns entered the room. Solomon pulled the table away from the wall, and Hannah slipped into a seat at the back. Sassy squeezed in beside her, sat on the floor next to her feet, and nestled her head in Hannah's lap. Ruth took a seat beside Hannah while Solomon sat at the head.

"Thank you for talking to us, Hannah," Mattie said, using a soft tone that she hoped would be soothing. "As you know, we're investigating Luke's case, and we need to gain as much information as we can from the people who knew him. Was he your friend?"

Looking down at the table, Hannah nodded, her eyes reddened and filled with tears.

"I'm so very sorry for your loss." Mattie paused, striving to impart all the sympathy she held for the girl in her gaze. She waited until Hannah glanced up from the table to look at her. "I know you'll miss his friendship."

Hannah nodded again before lowering her face to observe the tabletop.

"Do you know of anyone who might have harmed Luke?" Mattie asked quietly, feeling like she needed to use direct questions if she hoped to spark any kind of responsiveness.

Hannah shook her head, gathering a shaky breath. "I don't really know, but maybe . . . maybe the man who comes to shoe the horses?"

Mattie had to wonder if the girl had been coached while she was in the bedroom, and if so, she couldn't help but wonder why. Why would everyone point a finger at Randolph unless they themselves had something to hide about Luke Ferguson's death? "Why do you think that, Hannah? Why do you think the farrier might have meant him harm?"

Hannah lifted her gaze and looked Mattie in the eye. "Because Luke told me to stay away from him?"

Huh . . . now this was different. Perhaps the girl hadn't been coached after all. "Why did Luke tell you to stay away from Quinn Randolph?"

"Luke said he was a bad person, and that he said a lot of rude things to women and didn't treat them with respect." Hannah seemed to gain more confidence in her answers as she spoke, no longer turning them into questions. "Luke told me he didn't trust the guy and to stay away from the barn whenever he came."

A glance at Solomon told Mattie that this was probably the first time he'd heard this information as well. Anger infused his face. "Why didn't you tell me this, Hannah? There are other farriers we could use."

Hannah looked down at the table again, her face flushed. "It's embarrassing, Father."

"It's good to let your parents know these things," Mattie said, steering the conversation away from Solomon. "We'll follow up and talk to Mr. Randolph. And you don't need to worry that we'll mention your name, because we won't. Anything you tell us today will be kept confidential." Unless they needed the girl's testimony, but the reassurance would suffice for now. "Is there anything else Luke told you about him?"

Hannah shook her head. "But there was someone else that Luke didn't like. A man who gave the farrier drugs to use on the horses."

Adrenaline flooded Mattie's system. "Did he tell you the person's name?"

"Parker somebody. He said I wasn't likely to ever meet him, though." Hannah swiped at the wetness on her cheek, and Solomon handed her a folded handkerchief that he took from his shirt pocket. She raised her eyes briefly to meet his before looking back down at the table. "Thank you, Father."

The drug rep was named Parker Tate, and this bit of info connected him with the farrier. This had to be the guy who was supplying the xylazine, although Mattie didn't have proof of that yet. "Did Luke seem to be afraid of either of these men?"

Again, Hannah shook her head, and tears brimmed in her eyes. "I don't think anything frightened Luke. He was good and he was brave."

And Mattie would bet her next paycheck that the girl had been enamored with him. "So you knew Luke well?"

Hannah glanced at her father before nodding, her face lowered. "He liked to help me groom and train Sassy."

"Sounds like he loved dogs, like us," Mattie said, trying to establish mutual ground with the girl.

"He loved all kinds of animals, even the cats."

Ruth withdrew a feminine white hankie with a tatted edge from a pocket hidden somewhere within her skirt and used it to wipe her eyes daintily.

"Did Luke spend time in your home with the cats, Mrs. Vaughn?"

Ruth's face was drawn with sorrow. "On occasion. Especially right after we moved here. He seemed to miss his mother at first and hung around us women in the early days. But then he became busy with horse training and he liked to drive into town in the evening, so we didn't see much of him."

This seemed a bit off compared to Mary's comment that she'd seen Luke only at Sunday luncheon, but perhaps Mary and Luke hadn't been inside the trailer home at the same time. "So did you know him well, Mrs. Vaughn?"

"Some. He and the children played with the cats while I cooked, that sort of thing. He took his meals with the Graysons."

"Do you have information that might help us with his case?" Stella asked.

"No, no, not at all. I don't know anything more than what Hannah has told you."

Mattie directed the questioning back toward the girl. "Hannah, did you and Luke happen to share a friendship necklace?"

Hannah's eyes darted to her father before looking into Mattie's. "It's against our ways to wear jewelry."

Mattie had no doubt that she'd found the owner of the other half of the heart-shaped pendant, and the girl had kept it secret from her parents—and she also didn't want to lie about having it. It was valuable information that could raise serious problems between Hannah and her parents, so Mattie decided not to force her into a confession of ownership. It was enough to know she'd discovered their victim's best friend, and the subject needed to be handled with care. She met Stella's gaze, and the detective gave her a slight nod as if acknowledging some type of agreement. Perhaps she'd interpreted the delicacy of the situation the same as Mattie.

"I see," Mattie said. "Tell me, do you know anything about Luke getting beat up in town?"

Tears trickled from Hannah's eyes, and she wiped them with her father's handkerchief. "He didn't really get beat up. One guy held him while another punched him in the stomach. Luke said it was nothing, but I could tell he considered it a warning."

"A warning? About what?"

"About being different, I guess. Luke said some people are frightened by others being different, and these two men wanted him to stay out of their bar." She glanced at her father again, a child checking in on her parent's reaction. "Luke said it was a bar. I've never been there."

Mattie smiled gently. "The Watering Hole in Timber Creek?"

"I think so."

"Did he say if one of the two men who jumped him was Quinn Randolph or Parker Tate?"

Hannah's reddened eyes widened. "You know that Parker guy?"

"I've never met him, but it's a name I've heard before. I don't know for certain that it's the man Luke warned you about. I'm just checking to see if he's someone Luke mentioned that was connected to this fight."

"No, Luke didn't know the two guys, although he said he'd seen them before at the bar."

Great . . . two more unknown persons of interest to track down. A trip to the Watering Hole might give them a lead. Mattie knew the bartender there. She looked at Stella. "Any more questions, Detective?"

"Hannah, did you and Luke talk about his past, like his family or friends from back home?" Stella asked.

"Yes, he liked to talk about his mom and dad. It was different for him to be in a big family like ours, since he was an only kid."

"Did he ever say anything that would make you think he had enemies from his past? Someone who might have followed him here to hurt him?"

"No. He never said anything like that." Hannah's eyes spilled tears that wet her cheeks, which she mopped up with the balled-up handkerchief. "I think he had a happy life."

"Thank you, Hannah. You've been a great help," Stella said, reaching into her trouser pocket to extract a business card and then placing it on the table. "If any of you think of anything that might help us, please don't hesitate to call me. Day or night."

"Do you think we're in any danger, Detective?" Ruth asked, her brow puckered with concern. "Are the children safe?"

Stella's brow lowered with concern as well. "Do you have any reason to suspect that you or anyone else here might be in danger?"

"No," Solomon said, looking at his wife, reaching for her hand, which she met halfway and clasped in hers. "I don't think danger threatens the rest of us, Ruth."

"Mrs. Vaughn," Stella said. "Have you felt threatened?"

"Not since we moved here," Ruth said, clinging to Solomon's hand. "But, well . . . in other places."

"We have been threatened before," Solomon said, "but we thought we would be safe living here. Perhaps Luke brought this on himself by venturing outside."

"No, Father," Hannah interjected. "Luke didn't ask to be killed. He did nothing wrong."

Solomon frowned. "That's not what I meant, Hannah. He brought attention to himself, and perhaps that placed him in harm's way."

"We can't live isolated from others all the time."

"Enough. We'll discuss this later."

The interchange had been quick and intense, and it seemed like the argument could have been familiar territory for father and daughter. Mattie believed sheltering a teenager to this degree must be arduous work for both parents.

Stella leaned forward. "To answer your question, Mrs. Vaughn, I can't tell you for certain that your family is safe from future harm, because we don't have a full grasp on how or why Luke died yet. I don't think there's further danger, but it's always best to err on the side of caution. Please keep an eye out for any unusual traffic going by your place, cars that stop out on the road nearby, that sort of thing. And don't hesitate to call the sheriff's department if you have concerns of any kind."

Ruth's eyes were fixed on Stella. "Thank you, Detective."

Mattie took two of her business cards from her pocket and placed one next to Stella's on the table. She handed the other directly to Hannah. "Hannah," she said, waiting for the girl to make eye contact. "If you think of anything to help us find Luke's killer, please call me. And if you need help in any way, let me know. This card has my cell phone number written on the back, and you can call me anytime. Okay?"

Hannah nodded as she reached for the card.

"That goes for the rest of you too, Mrs. Vaughn." Mattie flipped the card on the table over to show her cell number. "Feel free to share this with the others. We're here to assure the safety of law-abiding citizens."

Mattie didn't completely understand the way of life these people had chosen, but as long as they weren't breaking any laws, it was her duty not to judge them but to protect them. And if any of them did break the law, it was also her duty to ferret that out. She hoped to get a chance to visit with Hannah alone, just to make certain the girl didn't feel threatened by her father or any of the other Brothers of Salvation.

"We need to move along and speak with the Grayson family," Mattie said.

"Let me show you to their home," Solomon said.

"I know where they live, but thank you anyway."

After Mattie and Stella left the house, closing the door behind them, Stella murmured her impressions in a soft voice meant only for Mattie. "She's the BFF. And her information leads us back to the drug rep and farrier. I'm going to contact Brody to see if he can rope those two guys in to the station so we can interview them there. Save us some time."

Stella dialed her phone as they walked to the Grayson trailer, while Mattie glanced at hers to check the time. Her stomach did a flip-flop as she realized there were only about four hours left before her family's arrival, and she still had a lot of work to do.

EIGHTEEN

Cole was stirring creamer into his coffee in the kitchen, wondering what chores around his place he should tackle this Sunday morning, when Angela strolled in.

"Hey, Dad," she said, heading for the refrigerator.

The greeting was music to his ears. It was the first time she'd acknowledged him without prompting in the past two weeks. He leaned against the counter in a posture that said he had all the time in the world to talk. "Hey. How are you doing this morning?"

"Good." She rummaged until she found a plastic container filled with slices of cantaloupe. "I thought I'd call Hannah and see if Riley and I can go out to see the kittens today."

Though he hated to put the kibosh on anything Angela wanted, he thought of Luke Ferguson, the dead man who'd been a part of Hannah's community. He felt like he was venturing into a field of land mines with this conversation, so he needed to tread lightly. "Sounds like fun. But I wonder if you might postpone that for a few days."

Angie frowned as she opened the container and arranged cantaloupe slices in neat lines on a plate, using her index finger to push them delicately into place in a pattern that evidently only she could imagine. "Why would we postpone it?"

He might as well be honest. "One of the people who lived out there with Hannah has been killed recently, and that concerns me. You know . . . my obsession with keeping you and everyone in my family safe kicks in. I can't help myself."

Angela gave him a long look before reaching for the salt-shaker and lightly sprinkling salt along the length of each slice. Cole loved watching Angie fix her plate, something she always turned into an art form.

"O—kay," she said, drawing out the word with teenage skepticism.

"But . . . I don't want to interfere with your plans." Cole was already kicking himself for throwing a monkey wrench into his whole day with what he was about to offer. "If Hannah says you can come over, I could go out with you and check on that horse. I'd stay out at the barn and visit with the guys while you girls spend some time together."

Angela gave him another one of her looks, one slender eyebrow raised, as she reached for a butter knife to cut a small bite. "Don't you have other things to do?"

"You know I've always got chores to do around here, but I'd rather take some time off and spend it with you."

Angela scoffed. "You mean as a bodyguard."

"Maybe." Cole shrugged. "Better safe than sorry."

Angela cut a few bites, arranged them into a circle, and then chose one to spear with her fork and place in her mouth. "I'll call Hannah and see what time we can come. Then we'll talk."

Feeling like he'd navigated this minefield pretty well, Cole decided to agree and retreat. "I need to go out to feed the animals. Just give me a call when you know what time you want to go."

Angie nodded and, carrying her plate with her, turned to head upstairs to her room, just as Sophie passed her coming through the doorway. She'd been in the den watching TV and must have overheard part of their conversation. "Where you guys going?"

"None of your business," Angie called from the stairs, her back turned as she climbed.

Evidently Sophie let the comment roll off her shoulders, as she ventured farther into the kitchen to question Cole. "Where are you going?"

It was too bad that Angie had felt the need to take a shot at her sister, but under the circumstances, Cole believed he had to pick his battles with his eldest and not reprimand her this time. "Angie and Riley want to go out to visit Hannah." He didn't dare mention the kittens. "And I have a horse to check out there, so I thought I'd take them."

"Can I go too?" Sophie was using that tone that was one step away from wheedling and could get on his nerves pretty fast. It was not something he wanted to encourage by giving in.

"Not this time. But do you want to go outside with me now to feed the chickens?"

"Okay," she said, apparently willing to be diverted. "But I'm hungry."

"They are too. Let's get the animals fed, and I'll come back inside and make you some scrambled eggs."

"Mrs. Gibbs said she'd make pancakes for brunch," Sophie said. "After she sleeps in. She said she has a book she wants to read in bed for a little while."

Their housekeeper was somewhere in her sixties and was typically the first one up in the morning, although Cole had told her to take it easy on the weekends countless times. He was glad that she was finally willing to do so on this rare occasion. "That all sounds great. She needs to get a chance to relax on the weekend too, don't you think? And pancakes! After we feed the chickens, you can have some fruit to tide you over until brunch."

Sophie grinned at him in agreement and went to find her shoes. Cole called the dogs, and together they all headed out to walk down the lane that led past their house to the clinic. He and Sophie chatted about all sorts of things while they filled the feeder in the chicken pen and replenished the water. Sophie was gathering eggs when his cell phone rang in his pocket.

It was Angie, and he connected the call. "City zoo."

She ignored his attempt at humor, speaking in a rush as if upset. "Hannah's mom almost didn't let me talk to her, but Hannah must have been there and convinced her to let us talk. She was crying. That man you said was killed? Hannah says he was her boyfriend."

"Her boyfriend?"

"Yeah. She was whispering, like she didn't want anyone to hear her."

"Huh." Cole didn't know what to say. Hannah was only fifteen, and he thought the dead man had been at least twenty. Not a huge difference in years but a big gap in maturity.

"Hannah wants me and Riley to come out."

"Did she say when?"

"After they eat lunch. About one."

"I definitely want to go with you, Angel. Mrs. Gibbs is going to fix a late breakfast, but I'll get it started. If you want, invite Riley to join us for pancakes at around ten. You could go pick her up."

"Okay, Dad."

As Cole disconnected the phone, he patted himself on the back for parenting on the fly. He'd come a long way since Liv had left him alone in the trenches last summer, and someone had to acknowledge his progress. Even if he had to do it himself.

★ ★ ★

Mattie's cell phone signaled a text as she and Stella were walking to the Grayson home. It was from Cole, and the content confirmed her supposition. "Angela just heard from Hannah that it was her boyfriend that was killed," she told the detective.

"That seals it." Stella gave her a gratified look. "Now, let's turn our attention to the family Luke lived with. Then we'll see where we go from there."

When Mattie knocked on the trailer door, Ephraim Grayson opened it immediately, his wife Rachel standing just behind him in the kitchen. "May we come in, Mr. Grayson?" Mattie said, stepping close to the threshold. "We'd like to talk to the adults in your family, including Abel, if we could."

"Certainly," Ephraim said, holding the door wide. "Isaac told us you had a positive identification of Luke. We're stunned, but we want to help in whatever way we can."

Mattie introduced Stella as they passed through the door into the kitchen. Rachel retreated toward the counter, her hands clasped in front, her eyes red as though she'd been crying. The succulent scent of roasting meat filled the small space, making Mattie's mouth water. She assumed Sunday luncheon was being prepared in all of the kitchens in the compound.

After Mattie greeted the woman, she said, "I'm sorry to bring such bad news. You have our sympathy for your loss."

Rachel dipped her head in acknowledgment and then met Mattie's gaze as she spoke. "We sheltered Luke and took him in as our son for the short time he was with us. We continued to hope that you would discover he wasn't the person who'd been killed. This is very sad news for us and our entire family."

Mattie assumed she meant everyone in the Brothers of Salvation. Stella stepped forward to extend her condolences, giving Mattie an opportunity to scan the living room. The sewing table and machine were still set up by the window, the empty playpen sat in the corner, and books were piled on the sofa, but there were no other people to be seen.

"We would like to speak with Naomi and Abel now too," Mattie said to Rachel. "Could you ask them to join us?"

Ephraim turned to stride across the living room toward the hallway that led to the bedrooms. "I'll get them," he said over his shoulder to Rachel. "Leah and Abigail can watch the younger children."

"Are there any other adults living here with you, Mrs. Grayson?" Mattie asked.

Rachel shook her head. "No, just my sister, Naomi. And of course Abel . . . he's an adult now."

"Is the girl who was here yesterday reading a book to the children Leah or Abigail?"

"That must have been Leah. Abigail was at the Taylors' house for a reading lesson."

"Is she younger than Leah?"

"That's right."

Mattie needed to assure herself that Leah wasn't Ephraim's wife. "And are both girls your daughters?"

Rachel answered without hesitation. "They are."

Ephraim reentered the living room with Naomi and Abel following. Mattie said hello and introduced them to Stella.

Like Rachel, Naomi looked as if she'd been crying, but Abel looked solemn and stoic. They all stood while Mattie grew uncomfortable waiting for an invitation to sit.

After an awkward moment, Stella took the matter into her own hands. "May we sit, Mrs. Grayson?"

Ephraim was the one who responded. "By all means."

After they settled into chairs, Stella explained their need to gather what information they could about Luke. She began with the standard question of whether they knew anyone who might have wanted to harm him. After they all murmured denials, Stella turned to Abel. "Did Luke tell you about the incident he had with the men in town?"

"When he got jumped outside the bar?" Abel asked, his face turning red, perhaps because he hadn't mentioned it himself when asked if someone might have meant Luke harm.

"That's right," Stella said. "What did he say about it?"

"Just that the guys were bigots."

"Did he know who they were or describe them to you?"

"He didn't know them, but he said it was two old guys and they weren't serious about hurting him. They just wanted to make a point, and it didn't sit right with him to be judged by his clothing." Abel's blush had receded to his neck, and he now looked more comfortable engaging with Stella. "I told him to get used to it."

"So I take it that your manner of dress was new to Luke?"

Abel nodded. "He hadn't been raised in our ways." He folded his arms and stared at his father, and the look on his face made Mattie wonder if he himself disagreed with some of the ways he'd been raised in.

Ephraim returned his son's stare for a few beats before looking at Stella. "Luke became unhappy living here. I think all of us were aware of that to some extent. We weren't surprised when he told us he'd decided to go home."

"Let me clarify something, Abel," Stella interjected. "What point did these two old guys want to make?"

"They didn't like people like us coming to Timber Creek. They didn't like the way we dress, and they didn't like the way we live."

"The way you live? What did they mean by that?" Stella asked.

Abel stared at the detective a moment before answering, his face filled with what looked like suppressed anger. "You would have to ask them that question. I don't know the answer."

Again, Mattie made a mental note to track down these two "old guys." They had become more and more important as persons of interest, perhaps even suspects.

The tension she felt between father and son made Mattie wonder if their home had been an uncomfortable place for Luke. She'd sensed a degree of tension between Hannah and her father, but it was more palpable here in the Grayson home. Perhaps some of the teenagers were growing dissatisfied with this way of living. Maybe Luke hadn't been the only one. She wondered how she could gain that information. "Did Luke discuss his decision to go back home with you, Abel?"

"He didn't really discuss it," Abel said, looking down at the floor, "but I knew he was considering it."

"And did he tell you when he made his decision to leave?" Mattie asked.

Abel looked at his father. "Not in so many words."

"You shared a room with him," Mattie said, "and he didn't tell you he was going to leave while he was packing his things?"

Abel continued to stare at his father. "He did not. I wasn't here."

"Where were you?"

"Luke left suddenly. I was out in the barn when he packed his things."

This was news to her. Somehow she'd gotten the impression that everyone had known Luke wanted to leave and that they'd supported him as he made his decision. She'd had visions of them fondly wishing him luck in his future. This sounded more like a sudden rift and then Luke was out. "Was there a farewell party? Did he say good-bye to everyone?"

Ephraim answered the question. "Luke's departure was not a happy occasion. There was no party, and only a few people said good-bye. Solomon took him to the bus stop."

Mattie thought Luke's sudden departure odd if they were indeed one big family as several of them claimed. She sent a pointed look Stella's way. "Any more questions, Detective?"

"Do any of you know a man named Tracy Lee Brown?" Stella asked.

"Never heard that name," Ephraim said, while the others shook their heads. "Why do you ask?"

"Mr. Brown was killed yesterday near the place we found Luke's body. Were all the members of your community here yesterday afternoon, Mr. Grayson?"

Ephraim's gaze turned inward as if he was thinking. "All of us were present and working at our various tasks all day yesterday. We rarely leave our property except to go into town or over to Hightower for supplies."

"All right, that's all the questions I have for now." Stella gave them her card along with the usual instructions to call if they remembered or discovered anything more. Then she said to Ephraim, "We'd like to speak with everyone who lives here, if we could. Could that be arranged?"

"I'll see to it," he said, and he rose from his chair to leave. "Abel, would you come with me to help?"

Mattie thanked Abel before he left and pressed her business card into his hand, asking him to call anytime. Maybe he didn't know more about Luke, but if he had other concerns about his way of life that should involve law enforcement, she wanted to know.

Mattie was about to leave when Stella moved across the room to look at a framed photo on the wall. Mattie turned to see a family photo exactly like the one in the Vaughn home except that the subjects in the image were members of the Grayson family. Naomi and Rachel were standing beside Ephraim with seven children clustered at their feet. "You have a lovely family here, Mrs. Grayson," Stella said to Rachel.

Rachel flushed, and she and Naomi exchanged glances. "Thank you."

"Seven children . . . that's quite a handful," Stella said with a soft smile.

"Not for the two of us," Rachel said, lifting her chin as she straightened.

She's bracing herself for us to ask about polygamy, Mattie thought.

"Abel looks like you, Naomi," Stella said. "He seems to be a fine young man. Growing up and getting independent, I would say. How old is he?"

"Nineteen," Naomi said, her face lowered in a demure way. "Yes, he's deciding which way he will go when it's time for him to have his own home."

"Which way he'll go?"

Naomi seemed to shrink away as if she'd said more than she'd intended, and Rachel placed an arm around her shoulders.

"When our children leave our homes," Rachel said, "they can decide if they'll follow our religious pathway or not. It's their choice and sometimes a difficult conclusion for us parents." Rachel started walking them toward the door, sending the message that the interview was over.

When Mattie followed Stella out of the trailer home, the group had assembled in the yard, standing in clusters that appeared to be family units: five men with two to three women aligned at their side and anywhere from seven to ten children gathered near.

While Stella spoke, Mattie scanned their faces, looking for expressions of hostility, fear, or furtiveness, something that might indicate hidden secrets. But for the most part, the men looked stern while the women wore their sorrow openly. Most of the children were younger than teenagers, and the men all looked younger than Ephraim.

She spotted Isaac in the crowd, standing beside three women who looked to be in their twenties, two holding infants and all three with a cluster of toddlers and youngsters clinging to their skirts. The women appeared to be of legal age for consent and the children well fed and clean. Unless they discovered something different that was of concern, there was no apparent need for Child Protective Services. Their current focus was Luke's homicide investigation, but this would be a community that warranted future observation.

Stella wrapped up her spiel by requesting help with their investigation and passing out what remaining business cards she had in her pocket. As the gathering broke up, Hannah caught

Mattie's eye. She was alone, evidently having left Sassy in the house, and she parted from her family to drift toward Mattie while she and Stella made their way to her unit.

Mattie slowed her pace and let Hannah catch up. "Do you want to see Robo?" she asked the girl, hoping to set up a diversion for them to be alone together for a few minutes.

"May I?" Hannah joined her as she headed for the back of the unit, where Robo was waiting with an eager doggy grin on his face.

Mattie opened the hatch. Grasping his collar, she turned to Hannah. "You can pet him, but you know not to put your face close to his, right? Dogs can take that as a threat."

"Right," Hannah said, offering her hand for Robo to sniff and getting a lick instead.

"Are you all right, Hannah?" Mattie murmured, still holding Robo inside the unit, where they had some shelter from the others. "I know Luke meant a lot to you."

Tears filled Hannah's eyes and spilled over her reddened lids. "We were going to get married. When I was old enough."

"I'm sorry. He was quite a bit older than you, wasn't he?"

"He said he would wait for my eighteenth birthday."

"Did he say good-bye to you before he left?" Mattie asked, pursuing the strange aspect of Luke's abrupt departure.

Hannah swiped tears from her cheek with the back of her hand. "The night before he left, he told me he was going and gave me a necklace to remember him by. I can't let my parents know I have it. He said he'd see if I could live at his parents' house until we could marry and he'd come back soon to get me. But Mother would never let me do that . . . never."

Mattie needed desperately to know the answer to one question. "Are you in danger, Hannah?"

Surprise lit Hannah's face before settling back into lines of sorrow. "No, but my heart is broken."

Mattie was about to ask about the day Luke had left when the sound of footsteps on the gravel road made her look. Solomon approached the vehicle but stood back a few feet behind his daughter. "He's a beauty, isn't he, Hannah?"

Hannah glanced at him as she stroked Robo. "Yes, Father. He's every bit as fine as Sassy."

"We should let these officers get on with their duties," Solomon said, placing his hand on the girl's shoulder.

Still holding on to Robo, Mattie didn't miss the fact that her dog stiffened and his ears pricked as he fixed his eyes on the man. She gripped Robo's collar and rubbed his fur to soothe him, aware that if Solomon made a wrong move toward his daughter, Robo wouldn't hesitate to spring. At one moment, Robo could be calm and loving, but if the need arose, he could in the next become as protective as a mama bear with her cubs. Mattie had to admit that she loved that about her dog.

But Solomon appeared to be aware of Robo's protectiveness too, and he dropped his hand from Hannah's shoulder and stepped back. "He's a fine shepherd, Deputy Cobb. I imagine he makes a good patrol dog."

"That he does, Mr. Vaughn."

"Thank you for coming out to talk to us, Deputy. Hannah, we should let them leave."

Hannah nodded and, taking her father's hand, turned to walk away toward the trailers. Mattie splashed water from Robo's supply into his bowl, closed up the back hatch, and joined Stella inside the Explorer.

"I figured she wanted to talk to you alone," Stella said. "What did she say?"

Mattie summarized their brief conversation as she started the engine and headed out to the highway.

"Do you have any suspicions of abuse toward her or any of these kids?" Stella asked.

"Not really. Hannah and her father may be of different minds when it comes to their way of life, but she doesn't seem afraid of him."

"I wonder if Abel is getting ready to leave the Brothers."

"That thought crossed my mind. I also wonder if the freedom of choice to stay or not applies to girls as well as boys." Interviewing the various members of the Brothers of Salvation had taken some time, but they'd gained some valuable information. "Ignoring the fact that polygamy is illegal in Colorado doesn't sit right with me, Stella. I wonder how jealousy plays out in a community like this. Could it have something to do with Luke's death? Could Abel have been jealous of Luke's relationship with Hannah? Or even one of the older men?"

Stella nodded. "I know, it's something to keep in mind. And we might have to investigate that angle sometime soon, but for now we have other leads to follow that appear promising."

"In addition to Quinn Randolph and Parker Tate, we need to identify and speak with these two older men who roughed Luke up outside the bar."

"I think Randolph might know who they are. He seems to be the one outsider who got to know Luke."

"I'm going to drop you off at the station and then go over to the Watering Hole to see if I can talk to Ned Dempsey. Sometimes he helps wait tables on Sundays during lunch. If he's not there, I'll talk to whoever's working."

"All right." Stella's cell phone pinged, and she took it out of her pocket to focus on the screen. She swiped and tapped before bouncing in her seat and turning toward Mattie. "Hot damn! CBI lab got a positive for xylazine on both Luke and Tracy Lee."

Her excitement energized Mattie. "That's great news. This points us toward Parker Tate and Quinn Randolph."

Stella checked her watch. "Brody has them lined up at the station for us to interview in about forty-five minutes. Let's hope they show up."

"If they don't, we'll track them down."

NINETEEN

Mattie stepped inside the dim interior of the Watering Hole and scanned the room, looking for bartender Ned Dempsey. The bar's dark log walls absorbed what little light its small windows managed to let in. She didn't come inside often, but she'd met Rainbow here for an occasional dinner of bar food. Neither of them drank much alcohol, but Rainbow had a penchant for the grill's cheeseburgers whenever she fell off her vegetarian wagon.

And Ned had a penchant for Rainbow, although the dispatcher swore she didn't return his affection. Her lack of interest didn't seem to stop him from flirting with her, and Mattie suspected that on some level Rainbow must enjoy it, since Mattie had watched her shut down other potential suitors numerous times while she allowed Ned to carry on.

She spotted Ned behind the old-fashioned wooden bar, filling mugs with beer from the tap. He was a handsome guy with dark-brown hair, dark-amber eyes, a scruffy beard, and a million-dollar smile that he gave out generously. He sent her one when their eyes connected, and he greeted her as she approached.

"Hey, Mattie. This is a nice surprise." He made a performance of ducking to the side and pretending to look behind her. "Where's your partner in crime?"

She teased him back. "You talking about Robo?"

"Ha! You know I'm talking about the lovely Rainbow Sanderson."

"I'm here alone today, Ned. Just wanted to see you."

"It figures . . . you must miss me. You haven't been in for a while." He grabbed a full mug of beer in each hand. "Just a minute. Let me serve these, and I'll be right back to take your order. Sit anywhere you want."

Mattie hitched up onto a barstool and watched Ned deliver the beers to two cowboys at a table near one of the windows. Many of the other tables were filled, and the scent of fried bacon and potatoes drifted from the kitchen. The place opened at ten and served a breakfast hash that drew a crowd any day of the week.

Ned went behind the bar, grabbed a white cloth, and polished off some wet spots near the tap. "What can I get for you?"

Mattie ordered a Pepsi.

"Are you sure you can handle the hard stuff while you're on duty?" Ned's brown eyes twinkled. "You want something to eat?"

"No, I can't stay long."

"Then have some of these." He plopped a tub of peanuts in front of her, giving her a look filled with curiosity. "Is this a social call or business? I'm guessing business, since Cole Walker seems to be taking up all your social time these days."

Mattie smiled. "It's always a pleasure to visit with you, Ned."

"Charmer." Ned pulled the handle on the soda fountain, filling the glass with liquid and bubbles that carried the sharp, sweet scent of cola. He fixed his gaze on Mattie, one dark eyebrow raised. "What do you want to know, my friend?"

Mattie took a sip, the fizz tickling her nose. "Do you know a young man named Luke Ferguson? Came in here occasionally for dinner, maybe drinks."

Ned leaned against the bar. "Don't recognize the name. What does he look like?"

Mattie gave a brief description of Luke, including the beard, the hat, and the rest of his clothing.

Before she finished, Ned was nodding his head. "I know who you're talking about. Came in here a few times with Quinn Randolph. Haven't seen him for a while."

"So you know Quinn?"

Ned's lips thinned into a downward-tilted crescent. "Yep."

She had questions she'd like to ask about Randolph, but she decided to stick to Luke for the moment. "Did you hear anything about an encounter Luke Ferguson had with two older men, oh, say, about a month ago?"

Ned picked up his cloth and absently polished the bar top. "What kind of encounter?"

"Met him outside and roughed him up a bit."

He frowned. "Hell no, Mattie. I didn't hear anything about that. Is that why the kid quit coming in here?"

Although she didn't need to withhold the fact that Luke had been killed, she didn't want to share that tidbit yet, not until she'd discovered some possible leads. "I guess they didn't hurt him too badly. I'm just trying to find out who the two guys are if I can."

Ned's gaze roamed the room while he rubbed the already shiny patina on the bar, and his eyes stopped suddenly as he stared toward the back by the kitchen. Mattie took a look and spied two old men seated at a table against the wall, both digging into plates of hash.

Ned's gaze returned to Mattie, and their eyes met. "Do you know those two?" he said.

"No."

"The Perry brothers, Keith and Kevin. Two cantankerous guys that stick pretty much to themselves. But they like the chow here, so they come in often." Ned shrugged. "I hate to point any fingers, because I really don't know anything solid, but I've heard those two grumbling about weirdos moving in on them. Evidently Luke's people moved onto the property across the highway from theirs."

This sounded promising. "Anyone else come to mind?"

"There are lots of old guys that come in here to drink, but none that I've overheard bad-mouthing Luke's group."

"And yet you know about this group of folks outside of town?"

Ned nodded slowly as his eyes drifted around the room again. "I hear a lot of talk in this place, and those folks attract attention with their old-fashioned dress. Most folks are just curious, you know. There hasn't been much mean-mouthing directed their way."

"So . . . you mentioned Quinn Randolph. What's his interest in befriending Luke, can you tell?"

Ned shook his head and quirked one side of his mouth. "Hard to say, but I think Luke seemed more interested in befriending Quinn than the other way around. Quinn's a big drinker. Luke tied one on one night and Quinn called one of Luke's buddies to come take him home, a tall guy who looked older than Luke."

"Did you get a name?"

"No."

Isaac was the leader of the Brothers of Salvation. Perhaps Luke had asked for him to be called. "Wears an eye patch?"

Ned frowned. "No."

Mattie thought of Ephraim next. "Dark hair with a lot of gray in his beard?"

"Nope . . . tall, thin, dark hair and beard."

"Okay." Mattie realized it was probably Solomon Vaughn. "Did Quinn get annoyed or angry with Luke when this happened?"

"Nah, he thought it was funny. Quinn likes to party, and he was egging the kid on." Ned scanned the café patrons again and then picked up a pitcher of water in one hand and a coffee-pot in the other. "Looks like I need to refill some drinks. I'll be right back."

Mattie swiveled on her barstool and watched the two Perry brothers for a few seconds. Both were graybeards, and even though they looked to be in their sixties, they appeared strong and heavily muscled, one taller than the other. They maintained a singular focus on their food, shoveling in bites as fast as they could chew and not talking to each other. She decided to catch them after they finished.

A family who'd been seated at a four-top rose from their seats, the mother and kids heading outside while the father came to the cash register.

Ned hurried back to his spot behind the bar, settled the man's bill, and turned to Mattie. "It's starting to get busy."

Mattie glanced at the Perry brothers and noticed that they were mopping up egg from their plates with their toast. Time for her to move on. She laid a few dollars on the bar along with her business card and lowered her voice to speak. "Ned, Luke Ferguson was found dead a couple days ago up at Hanging Falls. I wanted you to hear it from me. It's not a secret, but you might keep it under your hat and listen to what the town grapevine has to say."

His brows had risen with surprise.

"I'll leave my business card and number," Mattie said. "If you hear anything that might help us with our investigation, give me a call."

Ned picked up her card and slipped it into his jeans pocket. "Will do," he murmured. "I'm sorry about the kid. He seemed like a nice guy."

Mattie nodded. "That's what I've heard."

She lifted her hand in farewell, slid off her stool, and walked over to where the Perry brothers were starting to lay down their napkins and scoot back their chairs. Neither seemed to have seen her coming, and they both looked up in surprise, their shaggy gray eyebrows raised, when she stopped beside their table.

"Excuse me, Mr. Perry." Mattie looked at one brother and then nodded to the other. "Mr. Perry. I'm Deputy Cobb, and I need just a few minutes of your time before you leave."

Both rose from their seats as she introduced herself, and the taller one gestured to a free chair at their table. After Mattie sat, they followed suit.

"I'm Keith, and he's Kevin," the taller one said, first tapping his own chest and then pointing to his brother. "To what do we owe this pleasure?"

"I want to ask you a few questions about a young man named Luke Ferguson."

"Who?" Keith asked, apparently the older and the spokesperson of the two.

"Luke Ferguson, a young man that moved in with the people who bought property near yours."

Recognition dawned on both faces, Kevin's an open book while Keith rapidly shut his expression down to neutral.

"We don't know those folks, but we know who you're talking about," Keith said, caution evident in his tone. "What about him?"

Mattie kept her eye on the younger one's face, since he seemed to be giving the most away. "I heard he had an altercation with you two a few weeks ago."

Kevin's eyes widened, and he looked down at his plate.

"What? Who'd you hear that from?" Keith asked.

Kevin's reaction told her she was on the right track. Mattie stayed silent but leaned forward and placed her elbows on the table as she shifted her gaze to Keith.

Keith maintained steady eye contact. "Who said?"

"What can you tell me about it?" Mattie responded.

"Ain't nothin' to tell." Keith clamped his lips together.

Mattie fixed her gaze on Kevin, who fidgeted and stared at his empty plate, taking furtive glances at her beneath lowered eyelids.

"Is he gonna press charges?" Kevin asked, raising his eyes to blink a few times. "What did he say?"

"Kevin . . ." Keith sounded a warning.

Kevin looked at him. "We gotta tell our side of the story. We didn't really hurt the guy."

"Zip it, Kevin." Keith gave his brother a squelching look.

"All we did was give him a little tap in the breadbasket," Kevin muttered. "The guy was pretty soft."

"Why did you do that?" Mattie asked Kevin.

"I don't know. He was drinking and getting loud, carrying on. Just got on my nerves," Kevin replied before Keith could shush him.

"Dadburn it, Kevin, keep your mouth shut," Keith said to his brother. And then to Mattie, "The kid couldn't hold his liquor, and he was obnoxious. This bar is our place on Saturday nights, and we were just giving him a warning to shape up."

Mattie gave him one of her stern looks. "Assault is a serious charge. If you have a concern about rowdiness, tell it to the bartender. Don't take it on yourselves."

"Is the kid saying we assaulted him? We barely tapped him."

Mattie studied them both for their reaction to her next statement. "Assault is especially serious when the victim shows up dead a few weeks later."

Kevin's brows shot up. "What are you talking about? The kid's dead?"

Mattie nodded as she focused on Keith. No surprise on his face, merely a frown of concern.

"How did the kid die?" Keith asked, leaning forward to stare at Mattie.

"We're investigating his death as a homicide."

"Well, we had nothing to do with that." Keith kept his voice low but filled with fury as he pushed his chair back and stood, towering above her with clenched fists. "And you can't blame us for it neither. Come on, Kevin, let's go home." He turned on his heel and stalked toward the door, turning mid-stride to cross over to the cash register to pay the bill.

Mattie examined his boots—rounded toe with a low, square heel.

Kevin rose from his chair, giving her a look at his footwear, which was identical to his brother's. "We had nothing to do with killing that kid, Deputy Cobb."

Mattie stood and handed him her business card. "Assaulting an individual often leads to other violence, Mr. Perry, so we have to determine if you're involved in this or not. If you want to contact me, here's my number. Don't go anywhere in the next few days. We'll be in touch again."

Stiff lipped, Kevin stuffed the card into the back pocket of his jeans and followed his brother outside.

Mattie trailed behind, stopping on the sidewalk to watch the two climb into their beat-up old pickup and drive away. Stella needed to follow up and interview these two later.

She checked her cell phone for the time before hurrying to her unit, where Robo was waiting for her. Their next two persons of interest were due at the station, and she'd better get a move on.

TWENTY

When Cole and the kids arrived at the Vaughn place, it looked like a rodeo. A sorrel horse raced around the pasture outside the corrals, darting and bucking while men chased it. As he drew near, he could differentiate the men's faces and realized that Keith and Kevin Perry were on foot out in the pasture as well as several men who lived on the place, Isaac King and Solomon Vaughn included.

"Looks like they've got a horse loose," he said to Angie and Riley as he drove slowly up the lane.

"Isn't that the stallion we worked on yesterday?" Angie asked, noting what Cole had already concluded.

"Sure is." Cole parked outside the barn. "You girls go right to the Vaughn house and stay inside until we get this horse caught."

"Be careful, Dad," Angie said, a concerned look on her face that did Cole's heart good.

He smiled at her. "I'm always careful, Angel."

She made a sound of disagreement but opened the door on her side of the truck and climbed out, folding her seat forward so that Riley could exit the bench seat in the back.

"Be careful, Dr. Walker," Riley said over her shoulder as the two girls hurried away.

Cole grabbed a halter out of the mobile vet unit in back and headed around the corner of the barn to the pasture. He followed the men's voices until he spotted them. They were shouting at each other while the sorrel trotted freely around the periphery of the horse runs outside the barn.

Several mares inside the runs were squealing and pawing the ground, while one beautiful chestnut mare reared and struck out with her forelegs at the panel that separated her from the stallion. Cole sprinted toward the mare and shooed her away from the fence before she caught her leg between the rails.

He looked toward the others for help, but they were oblivious to him and the restless mares. Kevin Perry looked mad as a stout grizzly, squared off in front of Isaac King with his hands on his hips.

"What in tarnation are you doin' with that whip?" Kevin was shouting, his face red from his efforts. "If you go back inside the barn and leave this horse be, I can catch him."

"He's on our property. I'll do what I want with him!" Isaac glared at the older man as he shook a long black buggy whip in the air. "And you're trespassing! Get off our land!"

"Colorado is a fence-out state!" Keith Perry had joined the chaos, standing shoulder to shoulder with his brother. "If you want to keep animals off your property, build a fence around it."

Throwing his hands up toward the mare one last time to shoo her inside the box stall at the end of her run, Cole strode toward the knot of angry men. "Hold up," he yelled as he narrowed the distance between them. "Stop this before someone gets hurt!"

While the others glared at each other, none of them backing down, Cole made eye contact with Solomon and tried to enlist some help. "Solomon, you need to put those mares inside their box stalls before one of them breaks a leg."

Isaac cracked the whip. "If that stallion causes any damage to one of our mares, I'll kill him."

By this time, Cole had reached the group and waded into the center, getting between the Perry brothers and the rest of the men. "If we work together to solve this problem, your mares will be okay." He scanned the angry faces, picking out the men he'd already met. "Ephraim, Abel, go help Solomon secure those mares inside their box stalls. Isaac, put that whip away."

Isaac turned on Cole, fury consuming his face, his hand raised in a fist. "The wrath of God shall strike down those who trespass."

Cole lifted both of his open palms toward Isaac and spoke in a reasonable way. "Uh-uh. As I recall, the passage says we forgive those who trespass against us. Now, cool down and help get this situation under control. All we've got here is a horse running loose. Easy enough to take care of."

Isaac snarled. "That horse is the devil."

"He's a stallion and that chestnut mare of yours is in heat," Cole said. "Not a devil, just a stud horse doing what comes naturally. He could probably smell her a half mile away, which is just about the distance he came from."

The men Cole had told to secure the mares hadn't yet moved. Out of the corner of his eye, Cole saw the stallion, head up and nostrils flared, circling the area as if plotting his next blitz on the mare's pen.

"Isaac, we need to get those mares taken care of." Cole waved his hand toward the stallion. "Once they're penned inside, we can corral this one, get a lead rope on him, and get him off your property. But if we all stand around here shouting at each other, this isn't going to end well."

The others seemed to be waiting for Isaac to tell them what to do. The mare trumpeted a shrill whinny, making Cole turn on his heel and run toward the fence to head her off as she rushed it. "I need some help here," he called to the men.

Ephraim, followed by Abel, broke loose from the others and hurried after Cole, each of them going to the outside gate of a different run where they could let themselves in to push the mares inside the barn. Cole opened the gate that led into the chestnut mare's run and slipped inside, pulling the gate shut behind him. But Solomon, who'd evidently decided to help, caught the gate before it closed and followed Cole inside. Together they formed a human barrier and pressed the excited mare back through the narrow run and into her box stall, where they secured the solid door so that she couldn't get out.

"Let's leave this gate open to the run," Cole said to Solomon as he glanced back to where Isaac was still in a standoff with the Perry brothers. "If you can get Isaac to settle down, Kevin Perry should be able to catch his stud horse and lead him away."

Solomon raised his brow but didn't reply. "Leave the out-side gates open," he shouted to Ephraim and Abel as they fin-ished penning the other mares inside. "Then stand back to let the stallion go into one of these runs."

Realizing that Solomon would follow through with his plan, Cole strode back over to the other men. "Kevin, Keith, come with me and we'll see if we can move Rojo into one of these runs. The rest of you, stay still and be quiet."

Cole figured that removing the Perry brothers would defuse Isaac's anger. Kevin came away first, winding up his lead rope and looping it around his shoulder, where it would be less con-spicuous to the stallion. Throwing one last hard glare at Isaac, Keith followed his brother.

Isaac raised the whip handle in a threatening move toward Keith's back, and Cole quickly stepped up to intervene. He felt a rush of anger at the hardheaded man. "Isaac!" Cole pointed at the front of the barn. "Go inside and tend to your mares. Get that whip out of sight so this stud horse will settle down."

The sorrel continued pacing and circling while Solomon left the row of pens and approached Isaac. He murmured a few words that evidently made Isaac lower the whip. Tall and ram-rod straight, he and Solomon stalked toward the front of the barn, and the other men closed ranks to follow them. Ephraim and Abel backed away from the pens and joined the Perrys and Cole to form a loose semicircle around the stallion.

With a snort and a head toss, the horse rushed over to the run outside the chestnut mare's box stall and trotted through the open gate and into the pen. Cole hurried to secure the gate while the stallion snorted and reared outside the box stall door.

A wave of relief washed over Cole when the gate clicked into place. But getting this horse corralled was only half the battle. The stallion wore a leather halter, and it shouldn't be too hard to clip on a lead rope, but Cole had already seen this horse in action. He began to wonder if it might not need to be tranquilized.

Kevin slipped between the panel rails and began to speak to the stallion in a low croon. He put his hand into his jeans pocket and retrieved a piece of cake, sweet horse feed pressed into a bite-sized nugget. Kevin offered the cake but didn't try to approach the horse. Instead, he stood still and sideways, avoiding a full-front exposure, which the stallion might take as a threat or a challenge.

Rojo ignored him at first but gradually quit rearing and striking out at the air. Kevin's crooning seemed to calm the stallion, and he started pacing in circles near the box stall door, clearly more interested in the mare inside the barn than the cake Kevin held outstretched in his hand.

Slowly, Kevin sidled up to the horse, murmuring reassurance. Cole held his breath. The sound of heavy doors opening and closing came from within the barn, and Cole hoped that Isaac and Solomon had decided to help and were moving the mares over to the other side of the barn.

When Rojo settled, Cole decided that someone must have indeed moved the chestnut mare away from the door. Within a few minutes, Kevin was able to step sideways to the stallion's shoulder and stroke his glossy, arched neck. And when Rojo was offered the cake again, this time he took it, while Kevin snapped the lead rope onto the halter in a smooth, subtle movement. The horse snorted a bit but moved around Kevin in a restless circle while the man continued to stroke his neck and croon. Cole had expected the type of behavior he'd observed yesterday—pawing, biting, and striking—but instead he was observing the reaction of any nervous and excited stud horse.

Cole thought Kevin's display of horsemanship had been masterful. "Good job, Kevin," he murmured. "He's a different horse from yesterday."

"We spent the day and night together, didn't we?" Kevin crooned to the horse. "Come to an understanding."

Keith, who'd been watching from outside the pen, wore a look of pride. "Ain't no horse that Kevin can't tame."

Cole was still concerned. "That may be so, but how are you going to get him home?"

"I can lead him," Kevin said. "As long as these idiots stay away from us and don't get him riled up."

Ephraim and Abel were standing well within hearing distance, so Cole tried to dampen the tension. "You two go on home, then. You'll have to make sure he can't get out again."

"I know the fence he broke through," Keith said, opening the gate for his brother. "We'll make sure it gets shored up."

And without another word to Ephraim or Cole, Kevin led the horse away from the barn at a brisk pace, the red stallion trotting at his side, his hips flaring outward with an occasional side step until Kevin calmly moved him back into place, always heading forward.

Cole watched them leave, still amazed at the transformation. He turned to Ephraim and Abel. "Thanks for stepping up to help. Livestock crossing fences is common enough."

Ephraim harrumphed before answering. "Until one of our valuable mares gets hurt because of an untrained horse that no one can catch."

"Well, we prevented that today because you and Abel were quick to react." Cole decided to move on to the reason he was here. "Let me check on your gelding with the cracked hoof, and then I'll be on my way."

Ephraim turned on his heel and led the way around the barn to the entrance.

Cole could tell that bad blood had developed between these neighbors and wondered if there was anything he could do about it. Probably not. Keith and Isaac were the leaders in this clash, two men as hardheaded as he'd ever seen.

He wondered if he should alert Mattie to the skirmish. Surely the Perry brothers had had nothing to do with Luke Ferguson's death, but you never knew when these wars between neighbors would escalate.

Eager to check on the horse and take the girls back home, he followed Ephraim to the barn.

TWENTY-ONE

There were two unfamiliar vehicles in the station's parking lot, one of them a truck with *Randolph Farrier Services* stenciled on the front door. At least one of the two men had arrived for his interview, and the other vehicle possibly belonged to Parker Tate.

Robo beat Mattie to the door into the station and stood waving his tail as he watched her approach. "You wait," she told him, making him stand back so that she could enter through the door first. He seemed to be testing her frequently on this one small thing, but since his obedience was typically spot-on, it didn't concern her too much. It was his way of checking to see how serious she was about being boss.

The lobby was empty except for Sam Corns, the night dispatcher who shifted to days when covering for Rainbow. Light from the overhead glinted off his bald head. "Stella's got the guys you need to interview waiting. She said to meet her in the observation room when you get here."

Mattie hurried to the room, taking Robo with her. There she found Stella and Sheriff McCoy standing in the darkened space, the only light filtering in through the two-way mirrors from the interrogation rooms. "Sorry I'm late," she murmured.

Stella glanced at her. "Not a problem. These guys just arrived, and we're letting them sit for a few minutes while we decide which one to talk to first."

Mattie took a look at the two men: one, Parker Tate, the smooth guy with upswept, coiffed hair and office-casual clothing; the other, Quinn Randolph, a wiry, strong-looking individual with straggly blond hair beneath his cap, narrow-set eyes, and a pinched nose. But the thing that stood out most was the fact that both wore boots with rounded toes; the rep's new and shiny, the farrier's showing some wear. "Boots that could match our prints," Mattie murmured.

"Correct," Stella said. "And the sizes look like they fall into the range the lab estimated. Good thing to note, but we'll need more than that."

Parker appeared cool and calm, even motionless, while Quinn repeatedly took off his cap to swipe hair and sweat from his brow. Mattie briefed Stella and McCoy on her visit with the Perry brothers.

"They had on the same type of boots as these guys," Mattie added, gesturing toward the observation windows.

"Common style for horseback riding," McCoy said. "Makes the footprints less useful in our case."

"I'll follow up and grill them again this afternoon," Stella said.

"It'll help to separate them like you've done here," Mattie said. "Focus on the one named Kevin. He's most likely to talk."

"I know the Perry brothers." McCoy leaned one hip against a counter that ran along the wall beneath the observation windows. "You've read that right—Kevin is the one who would talk, while Keith would get mad and clam up. Keith manages the ranch, but Kevin has an uncanny way with horses. He does a lot of the work and training."

Cole must know them, Mattie thought, making a mental note to ask him what he thought of the two brothers. And if they might have access to xylazine.

Stella was watching the two men. "Let's talk to the pharmaceutical rep first and let this other guy sit and simmer a while longer."

"Do you want me to sit in on the interview?" Mattie asked.

McCoy pulled out a chair. "Sounds good. I'll observe and come in if I need to follow up."

Mattie settled Robo in her office and returned to Stella as she waited outside the door. She held a folder that Mattie knew from experience contained photos and notes pertinent to the investigation.

Parker Tate stood when they entered.

"Sorry to make you wait," Stella said, before introducing Mattie.

Mattie returned his firm handshake. "Thank you for coming in."

He nodded, tucking one hand against the front of his shirt as he bowed ever so slightly. "I don't know what this is about, but I'm happy to help law enforcement in any way I can."

A smooth talker in addition to his smooth looks. "Let's have a seat," Mattie said, taking a chair across the table from him.

The station's interrogation rooms were stark and airless, cold in the winter and hot in the summer. They contained plastic chairs with aluminum legs, a steel-topped table, and mounted cameras connected to recording equipment.

Parker waited politely for Mattie and Stella to sit before taking his own seat. "How can I help?" he asked, flashing them a smile that revealed even teeth, brilliantly white.

Stella started the interview and the recording by stating the date and time as well as the names of the people present. After her opening statement, she said, "Mr. Tate, I understand you're a veterinary supplies rep."

Parker stroked his navy-blue tie, which contained a slight checkered pattern within its satiny sheen. "Well, that's close, but I'm actually a veterinary pharmaceutical rep."

"How is that different?" Stella asked, leaning forward with apparent interest.

Mattie figured Stella already knew the answer and was warming the guy up.

"I represent a company that sells veterinary drugs and some other stuff like vitamins and prescription dog food, but we don't carry the many other items you'd find in a veterinary supply store. We only rep the stuff our company produces for sale."

"I see. So you carry mostly veterinary drugs?"

"Yes, ma'am. We go to veterinary supply stores and vet offices to introduce our new products and take orders if they're running low on stock."

"Do you sell to customers?" Stella asked.

"Those are our customers," he replied with a thin-lipped smile.

"Ah . . . I didn't make myself clear," Stella said, returning his smile. "I meant, do you sell directly to the consumers who use your products on their animals?"

"No, we don't sell directly to end users." Parker's smile seemed a bit strained around the edges. "But I know you didn't call me in here to talk about my job, Detective. How can I help you?"

"What can you tell me about a drug called xylazine?" Stella asked, placing one elbow on the table.

Parker fiddled with his tie again. "It's a sedative used primarily for horses."

Stella waited for him to add more, and Mattie waited with her.

Parker shifted his gaze from one to the other of them and back. "Dangerous to humans."

Stella nodded. "Do you carry bottles of it with you on your rounds?"

Parker placed his hand on the table and wiggled it back and forth. "That depends. It's not a new product, so I don't typically keep samples of it with me. But if one of our customers orders it and I know I'm able to deliver it on my rounds the next day, I might take it with me."

"Do you know a young man named Luke Ferguson?" Stella asked, changing the subject.

Parker squinted. "I do."

Stella raised a brow. "How well?"

Parker shook his head. "Barely know him. Had drinks at the Watering Hole with him a couple times."

"You met him there?"

"We just happened to be there at the same time, not an arranged meet-up." A frown creased Parker's brow. "I ran into Quinn Randolph in your parking lot. He's the one who came into the bar with Luke."

This information matched what they'd gotten from others, and Mattie saw an opportunity to clarify. "So Luke and Quinn are friends?"

Parker's frown deepened. "I'm not sure about that. Quinn said that Luke was one of his clients. I only saw him a couple times, and then I heard he moved away."

"You heard that from . . . ?" Mattie asked.

"Quinn."

"So you and Quinn are friends?" Mattie asked.

Parker shrugged, trying to look nonchalant, but there were beads of sweat that had formed on his brow that the room's temperature didn't warrant. "Sure. We're friendly. We've only known each other a couple months."

If this line of questioning had raised the heat, Mattie wanted to make sure they kept it on. "And you and Quinn met where?"

"The Watering Hole."

"Do you work together?"

"No." Parker looked down at the table. "We just happen to like the same bar at the end of the day."

"I guess your work does have something in common, though," Mattie said, figuring she might as well move into the topic that interested her most. "He works with horses, and you represent a company that manufactures a drug meant to sedate horses. Mr. Randolph might need that drug from time to time."

Parker looked up from the table to give Mattie a keen stare, as if trying to figure out if she had a hidden agenda.

Which, of course, she did.

Stella picked up the questioning. "Have you provided a bottle of xylazine to anyone here in Timber Creek lately?"

He shook his head. "My only customer here is Dr. Walker, and he hasn't ordered any."

"How about others? Say, Mr. Randolph or anyone who owns horses outside of town?"

Parker pooched out his lower lip and gave his head another shake. "Nope. Like I said, I don't sell to end users."

"How might an end user obtain the drug?" Mattie asked, wanting to keep the questions coming from both her and Stella.

"By prescription only. From a veterinarian." Parker shifted his gaze back and forth between them. "Why the interest in xylazine?"

"If an end user had a prescription, could they purchase the drug from you?" Mattie asked.

"No. They'd purchase it from a vet supply store or directly from a vet." He smoothed his tie yet again.

"All right," Stella said. "Do you know a man named Tracy Lee Brown?"

Parker squinted. "I've never heard that name."

"Do you like to hike, Mr. Tate?" Stella asked.

"Not really." He frowned at her.

"Do you ride horseback?" Mattie asked.

Looking at Mattie, he nodded. "I do."

When he didn't volunteer any more information, she prompted him. "Have your own horses?"

"I have two."

"Do you trail ride up in the mountains to places like Hanging Falls?" Mattie observed him carefully.

"It's one of the things I like to do on weekends. Why's that?"

That's interesting. "And have you been up to Hanging Falls this summer?"

"About a month ago before the heavy rain started, yes."

"Did someone go with you?" Stella asked.

"Well, yes. Quinn and I rode up there together."

So he and Quinn were better friends than he'd previously admitted. "Did you see anyone else up there when you went?"

"No." He paused a moment as if thinking. "Well, there was a guy on the trail just below the falls, but I didn't know him and we didn't stop to talk."

"What did he look like?" Mattie asked.

"Skinny guy, long hair pulled back into a ponytail, fanny pack. Jeans that were too big."

Sounded like Tracy Lee. "Did you pass this guy coming or going?"

"He was headed downhill as we were going up."

"And you didn't stop to talk?"

"Nope. We might have said hello as we passed each other. He stood off the trail to let us by."

"Did you camp up there?" Stella asked.

"No, it was just a day trip," Parker responded, looking at Stella. "Why all the interest in this, Detective? If you gave me a little more information . . ."

Stella might appear relaxed as she settled back in her chair, but Mattie could feel the detective's energy rocket beside her. She knew where Stella would go next. "Luke Ferguson was found dead at Hanging Falls a couple days ago."

Parker's brows rose, and his jaw dropped in a look of apparent surprise. Mattie wondered if it wasn't a case of overacting. She and Stella both sat and waited for him to say something.

He closed his mouth and opened it a couple of times before managing to speak. "Uh . . . good grief! An accident?"

"It was no accident," Stella said. "We're investigating his death as a homicide."

Parker frowned. "Well . . . I don't get it. Luke was just a kid. I mean . . . he was at least twenty-one . . . old enough to drink, but . . . he still seemed like just a kid, you know. Sheltered."

"Sheltered?" Stella asked.

"Well, yeah. He'd never been exposed to alcohol before, and it seemed like he wanted to party. He'd never had experience with girls or been away from home." Again, his gaze shifted between her and Stella, and Mattie wondered why it seemed he knew more about Luke than he'd indicated earlier.

She decided to assume he knew about the altercation in the alley. "What happened between Luke and the Perry brothers?"

Parker leaned forward, an intense frown on his face. "Did they kill him?"

Mattie shrugged. "What do you know?"

"Those old guys are loose cannons." Parker tapped a finger on the table. "Usually sit at a table by themselves and don't say a word. Couldn't believe they reacted the way they did to Luke."

"Which was . . . ?" Mattie waited for his answer.

"Told him to stay with his own kind where he belonged."

"Did you see it?" Stella asked.

"No, but Luke was shaken up enough to leave. Not long after that, he told Quinn he was going to go back home."

So far, they'd gleaned that Parker Tate owned horses, had been up to Hanging Falls, and had probably encountered Tracy Lee Brown at least once. But they didn't have anything on him at this point that felt incriminating. Mattie wanted to move on to Quinn Randolph.

Stella's next comment indicated that the two of them were in sync. "You've been most helpful, Mr. Tate. We need you to wait here a few minutes longer. I might have some follow-up questions for you before we let you leave."

Parker frowned as he leaned back in his chair. "How much longer might that be?"

"Not too long." Stella stood. "I'll return soon."

Mattie nodded at Parker as she followed Stella from the room out into the hallway, closing the door behind her.

"Knows more about Luke Ferguson than he originally admitted," Stella murmured. "And more friendly with Quinn Randolph than he'd like us to believe."

Mattie nodded and moved toward the door that led into the room where Quinn waited, stepping aside so that Stella could enter first. Quinn was wiping his brow as they entered, and he startled when the door opened, looking even more nervous than he'd been earlier.

"Thank you for waiting, Mr. Randolph," Stella said, as she took a seat across the table from him. She introduced Mattie, and although he wiped his hand on his jeans before returning her handshake, his palm felt clammy and damp.

"What's up, Detective LoSasso?" he asked, while Mattie sat next to Stella. "Why the long wait? Have you been talking to Parker first?"

"Actually, we have," Stella said in a pleasant tone. "So you know Mr. Tate?"

"Absolutely," he said, nodding as he leaned forward and folded his arms on the table. "We're friends. What's going on?"

"And you also know Luke Ferguson?" Stella asked, leaning forward to match his body language.

"Yeah. Parker and I had drinks with Luke at the Watering Hole."

"How do you know Luke Ferguson?"

"I met him when I went to his place to shoe horses." Quinn met Stella's gaze. "He was living out east of town with a bunch of folks who all dress alike. Do you know the people I'm talking about?"

Stella nodded. "How well do you know Luke and the people he lives with?"

Quinn shrugged. "I know their horse business. And I've seen enough to guess at their personal business, if you know what I mean."

"No, Mr. Randolph, I don't know what you mean," Stella replied, keeping her tone light and conversational. "Could you clarify that for me?"

"They're some kind of religious nuts," Quinn said, his gaze popping between Stella and Mattie. "And I'm sure they're polygamists, although Luke didn't say that in so many words."

"Oh?" Stella paused, and Mattie waited too, wanting him to go on, reading his body language to see how he felt about the information he was willing to share so readily. So far, he appeared eager to talk, as if he was sharing gossip more than passing judgment.

"Yeah. There's a lot of women and children out there and only a handful of men. It's like stepping into a different world, going back in time but with some kind of a kinky twist."

"And what did Luke say about it?" Mattie asked, genuinely curious about Luke's opinions prior to his murder.

"Actually, he didn't like it, and he decided to go back home." Quinn shrugged and rubbed a finger on the tabletop as if wiping a smudge. "Said he didn't care for the preacher, the guy named Isaac King. Wears an eye patch."

Mattie hoped Quinn would add more. "He didn't care for Mr. King?"

"Right. Said he was too intense about their religion."

"Did Luke say why he felt that way?"

Quinn paused as if thinking. "Nope. But that's the way I remember it. Too intense."

"Did he seem to like the others in the group?" Stella asked.

Quinn smiled in a way that looked more like a leer. "Oh yeah, he liked the others well enough. There was a purty little girl he liked a bunch, has a German shepherd that's with her all the time. Luke was taken with her. Said he planned to come back and marry her when she was older." Quinn was shaking his head as he finished talking, and he spread his hands on the table. "Kids."

"What do you mean by that?" Mattie asked.

"Luke was just a big kid, even when he was partying and carrying on. That's what got him into trouble."

"What kind of trouble?"

Quinn looked down at the table. "That's all I'd better say about that."

"In for a penny, in for a pound, Quinn," Stella said. "Go ahead and explain."

He looked up at her. "Well, he made some people mad because of his carrying-on when he was drunk, but I hate to talk about that, since they're my clients too."

"Tell us." Stella leaned back in her chair like she had all the time in the world.

Quinn darted a glance at Mattie. "The Perry brothers. They're a couple of old codgers who live out by the folks we're talking about. They threatened Luke, told him to stay with his own kind, but they didn't really hurt him."

That seemed to be the theme of the assault. Probably nothing the prosecutor could make stick, and charges would never be brought. But Mattie wondered if the Perry brothers would eventually be charged with murder.

"So why all these questions about Luke?" Quinn asked, looking at Stella.

Stella leaned forward again and crossed her arms on the tabletop. "Luke Ferguson was found dead up by Hanging Falls a couple days ago."

Quinn's head snapped backward, and he sucked in some air. "What?"

Stella nodded, while Mattie sat still and observed him.

"But he went home. He told us he was leaving." Quinn's gaze focused on the table, and he appeared to be searching his memories.

"When was that exactly?" Stella asked.

"I can't remember the date, but I might be able to find it on my calendar." He pulled his cell phone from his pocket, swiped, and scrolled. "Here. This is the last time I saw Luke at the Watering Hole."

He placed his phone on the table, turning it so that Mattie and Stella could see. Mattie took out her notepad and recorded the date. It was approximately two weeks earlier, and the notation was for six o'clock in the evening: *Luke—bar.*

"Thank you, Mr. Randolph," Stella said. "I just have a couple more questions. Do you have horses?"

"I have three of my own and board horses for other people."

"Where's this?"

"I have a property near Hightower."

"Have you ever ridden up by Hanging Falls?"

"A couple times."

"By yourself?"

"Once. And then again with Parker."

"Have you ever met a man named Tracy Lee Brown?"

Quinn's gaze lost focus as he thought. "No. Not that I can recall."

"When you went riding up to Hanging Falls with Parker, did you see a man on the trail?"

Quinn stared at Stella. "Parker said that, didn't he? Yeah, we saw a man. Skinny dude with a fanny pack. Headed downhill. Stepped aside so we could pass, said hello."

"You didn't stop to visit?"

"It was on a steep part, so there was no place to stop. Just enough room to pass."

"Okay," Stella said, and she looked at Mattie as if inviting her to jump in.

Mattie thought Quinn had been open and cooperative during their questioning up to this point. She cleared her throat and changed the subject. "Your work involves keeping horses calm enough for you to work on. Do you use any medications or drugs when you do?"

It was as if a curtain dropped over Quinn's face, and his expression went blank. "Not usually."

"But sometimes?"

"Well . . ." His gaze darted between Mattie and Stella and then landed on the tabletop. "Every once in a while, I have to give a horse an oral sedative that comes in a paste. It's an over-the-counter drug I can pick up at a vet supply store."

"How about xylazine?" Mattie asked, pinning him with her gaze.

"Nope. Don't use that." He shook his head as he clamped his mouth shut.

She probed further. "Do you know what xylazine is?"

He nodded. "The vet used it on a stallion at the Perry place just a couple days ago so that he and I could work on him. Big, mean horse . . . worked real well."

Mattie decided to go for the direct question. "Have you ever used the drug by yourself, or do you carry it with you?"

Quinn stared at Mattie for a few beats, and she could see the wheels spinning inside his head. *He's wondering what Parker Tate told us*, she thought. If Parker supplied Quinn with a pharmaceutical that could be obtained by prescription only, they both would be in violation of the law. With her cop face pasted on, she waited him out.

"Nope," he said finally, looking her in the eye. "That would be against the law."

He's lying. "What if I told you that we know you do carry this drug with you and have used it before?"

"I'd say you heard wrong." A slight smile lifted his lips and his worried expression cleared as if he'd just remembered something, and he leaned back in his chair and crossed his arms. "You can search my truck if you want to. You won't find anything like that."

His response made her wonder if he'd remembered he'd lost the bottle of xylazine up on the trail that led from Tracy Lee's campsite so that he knew she'd find nothing in his truck. "Thank you, Mr. Randolph. With your permission, my dog and I will search your vehicle before you leave here."

At the mention of Robo, Quinn swallowed, but he played it cool and nodded.

She figured they both knew she wouldn't find anything, but she needed to accept the invitation anyway. Robo wasn't trained to detect xylazine, but Quinn didn't need to know that. And you never knew when Robo would find something else unexpected . . . and illegal.

Mattie's cell phone vibrated in her pocket, and she took it out while Stella wrapped up the interview. It was a text from Julia. She and Abuela had arrived and checked in to the motel. They were in room ten.

Mattie's heart leaped to her throat as she texted back that she would finish her work and be there soon.

TWENTY-TWO

Mattie drove up to room ten at the Big Sky Motel and parked, her heart pounding and hands trembling as she turned off the engine. She paused, struggling to regain her composure. But a woman who could only be her sister stepped outside room ten . . . and snatched Mattie's breath away.

Time stopped as she and her sister stared at each other, unable to move. Julia bore a resemblance to the image Mattie saw each day in her mirror, but with one major exception—her sister was gorgeous. Whereas Mattie's nose had a slight bend in it from being broken in a fistfight when she was a kid, Julia's was straight and narrow and the perfect size. Her café au lait skin appeared flawless, and her hair, deep brown with a hint of auburn like Mattie's short bob, flowed below her shoulders in a silky curtain.

Tears sprang from Julia's eyes and she placed her hands to her cheeks to staunch them, the movement releasing Mattie from her daze. She registered the sound of Robo rushing to the front of his cage and then she bailed out of her SUV, running toward her sister. She and Julia collided, all arms and hugs and wet tears as they sobbed in each other's embrace.

My sister, Mattie thought. *This is my sister.*

A silver-haired lady, stooped with age, came up behind Julia, who loosened one arm so that both she and Mattie could gather the woman in and clasp her tightly in a three-way hug.

Mattie cried while her abuela murmured sweet endearments in Spanish, words that meant everything to Mattie, words she'd yearned for as a child. Words that a mother or a grandmother would utter to a little girl with a broken heart. They filled her with so much comfort and love that she thought she might burst with joy.

Eventually, Mattie pulled back to study her grandmother's face. Yolanda Mendoza was a tiny woman, her skin wrinkled like a walnut, perhaps from years in the sun. Her silvery hair was still thick, though fine in texture, which was apparent when a stray breeze tossed her short tresses and made them float about her head. Her eyes, such a dark brown that they were almost black, glittered with tears.

Mattie placed a hand on Yolanda's cheek and struggled to speak, her throat choked with emotion. "This is hard for me to believe."

Abuela covered Mattie's hand with hers. "*Mi dulce niña,*" she murmured. *My sweet girl.*

And then they were back in each other's arms until Robo started barking in the back of the unit. Julia chuckled softly, stepping back and wiping the wetness from her cheeks. "And I take it that's Robo."

Mattie brushed her tears away and tried to smile. Her heart was so full, she didn't know if she could contain the rush of adrenaline in her system. Her love for Cole and his kids had challenged her ability to remain in control of her emotions many a time, but this was different. She was way out of her element now.

She wanted to whoop, shout, and run circles around the motel. Instead, she answered her sister in an almost normal voice. "That's Robo. My partner."

Julia gestured toward the door to their room. "Bring him in so we can talk."

Mattie glanced at the motel office. "I'd better get permission."

Julia grinned. "I already did. Seems like you and your dog are celebrities around here. The manager said we couldn't have a dog in our room until I told him who we were here to visit, and then he couldn't be more accommodating. Said Robo was welcome anytime."

Mattie returned her sister's grin. "He's somewhat of a star. Hang on, I'll get him."

She needed to take a moment to breathe, because her agitation would make her dog nervous. She took in a deep inhalation through her nose, releasing it slowly from her mouth as she went to the back of the unit.

Robo bounced from side to side, showing how her excitement had lit him up. They were connected that way.

"Okay, buddy, settle down," she murmured in a soothing tone as she opened the hatch. Using a firm touch, she stroked his back, calming herself as much as him. Then she clipped a short leash to his collar and invited him to jump down to the ground.

He circled her ankles, looking up at her, his intelligent brown eyes telling her he was ready to do whatever she wanted. All their obedience drills and discipline paid off at times like these, and she couldn't have been prouder of her partner, even though her family had no way of knowing how much effort went into training a high-drive male dog like Robo.

She told Robo to heel and then to sit after leading him around the car, stopping about five feet away from her sister and grandmother, who stepped back behind Julia, her movement subtle but obvious to Mattie.

"Say hello, Robo," Mattie said, cuing him with the phrase that meant it was time to make friends. He stood, waving his tail gently, while Julia let him sniff her hand and then smoothed the fur on his neck and the top of his head. Robo acted like a perfect gentleman.

"He's gorgeous, Mattie," Julia said, and then spoke to Yolanda over her shoulder. "Don't be afraid, Abuela. He won't hurt you."

Mattie was quick to reassure her too. "He likes to meet new people. He's a good boy, aren't you, buddy?"

Robo looked up at Mattie and waved his tail before turning his attention toward Yolanda as she approached slowly.

After the introductions, Julia led the way to the motel room door. "Let's go inside where it's more private."

The curtains were open and the room decorated in cheerful red and blue shades, the double beds covered in white comforters and sheets that looked clean and inviting.

"Abuela, take one of the chairs." Julia gestured toward the two comfortable-looking chairs that sat next to a round glass table while she perched on the bed. "Mattie, you sit in the other."

Mattie waited while her grandmother took her seat and then sat, settling Robo beside her. This seemed like a strange ritual, visiting with family who would want to know everything about her life, information she'd always considered private. Mattie didn't know how to begin.

But Julia seemed like a take-charge woman. "I have pictures for you," she said, jumping to her feet and heading toward a suitcase that lay open on the bed at the far side of the room. "I can't wait to show you."

Mattie scooted to the edge of her chair, her hands itching to touch the photos. When Julia handed her the first one, her breath caught. It was a posed black-and-white photo of her mother as a teen, wearing a dark sweater and silver necklace. "Is this her senior picture?"

"*Si*," Yolanda said with a soft smile. "My darling Ramona."

Ramona had been as beautiful as Julia, with glossy black hair worn straight and long, pulled to one side and draped over her shoulder to flow halfway down her chest. She gazed into the camera with dark eyes framed by long lashes, a shy, sweet smile on her lips.

"She's beautiful," Mattie murmured, before memories rushed at her in flashes, filling her mind so that she couldn't speak. Memories of her mother bending over the bed that Willie and Mattie slept in, holding a finger to her lips, telling them to stay in bed no matter what and not to come out of their room. Mattie felt like she was about three, Willie five, and her mother had been trying to protect them from whatever abuse Harold Cobb had in store for her that night.

A trembling sensation started at the base of Mattie's rib cage.

Julia settled back onto the edge of the bed and offered another photo, which Mattie took with fluttering fingers. In this one, her mother looked older, and she held an infant wrapped like a peapod in a light-green blanket, proudly showing off the little wrinkled face and shock of dark hair by folding the blanket back. A sandy-haired man holding a boy who looked to be about two years of age stood with his arm around her, while a cute little dark-haired girl of about four cuddled between the two parents. A family photo—probably taken shortly after Mattie was born.

Mattie couldn't stand the pain that shot through her. She laid the photos on her lap and, covering her face, sobbed into her hands.

"Oh no, Mattie," Julia murmured, kneeling beside her and rubbing her back, while their grandmother made a sound of distress. "I didn't mean to make you cry."

Mattie struggled to control her emotion. Crying wasn't her go-to reaction to the sorrowful things in life, but the heart-wrenching sadness caused by the destruction of that happy little family overwhelmed her.

She stifled her sobs and swiped at her wet cheeks, raising her face so that she could meet Julia's gaze. "What happened to our dad?"

"Are you sure I should tell you now?" Julia looked worried, which made Mattie dread what she was about to hear, but nothing could be worse than Willie's death.

Mattie nodded.

Julia sighed and scooted back onto the edge of the bed. "That's our father, Douglas Wray."

Mattie had known that as soon as she saw the photo; she nodded again, encouraging Julia to continue.

Julia took a breath. "He worked as a border patrol agent back in the eighties when there was a big crackdown on illegal immigration. During that time, we lived in Mesa, California, just south of San Diego."

Mattie had heard of it, but she'd never been there. Well, evidently she had, but not when she was old enough to remember.

"You would've been two when he was killed. Do you remember him?"

Mattie shook her head. She hadn't yet explained her repressed memories to her sister.

"That's pretty young to remember anything," Julia said. "I remember him well. He was a good father. He worked the night shift, and I remember having to be quiet during the day while he slept. But then, in the evening before he went to work, he would play with us."

Julia's face took on a glow as she remembered those happy times. Mattie tried to recall something, anything, but her mind was a blank. She looked into the face of the man in the photo and saw a smiling image of a seemingly good-natured person behind the suntan, the grin, and the light-colored eyes. She wondered if they were green like the flecks in her own brown eyes.

"Money was tight. Mom didn't work, and we were a family of five living in a small rented cottage."

"Your papa worked hard," Abuela murmured. "He loved his family."

Mattie wondered why they were building him up, and she feared he was in for a fall.

"I was spending the weekend with Abuela when he was killed, the night the rest of you disappeared."

"I took care of Julia a lot," Yolanda said. "It gave Ramona a break to have two kids to take care of instead of three."

Mattie looked at Julia. "It all happened on the same night? His death and our disappearance?"

Julia nodded slowly. "I'll tell you what I've learned over the years. At first we didn't know anything."

Her sister and grandmother looked at each other, and the older woman dipped her chin in a slight nod, as if giving permission. "Our grandfather was working here in the U.S. with a green card, but Abuela was in the country illegally at the time. Grandpa passed away before they could become citizens, and well . . . she wasn't equipped to handle the system in those days."

"I was afraid," Abuela said softly, and her tone told Mattie that even remembering that time could still frighten her. Mattie understood that phenomenon completely.

"So was our dad turning a blind eye to that situation?" Mattie asked quietly.

"Yes and no. He helped support Abuela while they looked into getting her citizenship. She was cleaning motel units at a seedy place, being paid under the table, but without her having a real job with a green card . . . it was a tough situation."

"Your father was a good man," Abuela said. "He had a kind heart."

It was obvious that her father had been her grandmother's hero, but he had been walking a fine line for a man in law enforcement. "So what happened after he died?"

Julia frowned. "Abuela struggled to keep us both in the States, working what jobs she could as a laborer in fields, motels, or restaurants and getting help from the church we went to. Eventually, she married a man who was a U.S. citizen. It took some time, but he helped her establish citizenship." Julia and her grandmother locked eyes with each other, their look filled with love. "They raised me. Things might have been rocky at times, but I was always taken care of."

Mattie couldn't help but contrast the difference in their childhoods, hers overridden with fear while Julia's had been uplifted with love. She wished she'd been left at their grandmother's for the weekend along with her sister.

But then her mind did one of those crazy leaps back in time and flashed on a moment when her mother held her close and sang a lullaby, rocking her one night as they sat perched on the edge of the bed. Mattie might have been three or four.

She'd shared that moment with her mother only because they'd been together in the house of horrors that Harold Cobb had built. And her mind had given her back one of the good memories. A gift.

Julia continued her story. "Abuela tried to find out more about what happened that night but couldn't seem to get anywhere with it. The first time I went to the police to try, I was in high school. I connected with a lady detective, Sonia Alvarez. She was kind to me and said she'd look into it. It didn't take long for her to call me, because our dad's case was still in the files."

Julia's frown warned Mattie that the fine line her father had been walking had meant trouble for him and his young family.

"Detective Alvarez said that our father was shot to death at a checkpoint just inside the border south of San Diego," Julia said, her face filled with pain. Mattie reached for her hand and squeezed it, and they sat with their fingers gripping each other's. "She said the evidence pointed to his involvement with a smuggling ring. That he'd been on the take, allowing gun and drug runners that were buying him off into the U.S. through that checkpoint."

Mattie hadn't known this part of the puzzle, but she connected her father immediately to the ring that included the Cobb brothers. She could feel her features settle into her cop face, because she didn't want Julia and Abuela to know how much she despised learning that her father had been engaged in such dirty business. "How did our mother, Willie, and I get caught up in it?"

"We don't know." Julia hung her head, looking down at their clasped hands. "Detective Alvarez found a report in the file saying the initial investigation revealed that Dad's entire family was missing, and the detectives had filed a missing person report on all of us, me included. Ms. Alvarez questioned both me and Abuela, but we couldn't supply any new information. They'd never found his killers, but she said she'd kick it up for the cold case unit to take another look. We've been contacted off and on by various detectives over the years, but none of them have made any progress. Or at least not any progress that they've shared with us."

Mattie studied Julia while she spoke, taking in the nuance of her expression, the tone of her voice. She realized that her sister's life had been filled with pain too, a different kind of pain than hers, but still, her life hadn't been easy. All because their father had decided to play ball with a group of killers. Had he done it willingly, or had he been coerced?

"Can you give me the name of the last detective you talked to?" Mattie asked.

"Detective Jim Hauck." Julia raised her eyes and looked into Mattie's, her gaze filled with hope. "Will you contact him?"

"Sure. I even have a lead on someone who was probably involved."

Julia's eyes widened with surprise. "You do?"

Mattie bit her lower lip and nodded. "I don't know for a fact that this man was involved, but he certainly might have been. He's incarcerated in prison here in Colorado on multiple charges of murder and conspiracy to commit murder. Including killing Willie."

Tears brimmed in Julia's eyes. "Were you involved with capturing this man?"

Mattie nodded, reaching down to stroke the satiny black fur between Robo's ears, taking comfort from him as she remembered the awful time a few months ago when they'd investigated Willie's death. "Robo took him down, and we arrested him."

Yolanda moaned and then pressed her lips with her fingers. Mattie could tell her grandmother's tension rivaled her own and hoped the lady's heart was strong enough to take it.

"Tell us about Willie," Julia said, a determined set to her jaw, even though her brown eyes filled with tears. "We need to know."

Mattie settled back in her chair, sorting through what she could and couldn't share about Willie's death but knowing one thing for certain: she would never tell these two about the torture he had suffered. All they needed to know was that he'd been killed and his body had been found near Timber Creek.

Mattie's gut tightened as she told Willie's story. Even the abridged version brought memories rushing back, and the stricken expressions on the faces of her audience made her own pain even more intense.

Julia asked very few questions, darting glances at Yolanda as if wanting to make certain she could handle the information. When Mattie finished explaining that Willie's fiancée had wanted his remains cremated and had taken them with her to bury in a cemetery in Los Angeles, Julia asked if she could call her to find out where.

"I can tell you where," Mattie said, "but if you want to talk with her yourself, I'll call to make sure it's okay and then give you her number."

Julia stared at Mattie long and hard. "Why, Mattie? Why did this man kill Willie?"

This was one of the parts that Mattie had left out. "He wanted to find our mother, and he thought Willie and I could tell him where she was."

Yolanda gasped, covering her mouth with her hand.

Mattie was startled to see fear on her grandmother's face.

Did Abuela know where to find Ramona? Call it cop's intuition, but the notion that Yolanda knew something more struck Mattie square in the face. She studied her grandmother, who lowered her eyes to stare at the floor between them.

"Why did he want to find our mother?" Julia asked, her brow creased with concern.

Keeping her eyes on Yolanda, Mattie told what she knew. "He said she took money that belonged to him and disappeared. But I don't know if what he said was the truth."

Yolanda continued to hold her hand against her mouth and gaze at the floor. Mattie sat at a point in their close triangle where she could observe them both, and Julia seemed only puzzled, not fearful like their grandmother.

Mattie decided that confronting the older woman was not the way to go right now. She could tell when someone would clam up, and Yolanda definitely fit the description. There would be time over the next few days to gain her trust and get her to confide what she might know. Maybe Abuela knew nothing, but then again—and Mattie pinned all her hope on this alternative—maybe she knew everything.

"Anyway." Mattie decided to head the conversation in another direction. "The man who killed Willie is serving time, and I'll try to reach Detective Hauck today to inform him."

"Do you think you can reach him on a Sunday?" Julia asked.

"You never know when a detective will be on duty. Sundays are just as likely as any other day."

Julia gave Mattie the detective's phone number, which she entered into the contact list on her phone. She had tapped out emotionally, and she wanted to go to the station, where work was always a distraction. But Julia had taken the time to copy these photos for her, and she couldn't neglect her sister's effort.

She picked up the handful of photos that she'd placed in her lap and toiled her way through them. There was one of her mother feeding a baby girl in a high chair, and her openmouthed imitation of the child made Mattie bite her lip to keep from crying again. "Is this you or me?" she asked Julia.

"It's you." Julia smiled sadly. "Willie and I were sitting across the table, and Dad took the picture. I remember it."

There were other photos of family life—the three children running through the sprinkler in swimsuits that showed off their skinny legs and bulging little-kid bellies, one of all five of them around a Christmas tree, and one of Mattie and Julia posed on the couch, big sister feeding baby Mattie a bottle. By the time Mattie had struggled through viewing them all, she had a sense of the love the family had shared, the love her parents had given each other and their children.

Maybe her father hadn't been on the take; maybe he'd been framed for something he didn't do. The cop in her wanted justice for this man she couldn't remember but who'd brought her into the world.

By this time, Mattie felt herself bending under the emotional pressure of the little family reunion, and she needed a break. "I'm anxious to go to the station and make that call," she said. "My friends the Walkers have invited us for dinner tonight at six. Would you like a chance to rest before we go?"

To Mattie's relief, Julia glanced at their grandmother and nodded. She'd hoped the two would need a break as much as she did. She made arrangements to escort them to the Walker house later.

Mattie tried to hand the photographs to Julia as she stood to leave, but her sister pressed them back into her hands.

"I made these copies for you," Julia said. "Keep them."

Feeling like she'd been given hidden treasure, Mattie carried the photographs with her and set them inside her vehicle's console before taking Robo to the back to load him into his compartment. Her family stood at the doorway of their motel room, watching her get into her vehicle and waving as she drove away. Mattie returned their waves, looking into her rearview mirror to see them go back inside when she paused to turn onto the highway.

She felt absolutely wrung out. The information she'd learned about her father weighed on her heavily. It seemed filled with assumptions. She needed to review this "evidence" the police had. She would hate to discover that it was true, but if it wasn't, she needed to clear his name.

She headed for the station, a place that usually brought her peace in the form of work. She planned to seek out Stella, a friend who could hopefully point her in the right direction.

TWENTY-THREE

Mattie pulled into the station parking lot, relieved to see Stella's car still there. She took Robo with her and found the detective inside her office, working at her computer. Mattie tapped lightly on the open door and peeked in. "Do you have a minute?"

Stella pushed her reading glasses up on top of her head. "Of course. But you're supposed to be off duty and with your family right now."

Mattie quirked up her lip into a half smile. "They needed to rest before dinner."

Stella raised a brow. "And you needed a break."

She knows me so well. "Right. We've spent the past hour going over how Willie and my father died."

"Oh . . . pretty hard stuff."

"Yep." Mattie released a sigh. "Do you have time for me to tell you what I found out about my father?"

"Absolutely." Stella leaned back and gestured toward an empty chair beside her desk. "Have a seat."

Mattie sat and then summarized what she'd learned from Julia. As she did, Stella tipped her desk chair back a few inches and rocked on the spring, her lips pursed.

"So you're going to call the detective and tip him off about John Cobb, right?" Stella asked.

"Yeah, and I want to see how serious they've been about solving this case. Since it looks like my dad was on the take, they might have put it on the back burner all these years."

Stella studied Mattie, a furrow of concern between her delicately sculpted brows. "It might look like he was a dirty cop, but that's not always the case. And you never know what this smuggling ring had on him."

Mattie nodded. "Knowing John and Harold Cobb, that concerns me too."

"Do you want me to call this detective in California?"

Mattie didn't want to divert Stella's time from the Timber Creek investigation. "I'll take care of it, although he might want to speak to you sometime."

"Be sure to give him my cell phone number." Stella straightened and opened a notebook on her desk. "Now . . . do you want an update on our two cases?"

Mattie squared her shoulders, back in her element and feeling better. "Sure."

"Sheriff McCoy and I decided to interview the Perry brothers at their place so we could look around and get photos of their truck and trailer tires. They have a carriage whip hanging on the wall in the barn, similar to the one we saw this morning at the Isaac King place."

"I suppose they're common enough, just like the smooth-soled riding boots."

"And we didn't get anywhere with the pattern on the tires either. They're similar to the prints the sheriff found yesterday but not a definitive ID."

Unless tires had an unusual mark on them or an unusual tread, they weren't always helpful in identifying a vehicle. "I was afraid of that."

"But we did find one thing that'll knock your socks off."

The detective's excitement gave Mattie a spike of energy. "What's that?"

"An empty bottle of xylazine in a trash can by the barn door." Stella rocked back in her chair and gave Mattie a Cheshire cat grin.

Mattie was truly astonished, but she quickly thought of an explanation that might discredit the find. "Wait a minute. Was it theirs, or did Cole throw it away when he was at their place last?"

"Don't jump to conclusions, right?" Stella gave her a small salute. "The Perry brothers denied knowing it was even there.

They said that Cole must have thrown it in the trash or—get this—maybe Quinn Randolph threw it away after he trimmed their stallion's hooves."

"Quinn Randolph? Did either of them observe him using the drug on their horse?"

"Oh, yeah. At the very least, we've got this guy on illegal possession and use of a controlled pharmaceutical." Stella used her fingers to tick off the status of the case so far. "First, I talked to Cole and confirmed that he didn't throw away a bottle of xylazine at the Perry place, nor did he leave one for Randolph to use. Second, Brody and I contacted veterinarians in Willow Springs, and none of them have written a prescription for Randolph to obtain the drug. And third, we believe that Parker Tate is Randolph's supplier, but we can't prove that yet. We're working on it."

"Good job, Detective." Mattie held up a fist, and when Stella bumped it with hers, Robo sprang to his feet and shoved his way forward. It took a second to settle him down.

Stella laughed. "You'd better teach your dog to fist-bump, Mattie. Looks like he wants in on the action."

But Mattie's previous conversation with the Perrys and their reaction to their neighbors made her question whether the two were innocent. "So are the Perry brothers off the list of suspects? Are you sure they weren't lying?"

Stella had sobered. "They're not home free yet. We're still looking at them. Earlier today, the Perrys' stallion broke free from their place and went onto the King property. According to Cole, King threatened to kill the horse. Made both of the Perrys furious."

"Hmm . . . sounds like there's a lot of anger out there between neighbors. I guess we'll have to keep an eye on that."

"Yes, *we* will." Stella pointed at her. "*You're* going to spend more time with your family."

Mattie felt her eyes slide away from Stella's, only to return to be met by her friend's keen gaze. "It's tough" was all she could bring herself to say.

"I imagine it's real tough, especially having stuff like your father's death brought to light. Let me know if I can help."

It felt good to know that Stella was there for her. "I appreciate the offer. Right now, I'll go see if I can reach Detective Hauck."

Stella raised a hand in farewell and settled her glasses back on her nose as Mattie and Robo left her office.

With Robo trailing behind, Mattie went to the staff office to use her desk phone to make the call.

She'd think the detective would welcome having a suspect in a cold case dropped into his lap, but one never knew. Under the circumstances and if they'd left the case on the shelf, he might not appreciate hearing from the victim's long-lost daughter. But on the other hand, she could clear up the whereabouts of at least two of their missing persons: her and Willie. That should make him happy.

And if he was less than motivated to work on her father's case, she needed to know it.

She felt a twinge of nerves as she dialed the phone, but the only person she got to speak with was the dispatcher on duty. In the end, she was told that Detective Hauck would return to work tomorrow. She left her name, her phone number, and a message that she had information regarding the Douglas Wray cold case.

That would have to do for now.

TWENTY-FOUR

Fresh from the shower, Cole ran a comb through his closely cropped hair and then spiffed it up with a dab of gel that Tess had given him for Christmas last year, a gift that he'd thought might be a hint to step up his game in the grooming department. Satisfied that he'd achieved all he could, he slipped on a short-sleeved, mint-colored Western shirt above his jeans, fastening the pearly white snaps as he trotted down the stairs to the kitchen.

Mrs. Gibbs was at the stove, stirring a pot of green chili with pork, while Mattie's foster mother, Teresa Lovato, stood beside her, holding a spoon poised and ready to dip into the pot. Mrs. Gibbs had arranged for Teresa to join them for dinner as a surprise for Mattie.

Tension tightened Cole's shoulders as he wondered if Mattie would actually enjoy being surprised, but then he decided he couldn't worry about it. This home was filled with people who loved her, and she'd better get used to them doing things they hoped would please her. And he'd noticed that she was getting better at releasing the reins a bit when it came to control.

He grabbed a spoon from the drawer and stepped in beside Mama T, slipping an arm around her lightly. "Mmm . . . smells so good. I'm in line for a taste after you."

Mama T raised her round face to look him in the eye and gave him a wide grin that charmed him.

"You think you'll like my green chili, gringo?" she said in a teasing way.

"I know I will." Cole smiled at Mrs. Gibbs. "You don't have to be Hispanic to enjoy a bowl of green chili with home-made tortillas, do you, Mrs. Gibbs?"

"Aye, that you don't," Mrs. Gibbs said. "And the tamales you made are lovely, Teresa. Do you share your recipe?"

After taking a bite of the chili, Mama T smacked her lips and put her spoon into the sink. "Spicy enough, but it needs more salt," she murmured before replying. "I don't have a recipe, but if you'll come to my house some afternoon, I'll show you how to make a batch and you can take some home for your dinner."

"Sounds delightful," Mrs. Gibbs said, handing Teresa the container of salt.

Cole stood back until Mama T had finished measuring the salt in the palm of her hand and stirring it in.

"Now you try," she said, bumping the wooden spoon against the edge of the pot and then waving it at him.

He'd taken a tablespoon out of the drawer instead of one of the smaller teaspoons, and he filled it to the brim. After blowing on it a few seconds, he popped the entire spoonful into his mouth, letting the chunky, hot liquid pool around his tongue. The mixture of green Anaheim chili, onion, pork, and spices tingled his taste buds in a most pleasant way. He took his time chewing the bits of pork and savoring the bite while the two women watched him.

Finally he swallowed, his spoon poised near the pot. "That was fabulous. Can I have another bite?"

Mama T swatted the back of his hand gently. "Get a clean spoon, then, if you do."

He grinned, happy that his teasing had drawn a playful reaction from her. She was used to dealing with rowdy kids in her kitchen, so handling him was apparently nothing. "I'll wait until dinner. That one bite will serve to whet my appetite."

Out in the living room, Bruno barked, his nails skittering on the tile at the entryway to the front door. "Sounds like they might be here," Cole said. "I'll go see."

He went through the den to the front door, where Bruno bounced on his toes, looking up at the door and barking. "That's enough. Stand back now, out of the way."

Bruno gave him only a few inches, and he had to get stern, telling the dog to stop carrying on and give him more space at the door. He figured the Doberman knew it was Robo that had arrived, because the big dog's excitement had risen to a feverish pitch, behavior that accompanied Robo's visits. The two seemed to turn into a couple of knuckleheads when they greeted each other.

Cole let Bruno follow him outside, and the dog shot down the sidewalk to where Mattie had parked her SUV. The silhouette of Robo's head darted from side to side behind Mattie, and her mouth moved as she spoke words to her dog that Cole couldn't hear. Then Cole's and Mattie's eyes met, and when she pointed at Mama T's car, which was parked in front of the house, her lips parted in a brilliant smile that made all residual tension in his shoulders melt. He knew all would be well.

When Mattie was happy, he was happy.

Another car pulled up and parked beside her SUV, but like Bruno in his singular focus on Robo, Cole had eyes only for Mattie. He stepped off the porch and made his way down the sidewalk to greet the woman he loved and her family.

★ ★ ★

Mattie leaned back in her chair and scanned the faces around the table. Her heart was full of love for these people and her stomach full of the love that Mama T always put into her cooking.

She'd been nervous about this dinner, but her fears had edged away as the evening progressed. Yolanda and Mama T had hit it off immediately, Cole and Mrs. Gibbs made fantastic hosts, and Cole's kids seemed to be enjoying themselves.

Sophie had lightened the mood and kept everyone entertained with her lively chatter, and although Angie seemed quiet, she appeared drawn to Yolanda, making sure the older woman had everything she wanted at the table. In turn, Mattie's abuela seemed taken with Angie and asked her questions about school and her hobbies, trying to draw her into the conversation whenever Sophie slowed to take a breath.

Mrs. Gibbs was carrying her signature chocolate cake to the table when Mattie's cell phone vibrated in her pocket. Evidently hearing or feeling the vibration as he sat beside her, Cole turned to look, raising a brow.

"Excuse me, please," Mattie said, rising from her chair. "I'll be right back."

She went to the den with Robo dogging her footsteps as she removed her phone from her pocket. The screen displayed an emergency message from the station: *Missing Child Alert, Call Immediately.*

This was one of the most dreaded calls a police officer could receive. Mattie cringed while she swiped to her contact list and dialed the first number.

Sam answered her call.

"Calling in on the missing child message," Mattie said, her words clipped. "What's up?"

"I know you're off duty, but the sheriff wants to see if you and Robo can come in." Sam's voice was tight with stress.

Mattie was used to being called for emergencies, whether on duty or not. She started to head for the front door but stopped herself; Mrs. Gibbs and the others deserved at least an explanation and a thank-you before she left. Cole showed up in the doorway from the kitchen and studied her, concern evident on his face. "I can arrive in about ten minutes," she told Sam. "Who's missing?"

"Hannah Vaughn. Missing about two to three hours. Parents thought she was in her bedroom, so they aren't sure. The call came in a half hour ago. Sheriff McCoy called in Stella and Brody. Now you."

Mattie decided she needed to end the conversation so she could make her excuses and say her good-byes for the evening. "I'll be there as soon as I can," she said, and disconnected the call.

"What's going on?" Cole asked.

Mattie summed things up for him.

"I'll go with you," he said.

"You should wait here until we know if volunteers are going to be called."

Cole nodded, turning to follow Mattie as she headed into the kitchen. Everyone looked at them when they reentered the room.

"I'm sorry to have to leave suddenly," Mattie said. "There's an emergency at work, and I have to go."

"But you're on vacation," Julia said, her disappointment evident as she rose from her chair.

Mattie held out her hand. "A child is missing. They need a K-9 team and I have to go."

"Mattie's work is very important in this town," Mama T said, her eyes alight with adoration.

Mattie's heart swelled with gratitude for this woman who'd shaped her with advice, guidance, and sometimes criticism. She went to Mama T and dropped a kiss on top of her head. "Mama, thank you so much for cooking tonight, and thank you, Mrs. Gibbs, for baking a cake and having us over. I'm so sorry to leave early, but I need to run."

"Don't you worry about a thing, Miss Mattie," Mrs. Gibbs said, walking with her toward the door. "We shall have our cake and visit with your sister and grandmother in your absence. Be careful as you go."

Mattie paused, looking back at Julia, who'd resumed her seat. "Julia, I'll call you as soon as I'm free, unless it's too late. If it is, I'll call first thing in the morning."

Julia lifted her hand in farewell. "Take care, Mattie. See you soon."

Grateful that her sister didn't seem too upset about her abrupt departure, Mattie turned to leave, but not before the expression on Angela's face caught her eye. The girl looked positively terrified, her face white, her eyes wide. As Cole followed her to the doorway, she spoke to him in a quiet tone. "Take care of Angie. She looks scared."

"I will," Cole murmured. "Take care of yourself. Call if I can help."

He opened the door, and she and Robo stepped out onto the porch. She gave him a tight hug, a quick kiss, and told him thank-you for hosting her family, and then she and Robo sprinted out to her vehicle.

She loaded her dog, then took a moment to unlock the compartment that held her utility belt and service weapon so she could strap them on. She waved at Cole as she fired the engine in her unit and headed down the lane.

She set aside all thoughts of family and friends and focused completely on a teenage girl with a German shepherd, a dog that would probably protect her if she could. She prayed that Hannah was in a safe place and didn't need that protection.

TWENTY-FIVE

At the station, Mattie found the sheriff in his office, wearing a worried expression on his typically composed face. "Thanks for responding, Deputy," he said, his voice deep and resonant with concern. "Sorry to interrupt your vacation."

Mattie waved her hand in dismissal. "What do we know?"

"Ruth Vaughn reported Hannah missing around six thirty. Detective LoSasso and I responded by going out to her house, where she and her husband provided information. The last time they saw Hannah was around three, when she and her dog went into her bedroom to read and for prayers. They thought she remained there until dinner time, but when Ruth checked, the bedroom window was open and she was gone."

"Runaway?"

"That's what it looks like, and that's what Mr. Vaughn seems to think. But because of Luke's recent homicide, his wife is afraid it's a kidnapping," McCoy said. "And I agree that we don't want to assume anything here."

"So you want us to see if Hannah left a scent track outside her bedroom window?" Mattie asked, thinking that should be the next move.

"Exactly. And since we still haven't discovered how Luke ended up at Hanging Falls, we need to make certain Hannah actually left the property instead of someone taking her. I know that's not within Robo's capabilities, but I hope you know what I mean. I want to see where a scent trail starts and ends, or even if there is one."

Mattie nodded acknowledgment. The community itself was still suspect, and they shouldn't overlook the possibility of some insider being dangerous. But things didn't sit right on this one. "Where is Sassy, the German shepherd?"

"She's gone too."

"I'd be surprised if that dog wasn't protective of Hannah. If they're together, it indicates Hannah left her house willingly." But then, if the two had been separated, it was possible they would find Sassy injured or dead somewhere along the scent trail, something else that Mattie dreaded. She tucked the thought away, not wanting to verbalize it. "We're ready to go."

"Deputy Brody and Detective LoSasso are already out there securing the scene and conducting interviews," McCoy said as Mattie turned to leave.

She hurried out to her vehicle and loaded Robo. After leaving the station, she flipped on her overheads and headed to the highway, driving with flashing lights but no sirens.

She checked the time—almost eight o'clock, and the sun had dipped below the western horizon. In July at this time in the evening, she could count on less than an hour of good visibility left. She needed to depend even more on Robo's nose, since she doubted she could see much disturbance in the natural grasses that surrounded the trailer home.

At the highest speed she dared travel, it took about five minutes to reach the property. Relieved to see the place lit by porch lights, she turned in and drove as fast as she could up the bumpy lane. There, she found Brody's cruiser parked near the cluster of trailers. She pulled up behind his vehicle and parked.

He met her as she exited her unit. "No one has been behind the trailer near the window in question since I arrived, but I would guess at least half these folks tramped through there before I got here."

Mattie acknowledged his attempt to give her an uncontaminated scent trail with a nod. "If she went out that window, Robo will probably be able to pick up the scent. We'll see."

Stella came around the front of the Vaughn trailer, carrying a paper evidence bag. "I have a scent article in here. A dress from her laundry basket."

"Thanks. Hang on a minute while I get Robo ready."

Robo pressed his nose against the window of his compartment, watching Mattie's every move as she went to the back and opened the hatch. He met her at the open door, doing his happy dance. He knew he was going to work even before she began the chatter meant to rev him up.

She made him wait long enough for her to put on his search harness and give him a drink of water. After she snapped a leash on the harness ring, he hopped out of the Explorer and moved to the end of the leash toward Stella, his nose seeking the bag with the scent article in it. Robo never failed to amaze her; he was wearing his search harness, which to him signaled a human search, and he was raring to go.

Mattie took the bag. "Where's her window?"

Brody led her into the shadows to an open window in back. A square of light shining from within lit the ground beneath it enough to show a window screen leaning against the under-skirt of the trailer. "So this window was open when they discovered Hannah missing?"

"Right. There's no sign of forced entry," Stella said, having followed them. "The screen has tabs that you unclip to remove it. They were all opened from the inside, and then it looks like it was dropped down here underneath the window."

Mattie could tell Stella was thinking runaway. Well, that's what she was here to determine. Robo was already waiting at her left heel, so she opened the bag and lowered it for him to get a sample of Hannah's scent. He poked his nose in the bag, whiffed several times, and withdrew his head. Mattie passed the bag to Brody, then leaned forward to unclip Robo's leash and told him to "search," his command for finding a person.

Robo surged forward, and Mattie moved quickly to direct him to the area beneath the window. He entered the square of light, giving her a view of him sniffing the area, including the side of the trailer.

Rising up on his hind feet, he placed his paws on the windowsill before lowering back on all fours and working his way along the ground. His head moved side to side as he gave the area a thorough going-over. Mattie could imagine him sorting through the various scents of all the people who'd crossed through the grass behind the trailer.

Although she was tempted to move Robo out farther to where the scents might not be so congested, she told herself to be patient and give him time. And she was glad she did, because within another minute, he seemed to pick up a track that ran along the side of the trailer close to the wall.

Mattie followed while Robo took a few steps. With his nose to the ground, he gingerly sorted out the track that matched the Hannah scent he'd cataloged in his brain. Raising one paw at a time, he made his way to the end of the house and then picked up speed as he quartered the area beyond. He trotted along the back side of the next trailer until he took Mattie to the Graysons'. There he moved down the trailer's side to a window set at a point midway.

Remembering the floor plan inside the home, Mattie thought this window might correspond to Abel's bedroom. A dark thought struck her: had Hannah and Abel conspired to kill Luke and now run away together? Or had Abel killed Luke and now kidnapped Hannah?

"Have you questioned Abel Grayson yet?" she murmured to Brody, who was close behind her.

"Nope. We talked to the girl's parents and the guy named Isaac King."

"Do you know if Abel Grayson is on the property?"

"No, I don't."

"Tell Stella to find out."

Brody radioed Stella while Robo circled the area beneath the window. She wondered if he'd come to the end of the track and Hannah was hiding inside. She kept still and observed.

Robo wasn't ready to sit and call an end to the search yet. He headed across the grass toward the back of the next trailer. The light had faded, and it was now dark enough that Mattie could barely see his shadow, so she hurried to stay close.

Robo left the edge of the trailers and struck out, leading her into the grassland that surrounded the buildings. Once she moved away from the porch lights and the light streaming from windows, she was relieved to find that her eyes adjusted to the semidarkness and she could keep an eye on her dog. He moved steadily, nose to ground, acting sure of himself as he followed a scent track. And she felt certain the track belonged to Hannah.

As they moved, Brody stayed close at her back. Mattie hated going into the darkness where she and Robo could be a target for an ambush or a sniper. Robo took her across the field directly to the highway, which seemed deserted at the moment. With no traffic to worry about, she let him search the shoulder until he assured himself that he could find no more scent. Then he sat down at the edge of the road and raised his head to stare at her.

This represented the trail's end. An open spot on a highway where Mattie could imagine a car stopping for the young girl—and probably her dog—to climb inside.

"Someone picked Hannah up right here." A wave of anxiety rolled through her while she patted Robo and told him what a great job he'd done. She turned to Brody, who'd taken out his phone to report to the others. "We just have to find out who."

"And if that person was friend or foe," Brody said as he dialed.

★   ★   ★

Around nine o'clock, Cole and Mrs. Gibbs walked their guests out to their cars, saying good-night. He hadn't heard from Mattie yet, and his anxiety had grown throughout the evening.

He felt an obligation to take care of Mattie's family and to not abandon his hosting duties until the evening ended. But as soon as he had a free moment, he planned to touch base with Sheriff McCoy to see if there was anything he could do.

"Thank you for such a wonderful dinner and for sharing so much about our Mattie with us," Julia was saying as they reached her car. "I feel like we've gotten to know her better by visiting with her friends. Perhaps it was a blessing in disguise that she had to go back to work."

As closemouthed as Mattie was about herself and her private life, Cole had no doubt that Mrs. Gibbs had supplied way more information about Mattie than she herself would have allowed this evening. Even Mama T had provided insight into the teenage Mattie and how she'd overcome her rebellion by channeling it into her cross-country training, and it had become apparent that Mama T was as proud of her accomplishments as any mother could be.

Mrs. Gibbs responded to Julia's statement. "Mattie is a special person. We couldn't be more thrilled that she's found you."

Cole steered the conversation to its end, said his good-byes, and hurried back up the sidewalk, thinking that the evening had gotten away from him and that now, finally, he could call the sheriff.

But Angela stood blocking the front doorway, the porch light casting its beam across her worried face as she sought him out. "Dad," she said, her voice quivering with tension. "I need to talk to you about something. It's real important."

TWENTY-SIX

Mattie and Stella had sequestered Abel between the K–9 unit and Brody's cruiser. He stood in the light from Mattie's low beams, and his body language screamed defensive, his arms crossed over his chest, his eyes focused anywhere but on his interrogators.

"Abel," Stella was saying, "we know that Hannah came to your bedroom window. Are you saying she didn't?"

He glanced at Mattie, but his eyes slid off sideways while he spoke. "Maybe she did, but I wasn't in there. I never saw her."

Mattie wondered how she could get him to tell the truth. "We're concerned about Hannah. I know she went across that field, got into a car, and drove away. We need to know if she's somewhere safe or if she's with someone who might hurt her. What can you tell us?"

"Nothing. I don't know anything."

Mattie decided to play the religious card. "Would you swear to that on a Bible? Because I'm having a hard time believing you."

Abel looked down and toed the ground with his boot.

Stella went a different direction. "Could I see your cell phone, Abel?"

He looked at her in alarm. "My cell phone?"

His reaction gave Mattie hope. She hadn't realized that he owned a cell phone. Perhaps Stella hadn't known either, but her guess had struck pay dirt.

When Abel didn't move, Stella repeated herself. "I want to look at your cell phone. Now."

"What if I don't want to show it to you? I have a right to privacy, don't I?"

"You certainly do." Stella straightened, squaring her shoulders and giving him the full force of her penetrating stare. "But we have a missing child here and evidence that she visited your bedroom window before she disappeared. If this is a kidnapping, you've been implicated. It's best if you cooperate now, because I have exigent circumstances on my side and it will be only a matter of time before I see it."

Abel gazed out toward the barn as if looking for a way to escape. Then he shrugged, removed a cell phone from his pants pocket, and handed it to Stella.

She swiped the screen and found the phone locked. "Unlock it for me," she said, holding it out toward him.

He traced a zigzag pattern across the screen. Stella swiped to the call history and pulled up the latest call. As she read the number aloud, she glanced at Mattie, letting her know it was for her benefit. The number had a Colorado area code and perhaps even sounded familiar, but she couldn't place it.

"Whose number is that, Abel?" Mattie asked. "Who did you call?"

He looked away. "I don't know whose number that is."

Stella stepped forward. "You must know, if you dialed it. There's no name, only the number, so I won't find it in your contact list, will I?"

Abel shook his head.

Mattie thought she knew what he was trying to hide, though not very successfully. "Did Hannah use your phone?"

He shrugged and wouldn't meet her eyes.

"I have a feeling you're trying to protect Hannah for some reason," Mattie said. "But we're not going to leave you alone. Whose number is this?"

He shrugged again. "I told you I don't know, and that's the truth."

Mattie toned down her frustration and applied a soft touch. "Did Hannah come to your window to use your phone?"

He nodded reluctantly. "But I don't know who she called."

She stepped closer and pressed for more. "What did she tell you when she asked to use it?"

For the first time, Abel made eye contact with her. "All she said was that she needed to borrow my phone. It was during prayers, and I was in my bedroom. She knocked on the window, I gave her the phone, she gave it back to me. That's all I know."

"Did you listen to her side of the conversation?"

Abel maintained eye contact. "She took the phone toward the back of the trailer where I couldn't hear her. I don't know who she called or what she said. And I could swear to that on my Bible."

He'd convinced Mattie he was finally telling the truth. "What was her demeanor? Did she act afraid, angry, sad?"

He frowned, apparently replaying the memory of the encounter. "Hannah sometimes acts . . . well . . . dramatic. She acted dramatic, like she didn't want to tell me anything, even when I asked her what was going on."

Mattie wondered about the relationship between these two. "But you were willing to share your cell phone. Why's that?"

"Hannah's my friend. I just got a phone this summer. She'd never asked to borrow it before now, so I thought it must be important."

Mattie's phone jingled in her pocket, and she slipped it out to see who was calling. Cole. She started to push the call through to voice mail, but something stopped her. Cole wouldn't call unless it was important.

"One moment," she said to Stella. "I have to take this call."

She walked away from the two, heading for the rear of her vehicle, where Robo waited in his compartment, ears pricked. He bounced side to side, obviously thinking she was coming to get him out again to work. She kept her gaze on him through the window to settle him down while she connected the call. "Hi, Cole."

"Mattie, have you released an Amber Alert yet?" Cole's voice was tight with tension.

"Not yet. Looks like we will soon."

"Hold off on that. Are you alone?"

Mattie glanced at the others. No one was within a twenty-foot radius where they might overhear Cole's words coming through the speaker. "Good enough."

"I know where Hannah is, but she's afraid and needs protection from her family and the others. Can you free up to come talk to her?"

She felt sideswiped, but she held it together. If the girl had run because she needed protection from the Brothers of Salvation, Mattie didn't want to give away anything that would tip off these people. While she did a 360-degree scan of the area to make certain that she was still alone, she kept her voice low. "I'll do that. Where?"

"Riley's house. I'm almost there now. Hannah's safe."

"Good."

She disconnected the call and rounded the vehicle to rejoin Stella, who was still asking questions that Abel either couldn't or wouldn't answer.

"Detective," Mattie said, "I think I've gleaned what I need to here at this site, so I'm preparing to leave. But I need to speak with you privately for a moment about the Amber Alert."

Stella shot a quizzical look in Mattie's direction but went ahead and wrapped up her interview with Abel before turning back to her. "What did you get from that phone call?"

"Let's get inside the Explorer." Once they were tucked away inside the unit with only Robo pressed up against the front of his cage to listen, Mattie shared the cryptic message she'd received from Cole.

"Good grief," Stella said. "This makes me think that Luke's killer is right here. What if Hannah knows who it is?"

"That's possible. We need to keep everyone here while we clear up what's happening with Hannah. She might provide evidence that we could use to make an arrest."

"And she's reportedly afraid of her parents too?" Stella asked, her eyes skeptical.

"That's what she told Cole." Mattie realized she was repeating hearsay and felt anxious to get the story straight from Hannah. "I need to go talk to her."

"As you go, call Sheriff McCoy and tell him we're holding off on the Amber Alert and why. I'll stay here with Brody to keep an eye on things, and we'll tell the parents that we're done with your part of the investigation."

"I'll call as soon as I have details." Mattie started the engine, eager to be on her way.

Stella stepped out of the car.

Mattie had a bad feeling about leaving Stella and Brody here with a group of people who might be killers. "Be careful."

"You too," Stella said, then closed her door and tapped on it twice. She lifted a hand in salute while Mattie steered the SUV into a turn and headed up the lane.

Out on the highway, she brought her unit up to top speed, hesitating to turn on the overheads until she'd driven far enough to be out of sight. She had about five miles to go before she could discover any answers.

And now she suspected why that phone number had sounded familiar to her. Keeping her eyes on the road, she swiped to her contact list and glanced at it while she scrolled down to Angela Walker and found the number she was looking for. It matched the one on Abel's cell phone.

Hannah had called Angie. And now the girl was safe at Riley's house. In this case, one plus one added up to three— two girls sheltering a third. Thank goodness Angie had had enough trust to tell her father about it.

TWENTY-SEVEN

Mattie parked beside Cole's truck in front of Riley Flynn's house, a log cabin with light streaming from most of its windows. Robo woofed softly behind her, and she wondered if he could detect Hannah's scent here in the yard or if he was just excited to see Cole's familiar truck. It could be either.

Cole must have been watching for her, because the porch light came on and he stepped outside. Angie followed him, hovering behind, her hands clasped together at her chest. She looked so distressed that Mattie's heart went out to her. Father and daughter came down the sidewalk toward her.

"You're going to stay here," Mattie told Robo, stopping his happy dance midbounce. "I'll be back soon."

She exited her unit and met the two Walkers in the darkness at the end of the sidewalk. But the moon provided enough light for her to see the lines of anxiety drawn on Angie's pale face. She reached for the girl with one arm and was grateful when Angie let her draw her in close for a quick hug.

"I'm sorry," Angie said. "I should've called you sooner."

"You can always count on me, Angie," Mattie said softly.

His movements clandestine, Cole ushered them up the sidewalk toward the porch. "Let's go inside."

Mattie had been inside this living room before, and nothing much had changed. Inexpensive furniture including a sofa, two chairs, and a coffee table clustered around a small television near the front window. Riley and Hannah were sitting on the couch with Sassy lying on the floor, but when Mattie came into the room, Riley shot to her feet, sending Mattie an anguished look.

She felt like this girl was one of her special kids. She'd met Riley at school, had grown concerned about how the child had no supervision at home, and had arranged jobs for her at Cole's clinic and Mama T's house. And Riley's face told her how much she feared she'd risked their friendship this day.

Sending Riley a reassuring look, Mattie murmured, "It's okay, Riley."

The girl's shoulders sagged with relief. Riley's father was absent as usual, since he worked as a bartender at night in Hightower.

Mattie went to the sofa where Hannah remained, her head bowed. "Let's sit here together, and you girls can tell me what happened."

Cole was still standing by the front door. "Shall I step outside?"

Mattie considered the options and decided that since she was talking to minors, it would be best if he remained. At least he was the parent of one of the kids and had a supervisory connection to another. "Is it all right with you, Hannah, if Dr. Walker stays?"

Hannah nodded, her eyelids swollen and red. "He already knows everything."

Once they were settled, Mattie focused on Hannah. "You don't really know me, but my biggest mission in Timber Creek is keeping kids safe. What happened to frighten you? Why did you decide to run?"

Hannah's face crumpled, and fresh tears streamed down her cheeks. "M–m–my parents want me to get married."

Mattie rocked back in her seat while Hannah covered her face with her hands and cried. She thought she needed to clarify what she'd heard. "Do you mean they want you to get married now, even though you're only fifteen?"

"Next week," Hannah said through her tears, fighting for self-control. "I'll be sixteen next week."

"That's still under the legal age," Mattie said, glancing at Cole. He looked uncomfortable, a dark frown on his face. A sixteen-year-old could marry in Colorado with parental consent, but not if it was against the child's will. Age didn't matter without the child's consent. "Are both your parents willing to sign the consent form?"

Hannah sniffed, working hard to control her tears. "There's no consent form in our church. It's a spiritual marriage."

Mattie should have known that's what was going on. She thought of Abel and his willingness to let Hannah use his phone. "Who do your parents want you to marry?"

"Isaac!" Hannah's attempt to control her emotion dissolved, and she hid her face while she sobbed. "And he's already got three wives. Besides, I don't love him. I don't want to be with him like that. I mean . . . ewww . . ."

Blown away by Hannah's answer, Mattie took a moment to gather her thoughts and let the girl regain control. *I shouldn't be surprised*, she told herself. *It's obvious that Isaac is the one in charge out there.*

"Besides . . . Isaac's crazy," Hannah said, removing her hands from her face. "He ripped out his own eye."

Mattie struggled to take that in. "He what?"

"That's how he lost his eye." Hannah's face screwed up in distaste. "You know how the Bible says, 'If thy right eye offend thee, pluck it out, and cast it from thee'?"

Although it sounded familiar, Mattie didn't know the line or the exact context. "I really don't know it, Hannah."

"Well, Isaac said he once looked at a woman with lust, so he plucked out his right eye. My dad said it's true, and he watched him do it. They say it shows how dedicated he is to following God's word, but I think it just means he's crazy."

"I'm glad you think for yourself on that one, Hannah." Mattie felt like she must've missed something during the time she'd spent at the compound. She'd seen no evidence of a child bride on the property and wondered if this had been a regular practice prior to their arrival in Timber Creek. "Is there a written record of the marriages in your group?"

Hannah nodded. "Isaac keeps the records in his house."

Mattie was glad to hear it. Perhaps records would provide evidence of these underage marriages to support child abuse charges. "Is your mother in favor of your marriage?"

Hannah took a shaky breath. "She doesn't seem happy about it, but she said that if that's what my father wants, we should obey."

"That's not true, Hannah. There are laws that protect children in situations like this. No child can be forced into marriage against her will." *Or into having sex with an adult*, she added silently.

From her seat on the floor, Angie reached up to touch Hannah on the knee. "I told you, Hannah. I knew Mattie would protect you."

Angie's words stirred a warm glow in Mattie's heart. "You were right to ask for help, and you girls did the right thing by helping her. We'll get to the bottom of this, but meanwhile, you'll need a place to stay."

Riley was quick to speak. "She can stay with me."

Mattie made eye contact with Cole, hoping he would read her mind. She knew that county CPS would not allow Riley Flynn to act as foster parent, no matter how generous the girl was with her home and friendship.

"You'll come stay with us, Hannah," Cole said. "Until this gets sorted out."

Mattie worried that there was more than this threat of marriage to sort. Hannah had considered herself in love with Luke Ferguson while evidently her father and his leader had been plotting for her future. She wondered if Luke's death had been a way to force her to see things their way. "Hannah," she said, "is there anything you know about Luke's death that you should tell me?"

The girl looked startled. "Nothing more than I've told you before."

Mattie thought of the word *PAY* carved onto Luke's chest. "Does the word *pay* mean anything to you, either related to your religion or to Luke's death?"

Mattie waited, hardly daring to breathe, while Hannah thought about it.

Finally, Hannah responded, her demeanor matter-of-fact, apparently unaware of what her answer might mean to Mattie or how it might relate to Luke's death. "Isaac talks about paying retribution for our sins all the time when he gives his sermons."

Mattie tried to project a calmness she didn't feel. "Who's responsible for making sure that sinners pay retribution?"

Hannah shrugged. "Isaac. Or if it's a kid that's sinned, then that kid's father."

"What punishments are used to pay retribution?"

"It depends. Maybe extra prayers, maybe you have to stay in your room, sometimes a paddle on the rear end, but that's mostly for the boys."

Those types of punishments were a far stretch from whipping and death. "How about with the adults?"

"I don't know for sure." Hannah squirmed in her seat. "When I was small, my mom had to stay in her room for a long time, or it seemed like it to me. I think that was punishment for something she did."

Hannah looked down at her lap and picked at the fabric of her skirt with shaky fingers while Mattie waited for her to continue. Finally, she looked up and met Mattie's gaze. "Luke told me that sometimes Isaac uses a whip on the men . . . out in the barn. We're not supposed to talk about it. It's private, just between him and the one who's sinned."

This was what Mattie needed to tie Isaac to Luke's homicide. So far they had no hard evidence, but at least she could get a warrant to search on the child abuse charges. And she could get a warrant to have the lab take a look at that whip she'd seen in the barn.

"Do you know of anyone younger than eighteen who's married to one of the older men?" she asked Hannah.

Hannah shook her head. "Not now. Isaac's third wife was sixteen when she came to join us. She didn't like living with us at first, but once she got pregnant and had her first baby, she seemed happier." Her face flushed with embarrassment. "Mother says it's our duty to bear children and to build a legion of true believers to populate Heaven." She lowered her eyes. "But sometimes I have trouble believing all that. I mean, I want to have a life where I do things besides having kids. Like getting a job as a flight attendant or something like that."

Mattie thought it ironic that here was a girl, sitting before her in her unusual clothing, who'd led a sheltered life with strict rules and expectations, and what she wanted most was to have a normal job. "So you'd like to travel and see the world, huh?"

"Yeah. Luke and I talked about driving to Mount Rushmore on our honeymoon. He wanted to see more of the world too." Hannah's lip trembled.

"Thank you for sharing this with me. You've done the right thing, sweetheart." Mattie felt an urge to get back to Stella and Brody. She'd gleaned enough to know that she'd left her colleagues in a place that harbored a killer, possibly an entire gang of killers.

She turned to Cole. "I have to go, but you all need to be careful. Ruth Vaughn might figure out that Angie helped Hannah. Someone could come after her."

"We'll go home and batten down the hatches." Cole followed her out the door. "Isaac King has a buggy whip that he threatened to use on the Perry horse. Make sure you find that—it could have Luke's DNA on it."

Mattie nodded. "Maybe you should take everyone to the station. You'll be safe there."

"We'll be all right," Cole said, taking her hand as she turned to leave. "*You* be careful."

"Always." Mattie squeezed his hand and hurried out to her unit, where Robo was waiting.

TWENTY-EIGHT

Mattie called Sheriff McCoy as she drove away from the Flynn house. When he answered, she summed up everything she'd learned during the past half hour. "What do you hear from Stella and Brody?"

"I decided to have them pull away from the property, and they're parked on the highway, watching the place and waiting for me to get back to them. The distance made more sense under the circumstances. Folks out there think we're searching for Hannah, and I didn't want them to know they were under suspicion."

Relieved to hear it, Mattie wondered about next steps. "How should we approach this?"

"We've got enough to get a search warrant now. Come to the station, and we'll set up a plan."

★ ★ ★

Lightning flared toward the east while the entire Timber Creek police force drove to the compound. They moved quietly without flashing lights. No sirens. Just a string of four vehicles with headlights piercing the darkness as they went to meet Stella and Brody—Deputies Johnson and Garcia in their cruisers, Sheriff McCoy in his Jeep, and Mattie and Robo in their unit.

Mattie spoke to Robo as they drove, and he stood at the front of his cage as if listening to her every word. This time there would be no prep, no time when she changed out his equipment and revved him up to search.

This time she and her partner would be in full apprehension mode. They both wore Kevlar, and it would be their role to intimidate and control, not befriend and win over a community. They'd been granted a warrant to search the premises for evidence of child abuse and any items that were part of a criminal act or illegal in nature, and those included whips, knives, and bottles of xylazine.

Mattie pushed images from television footage of past law enforcement raids on compounds like this one out of her mind. Instead, she explained the action plan to her partner as they drove, partly to settle her nerves and partly because Robo was so smart that she remained convinced he understood everything she told him.

A half mile from the compound, Stella and Brody joined their lineup in his cruiser. As they turned onto the lane that led to the buildings, all but Sheriff McCoy in the lead car turned off their headlights. Garcia and Johnson stayed parked in the lane and took to the field on foot to hold the perimeter.

Lights were still on in the five trailer homes. Mattie would be watching those windows for anyone with a gun or weapon.

Once parked, they exited their vehicles swiftly. She popped open the door at the front of Robo's cage and he bailed through, leaping down to circle at her feet.

Without a word, the sheriff and Stella headed toward the Vaughn trailer, while she and Brody went to the Kings'. They had the right to detain everyone living on the property while they executed the search warrant. If others came from their homes, they would make them stay in the yard where they could be observed.

Although Hannah's statement about child marriage provided impetus for law enforcement to act, it was still important to get their hands on those marriage records. They would provide proof to support Hannah's statement.

With Robo off leash and at heel, Mattie remained in the yard to back up Brody as he mounted the wooden stairs and paused.

She heard McCoy's knock on the door of the next trailer, followed immediately by Brody's rap on the Kings' door. She became hypervigilant, her ears focused on every sound and her eyes on every movement at the trailer's windows.

The porch light flicked on, and a young woman whom Mattie had seen with King earlier came to the door. "Yes?"

"Sheriff's Department, ma'am," Brody said, his voice quiet and polite. "I need to speak with Isaac King, please."

A furrow of concern etched the woman's brow in the dim light. "Isaac isn't here."

Brody straightened. "Where is he?"

"I'm not sure."

Mattie felt her muscles tighten as if warding off a bullet to her back. She angled away from the door, scanning the darkness around her for Isaac, watching Robo out of the corner of her eye for any sign that he sensed immediate danger.

Nothing.

Stella appeared in the glow from the porch light, hustling Ruth around the corner of the Vaughn trailer and across the lit space, disappearing behind the Kings' trailer as she headed toward their vehicles. McCoy followed, escorting Solomon, who protested loudly. Mattie knew they would secure the two parents in different vehicles and come back to assist with the search warrant, but with Isaac still loose, their plan threatened to fall apart.

The woman's eyebrows raised in alarm as she peered beyond Brody to the edge of her yard. "What's happening? What's wrong with Solomon?"

Brody took a step forward. "I have a warrant to search the premises, ma'am. I need to come inside."

At the same time, Mattie used the radio transmitter at her shoulder to alert the others. "King is missing and unaccounted for."

Thunder rolled, and a cold breeze quickened. Mattie glanced upward to see clouds cover the moon—another storm moving in.

McCoy rounded the corner of the trailer and mounted the steps to stand beside Brody. "I'm Sheriff McCoy, ma'am. We need to come inside."

And with that, he pressed his way inside the trailer with Brody on his heels. Mattie waited. Stella came to the edge of the lit space and paused there, scanning the yard.

A man's voice came from a short distance. "What's going on here?"

Stella spoke, her voice firm. "We have a search warrant for the premises, Mr. Grayson. Stay right here, please, where I can see you. Are you carrying a weapon?"

"Of course not," Ephraim said, sounding offended. "Why would you search our property? Is this about Hannah?"

Mattie focused on the open trailer door, through which Brody had disappeared and she could still see McCoy's back. At the same time, she kept an eye on Stella, who appeared to be dealing with Ephraim on her own and was not yet in need of assistance.

Robo hovered at her left heel, restless and tense, a spring ready to launch. She steadied him with a touch and a quiet command. "Wait."

Brody came back outside, carrying an evidence bag, which he handed to Mattie. "King's socks. He's not here. She says he left about ten. The records are gone."

"Did he drive away?"

"She says he didn't. She doesn't know if he's in one of the other homes or the barn."

McCoy came through the door, speaking to the woman as he left. "You and the others stay inside. Don't leave the premises."

"Our babies are asleep. Why would we leave? We have nothing to hide," she said, her voice angry as she closed the door firmly behind him.

Other men were coming from the trailers, and McCoy went to help Stella with them, telling Mattie, "See if you can find King," as he hurried past.

She walked Robo a few steps away and placed the evidence bag on the ground. She squatted beside him and took his head in both hands, beginning the chatter with "Do you want to find a bad guy?" She didn't want Robo to have any doubts about the man they were hunting. She wanted him to know they were looking for an enemy, not a friend. She wanted him prepared for anything.

Robo pranced in place before nosing the bag. Mattie picked it up, held it for him to sniff, and then stood, leaving the bag on the ground.

She said his name to get his attention before she raised her arm and flung it out in a gesture that encompassed the area. "Search."

Robo sprang, ears pinned, his nose scouring the ground in fast sweeps. He darted back and forth, heading away from the porch.

Mattie imagined all those skin cells that Isaac had shed over the past days, clinging to the grass and dirt as he came and went going about his daily routine, leaving a trace of his scent everywhere. She knew that Robo was searching for the hottest scent, the freshest track that the man had laid down tonight. Her dog knew how to go after a bad guy. He knew what he was doing.

Robo quartered the track, pinging back and forth as he homed in on the scent. Nose to the ground, he left the light around the trailer and headed into the darkness. Mattie rushed after him, sticking close, and she felt Brody fall in behind.

Robo trotted toward the barn, and she ran to keep up. As soon as she realized he was heading toward the open double doors at the front, she pushed up next to him and grabbed the handle on the back of his Kevlar vest. She kept pace beside him until she pulled him to a stop outside the open door, taking shelter behind the barn wall while Brody settled in beside her.

Bam, bam, bam!

Three shots fired. Bullets whizzed through the doorway past her head. One struck the doorframe next to her, splintering the wood.

"Shit," Brody muttered.

Mattie struggled to hold on to Robo. Shots fired meant "take down" to him. Her eyes had adjusted to the dim light, and she could see Brody reaching for his service weapon. "Call him out."

"Timber Creek county sheriff," Brody shouted. "Isaac King, come outside. Hands up where we can see them."

Silence.

"Come outside the barn, or we'll send the dog," Mattie shouted, hoping she wouldn't have to.

No response.

Standard operating procedure would be to send Robo in alone, but Mattie couldn't do it that way. He was her partner, and they acted together. Her heart rate in overdrive, Mattie shouted to Robo, "Take him, take the bad guy!"

Robo disappeared into the black hole beyond the barn door, and Mattie leaped in behind him. She darted to the left just inside, flattening herself against the wall. She sensed that Brody had moved in and headed right.

Thunder boomed overhead, making it impossible to hear her dog. She strained to see, but her eyes could detect nothing in the inky void. Brody's flashlight flicked on for a few seconds, giving her time to scan the alleyway. Empty.

Brody switched the light off. Mattie edged along the concrete, listening for Robo between crashes of thunder. Lightning forked outside the barn ahead of her, and she realized there was an open doorway at the other end. If King had been inside this barn, Robo would have taken him down and she would be hearing the scuffle and his growl.

Her heart swelled with fear as she realized that her dog must have run through the barn to the other end. Now he was outside, alone and in full apprehension mode. He wouldn't hesitate to take a person down on his own. "They've gone out the back door," she shouted to Brody, pulling her own flashlight from her belt.

Guided by the beam, she sprinted down the alleyway. To avoid being a lit target, she turned off the flashlight when she hit the door's threshold.

Still no sound. Lightning filled the sky and a wave of rain splashed down, drenching her at once. Thunder cracked. Relying on the small amount of light coming from the electrical storm, she scanned the grassy field.

And then she heard it. A yelp, followed by her dog's furious growl. She knew what that sound meant. Robo always glided toward his target like a silent missile, but once he hit, he would bite and hold on to the fugitive, his ferocious throaty snarl rumbling from his chest.

Robo's growl filtered through the driving rain, giving her an auditory beacon to home in on.

She switched her flashlight back on as she heard Isaac King yell. Running as fast as she could, she bolted into the field, the beam lighting her way.

Robo's growl intensified, and King screamed with pain. Mattie swept her flashlight's beam and spotted them, both down on the ground fifty feet away. Robo had King by his right arm and was tugging hard, trying to stretch the man out on the ground.

Her beam glittered off a silver blade that King gripped in his other hand, slashing down at Robo.

Running full tilt, Mattie jumped onto King's back, dropping her flashlight and landing with a thud. His breath whooshed out as she struggled blindly to reach his left hand. His fingers were empty.

He dropped the knife, her mind screamed at her. *Where is it? Keep him away from it.*

Robo still clung to the man's right arm. Mattie grabbed King's left wrist while she shoved his hand down into a hard flex, immobilizing it. Still he struggled to get free.

Brody ran up, his flashlight beam bouncing across the ground and then over them. "Give it up, King," he shouted. "You're way outnumbered!"

Mattie applied more pressure to the man's thumb, bending it down toward his forearm as she shouted into his face. "Stay still! Give up and I'll call off the dog!"

King groaned and quit moving. Mattie shouted at Brody to find the knife. His light glanced off the seven-inch blade of a hunting knife, and he kicked it away from King's reach while pulling his cuffs from his belt.

Brody snapped a cuff on King's left wrist while Mattie told Robo to let go of his right. Robo backed off a step, crouching in guard position, his teeth bared.

Mattie grabbed King's right wrist—slippery with rain and blood—and gave him a few inches of space. "Turn over to your stomach," she said, pushing him into place so that Brody could cuff the man behind his back and pat him down for other weapons.

Only then did she notice that King's clothing was saturated with the red color of fresh blood. Alarm bells went off as she realized that Robo must have torn up the man's arm far more than usual. Her dog had been taught to bite and hold when apprehending a fugitive to lessen the skin damage.

Does King need first aid? Was an artery torn? She pushed up King's right sleeve. "Shine the light here on his arm, Brody."

Deep indentations marked King's forearm, but she found only one puncture wound, with a small trickle of blood. It took a split second for her to remember Robo's yelp. Cold terror washed through her as she staggered up from kneeling beside King.

"Give me the light," she said, grabbing Brody's flashlight from his hand and striding over to Robo. She knew before she got to him that he was hurt. Instead of being up on his toes in guard position, Robo remained crouched on the ground. She murmured soothing sounds as she knelt beside him in the pouring rain.

His fur was wet and matted, his Kevlar vest still in place, protecting his chest. She ran the light over his head, figuring that would be where the knife had struck. In the beam, his eyes were narrow, his brow puckered, his pain evident. Stroking the top of his head with one hand, she continued to move the flashlight down to his neck to search for bleeding.

A tear at the top of the Kevlar vest tipped her off. The vest hadn't been penetrated; it looked more like a glancing blow. But underneath the vest at the base of her dog's neck, the knife had done its damage. Bright-red blood oozed from a gaping wound.

"He's been cut, Brody," she said, fear gripping her throat. "He's bleeding. Bad."

Kneeling in the bloody grass with rain pelting her shoulders, Mattie leaned over Robo, trying to shelter him while she struggled to get to her first-aid kit inside a pouch on her utility belt. Her bloody fingers slipped against the leather as she fumbled with the straps.

Brody's radio transmitter crackled to life. "Priority air. K-9 down. One in custody. Need assist fifty yards east of barn."

Lights flared on the east side of the barn as two others ran toward them. After seconds that seemed like hours, Mattie managed to open her kit and extract gauze pads. She pressed them against the wound, pinching the gaping edges shut and applying pressure to try to stop the bleeding. Robo whimpered and sank lower onto the ground. "We've got to get him to Cole, Brody."

"We will." Sheriff McCoy and Garcia ran up, and Brody used a few curt words to report their situation before barking orders. "Garcia, take charge of the prisoner, secure that knife that's over there on the ground. Find the gun—he must've dropped it when Robo hit him. Sheriff, call Dr. Walker. Mattie, keep up the pressure while I carry him."

Brody squatted and scooped up Robo, clasping him at his chest and haunches. With a groan, he lifted the one-hundred-pound dog while Mattie supported him from below and maintained pressure on the wound. Together they set off toward the barn and the K-9 unit.

Mattie prayed that they could get her partner to Cole's clinic in time.

TWENTY-NINE

Cole had taken the kids home, telling them to go to bed upstairs in Angie's room while he and Bruno stood guard on the main level. He wasn't afraid of Isaac King or the others, and he knew that Bruno would sound off if anyone tried to break in.

When McCoy called, Cole had been shocked to learn that Robo was injured and on his way to the clinic. The news that Mattie remained unhurt and that Isaac King was in custody steadied him, letting him think and move quickly.

McCoy had said there'd been serious blood loss, so Cole didn't waste any time. He called Tess at her home, woke her up, and asked her to come to assist. Taking the stairs two at a time, he went to awaken Mrs. Gibbs. With King under arrest, he no longer feared for the safety of the kids, but he wanted her to be awake and alert just in case anyone came to the house.

Assured that Mrs. Gibbs had things under control, he started to head for the garage, but he paused when he spied Bruno waiting at the bottom of the stairs. Cole feared he might need a blood donor and decided the big dog should be close at hand.

McCoy had said Robo was in bad shape, so sedatives would need to be avoided. Tess would be busy assisting him, which meant he needed another person to handle Bruno.

Torn, he debated for a split second. On one hand, he wouldn't want Angie to have to suffer watching Robo die if things headed south, but on the other, his daughter would be able to keep Bruno calm.

He knocked softly on her bedroom door, making Sassy bark from inside while Hannah told her to be quiet. Within seconds, the door opened and Angie peered through. "Have you heard from Mattie?"

She was still awake and fully dressed, as were the other girls. "I need help at the clinic for an emergency. We've got to leave right now. Can you come?"

Her eyes widened. "Sure. Let me grab some shoes."

"Do you need me too, Dr. Walker?" Riley said, getting up from where she'd been sitting.

"No, you girls stay here and take care of Sassy. Riley, Mrs. Gibbs is awake if you have any concerns. Keep the outside doors locked."

"Have you heard from Mattie about my parents?" Hannah said, coming to the door.

Cole had no information to share, and he needed to hurry. "I don't know anything, Hannah. You girls stay here and try to get some rest if you can."

Angie and Bruno followed Cole to the garage. After they all climbed into the truck, he shared more details. "I really need your help with this one. Robo's been hurt, and he's in bad shape."

"Oh no! Dad, is Mattie okay?"

"She isn't hurt, but I doubt if she's okay, if you know what I mean. Robo is everything to her."

"I know."

Cole drove the short distance to the clinic. The cloudburst from earlier had slowed to a drizzle. Bruno hopped out of the truck, trailing after Cole as he hurried through the rain to unlock the front door. "Angie, if you'll get a leash for Bruno and keep him close and calm, that would be great. We might need him as a blood donor."

Angie grabbed one of the leashes they kept hanging near the door in the lobby and called Bruno over to her. After she snapped it onto his collar, he leaned against her for petting.

Cole flipped on the yard light that lit the front doorstep and then made his way through the clinic to the treatment room, turning on overheads as he went. By the time Tess arrived a few minutes later, he had his supplies lined up on the counter.

Tess headed over to their rack of lab coats. "Headlights coming down the lane. They're here."

Cole hurried outside, meeting the K-9 unit as it pulled up to park. Brody hopped out of the driver's seat and ran for the back while Cole followed. As Brody opened the hatch, interior lights flicked on and revealed Mattie holding her dog. She was drenched, her dark hair framing her pale face in wet tendrils, blood smeared across her cheek where she'd probably swiped at tears that were still evident. She was applying pressure to blood-soaked gauze on the wound.

A quick assessment of Robo told Cole what he needed to know. Gums—blanched white. Demeanor—conscious but shut down in survival mode. Heart rate—rapid and thready. Breathing—rapid and shallow. Time was of the essence.

He squeezed Mattie's upper arm in a gesture of support and tried to project confidence. "Has Robo ever had a blood transfusion?"

"Not that I know of. No, I'm sure he hasn't. They would've told me." She sounded terrified but steady.

Mattie will keep it together, he thought. *It's in her nature.* "We're going to have to give him some blood, and we don't have time for blood typing. His first transfusion shouldn't be a problem, and we really don't have a choice."

"Do whatever you need to, Cole." Her breath caught.

He turned to Brody. "Let's get him inside."

Brody stepped forward. "I can carry him."

"Let me take over with the wound, Mattie," Cole said, ripping open a packet of fresh, sterile gauze. "You've done a great job."

Brody hoisted Robo out of the back of the vehicle, and with Cole applying pressure to the wound, they walked in tandem toward the clinic while Tess held open the door. Cole directed Brody to the surgical table in the treatment room, where they laid Robo on his side. Mattie came around to hold him, smoothing the wet fur on his head.

First, Cole needed to staunch the blood flow. He removed the gauze, dabbing at the blood as it refilled the wound. He could see several of the wormlike vessels that had been severed.

Grabbing hemostats from a nearby tray, he used gauze to soak up enough blood to locate and clip off the bleeders.

"Tess, let's insert an IV." Cole looked into Mattie's dark, frightened eyes. She would probably do better if she had a task. Being careful not to dislodge the hemostats, he placed fresh gauze in the wound. "Take over the pressure again here."

He showed Mattie how much pressure he wanted her to apply. Tess turned on the razor, which whirred as she shaved a patch on Robo's foreleg. Cole grabbed the IV supplies from the kit he'd opened earlier.

"Hold the leg," he told Tess. But when she grasped the fore-leg to occlude the vein, it didn't plump like it should. Robo's veins were starting to collapse.

Cole clasped the leg himself, exerting maximum pressure while probing with the needle to try to enter the vein. He felt a wave of relief when blood dripped from the needle's end. He snatched a pipette and took a sample, handing it to Tess. "Run a packed cell volume on this."

Tess set up the test, and the noise from the centrifuge filled the quiet room while Cole concentrated on securing the IV catheter in Robo's vein. When finished, he attached a bag of saline fluid to the tubing before hanging it from an IV pole.

The PCV test took about sixty seconds to complete, and the news was grim. Red blood cells per volume were below ten percent. He needed to start the transfusion now.

He looked up to find Angie, her face pale, squatting against the wall, holding Bruno and stroking his delicately shaped ears. She was doing a fine job, because the usually rambunctious Doberman was standing stock-still, watching his fallen buddy.

Cole grabbed a strappy red nylon muzzle and slipped it onto Bruno before the big guy knew what was happening. Cole murmured soothing sounds, stroking Bruno's head and patting his chest.

"Let's put him here on the treatment table," he said to Angie, and they both lifted the dog up to the table. He went without protest while Angie took over the petting. Cole snatched up the contents of the other IV kit and found a full, plump vein underneath the short hair on Bruno's foreleg.

Tess grasped the leg to stabilize it. Bruno flinched when Cole inserted the needle, but Tess held him steady, and it took mere seconds to establish the IV. Healthy, red blood flowed through the tubing and into the collection bag that Cole attached.

"Great job, Angie," he murmured to his daughter, relieved that he'd made the right decision to ask for her help. "Tess, keep an eye on Bruno while I tie off some bleeders."

"Give me a job too, Doc," Brody said.

"Stand by, Ken. I might need to." Cole hurried back to Robo.

The saline solution was building some volume in Robo's veins, which would help carry the blood after they collected it. The gauze beneath Mattie's hand had become saturated with blood.

"I can't sedate him," he said to Mattie. "We'll use a local."

He injected lidocaine to numb the area around the gash. Robo's limbs trembled, but he'd retreated into that space where wounded animals go to suffer. He didn't even flinch as Cole pricked his skin numerous times.

He used internal suture to tie the clipped vessels one by one, removing the hemostats as he finished.

"We've got enough blood," Tess said from across the room.

"All right." Cole pressed the edges of skin together with gauze and looked at Mattie, reaching for her hand to place on top. "Light pressure now, here."

At Bruno's side, Cole stroked the Doberman's head, telling him what a good boy he was as he closed off the IV flow valve and disconnected the bag of life-giving blood. Bruno looked a little sad about the whole situation, but he was bearing up while Angie stroked him.

"You're going to be Robo's blood brother now," Cole told him, before turning to Tess. "Let's leave the IV intact in case we need it."

Cole hung the bag of blood on the pole, attached it to the IV tubing, and started the flow that he hoped would save Robo's life.

"This should give him what he needs," he said, trying to reassure Mattie.

Her tears had stopped, and the look she gave Cole was so full of trust that it set him on his heels for a moment. He considered the pressure he was under when taking care of this dog. Not only did he love this valuable animal, but he loved his handler as well. *How could I ever forgive myself if I made a mistake?*

He pushed the thought aside, unwilling to be distracted by it. "Let me take a look again," he said, pressing her hand as he took over.

When he lifted the gauze square, the wound seeped slowly, but he felt certain he'd found and tied off the main vessels. He worked with needle and suture to repair the muscle layer, dabbing at the small amount of blood and feeling satisfied that he'd staunched the major flow. He asked Tess to get him the right suture for closing the skin.

By the time he finished placing the external stitches, enough of the new blood had dripped into Robo's circulatory system that his gums were starting to show a light shade of pink.

Cole prayed the procedure would be successful, but they weren't out of the woods yet.

"Mattie," he said quietly. "Everything looks positive so far, but he could still have a reaction to the transfusion. I'll need to watch him here at the clinic tonight."

"I'll stay with him." She ran her hand down Robo's side in long, firm strokes.

"Do you think you'll need my help, Doc?" Brody asked.

"No, we've got this under control. Thanks."

Brody was pulling his cell phone from his pocket as he spoke to Mattie. "Then I'll have Garcia come give me a ride to the station and leave your unit here for when you need it. Call if you need me to come back."

"Thanks for everything, Brody," she told him, tears brimming in her eyes.

Brody shrugged, muttering, "He's one of us," as he stepped away to make his call.

Cole checked in on Angie. She'd succeeded in keeping Bruno on the table, calm and at ease while he lay there and watched the flurry of activity around Robo. "Well done, Angel. I'll take out his IV, and you two can go home."

"I'll stay and help you clean up." Her eyes were filled with nothing but respect, giving Cole hope that they'd found new ground to meet on. "Maybe I should make some hot cocoa for you and Mattie while you wait."

Tess was busy cleaning, but she glanced up at Cole and gave him a quick smile. He figured she knew how much Angie's turnaround meant to him.

Murmuring a thank-you to Angie, Mattie glanced down at her hands and clothing, a stunned look appearing on her face as if she was only then becoming aware of the bloodstains.

"I'll lay out a pair of my scrubs that should fit you," Tess said to Mattie. "You can clean up in the utility room."

Cole headed for the kennels in back to get a dog cushion for Robo. While he was at it, he'd bring a few for them to sit on too. It was going to be a long night.

★ ★ ★

Mattie sat on a thick dog cushion, her back against the wall and Robo stretched out beside her. Cole had disconnected the bags of blood and fluid that had dripped into her dog's veins, though he'd left the capped IV in place. Robo seemed to be asleep and breathing in a normal rhythm. Cole had covered him with a blanket, and he'd quit trembling. She rested her hand on his chest, relishing the slow, steady thump of his heart.

Cole sat on her other side, snoring lightly as he rested his head back against the wall. The others had gone home and all was quiet, but Mattie couldn't sleep. She couldn't shut down the adrenaline surge from the events of the evening, and she wondered how Stella's interrogation was going at the station.

A knock resounded from the outside door, and Cole startled awake. "I'll see who it is," he murmured, getting up from the cushion beside her.

Within seconds, he ushered Stella into the room.

"How's the champ?" Stella spoke quietly, as if not wanting to disturb the sleeping dog.

"He's doing well." Cole pulled up the rolling stool to offer Stella a seat. "I think it's safe to say he's going to be fine. Should be healed up within a few weeks."

"I thought you'd want an update," Stella said as she sat on the stool.

"Thanks for coming by," Mattie said. "I was wondering how things were going."

Stella nodded. "I figured you'd still be awake. Isaac King clammed up and won't say a word, asked for a lawyer. But Solomon Vaughn has been singing like Frank Sinatra. He and King have both been charged with two counts of first-degree murder."

Mattie was stunned. "Solomon confessed to killing both Luke and Tracy Lee?"

"That's right." Stella looked like she couldn't have been more pleased.

"So what did he say?"

"Killing Luke Ferguson and Tracy Lee Brown was King's idea."

"I guess that isn't a surprise," Cole said.

"True, but Solomon did admit to his part in the murder. They sedated Luke with the xylazine and took him to Hanging Falls. By the time he came out of it, they forced him to climb to the area above the falls, tortured him with the whip and the letter carving on his chest, and then killed him with another dose of the drug. They buried him up there."

"And their motive was Hannah?"

"It was more than that. Evidently Luke broke the laws of their society when he tried to tempt Hannah away from the group. That's what he had to pay for—blood retribution, according to Solomon. Supposedly men have free will to stay or not, but women don't, especially if they're destined to become the leader's child bride."

"Good grief," Cole muttered, his disgust evident.

Nodding, Stella went on. "Tracy Lee was in the wrong place at the wrong time. They knew someone had seen them taking Luke up to Hanging Falls, but it took a while to find out who it was and where he lived. That's why we can charge them with premeditated murder for him too. They literally hunted him down to kill him. Sedated him with the xylazine and hanged him from a tree."

Anger fueled by guilt shot through Mattie. "I wish Tracy Lee had told us what he knew. Things could have been different."

"I know, it's frustrating," Stella said. "My guess is that Tracy Lee didn't realize they'd seen him."

"Don't tell me *we* led them to Tracy Lee's campsite."

"They'd ridden up there trying to find him before. It's possible they found his campsite while we had him in jail."

Mattie felt defeated. It would take some time to work through her feelings about this one. "What will Solomon get for his confession?"

"He says he was coerced and wants leniency, but I guess that will be up to the prosecutor. I think he's as manipulative, secretive, and dangerous as King, so I've put in my two cents to go as hard on him as they can."

Mattie hoped he would get enough years to last his lifetime. After all, this was two counts of first-degree murder they were talking about. And she never wanted him free to threaten Hannah again.

"Were any of the other men involved?"

"Solomon says not, but they were willing to give a false alibi for those two the day they went after Tracy Lee. We'll probably file charges against several of the others for interfering with a police investigation." Stella stood up from her chair. "I need to get back to the station. We brought in the entire community and are still in the process of interrogating them. Jail's full to the brim. Ephraim and Abel Grayson seem the most willing to cooperate. They've been unhappy with King's leadership for some time now. Brody and Garcia are still at the property, searching for evidence to build a solid case. They haven't been able to find the records yet."

"I should be out there helping them," Mattie said.

Stella's reply was quick and firm. "Your job is to keep our K-9 quiet so he can heal. We can handle the rest of it. We've gathered up riding boots from both men's closets that should match the prints at Tracy Lee's crime scene, and we've sent a half dozen whips of various sizes to the lab. Surely one of them will have Luke's DNA on it. The case looks good, Mattie. We'll be able to put these two scumbags away, even if Solomon recants his confession."

Mattie stroked Robo softly on his side. "That's good."

Stella looked at Cole. "So you're keeping Hannah overnight?"

"She's welcome to stay as long as she needs to."

"We'll work that out with Child Protective Services. We plan to hold the men while we sort this out, but unless we find evidence of complicity, I think we'll release the women and children as soon as we can. It's different with Ruth, though. She might be charged with child abuse or conspiracy to commit child abuse. We'll know soon."

"Was she a child bride herself?" Mattie asked.

Stella nodded, her eyes strained at the corners, the only sign of her inner turmoil.

"For what it's worth," Mattie said, "I think she genuinely cares for her kids, and from what Hannah told me, Ruth wasn't a willing participant."

Cole spoke up. "From my observation, I agree with that."

"I'll pass it on to the prosecutor," Stella said, before saying good-bye.

After Stella left, Cole switched off the overhead light. A plug-in nightlight filled the room with a gentle, comforting glow. He sighed as he settled back against the wall. "We might as well try to get some sleep. It'll be morning before we know it."

"I guess you're right." But Mattie's feelings about this case were in such upheaval, she doubted if she could sleep. Guilt about Tracy Lee, worry about the women and kids, and concern that they still needed to lock in all the evidence made her gut churn.

Exhaustion overcame her, and eventually she dozed, one hand on Robo, the other within Cole's. When a text pinged her phone, she awakened suddenly to rose-colored light streaming through the window. She moved to check the text, making

Cole groan and peer at her with sleepy eyes. Robo raised his head and thumped his tail on the floor, a very good sign.

The text was from Julia. It said, *Come when you can. Abuela has something to tell us that must be very important. She says she's getting old, and she knows a secret she doesn't want to take to her grave.*

THIRTY

Two days later, Wednesday

The briefing room felt cold and empty without Robo. Even though he'd given her sad eyes, Mattie had left him at home to spend the morning on one of his many dog cushions. Cole had recommended rest with no jumping in and out of the unit for two weeks while his wound healed, so Sheriff McCoy had officially placed him on sick leave.

Mattie's sister and grandmother had returned to California, and Mattie planned to take some time off while the Timber Creek K-9 unit was out of commission. Tomorrow she would leave Robo with Cole and fly to San Diego to meet with Detective Hauck and take care of some family business. But today, she wanted to tie up some loose ends.

Though officially on vacation, Mattie sat at the table with the rest of the team, wrapping up details in the cases of Luke Ferguson and Tracy Lee Brown.

Sheriff McCoy leaned back in his chair, shaking his head in frustration. "I managed to get a lead on Tracy Lee's parents, and his father finally returned my calls early this morning. I'm sorry to say, they refuse to come forward to claim Tracy Lee's remains. He'll be buried here in the Timber Creek cemetery, and the county will assume the cost."

The fact that no one in this victim's family cared enough to claim him saddened Mattie and did nothing to assuage her guilt. "I'll pay for his funeral service," she murmured.

McCoy responded quickly. "That won't be necessary. I already have preauthorization for cremation and burial. If you want, we'll wait until you return and hold a private service at graveside when his ashes are interred."

Mattie met the sheriff's gaze. "I'd like that. Thank you."

Brody cleared his throat. "I'll be there too."

"We all will," Stella said. "But you two need to quit beating yourselves up over this. There was no indication Tracy Lee needed protective custody, and we had no reason to hold him. We made decisions based on the information we knew at the time."

"Agreed," McCoy said. "Legal protocol dictated your actions, and you performed your duties responsibly."

In light of Tracy Lee's lack of family support, Mattie felt even more grateful that she'd connected with her own. She had already bonded with her sister and grandmother to the point that they could share their deepest secrets.

"Go ahead and sum up the investigation, Detective," McCoy said. "What's the current status?"

Stella glanced around the table. "Solomon Vaughn confessed that they obtained xylazine from Quinn Randolph, who named his supplier as Parker Tate. We've pressed charges against both Randolph and Tate for violations of the pharmaceutical act. They've lawyered up, but if this goes to court, the Perry brothers will testify that Randolph had the drug in his possession and used it on their horse."

Mattie doubted if it would go that far. She suspected the two would eventually pay their fines and move on, albeit with a drug-related felony on their records.

Stella continued. "Ephraim Grayson helped search for the Brothers of Salvation's records. He suggested we sort through a pile of hay that seemed out of place in the barn, and we found a leather-bound Bible containing recorded unions. The records proved that only Solomon Vaughn and Isaac King had formed spiritual unions with underage girls in the past. We've added child abuse and conspiracy to commit child abuse to both their charges."

Combine those charges with two counts of murder one, and both should be put away for life, Mattie thought.

"Extensive interviews with the women revealed that no one was being held in the group against their will, and all of them want to keep their families intact," Stella said. "There are no marriage licenses involved. These unions were formed according to the rituals of their religion, so no state or federal laws have been broken. We found no current abuse of the social services or legal systems, and everyone has returned to their homes. Except, of course, for Vaughn and King."

"I heard from Cole that he's taking Hannah out to visit her mother later this morning," Mattie said.

"She'll be allowed supervised visits until it's determined safe for her and the other teenage girls," Stella said.

"How will that be determined?"

"Child Protective Services is working through that. Ephraim has stepped up as new leader for the time being. Evidently he's been on the fence for quite some time about the direction Isaac King and Solomon had taken. Abel Grayson is adamantly opposed and has become very vocal about it with authorities and other group members. I expect there will be a falling-out soon and this particular branch of the Brothers of Salvation will disperse. Until then, Ruth is going to have to prove that she has the best interests of her children at heart if she's going to be allowed to keep them."

Despite Ruth's prior failure to protect Hannah, Mattie hoped it wouldn't come down to her losing custody. She planned to stay involved until she felt satisfied that Ruth and her fellow sister wives could be trusted with the safety of their daughters. And Cole would watch over Hannah until Mattie returned from taking care of business in California.

"I'm going out there with Cole later today," Mattie said. "I'll report back afterward."

Stella nodded. "There will be a social worker present too. Let me know what you think."

★ ★ ★

Mattie left her unit at Cole's house and rode with him and the kids in his truck. She turned in her seat to give Hannah a smile of encouragement as she studied her face.

Sharing the back seat with Angie, Hannah looked pale but composed. She was dressed in loose jeans and a tee that she'd evidently borrowed from Angie. Mattie felt grateful that the kids were mature enough to realize that Hannah's clothing choices should be conservative for this visit, and she'd chosen not to flaunt her newly found independence by dressing radically.

Hannah looked nervous as she attempted to return Mattie's smile.

"How are you doing, Hannah? Do you feel ready to see your mother?" Mattie asked.

"I talked to her on the phone, so it'll be okay." Hannah glanced at Angie before resuming eye contact with Mattie. "She might be mad that I decided to dress this way, but I might as well show her I meant what I said when I told her I'm done with all that."

"It could take her a little while to get used to it. But do you think she'll adjust?"

Hannah raised crossed fingers. "I hope so. I'm going to tell her that I want to go to regular high school too. I'm going to get everything out in the open."

Angie joined in hesitantly. "I told Hannah she might as well speak up for what she wants."

"I think that's a fine plan." Mattie smiled at both girls, trying to put them at ease. "You're old enough to speak up. Just do it respectfully and listen to what your mother has to say."

During the pause in the conversation, Hannah broke eye contact with Mattie and gazed out the window, a troubled frown on her face. "At first I was mad at Mother for being willing to sacrifice me for the cause." She sighed. "But now I guess I just feel sorry for her. Her parents belonged to the Brothers of Salvation too, and it's all she's ever known."

"That's a very grown-up conclusion you've drawn, Hannah," Cole said. "I'm proud of you."

Hannah shrugged, and though she continued to gaze out the window, her face relaxed somewhat.

"Let us know how we can help. You don't have to hold in your feelings around us," Mattie said, before facing forward, leaving the girl to her thoughts as she prepared for what might be a difficult reunion.

Mattie exchanged glances with Cole as he slowed to turn into the property. She steeled herself for facing feelings that might surface this first time back since Robo had almost been killed. Whatever might arise, she would deal with it and force herself to remain neutral. These remaining people had been cleared of wrongdoing, and it wasn't her place to judge them.

As Cole drove up to park beside the trailers, a social worker whom Mattie recognized stepped out of her car to meet them.

"There's Mrs. Elliott," Hannah murmured as she opened her door. "Are you guys coming inside with me?"

Mattie returned the social worker's wave. "I think it's best if we wait for you out here," she told Hannah. "Unless you really want one of us to join you."

"No," Hannah said, squaring her shoulders. "I'll be all right."

Angie reached out and squeezed Hannah's hand before she exited the car. When the door closed behind her, Angie heaved an audible sigh. "I hope everything will be okay."

Cole glanced at Mattie as he turned to face his daughter. "We'll be here for Hannah no matter what, but I think her mother is a good person at heart. I think this will work itself out."

"Me too," Mattie said quietly, before noticing a man step out of the barn. She gestured in his direction with her head. "Cole, there's Ephraim."

"I'll go talk to him and check that lame horse," Cole said as he exited the truck.

But Ephraim paused to speak to Cole only briefly before approaching Mattie's side of the truck, and Cole came along with him. Since the engine had been turned off, Mattie couldn't power down her window, so she opened her door to speak with him.

Ephraim's expression was grave. "I want to apologize to you specifically for what happened out here the other night. Our church is not about violence, and I'm sorry that Isaac endangered you and your dog."

Mattie acknowledged his apology with a nod. "I'll be honest with you, Mr. Grayson. My primary concern is for the women and children here. I want to be certain that no one is being forced into any relationships against their will and that these children are all safe."

He winced as if her words caused him pain. "That's my focus too. Children are precious to the Brothers of Salvation, and women should be honored. Solomon and Isaac lost their way."

She hoped he was speaking the truth, but she planned to do more than hope. As long as this brotherhood remained in Timber Creek County, her department would be keeping a close watch. "I hope you can take your folks in a better direction."

He lowered his gaze. "We've lost heart. Our trust has been broken. Once things get settled here, we'll probably split up."

Mattie refrained from voicing an opinion. Ephraim was cooperating with law enforcement now, but he'd been willing to ignore his better judgment before and follow two men who were killers. The prosecutor seemed inclined to refrain from pressing charges against him in exchange for his cooperation, but Mattie remained unable to accept him as fully law-abiding. She would continue her plan to wait and watch.

Cole ended the conversation by suggesting they go out to check the horse, and Mattie climbed back inside the truck to wait with Angie. Shortly after Cole returned from the barn, Hannah came around the corner of the first trailer, followed by Ruth and the social worker.

Ruth appeared haggard, her eyes reddened and swollen from crying, and dark circles beneath them suggested sleepless nights. She snuggled a Siamese kitten against her chest, its brilliant blue eyes standing out against its dark-chocolate mask.

"That's the kitten that fell asleep in my lap," Angie murmured as she scooted forward in the back seat.

Ruth approached Cole's side of the vehicle, and he opened his door to step out and greet her. With the door open, it was easy for Mattie to hear their conversation.

"I'm forever in your debt for taking care of Hannah," Ruth said, her voice choked with tears. "I want Angie to have this kitten as a very small token of my appreciation for helping my daughter when I wasn't able to."

Mattie heard Angie gasp.

"You owe us nothing," Cole said. "We're happy to take care of Hannah as long as she needs us. Besides, I thought you had this litter sold."

"I have one customer who wants to wait for the next one." She held the kitten out toward Cole, the small bundle of tawny fluff squirming as it mewed. "Please take her. She's been weaned and litter-box trained."

Cole took the kitten and held her close, where she settled down, supported by his large hands. Mattie could feel the anxiety coming from Angie as she watched the exchange silently. The girl really wanted this kitten, and Mattie hoped Cole would decide in favor of keeping it.

"But this is your livelihood, Ruth—now more than ever. We can't accept her as a gift," Cole was saying.

Angie leaned forward between the two bucket seats. "I'll pay, Dad. I have enough money saved up."

Cole glanced at his daughter, and Mattie could tell by the look on his face that he was going to give in. Her heart filled with joy. With Belle so attached to Sophie and Bruno to Cole, Angie needed a pet for herself.

"It's my gift to Angie," Ruth said, her lips slightly upturned in a tremulous smile. "It would make me happy for her to have it."

Angie projected her voice for Ruth to hear. "I'll pay for the kitten, Mrs. Vaughn. I'll bring the money out here soon."

"Well, I'll leave that up to the two of you," Cole said, passing the kitten to Angie, who slid back in her seat to cuddle and soothe the tiny animal. "Are you going back home with us, Hannah?"

The social worker spoke up. "For now. I hope it will only be for a few more days."

Mattie assumed the visit had gone well, and this exchange with the Walkers made her think that Ruth regretted not protecting her child when she should have. Mattie hoped the two could be reunited, because deep in her heart, she couldn't help comparing her own past with Hannah's current experience.

She wanted a happier ending for this girl than the one she'd suffered during her childhood.

THIRTY-ONE

Several days later
A small village in Mexico

The heat was oppressive. Sweat trickled down Mattie's back as she strolled down a boardwalk that edged the packed-dirt street. People cluttered the walkways. A small boy filled empty plastic bottles with water from a spigot on the side of a building—the kind of bottles she'd seen another kid hawking as purified water a few blocks down the street.

She entered a *panadería* to buy some bread. A bell jingled as the door swung open, and she scanned the half-empty glass cases on the other side of the room. She was wearing ragged cutoff jeans and a black tee, trying to blend in—just another villager shopping at the local bakery.

She'd been cautious. No one had followed her when she drove an old beater car across the border. No one had followed her since she'd arrived. No one seemed to even notice her.

The clerk came through a doorway from what must have been the kitchen, the delicious scent of baking bread wafting along with her. Mattie greeted her in Spanish, complimenting the contents of the lady's display before buying a loaf of warm bread and a half dozen sugar cookies.

The clerk seemed bored and uninterested as she took Mattie's pesos and made change. Mattie hoped she'd pulled it off—just another local buying food.

After she left the store, she paused outside and scanned the street. A handful of cars parked at the edge, all of them old like hers. She moseyed down the sidewalk to the end of the building and entered the alley. Pausing a few seconds, she scanned the crates, boxes, and trash bins before walking down the alley to the next street. She encountered no one and no one followed.

Nondescript adobe houses lined both sides of this dirt road—very small buildings with yards that were bare or planted with a few succulents. Chickens scratched and pecked as she went past, making the throaty sound hens made, searching for food on a hot summer day.

At the end of the block, she found the house she was searching for, and her heart leaped to her throat when she spotted a woman out front. The woman wore a gauzy, russet skirt that flowed to below her knees, its hem waving in the slight breeze, and a loose tan peasant blouse made of thin fabric meant for the hot climate. A large bun was pinned at her nape, and strands of gray were noticeable within the tight, shiny, black hair scraped back on her head. She carried a bowl on her hip and was throwing potato peelings to hens while they flocked around her.

As Mattie approached, the woman glanced up and froze. She recovered quickly and greeted Mattie in Spanish. "Hello, my friend. It's good to see you. You must be thirsty on this hot day. Please come inside for a nice, cold drink."

Mattie would have recognized her mother anywhere. She swallowed the lump in her throat and responded in kind as she held out the bag she carried. "*Gracias*. I've brought some bread and cookies from the bakery."

Ramona turned and sauntered down the side of the brown adobe house, tossing the last scraps of food as she went while Mattie followed. If any neighbors happened to be observing, they were two friends greeting each other and about to enjoy some baked goods with a refreshing drink. But Mattie's gut fluttered with a swarm of butterflies.

They entered the side door that led directly into the kitchen. As soon as Mattie stepped inside the small space—tidy and furnished very much like Mama T's with a wood-burning stove and a small refrigerator—Ramona shut the door behind her.

Ramona's eyes widened with wonder. "Julia?"

"I'm Mattie."

Her mother's face filled with shock, and tears sprang from her eyes as she pulled Mattie into her embrace. "Oh, my baby girl."

For the second time in only a few weeks, Mattie sobbed in the arms of someone she'd longed to see. The pain was exquisite, and her mind seethed with unanswered questions. She set those aside and focused solely on her mother: the touch of her skin, the scent of her hair, and the heat from her embrace in the small, warm room.

Time became meaningless as they clung together and cried for what seemed like seconds or maybe hours but was probably only minutes. When they pulled apart, Mattie felt wet from tears and sweat, and she wiped her cheeks and forehead with her hands.

Ramona stepped over to the counter, opened a drawer, and handed Mattie a clean towel. "Use this. I'll get you a cold drink." She grabbed a towel for herself and wiped the back of her neck as she reached into an upper cabinet for glasses.

Ramona spoke quietly in accented English, her voice low and melodic as she took ice trays from the top of the refrigerator and carried them to the sink. "I thought I'd never see you again. I thought I'd never see any of my children again."

Fresh tears streamed down Mattie's cheeks as she thought of Willie. She would have to be the bearer of bad news here, but she wanted some time before she broke her mother's heart. Together they fixed glasses of ice and twisted the sealed caps on bottled water, and then Mattie followed Ramona into a tiny living room set up with a sofa, two chairs, and a small television. Mattie sat on the sofa while Ramona went over to turn on an oscillating fan before settling in beside her.

She took Mattie's hand. "Tell me how you got here."

Mattie told her about meeting Yolanda and Julia in Timber Creek and how Yolanda had told her where to find her. "Abuela said we'd all been apart too long, and she needed to know you were safe before she died. She said I could be trusted since I was a police officer."

This prompted questions from Ramona about her mother's health, and Mattie assured her that this death Yolanda anticipated was not imminent. Then Ramona asked what Mattie's life was like in Timber Creek, followed by what her life had been like growing up. Mattie answered her mother's questions as succinctly as possible while she struggled with impatience, wanting to move on to her own.

After all, how could she explain a lifetime of not knowing anything about her family, her feelings of abandonment over the years, and the horror of discovering her past the hard way?

Ramona used her towel to wipe her tears. "What about Julia and Willie?"

Mattie's heart sank, and she hoped to buy time before having to talk about Willie. "Julia's a housewife and mom of two boys. She wanted to come, but I stood a better chance of travelling unnoticed if I came by myself." Although she left the words unsaid, she'd also feared this visit might be too dangerous to bring her sister. "I have a picture she sent to you," she said, removing it from her pocket.

Ramona took the photo of Julia, her family, and Abuela and gazed at it as she swiped at her continuous flow of tears. "Oh, my mama looks good. You said she's well?"

"She is."

Ramona nodded, hanging her head and avoiding eye contact. "I feel so ashamed. I abandoned you kids and my mother all those years ago, and I've been too afraid to go back."

This led Mattie to the question she most needed answered. "Why . . . why did you? Why did you leave all of us?"

When Ramona finally raised her eyes, they were awash with sorrow and terror from years past. "They were very bad men, Mattie," she said, her voice barely above a whisper. "I saw them kill my husband, and you know how we all suffered. I couldn't protect you. Harold Cobb was one of many who would come after me. So I ran."

Mattie's stomach ached from the tension. "Harold Cobb is dead, and John Cobb is in a maximum-security prison in Colorado."

Ramona shook her head, leaning forward as she squeezed Mattie's hand as if for emphasis. "They were only two, sweetheart, and there are many more. It will never be safe for me. It might not be safe for you."

Mattie had already discovered that, but she didn't want to mention it to her mother. She returned her mother's grip. "What happened? How did my father get wrapped up with this gang?"

Ramona hesitated, looking around the room as if suspicious she could be overheard.

Mattie believed her mother still lived in fear every day. "You can tell me. I need to know so I can fix this."

Ramona shook her head, her face crumbling with pain. "You can never fix this, Mattie. It's too big."

"Tell me."

"Your father, Douglas, worked in border patrol at night. I used to take him meals when I could, and you kids would ride in the car."

"Is that what happened the night we were taken?"

She shook her head quickly. "No, not that night. But these guys, these smugglers, had seen us there, and they used us to get to your papa. They threatened to kill us if he didn't cooperate. It went on for only a few months. Douglas warned me to stay away, and I did."

Mattie's gut, already clenched, tightened even more. "What happened that night?"

"Julia was staying with my mama. Someone called and told me to come get Douglas, that he was ill and couldn't drive home. I thought it was a guy he worked with, so I loaded you and Willie into the car and went to get him. A man in a border patrol uniform met us and made me take you kids inside. There were six of them, and they were holding your papa and another guard at gunpoint."

Mattie's chest ached. She knew what was coming next.

"They shot him in front of me, in front of you and Willie." Sobbing, Ramona stopped to catch her breath. "It was horrible. I still have nightmares."

Mattie moved closer and held on to both her mother's hands. "And they took us."

Ramona tipped her head down and stared at her lap, her shoulders slumped. "To Colorado . . . in the back of a van. There were three others, two Mexican men and a boy. None of them spoke English. One of the men was the boy's father."

Mattie knew this part of the story but still needed to hear it from her mother. She waited in silence, the whir from the fan the only sound in the room.

"The Cobb brothers took over when we got to Colorado, and we went by horseback up into the mountains. They shot the others in the back of the head, even the child, and burned their bodies. But I begged for our lives." Ramona's voice had begun to quiver. "I told them I would do anything they said if they would let us live. There was nothing I could do to stop Harold from hurting you kids except try to draw his rage back onto me."

The image of Ramona fighting Harold Cobb came to Mattie's mind, this time slightly different. Ramona had started the fight—she'd come at Harold wielding a knife. He'd overpowered her and beaten her to within an inch of her life, stopping only after Mattie sneaked away to dial 911 and the deputies arrived. She shivered, her muscles so tightly bunched that they were quivering.

"I'm sorry I left you and Willie." Ramona raised her eyes to meet Mattie's. "I was injured. I was afraid. And I didn't trust anyone."

Mattie wondered if her own inability to trust was partially inherited or simply born out of their mutual experience. "Did you have any money? John Cobb said you had taken money from Harold."

Ramona's eyes widened. "No, I never had money. I don't know what he's talking about."

Mattie had suspected as much. Harold had probably hidden the money from John or taken it for himself before being sent to prison. "I believe you," she told her mother, encouraging her to go on with her story.

"I hitched a ride to San Diego with a trucker, told my mama what had happened and that I was going to hide in Mexico. I only contacted her one other time, and that was to tell her where I was. We haven't seen each other since the night I left Julia sleeping in her bed."

Unable to speak, Mattie sat holding her mother's hands and staring into her eyes.

Ramona leaned toward her. "Now, what about Willie?"

And that question brought the inevitable moment she'd been avoiding. Mattie shared what she could with her mother, giving her only the information she needed to know about her son's death. Together they grieved, their hoarse sobs mingling with the quiet shushing noise of the fan.

★ ★ ★

Mattie stayed for two hours. She learned that her mother had married one of two brothers who owned the local car repair shop. She'd never told him her story and wanted Mattie to leave before he came home from work—which was fine with her, since she needed to get back across the border before nightfall.

When it was time for Mattie to go, Ramona gave her a long hug. "I love you, but please, don't come back," she murmured in Mattie's ear. "It's not safe for either of us."

"I'll keep you and where you live a secret, but I'm going to look into some things to see if you're safe now."

Shaking her head, Ramona clasped Mattie's upper arms and held her at arm's length. "No. You need to leave things as they are. It's not safe for any of us. You know what they did to Willie."

"But that man is in prison. He can't hurt you."

"You can't be certain, Mattie. There are others, I tell you. And we don't know where they are."

Mattie tried to reassure her mother, gave her another hug, and left. She scanned the area as she took a roundabout way back to her car. She noticed no faces peering from windows, no one following her footsteps, and by the time she reached the car, she felt satisfied that she'd not brought any of her mother's demons to her doorstep. Only then did she start her engine, drive around a few blocks to make certain she didn't have a tail, and head out of town.

The day had been a huge drain on her energy, but she felt restless while she drove the narrow highway north toward the border. As she moved farther away from her mother and their emotional reunion, an itch of discomfort began to build inside her.

She didn't doubt that her mother feared her captors, had back then and did even now. But did that justify abandonment of her children?

Her mother had left her family decades ago. Why had she never reached out to check on Abuela? Why had she done nothing to help Abuela find her lost children? Was fear a large enough factor to have kept her from doing the right thing?

Mattie tried to put herself in her mother's shoes, and even then, the answer was no. No person and no thing could ever keep Mattie from protecting her children or her family. She knew that for certain.

She knew she struggled with perfectionism, and she tried not to judge her mother too harshly, but still . . . Her mother had expressed shame and regret, but how could her fear have immobilized her for decades?

Or had living without the entanglement of children been more convenient?

Mattie fought resentment as she drove, occupying her mind with other mother–child relationships. Hannah and Ruth, now reunited and trying to find a way to support themselves and the rest of their family so they could stay in Timber Creek. Angie and her mother, trying to repair the rift between them. The many parents and children who called law enforcement to help straighten out domestic disturbances.

Issues within families weren't all that unique.

Family. Cole, his kids, Mrs. Gibbs, Mama T, Robo, and the other dogs were her family now. She could hardly wait to get back to them. She would spend tonight with her sister and grandmother and then fly home tomorrow.

And soon, Detective Hauck would come to Colorado to interrogate John Cobb about her father. She needed answers about her father's death and the status of this alleged smuggling ring. Was it still in existence? Were her mother, Julia, and Abuela in danger? Mattie needed to know.

Robo came gently to her mind, and she relaxed back into the car seat, the smile on her lips making her feel better. Before leaving home, she'd asked Sheriff McCoy to request permission from the county commissioners for a mating between Robo and Sassy. If it was approved, there would be puppies sometime during the next few months. Robo's offspring—little fuzzy balls of black-and-tan fur. She could imagine them now, and the image brought joy to her bruised heart.

Despite the pain, her life was good.

Acknowledgments

First, I'd like to express my gratitude to the readers of the Timber Creek K-9 Mysteries. Your leisure time is precious, and I appreciate you sharing those moments with me. Thank you to those of you who've written to encourage me to keep adding stories to the series. You keep me going back to the keyboard.

I owe a huge, heartfelt thank you to the many professionals who helped bring *Hanging Falls* to print:

To Lieutenant Glenn J. Wilson (Ret.); Charles Mizushima, DVM; and Tracy Brisendine, Medicolegal Death Investigator, for their time and assistance with procedural content. As always, any inaccuracies or fictional enhancements are on me.

To Terrie Wolf of AKA Literary Management, for her encouragement and guidance; to publisher Matthew Martz, for his vision, insight, and support; to the fabulous team at Crooked Lane Books—Jenny Chen, Melissa Rechter, and Madeline Rathle—for helping me in an endless variety of ways; to my editor, Martin Biro, for guiding me toward a better novel; to my copyeditor, Rachel Keith, for her unflagging attention to accuracy and detail; and to publicist Maryglenn McCombs, for helping spread the news about the Timber Creek K-9 series.

To Scott Graham, author of the National Parks Mysteries, for his early input; and to Susan Hemphill and Bill Hazard, for their assistance with drafts.

And last but by no means least, I want to express my love and gratitude to friends and family who've supported me throughout the years. Like most of my stories, the theme of family, both by blood and by choice, runs through this episode. I'm so grateful for those of you who've shared my life's journey with me.

And to my husband, Charlie; daughters, Sarah and Beth; and son-in-law, Adam: thank you for providing a safe place to land and for always cheering me on.